# A New Kind
# of Bliss

Also by Bettye Griffin

ONCE UPON A PROJECT

IF THESE WALLS COULD TALK

NOTHING BUT TROUBLE

THE PEOPLE NEXT DOOR

Published by Kensington Publishing Corporation

# A NEW KIND OF BLISS

## BETTYE GRIFFIN

KENSINGTON PUBLISHING CORP.
www.kensingtonbooks.com

DAFINA BOOKS are published by

Kensington Publishing Corp.
119 West 40th Street
New York, NY 10018

ISBN-13: 978-0-7582-3161-1
ISBN-10: 0-7582-3161-X

First Printing: May 2009
10  9  8  7  6  5  4  3  2  1

Printed in the United States of America

*For my mother*

# Acknowledgments

Bernard Underwood, Eva Mae ("Bettye") Griffin.

My agent, Elaine English.

My story consultant, Kimberly Rowe-Van Allen.

My editor, Rakia Clark. I'm usually *much* better at meeting deadlines than I was with this one, and with the next book I'll prove it to you!

Special thanks to Reon Laudat and Patricia Woodside.

Everyone who is reading a copy of this book.

There was an unfortunate typo made in the e-mail address of my last book, *Once Upon a Project*, so if you e-mailed me and it bounced back, I'm so sorry. Go to my website (www.bettyegriffin.com) and you'll be able to contact me for sure.

The Almighty, from whom all blessings flow.

"They don't call him 'Big Sid' because he's six foot three, you know."
—Billie Holiday, admiring a musician boyfriend

"I love Clark [Gable], but he's a lousy lay."
—Carole Lombard, on her matinee idol husband

# Chapter 1

Maybe I just imagined the huge cloud of doom and gloom over New York City as the jet headed toward the runway at LaGuardia. It might have been one of those symbolic things, a metaphor, I think it's called. But I was feeling pretty damn low, so it seemed appropriate.

Anything could have happened while I was in the air. I didn't know if my father was still clinging on to life or if he would be dead by the time I got to the hospital. Even if he pulled through this respiratory failure, there would probably be another one waiting next week or next month. That's how emphysema works. It doesn't go away; it just keeps getting worse until it kills you.

Pop's health was my first concern. My mother, Ruby Yancy, was my second. She was seventy-eight years old and had never lived alone in her life. She'd been a wife for most of her adult life, always seeing to it that the cupboards and refrigerator were stocked, serving a hot meal at six P.M. every night, keeping the apartment tidy, and notifying the building superintendent whenever repairs were needed. She could work within the confines of a budget, too, but she had never put gas in the car, never taken it in for maintenance or repairs, never even written a check to pay a bill. My dad, Earl Yancy Sr. has always been the real take-charge type who always insisted on handling all the household business. He continued to do so even after his breathing difficulties got worse.

The bottom line was that after the inevitable happened, Mom wouldn't be able to live alone unless someone taught her how to balance a checkbook and check the oil. But neither I nor my siblings lived in our hometown of Euliss, a city along the Hudson River, just north of the New York City limits. I'd moved to Indianapolis after college, because that's where Al Davis, my ex, whom I'd met at Cheyney University, lived. Two years later we got married, and I remained in the city after we got divorced six years after that. My sister, Priscilla— we call her "Cissy"—lived in Pittsburgh, and my brother, Earl Jr., lived upstate. The three of us had never sat down and discussed what was going to happen when Pop's gone. We may be separated geographically, but we could have done it easily with that marvelous innovation known as three-way calling.

Still, I didn't feel too guilty about not having initiated that conversation. I suspected that one of them would suggest that *I* be the one to spend three or four months in Euliss getting Mom settled. "Let Emily take care of it," they would say. "*She* doesn't have a husband. *She* doesn't have kids."

Bullshit. Sonny—my brother's nickname from childhood, which I thought was silly, considering he was now fifty-five years old and a grandfather—and Cissy were eleven and thirteen years my senior, respectively. They both had kids, most of whom were grown and out of the house. Sonny taught mathematics at SUNY New Paltz, but it was only early June and there wouldn't be classes until the fall. Cissy was general manager of a big convention hotel in Pittsburgh, but it wasn't like they couldn't find someone to fill in for her, somebody like, if I had to guess off the top of my head, the *assistant* general manager. I saw no reason for *me* to be the one to have to make a major sacrifice. Being divorced meant the only household income was the one *I* brought home, and in my opinion that made me the least likely candidate—that is, unless Sonny and Cissy planned on paying my mortgage, car note, and other bills.

The plane was really low now, and all I could see out of my window was water. I heard a loud clicking sound as the landing gear dropped into place. Just when I was certain we were headed for the bottom of Long Island Sound, the runway appeared, seemingly out of nowhere. I knew the pilot had been able to see it the whole time. Still, I held my breath until I felt us touch down with that familiar thump. Landings under ordinary circumstances weren't as dangerous as takeoffs, but they make me uneasy just the same.

The engines roared now as the jet barreled down the runway, and I didn't truly relax until it slowed to taxiing speed.

I sat out the mad rush to deplane, most of which was spent standing up, holding carry-on luggage in hand, and grumbling about what was taking so damn long. Some of the passengers held packages of cigarettes, and one especially impatient man already had an unlit Salem in his mouth. He'd probably make a mad dash for the exit so he could get in a few puffs before claiming his luggage. But I wasn't about to let the people standing in the aisles behind me get off before I did. I put my foot in the aisle to block it as I got to my feet and retrieved my garment bag from the overhead bin.

Cissy stood waiting, an impatient scowl on her face, when I emerged at the baggage claim area downstairs. Instead of a standard greeting, the first words out of her mouth were, "Look at all the people already waiting at the belt for the bags to come out. Did you *have* to be the last one off the plane?"

"Lighten up, Cissy; there's a good forty people behind me. I was sitting in the back," I said calmly. "But even if I was the last, we can't leave until I get my bag, and nothing has come out yet," I pointed out as we stopped in front of the silent carousel. I grasped her forearm. "What's the latest on Pop?"

"He's hanging in, but he could go any minute. He already

went into respiratory arrest at four o'clock this morning, but they revived him. We've been at the hospital ever since."

"Did anyone at the hospital talk to Mom about a DNR order, 'do not resuscitate'?"

"Yes. We made him a full code for the time being, so you'd be able to see him. Now that you're here, I guess we can reverse it, although it's a hard topic to discuss. I'd be hesitant to bring up the subject to Mom." Cissy looked a little embarrassed. "How've you been, Em?"

I was wondering how long it would take my sister to get around to basic civilities. "I'm fine." Then I asked about Cissy's family. She and her husband, who was waiting in the cell phone lot, were staying with their daughter, son-in-law, and two-year-old grandson. Everyone was well, but anxious about Pop.

The crowd at the carousel was the same people who were practically knocking each other over to get off the plane. Now the gripe had changed from "why isn't this line moving" to "where's my damn luggage." I got lucky. When the buzzer finally sounded and the belt started moving, my bag was the third one to come out. Cissy promptly called her husband, and five minutes later we were in the car and on our way to Euliss.

Traffic was light, which was a relief. But I winced when I saw the toll for the Triboro Bridge was up to five dollars. It made me feel old to remember those exact-change lanes that existed back when the toll was just seventy-five cents.

It was too hazy to see the Manhattan skyline from the bridge, and since there wasn't anything else to look at but one of the most hideous parts of the Bronx, I stared straight ahead at the back of my brother-in-law's head of straggly salt-and-pepper hair. "Has Mom really been at the hospital since four this morning?"

"We all have," Cissy answered. "They normally have just two visiting periods a day for intensive care, but since Pop's situation is so grave, the staff usually lets us in any time we want." She paused, possibly to make her next words have more impact. "He really could go at any time, Em."

That explained why her husband was driving like his foot was weighted with a cement block. David, a retired police lieutenant, zoomed past traffic like he was on a high-speed chase. I barely had time to get a whiff of the sweet smell of baking cakes and cookies from the Stella D'oro plant at 238th Street before we crossed into Westchester County.

The Euliss Medical Center, formerly Euliss General Hospital and usually still called that by locals, had been the recipient of a complete expansion and face-lift. Gone were all traces of the eighties—*eighteen* eighties, that is—haunted castle look I remembered in the main building, which had looked every bit of its hundred-plus years before the remodeling.

We had to drive a block past the main entrance to get a parking space. David dropped a few quarters into the meter and we rushed to the hospital entrance.

Mom and Sonny were waiting in the lobby, and they greeted me with strong, tight hugs. Mom looked older and smaller than she had the last time I'd seen her during the holidays, just six months before. The illness of her life's partner of more than a half century had been taxing for her. I felt a twinge of guilt that quickly grew to encompass my whole being. As the youngest of the three, with a considerable age gap between me and my older siblings, I had enjoyed having our parents all to myself during my adolescence and teenage years and had lived a semipampered existence, at least as much as a lower-middle class kid could. I knew they hoped I would return to Euliss after my divorce, but the truth was I liked Indianapolis. I usually got back home about twice a year for quick visits. Because of that I had missed much of Pop's decline. Sonny and Cissy got to town more frequently, especially Sonny, since New Paltz was only a few hours' drive away. He'd driven down fairly often in recent months after receiving hysterical telephone calls from Mom, usually telling Cissy and me that Pop had improved and there was no reason for us to travel to Euliss. Until now.

David took a seat in the waiting room outside the ICU, while the rest of us walked to the desk. I eyed the sign that stated each patient was restricted to two visitors. "Will they really let all four of us in to see him?" I whispered to Sonny.

"We're here to see Earl Yancy," he said to the nurse as he gave my shoulder a reassuring squeeze. "There are four of us."

The woman didn't blink. "Yes, of course. Go right in."

Pop's eyes were closed. He had tubes going down his throat. He had never been a large man, but his outline under the sheet looked thin and wasted.

Mom leaned over the bed's guardrails, talking to him and becoming visibly upset when he didn't respond. I pulled her to me and hugged her tightly. "Take a break, Mom," I whispered; something about all that machinery alternately clicking and flashing his vital signs in the background made hushed tones appropriate. "Let me try."

Again he was unresponsive. I couldn't even get him to squeeze my hand. I work as a physician assistant, and my trained eyes automatically went to his vital signs on the monitor. His pulse was steady, his blood pressure was normal, and so were his oxygen levels, but the latter was only because of those four liters of $O_2$ he was receiving every minute.

"Pop," Cissy whispered near his ear after fifteen minutes, "visiting time is over. We have to leave, but we'll be back at three o'clock."

He suddenly opened both eyes. "Earl!" Mom squealed, rushing to his bedside from where she stood between Sonny and me.

We all moved in closer. Pop's gaze shifted to all four of us, and I thought I saw him smile. Then his eyes closed in a slow fade very different from the haste in which he had opened them. We all kissed him good-bye, even Sonny.

I rode to my parents' apartment with Mom and Sonny, while an exhausted Cissy returned with David to the apartment of their daughter and son-in-law.

"There's some tuna fish for you in the fridge," Mom said to me when we arrived. "I'm going to lie down for a bit."

"Okay, Mom." I sighed as she disappeared down the hall. "This is tough on her," I said to Sonny. "It's not going to get any easier. It doesn't look good."

"No, it doesn't."

"Do you know if she's prepared? I mean, does she know where the will is? The life insurance policy? Have she and Pop discussed what kind of funeral he wants?"

"All that's been addressed. The problem is what's going to happen to Mom."

My shoulders automatically tensed as I waited to hear what he would say next. When he remained silent I prompted him. "You have any ideas?"

"Well, I know she wants to stay here in Euliss. All her friends are here, and the church is here. Of course, Nelly and I would love to have her come live with us, but Mom won't consider it. I don't think a college town is the right setting for her anyway."

I noticed that he didn't say that he'd actually *invited* her to live with them, only that she wouldn't consider it. "I don't know if she has a choice," I said. With a sigh, I added, "I wish she'd listened to me when I tried to get her to take a more active role in running the household. If she had, she wouldn't be facing such a hard time in the first place. It'll be hard enough for her to lose Pop. But considering that all three of us live out of town and she wants to stay in Euliss, her only other option is to live alone."

He shook his head. "I don't think she can."

"Of course she can, Sonny. You do what you have to. We all do, no matter how old we are."

"She'll have a terrible time of it. Do you really want to put her through that, Emily?"

"I don't see any way out, unless you're planning on coming down here to teach."

"Don't be ridiculous. I couldn't possibly do that. But Cissy and I figured *you* could come back."

I raised an eyebrow. They sure didn't waste any time. How long had I been in town, forty-five minutes?

I raised my chin defiantly. "Well, that's interesting, considering I live farther away than either one of you. How did you come to the conclusion that my relocating would be easier than it would be for either of you?"

He shrugged. "Well, you're not married. . . ."

There it went. "Which is precisely why I have to work to support myself," I snapped. "It's June, Sonny. College is out of session for the summer. Are you saying you can't spend the summer here with Mom? It shouldn't be necessary to pull up stakes and move back permanently; she only needs time to get used to the idea of being alone."

"And then just abandon her?"

His righteous indignation was starting to get on my nerves. "You're here all the time anyway, Sonny; New Paltz isn't that far away. She's not being abandoned. Most of her friends are widows; they all manage."

"They all have kids living here. Mom has no family except us."

"She has grown grandchildren living right here in Euliss." That's the kind of place Euliss was; if you didn't leave by the time you were thirty or so you would probably spend your entire life within the boundaries of a single zip code.

"That's not the same as children," Sonny insisted.

"I'm not moving back here, Sonny, not even temporarily, so forget it." I held his gaze for emphasis until he looked away.

I was still glaring at him when the phone rang. "Hello?" I listened to the caller, a female, identify herself as a representative of the hospital, and I in turn identified myself as the daughter of Earl Yancy. "I'm terribly sorry," the woman said. "We did everything we could. We were unable to revive him."

# Chapter 2

People started arriving at the stroke of seven. In a way I was glad; it gave me something to concentrate on other than the casket, just a few feet away. I had looked at Pop when I first arrived at the church. Some people truly do look as if they are merely sleeping when they are laid out. Others look like there isn't an ounce of life left in them, like they've been stuffed by a taxidermist like a moose. I'm sorry to say that my daddy fell in the latter group, which I found depressing. I reminded myself of how at the hospital he had opened his eyes and smiled at all of us, the family he loved so much. In my heart I felt that he'd known all of us were there and that he only had another half hour or so of life left. It was like he was trying to tell us that it was all right, that he was ready to go and we shouldn't be sad . . . words he could not audibly express because of the tube in his throat. Thank God I'd gotten into town when I did and was there to see the face I knew so well that one last time. But I'd give anything if I could have heard his voice as well.

"Emmylou," he used to call me. His mother's name had been Louise, and he made that my middle name, in honor of her. She'd died when he was a boy, and now he was with her after a separation of nearly seventy years. Could that have been why he died with a smile on his face? Big drops of tears spilled from my eyelids. I didn't bother to wipe them away.

The wake and funeral were being held at the A.M.E. church our family had attended for as long as I could remember. We opted for only one wake; more than that would be too much of an emotional burden. Telephone calls had been made to close family friends, and the obituary had run in the Euliss *Daily Dispatch*.

I recalled the countless times I had opened letters from Mom and a folded piece of newsprint paper had fallen out, making me ponder, *Who died now?* always holding my breath a little as I unfolded it, knowing I would see a familiar name. Even miles from home the *Dispatch* was still part of my life. I'd be forty-three in a few months, and many of my friends had lost one or even both parents by this point in their lives. Now it was my turn.

It soon became apparent that we were going to have what is generally referred to as a good turnout. For some reason folks in Euliss like to brag about how many people show up at wakes and funerals, the same as they do about how late people stay when they give a party. Does it really make a difference how popular a person is when they're dead?

The first arrivals were relatives, longtime friends, neighbors, and people from church, folks my parents' age whom I'd known all my life. I hadn't seen many of them in years, and they all looked a little smaller, a little grayer, and moved a lot slower.

The younger set showed up a little later. Even my brother's and sister's friends had that definite over-fifty look. I saw a lot of matronly looking women, and men with bulging bellies, raggedy gray hair a lá Fred Sanford, or shaved heads, which I suspected was their way of coping with receding hairlines. Where had the time gone? Even my nieces and nephews were adults now. Cissy's daughter, my parents' oldest grandchild, was thirty-one, a mere dozen years my junior. Sonny's two boys and Cissy's son were all in their mid- to late twenties. Only Sonny's seventeen-year-old daughter still seemed young enough to feel like a niece.

I sat in the first pew with my arm draped around Mom's shoulders, periodically asking, "You all right?" and looking at the nearly two dozen floral designs, including the ones purchased by Mom, Sonny, Cissy, and myself, and the grandchildren. Only two were blanketed, but despite having cheerful colors, they practically screamed out, "Funeral!" The others were in wicker baskets or plastic containers and came in different colors, shapes, and sizes.

Mom was handling her stress and grief just fine, and I was proud of her. My own marriage had become a statistic after six years, and I couldn't imagine being married to someone for five-and-a-half decades. You've got to feel like you've lost a part of yourself.

Mom eventually went off to huddle with her closest friends, the group from her twice monthly bid whist game. They were too far away for me to hear what they were saying, but I could just imagine the inane remarks being made. I was surprised that older folks, who surely had been touched more by death than the young, didn't seem to have anything better to say than how "good" the deceased looked. "Oh, Ruby, Earl looked beautiful." "Ruby, he looks just wonderful." "He looks like he's going to sit up and talk." *He's dead,* I wanted to shout. *Don't you get it? He's* through *with talking!*

I'd lived in Euliss for the first eighteen years of my life and had known many people, most of whom I'd eventually lost touch with after I moved to the Midwest, if not before. Because so many years had gone by I wasn't expecting to see any faces from the past, and it came as a pleasant surprise when I recognized old friends who came to pay their respects. Some of them I hadn't seen in ten or fifteen years.

I'd kept in touch with Rosalind Hunter, and even though I didn't have time to inform her or anyone else, I wasn't surprised to see her approaching. I'd know her anywhere. Even as a teenager, Rosalind had always stood out in a crowd. She was striking, tall and slim with wide-set eyes and long black hair, only now that hair was short and auburn.

"I love your haircut!" I exclaimed as we embraced. "And the color, too. If I didn't know better I'd swear it was natural."

"Thanks. It took John a while to get used to it, but now he likes it." She squeezed my shoulder in concern. "How are you, dear?"

"Oh, I'm doing all right. Let's move down here so we can sit and talk." Mom, Cissy, and Sonny were all involved in conversations of their own, and I saw no reason why I shouldn't do the same. The wake had turned into a social event of sorts, a cocktail party without the cocktails. But I'd rather chew the fat than sit and sob for two hours, and I knew Pop would prefer it that way as well.

"I'm sorry I didn't get a chance to call you, Rosalind," I said after we were seated. "How did you hear?"

"The notorious Euliss grapevine. Valerie Woods called me." Rosalind scanned the room. "I see a lot of people came out to pay respects."

"Yes. I haven't seen Valerie, though."

"She said she plans to stop by tomorrow morning, before the service. She's got . . . she's awfully busy at home."

I wondered what Rosalind meant—Valerie was single with three children, but the oldest was about sixteen, certainly old enough to give her mom a hand—but before I had a chance to ask, a male voice greeted, "Hello, Emily."

I stared at the man with the close-cropped sandy brown hair, long nose, and close-set eyes, who was clearly enjoying my confusion. I watched as he and Rosalind exchanged amused glances.

My mouth dropped open in a lightbulb expression when I finally realized who he was. We all thought Wayne Pittman was incredibly handsome in junior high, as we did with every guy who was light skinned and had a big 'fro. His being a football player by the time we got to high school didn't hurt, either. I ran into him and his wife—not a Euliss girl—at the annual Thanksgiving morning football game about ten years after graduation, long after Afros went out of fashion, and then it struck me that he was about as good-looking as Godzilla. But Wayne had always been a nice guy, easily able to straddle the line between being friendly and a come-on. To this day he was the closest I'd ever come to having a male friend, except for my ex-husband before our marriage went the way of the rotary dial.

I stood to hug him. My arm muscles were sure getting a hell of a workout tonight, and so were my cheekbones. "Wayne, it's good to see you. Thank you for coming."

"I'm sorry about your father, Emily."

"I know. Sit down with us. I haven't seen you in how long, fifteen years?"

"That's about it. At the Euliss–Horace Mann Thanksgiving game, wasn't it? You and your husband." His eyes darted about, like he was looking for said spouse.

"Yes. We got divorced a couple of years after that."

"Oh. Me, too." Wayne leaned forward so he could see Rosalind. "What's up, Slim?"

"Not a thing. How're your boys?"

"Everybody's well. My youngest son is in middle school already."

"They grow so fast," Rosalind remarked wistfully.

"Tell me about it," I added. Of course, I had no firsthand knowledge of raising children. After a miscarriage I had difficulty conceiving again. In hindsight it had been a hidden blessing, especially after I learned that Al Davis, my dearly beloved husband, was cheating on me. I left him shortly after. At this point in my life, less than ten years away from hot flashes, I felt it was safe to say I wouldn't be having any children, but my friends' words reflected my earlier sentiments about my nieces and nephews.

So Wayne was divorced, too. Knowing that he hadn't lived that storybook existence like Rosalind comforted me in an odd way. I guess nobody wants to be the only divorcée in the bunch.

When Rosalind got married people predicted it wouldn't last as long as, well, pick any short-lived celebrity marriage. She and John Hunter had been the talk of Euliss High School twenty-five years ago because John was white. People in Euliss, both black and white, tend to view interracial dating like smoking on the street—it just wasn't done, at least not by anyone who had any class. At least that's how it used to be back in the day, but knowing Euliss, I doubt much has changed.

Rosalind glanced at her watch. "I see it's almost eight. I promised my oldest that I'd look at his math homework when I get home." She turned to me. "Emily, how long will you be in town?"

"Until Sunday. I hope we can get together before then."

She brightened like someone had turned on the lights inside her head. "Why don't both of you come over for dinner Friday? I'll put together a small dinner party. Maybe I can introduce you both to some nice people."

Wayne chuckled. "No, thanks, at least to being set up. I'm still convinced that the last so-called woman you matched me with at one of your parties either was a transvestite or had a sex change."

Rosalind made a face. "We've already been over that, Wayne. I thought she'd be good for you. You've always gone for tall women. How was I supposed to know? She seemed like a nice girl . . . who just had really big feet."

"So which one was it, Wayne?" I asked. "Transvestite or surgically altered?" I playfully wiggled my eyebrows up and down.

"I didn't stick around long enough to find out. The size of

those hands and feet were a real turnoff. At the end of the evening I shook her hand and ran for my life. Her grip was stronger than mine." He laughed.

"Oh, all right. I'll give you a simply platonic dinner partner, Wayne. Tanis Montgomery doesn't live far from me, and I think her husband is out of town."

As I thought of Tanis, who'd gone through school with us, it was now my turn to want to make a face. Our mothers were good friends, and there'd always been a competition of sorts between both Tanis and I and our mothers, who were eager to brag about our accomplishments. I'm sorry to say that I was behind in the race.

"But I've got just the man for you, Em," Rosalind continued. "Aaron Merritt. He's the most eligible over-forty-five-year-old bachelor in Westchester County."

"What's wrong with him?" I promptly asked, and I wasn't joking. I figured if he had credentials like that, it had to be because nobody wanted his ass.

"Well, let's see. He's about six one with a nice build, sexy eyes, he's a doctor, a few years older than us . . . ," Rosalind began.

"Back up. He's a *what?*"

"A doctor. He specializes in oncology at John's hospital." Anyone who heard Rosalind refer to "John's hospital" and didn't know better would think John's last name was Hopkins, but John was actually an administrator at the Columbia University complex in upper Manhattan.

My heart began thumping in excitement, in spite of my efforts to stay calm. But I'd never been one of those people who saw the glass of milk as half full. Instead, I told myself that this milk had to have a sour taste to it. "And how is it that no one has snapped him up?"

"Somebody did. He met his wife when they were in college. But she died the beginning of last year," Rosalind replied.

"Has he dated anyone else since?" The idea of breaking in

a widower made me a bit uneasy. I pictured some faceless man telling me all about his late wife, then breaking down while I tried to comfort him. Not exactly my idea of a roaring good time.

"Not that I know of. I do know that a lot of women have been inviting him to their dinner parties as the 'extra man,' and that he's been turning them down. So I'll downplay the part about wanting to introduce him to my girlfriend and just say John and I are having some old friends over for dinner." Rosalind stood up. "We'll talk about it later. I've got to run, and I want to say hello to your mother on my way out. I'll be in touch." She blew Wayne and me a kiss and headed for the far end of the pew, where Mom continued to hold court.

The funeral service was a lot smaller than the wake—it was a weekday after all—and a lot sadder. Sonny and I flanked Mom. We all cried, and I found it heartbreaking when Mom broke down and cried on my shoulder, squeezing my hand like she'd never let go. I tried as best I could to comfort her, and suddenly I knew Sonny and Cissy were right. She shouldn't be alone right now.

Sonny gave the eulogy, and his words made all of us feel a lot better. Pop died confident in the knowledge that we, his family, would never forget him, how well he took care of us and all the things he taught us. He would want us to go on.

"He knew that his one concern, namely that we siblings take care of our mother, would be taken care of," Sonny said.

I knew I didn't just imagine his gaze lingering on me with all the subtlety of church bells striking twelve, but what really worried me was Mom's increasing the pressure on my upper arm in a silent plea. She *wanted* me to stay with her.

There had been no more talk of what would happen to her since we'd gotten the phone call from the hospital. I knew Cissy wasn't going to take a leave of absence beyond the time she was spending in Euliss now, and I couldn't half blame her. She'd worked hard to get that general manager position, which was largely dominated by men. She said that she never expected to advance to running a tony New York hotel because, for some reason, they were all helmed by accented Europeans, but that calling the shots at a convention hotel in Pittsburgh with a thousand guest rooms was a satisfying challenge.

On the other hand, it seemed terribly unfair to me for Sonny to refuse to spend the summer down here when he was obviously the best one to do so, because his position gave him paid time off.

Back at my folks'—no, that wasn't right anymore—at *Mom's* apartment, I pulled Cissy aside the first chance I got. "Did Sonny tell you he asked me to stay with Mom?"

"Yes, he did."

"Well, I wish the two of you had included *me* in the conversation when you decided I'm the best one to put my life on hold and come to Euliss indefinitely. Sonny's a college professor, Cissy! He's off the next couple of months. Doesn't it make sense for him to be the one to come down here instead of me uprooting from Indiana? What the heck am I supposed to do with my condo?"

"He didn't tell you?"

"He didn't tell me anything. What's going on?"

Cissy sighed. "Sonny's been having an affair. Some woman who lives down here. They were meeting each other somewhere near West Point. Nell found out about it and raised Cain. Sonny's trying to keep the peace with her by staying close to home. There's no way she'll consent to his spending any extended amount of time in Euliss, even if she comes with him. That woman is here, and it's not like Nell can watch him every minute."

"Oh, for crying out loud." No wonder he didn't tell me. "What's wrong with men today, anyway?" I said, thinking of my ex. "Pop never did anything like that."

"Neither has David," she said quickly, in defense of her husband. "But everybody's different, Emmie. And it's nothing new. This type of thing has been going on for a long time."

I made an unintelligible grunt in response. I'll never forget how shocked I was to learn that Al had a chick on the side, while the blissfully uninformed me had been steadfastly trying to get pregnant, all but standing on my head after sex because a little bit of balance in the right direction helps the semen go down. I couldn't divorce his sorry ass soon enough, but it had hurt something awful. I hadn't realized that my brother was also the type who couldn't keep his pants zipped. I felt sorry for Nell.

But Sonny's future wasn't the main topic. I recalled how Mom clutched my arm at Pop's funeral, how she buried her face in my shoulder, almost as if I had suddenly become the mother and she the daughter. I kept remembering the words of Sonny's eulogy. All Pop wanted was for Mom to be taken care of. And he'd known he didn't have to worry, because he knew we'd take care of her.

Knowing what I know now, I saw only one possible solution. I sighed. "All right."

Cissy's head turned so fast I thought she might have snapped her neck. " 'All right'? Does that mean what I *think* it means?"

"Yes. I'll come back." I hadn't the faintest idea how I was going to pull this off, but I knew it was the right thing to do.

"Oh, Emmie, that's wonderful! Mom will be so happy!"

I knew she would. Although Mom had lived with the inevitable for some time, in the few days since becoming a widow she seemed almost childlike, continually reaching out for my hand, hugging and kissing me for no reason, and, hardest of all, saying things like, "You're my baby," and "I don't know what I'd do if you weren't here with me, Emmie." I'd known in my heart what I had to do the first time Mom reached for my hand, but I'd tried to ignore it. Of course, that was a tactic that never worked, and guilt had been picking at me like late-night nibblers to leftover roast chicken.

Even at the wake, Mom had proudly pointed me out to all her friends. I smiled at the memory, but as I remembered what Cissy and I were discussing my smile faded. "Sonny will have to cut me some slack and fill in for me in the beginning," I said. "It's going to take me some time to pack up my stuff, and I don't know what I'm going to do about my house." I'd bought a two-bedroom town house seven years ago and spent that time lovingly decorating it.

"Maybe you can rent it out."

"I doubt it. Space in Indy isn't at the premium it is in New York. From what I understand, no one in Euliss ever moves." I'd actually heard of elderly people adding their children to their leases so their apartment would stay in the family after they died. Rich people will their jewelry. Po' folks leave their heirs apartments that rent for six hundred dollars when the going rate is sixteen hundred. "In Indy there are plenty of vacancies. But I'll talk to my friends and coworkers. Maybe someone knows someone who needs a furnished rental for a couple of months."

"How long do you think it'll take you to get everything done out there?" Cissy asked.

"It'll take as long as it takes," I said testily. I wouldn't stand for being rushed, and Cissy's eagerness to wrap this up so she could return to Pittsburgh with a clear conscience annoyed me. Her disregard for how a move to Euliss would affect my life and my wallet was glaring. I couldn't believe she and Sonny could overlook a detail this important, since they seemed to have worked out everything else. Money made things happen. It's the flour in the cake.

"It depends on what I do with the house," I said. "I'd like to rent it furnished, but I might not be able to. If that's the case, all my furniture will have to go in storage," I said, the very thought of packing up seven years' worth of accumulated possessions making my stomach twirl more violently than a ride on the Octopus at the amusement park. "I'll have to check the job market here, too. My mortgage and possibly storage bill will have to be paid, whether I have a tenant or not. That might be difficult to do without a job," I added pointedly.

"Sonny and I already talked about that, and we decided to give you some money if you came back, a total of five hundred a month for three months. It's the least we can do, with you making such a big sacrifice. But you know Mom won't accept any money from you. She doesn't really need it; Pop took good care of her financially. She just wants you to make sure you've got all your stuff covered.

"And you won't have much of a problem finding work," Cissy continued. "There are plenty of doctor's offices, clinics, and medical centers here in Westchester, and of course some of the best hospitals in the world are in the city, if you're willing to commute. Health care is a great field, one of the few that's growing."

"Yeah, right." I knew it wasn't going to be easy, in spite of Cissy making it sound like I was moving to Sesame Street. God, I couldn't believe I'd consented to returning to Euliss, a city I hated. I liked living in Indianapolis, but it wasn't like I was leaving anything—or anyone—of tremendous importance behind. But I had a good life in Indy.

And in Indy I had my own place. I never thought I'd come back home at age forty-two to live with my mother, and that would take a lot of getting used to.

Mom lived in an early-twentieth-century house, originally a large private home that had been converted into apartments. She and Pop downsized from a larger two-bedroom unit to a one bedroom after I moved to Indy. It was on a quiet cul-de-sac off of the main drag, and because of that it looked like less of a concrete jungle than other parts of the city. The parking situation wasn't too bad, either. At least the city hadn't yet gotten greedy enough to install parking meters, like it had in other residential areas of the city, usually around high-rises with large populations. But because there was only one bedroom, I would have to sleep on the sofa bed. I was a little old to be camping out on anybody's Castro convertible, even on a temporary basis, but I supposed it couldn't be helped.

# Chapter 3

The bloom, as they say, was off the rose.

It certainly hadn't taken long. We buried Pop the day before yesterday, and already I was wondering how I was going to cope with living in Euliss again. The old town was dirtier and noisier than ever, a fact I was made aware of every time I left my mother's quiet street. Crumpled milk cartons and soft drink cans and bottles missed by the alleged street-sweeping machines lined the curbs. A variety of hip-hop CDs, with language too raw to be played on the radio, competed for listeners at top volume on boom boxes positioned in windows like fans. And the street was full of vehicles in desperate need of Midasizing.

I went to the supermarket for Mom the other day. Residents on the black side of town—Euliss might be in New York, but it's segregated, just like 1950s Alabama, with blacks and Latinos for the most part kept west of the dividing line—were thrilled when a major chain opened in the neighborhood with the promise that its prices would be the same as they were at its location across town. This was a novelty, because its competitors' prices at their stores in the black and Latino neighborhoods bordered on larceny, like two dollars for a single green pepper. Not a more exotic red or yellow pepper, but an ordinary green one. I doubt Leona Helmsley would have paid two dollars for a single green pepper . . . unless it was for that dog she left all her money to. I can hear her telling her maid, "Skip the green peppers. Only the little people eat them."

Anyway, the first thing I saw upon entering the market that was the crown jewel of Euliss's west side—a windowless dull brown brick structure that reminded me of a prison—was a crudely hand-lettered sign that said, PLEASE DO NOT SPIT ON THE FLOOR. I rolled my eyes. People in Scarsdale don't have to put up with this shit.

I kept reminding myself why I was here. Mom needed me. Sonny's circumstances in terms of proximity and time off made him the ideal candidate, but I also didn't want to contribute to any more problems between him and Nell. They'd been married thirty years, and I was fond of my sister-in-law. I also knew firsthand how difficult it was to survive infidelity. Nell must be a better woman than I, because I couldn't bring myself to do it. If I'd stayed married to Al, I would have spent the rest of my life worrying about what he was doing every minute he was out of my sight. Frankly, I felt I deserved better. But staying with Sonny was Nell's choice, and I respected it.

I found myself looking forward to dinner at Rosalind's. We'd spoken on the phone, and I knew she'd kept the gathering small, six people. Besides Wayne, Dr. Merritt, and me, the only other guest would be our old classmate Tanis Montgomery. Tanis was married, but her husband, an agent who represented both East and West Coast actors, was often in California.

Because we were on the phone, Rosalind couldn't see how my lip curled when she said Tanis's name. Not that I disliked Tanis. It's just that I'd been hearing about her most of my life, and I was sick of her.

Her mother, Mavis Montgomery, and mine, plus two other women, including Mavis's sister, Winifred Woods, had been getting together twice a month—right after their husbands got their paychecks—to play bid whist for as long as I could remember. Since it was impossible to put four women in a room without some bragging taking place, I always heard about

Tanis's accomplishments. From my childhood, my mother, wearing an animated expression like she was a news anchor, regularly passed on tidbits like, "Tanis is going to do a solo at the dance recital," "Tanis is entering the contest to win Miss Euliss High," "Tanis is dating that star football player," and "Tanis was voted Best Personality for the yearbook." I knew Mom didn't consciously mean to, but her recounting of Tanis's achievements only served to make me feel like an also-ran.

I'd gone to the same dance school as Tanis had, but while she was graceful, my skills were merely adequate. Even at the age of nine I seriously considered tripping her so she'd sprain her ankle and wouldn't be able to do her solo. Conscience prevailed, and I wisely left it alone. By high school I wasn't much interested in extracurricular activities. All I wanted to do was keep my grades up so I could get a scholarship, and I enjoyed hearing my mother brag to Mavis how I'd made the honor roll. I worked as a volunteer candy striper, and Tanis took a job at a local supermarket and managed to get promoted to the customer service desk after just a few months. Hearing my mother's muted response to Mavis's news about Tanis's promotion ("Emily works for no pay because she wants to be a nurse, Mavis") nearly broke my heart.

It didn't help that people sometimes got us confused. We were about the same height, both of us had skin the color of a walnut, and both of us had long hair, which we'd worn in braids as children. My hair was coarse, but Tanis's hair had waves in it, which she'd inherited from her father. Of course, she'd gotten her oversized nose from him as well.

While we were in college I got a break. I was the one to make the dean's list while Tanis was busy being sociable, and Mom actually snickered at Tanis being a theater major. "She needs to study something she can fall back on, like teaching," she had said. Unfortunately for me, the feelings of being on top ended when Tanis went out to California to pursue an acting career. Mom now delivered her news with increasing excitement. "Tanis got a McDonald's commercial." "Tanis is going to be the model on that game show, *Go for the Gold.*" "Tanis is doing a guest spot on that TV show I always watch."

Oh, yes, I knew all about Tanis. I heard about her husband, Rob Renfroe, even before they got engaged. Originally he'd been her manager, or agent, or whatever they call it. When they got married I heard about what they served at the reception (prime rib), and when her children were born Mom told me all the details, that her son, whom she'd had first (naturally), weighed eight pounds five ounces, and that the daughter she gave birth to a few years later entered the world at a dainty six pounds nine ounces.

I knew that Tanis and Rob moved back to New York when he decided to go bicoastal and manage the careers of East Coast stage actors as well. I heard all about their fabulous house on Long Island Sound, and how Tanis landed a recurring role on a drama filmed in New York. The big news that had come out just before Pop died was that she now had a regular part, a supporting role on a new show from the same producers.

I'd seen her on TV a couple of times. She hadn't changed much since high school except for one thing. Funny that with all the details of Tanis's life Mavis Montgomery proudly proclaimed to my mother, she forgot to mention that Tanis had gotten her nose thinned.

It would be interesting to see Tanis in person after all this time. She was a working actress trying to keep steady employment. I worked as a physician's assistant in my white smock, performing physical exams and writing prescriptions, often for people who sneezed uncontrollably on everything in sight, including me.

Okay, so the competitive edge in me was alive and well. But maybe when I saw her this time I could finally drop the feeling of being second best.

*    *    *

"I'm going out tonight, Mom," I remarked Friday morning as I made my breakfast in the kitchen and she sat eating hers at the adjoining dinette.

"Oh, Emmie, I'm so glad. You don't want to sit around the house all the time. Where are you going?"

"To a small dinner party at Rosalind Hunter's. She used to be Rosalind Gill. You remember her; she spoke to you at Pop's wake."

"Oh, yes. The girl who married the white boy."

My mother and her friends might not know Rosalind's name, but they all remembered whom she'd married, even after nearly twenty years. Rosalind had become a Euliss legend.

"Yes. They live in New Rochelle now."

"Ooh, nice. Maybe you'll meet a nice man there."

I hesitated, not sure if I should mention Aaron Merritt or not. After all, even he didn't know Rosalind's motives. "Uh . . . actually, Rosalind is sort of pairing me with someone eligible. He's an oncologist."

Mom put down her coffee cup with a suddenly shaking hand. Under other circumstances I would have been concerned that she was having a seizure, but since I'd just announced I'd be dining with a single physician I knew it was excitement, not anything medical.

"An *oncologist!*" she exclaimed, her eyes shining. If she was a cartoon character her pupils would have transformed into dollar signs. "How wonderful! What are you wearing?" And then the question I knew was coming: "And what on earth will you do with your hair?"

I'd always had difficulty managing my hair, so I'd worn it natural since deciding that I had neither the time nor the money to invest in monthly salon visits. Mom disapproved, believing nappy hair was suitable only for little girls. But at least now they made Afro combs with thick, wide teeth, which made combing it a snap. Until that product became available when I was about four, all Mom could do was brush it because those combs they made for white folks just didn't work on us.

"I figured I'd wear my black and white polka-dotted dress. It's the only other one I brought, and that solid black with the peplum I wore to Pop's funeral is too somber, don't you think?"

"Yes. But what about your hair?" she persisted.

"I'll just pin it up, I guess."

Mom took a casual bite of her buttered kaiser roll. I knew she was thinking. I just hoped she wouldn't start with something like, "I don't want you to take this the wrong way," and then proceed to say something insulting. I loved my mother, but Miss Manners she wasn't. I swear, I remember someone once telling her they were receiving obscene phone calls, and damned if Mom didn't ask what the caller had said.

"Emmie," she began, "go to the beauty parlor. I'll get my regular operator to squeeze you in, and I'll even pay for it. Try a relaxer again. It'll look beautiful, especially with your streak."

Over the years I'd developed a gray streak about a half inch wide that ran down my crown and was slowly extending. I didn't mind it getting longer; I just hoped it didn't get any wider. I didn't relish looking like a damn raccoon.

"I don't know, Mom."

"It'll be my gift to you. You can even get your nails done."

"I can afford to pamper myself a little, Mom." My, I sounded confident for someone who had a mortgage to pay and who was about to quit her job. "But I always look so perfect when I leave the salon, and then when I wash it myself it loses its luster."

"You'll be fine, Emmie. You have me to help you." She leaned in, placing a slightly gnarled hand on my forearm. "Think of the possibilities. He's a doctor, so you already know he's rich and successful. If he turns out to be good-looking, too, that's a bonus." Her forehead wrinkled. "Why do you suppose no one has snapped him up yet?"

I didn't tell her he'd been widowed because I didn't know how she'd react, so I merely shrugged.

"I want you to look perfect tonight," she said. She pulled her hand away and leaned back in her chair, staring at me meaningfully as she sipped her coffee. Finally, she shared her true thought with me. Not that I really needed to be reminded of it.

"Besides, this might be your last chance."

At six o'clock I ran my newly manicured fingers through my newly relaxed and wrapped hair. Mom was right—it did look nice. I'd gotten the stylist to even out the ends, but even after the trim it still fell nearly to my shoulder blades. I shook my head, and my hair bounced. I felt just like one of those Breck girls from the old TV commercials.

"You look lovely, Emmie," Mom said.

"Do you think I should pin my hair up?" I knew that, having been an old wife herself, Mom subscribed to that old wives' rule about forty being the absolute cutoff for women to wear long hair loose.

But she surprised me. "No, I think it looks perfect just the way it is. You can get away with it. They do things differently now. Years ago, if a woman in her forties wore her hair loose it would be the talk of the town. . . ."

Didn't I know it. There was nothing like a fashion faux pas to get the people of Euliss talking. "Do you remember the time Valerie Woods showed up in church in slacks and no hat?" I asked. Even after twenty-odd years, rumors still persisted that she was on drugs. Like a drug addict is really going to show up regularly for Sunday services. Now slacks on women in church are commonplace, and no one wears hats anymore.

Mom chuckled. "Oh, yes, I do. You know, that girl was always a handful. She broke her father's heart. If you ask me, that was what killed him."

I rolled my eyes. Why did people of my mother's generation believe that heart attacks were caused by anything other than a bad heart? Still, there could be no question that Valerie's handling of her private life had disappointed Paul and Winifred Woods. I never understood Valerie's desire to have all those children as a single parent. I remember seeing her and her first daughter during a quick visit home to check on Mom, who'd been hospitalized with a severe sinus infection. Valerie looked so happy, and the chubby-cheeked baby was so cute. Looking at her all dressed up in pink made me actually want to lean over her and mumble baby talk to her, an action I'd always previously dismissed as, well, stupid. "I know you're wondering why I did it," she'd said to me. "I figured it this way. I'm twenty-seven with a good career and no prospects for marriage. I don't want to miss out on being a mom, and I also don't want to do it when I'm forty."

I could sympathize with how she felt, but I couldn't help feeling that she'd given up way too soon. So what, she was twenty-seven. Unlike her Halle Berry wannabe cousin Tanis, Valerie majored in business in college. She'd been working as a seminar instructor and, according to Winifred Woods's bragging to my mother, was doing rather well. Didn't her job bring her into contact with eligible professional men? And wouldn't having a baby make it more difficult for her to land a husband?

Valerie's attitude toward marriage did raise an obvious question, and I had decided to ask, since we went back to the playpen. "What about the baby's father?"

She'd brushed it off with a grin. "Not husband material, but he had great genes."

So she'd found herself a good-looking, worthless stud to impregnate her. I wonder if he'd known she was only in it for his sperm. Did she even bother to tell him he was about to become a father? Somehow I doubted she'd go after the poor sap for child support.

I did hope that one day she would meet her Mr. Right and live happily ever after. I was happily married at the time—at least I *thought* I was—and believed everyone's soul mate was just waiting to be uncovered. I've since removed those glasses that tinted everything rose colored.

Apparently Valerie never had any delusions. When her daughter was six, she had another baby, a son. And when her son was six and her daughter twelve, she had one more daughter. Since none of the kids looked alike and there was no steady man in Valerie's life, rumor had it that they all had different fathers.

My mother had told me about each of Valerie's successive pregnancies as soon as she learned of them, adding in a confused voice, "I don't understand. Why doesn't she just marry one of the men she's been sleeping with?"

I didn't understand it myself. By the time Valerie had her youngest child, her career had advanced, and she had become a highly sought after motivational speaker. She was well paid and had a lifestyle to match, with a spacious house on a quiet street on City Island.

"It puts Winnie in an awkward situation," Mom continued. "She's always talking about Norman's kids and Wendy's kids, but she never says anything about Valerie. In fact, if I hadn't known her for so many years, I'd think she had only two children, not three. And Valerie's got everything going for her. I wonder what makes her have all these babies. It's like as soon as they outgrow their babyhood she gets pregnant again."

"Well, she's in her forties now, Mom, so I think she's shut down production."

"Yes, but that doesn't mean there won't be more babies in her family. Bea Pullman told me that she saw Valerie and her kids at a restaurant on City Island and that the oldest daughter looked like she was pregnant."

Bea Pullman was the fourth member of their card-playing group. "Oh, I'm sure she was mistaken. Valerie sends all those kids to parochial school," I said.

"I doubt she got this baby during school hours," Mom said in a droll tone.

* * *

Wayne came for me at seven-fifteen, looking quite handsome in a navy blue suit, which, since he worked as an electrician for Con Edison, I suspected was his standard outfit for weddings, funerals, and dinner parties. Although for a funeral I supposed he'd skip the snazzy geometric red and blue tie and matching silk hanky in favor of something more solemn.

We said good night to a beaming Mom and set out on our way in Wayne's Grand Marquis. The day had been warm, but the night was cool. June in New York had always been iffy, and I was grateful the shawl I borrowed from Mom was a knit blend and not the oversized lace doily type that provided no warmth whatsoever.

"Your mother seems to be doing pretty well," he remarked.

"Yes. I think it helped her a lot when I told her I'm staying on."

"You're moving back to Euliss? Hey, that's great!"

I shrugged. "Well . . . I don't know if 'moving' is the appropriate word. I'll probably be here for about six months to help Mom adjust to taking care of things herself." In the back of my mind I was already dreading having to change locations twice in six months.

Then again, after six months in Euliss I'd probably be ready to run for my life.

Rosalind and John lived in an ivy-covered thirties Tudor on a quiet street. The house had belonged to the senior Hunters after they left Euliss—the scuttlebutt was they were ashamed to face their neighbors after John married Rosalind—and they sold it to John when they retired and moved to Florida. I noticed three other cars parked in the wide driveway. One undoubtedly belonged to Rosalind and one to John, but what about the third one? Did that maroon Mazda 929 parked next to us belong to Tanis or to Dr. Aaron Merritt? My palms suddenly felt damp.

Rosalind answered the door, looking stunning in a tan short-sleeved knit dress with a gently draped neckline and white paisley print. Her low-heeled pumps were a standard for her, for as children she had towered above most of the fellows at school, eventually growing to five feet nine and marrying a man who stood only two inches taller. She kissed both of us hello. "I'm so glad to see you guys." She added, "Oh, thank you!" when we presented her with her hostess gifts, by Smirnoff and Bacardi, respectively. "Come on in. Tanis is here already."

I let out my breath as softly as I could. Aaron hadn't arrived yet.

John Hunter, sitting in the living room with Tanis, rose to greet us. Never thin, even as a teenager, he'd become nicely broad in early middle age. With curly blond hair, round cornflower blue eyes, and a nose that didn't get in his way, he was still good-looking. In high school all the girls had crushes on him. The black girls were thrilled when he showed an interest in one of us. The white girls, on the other hand, were shocked. A jealous Mary Alice O'Brien started a rumor that Rosalind was putting out for him, and when Rosalind heard her say it after gym class she slammed Mary Alice against a locker and made her take it back.

Wayne turned to greet John, leaving me facing Tanis. I was surprised at how small she looked in person, maybe a size six. At a size ten, I can hardly be referred to as full figured, but I felt like a lumberjack next to her.

She wore a simple drop-waisted, sleeveless berry-colored dress with a V-neck and pleated bottom, and matching pumps. Her trademark long, wavy hair had been relaxed into a texture as straight as railroad tracks, losing none of its lush thickness along the way. She wore it in a layered style that brushed her shoulders at its longest length, and of course no gray showed.

She took one of my hands in both of hers and pressed her

cheek to mine, careful not to get too close. "Emily, I'm so sorry to hear about your dad. I'm sorry I wasn't able to get to the wake or the funeral. I was shooting that week."

She seemed sincere, I thought, but who knew? The woman role-played for a living.

"It's been ages, hasn't it?" she added.

"Yes, it has. I heard about your new show. Congratulations."

"Thanks. Fortunately, we were picked up for a full season. The network made that commitment to Bob." She spoke about the veteran TV actor who'd signed on to star in the hourly drama.

I resisted the urge to point out that many a star had gotten a full-season commitment for new shows that tanked. I wanted to keep things pleasant, but so help me, the first time she said something bitchy, the gloves would come off. "Congratulations," I said with as much warmth as I could muster.

We sat on the sofa, and I reached to help myself to a cheese puff from a tray Rosalind had set up on the coffee table. I hadn't eaten lunch, and it melted in my mouth in seconds. I promptly reached for a stuffed mushroom.

John fixed drinks, and I helped myself to hors d'oeuvres at ninety-second intervals, hoping no one would notice.

"Feeling a little peckish, are you, Emily?" Tanis asked, her eyebrows raised in amusement.

I flashed an uncomfortable little smile. I decided I liked Tanis better when she smiled at refrigerators and cuddled up to bottles of shampoo on that game show she used to do.

My fingers gripped the arms of my chair when the chiming sound of the doorbell reverberated through the house. I felt Tanis's eyes on me and because of that resisted the urge to smooth my dress. Why was she watching me like a lazy worker eyes the clock? Had Rosalind told her she hoped Aaron and I would hit it off? And even if Rosalind had seen fit to share that information, what did that have to do with Tanis?

I took a sip of my wine, the warm liquid calming me. It

had been years since I'd been set up with anyone, but I don't ever remember feeling so nervous. Maybe it got harder when you got older because you knew opportunities were fewer.

"I'll get it," John said.

I took a bigger sip, and then, suddenly panicky, I took a gulp. This was it.

A minute later John returned with one of the best-looking men I'd ever seen.

# Chapter 4

Rosalind had been right. He was about six one, light brown–skinned, with a mustache and neat goatee. But it was his eyes that stood out to me. Not the color, which was an ordinary brown. Their shape commanded my attention. They were narrow, like he'd just gotten out of bed. I've always been a sucker for a man with bedroom eyes. Al had them.

The marvelous specimen standing just a few feet away from me looked like he belonged on the cover of *GQ*. Instead of a suit he wore a navy blazer over tan pants, a white shirt, and a navy-and-red print tie.

Aaron greeted Rosalind first, then shook Tanis's hand. "I'm sorry I missed Rob. He's spending a lot of time in California these days, isn't he?"

"Oh, he'll be back Sunday," she replied breezily.

As Rosalind introduced Wayne to Aaron, I hoped she'd be subtle when it came my turn and would remember that it's not just what you say but how you say it. If she injected too much enthusiasm she might as well put her arm around me and announce, "And right here we have the answer to All Your Problems," like some spokesperson hawking a vitamin supplement on a TV infomercial.

Rosalind didn't let me down. "Aaron Merritt, Emily Yancy," she said simply.

"Nice to meet you, Emily," he said melodically.

I managed a cordial hello, mentally giving him five points for his speaking voice. His grip was firm and strong, reminding me of how long it had been since I'd been on the receiving end of masculine attention. But it didn't feel like it would break my hand. I hated it when men pumped my hand like they were greeting Lennox Lewis. Five more points for consideration.

Aaron's eyes and smile didn't belie anything other than casual friendliness, and I hoped mine were equally unrevealing. I didn't want to appear overeager, or even particularly impressed, even if my heart was doing somersaults.

John asked Aaron if he wanted a cocktail. "After dinner," he replied.

"All right. In that case why don't we go in?"

I watched with annoyance as Tanis chose that moment to strike up a conversation with Aaron, slipping her arm through his companionably as we all walked toward the dining room, leaving me to pair off with Wayne. But Rosalind had made place cards, and Tanis was assigned next to Wayne, across from Aaron and me. Rosalind and John sat at the respective heads of the gleaming brownish red cherrywood table.

"So, Emily," Aaron said over the French onion soup, "are you a friend of Rosalind's or John's?"

Damn. He started to make conversation just as I took in a rather large ring of onion. I quickly cut it with my teeth and allowed the uneaten portion to drop back into the bowl. "Technically both of them, but Rosalind and I go all the way back to grammar school."

"Wayne and I, too," Tanis interjected.

"Yes, that's right," I agreed, trying to conceal my growing impatience. "The four of us went all through school together."

"That's impressive," Aaron observed. "Most people from that far back are out of touch. Do you live here in New Rochelle?"

"No, we all grew up in Euliss." Euliss is generally regarded as the shabbiest city in Westchester, and I watched his face to see if he would flinch, but his expression didn't change. Five more points. "Wayne still lives there, and I'm in the process of relocating from Indianapolis for an extended time. My father just died, and my mother's having a hard time with it."

"Oh, I'm sorry. I didn't know. Was it sudden?"

"No, he'd been failing for some time." As an oncologist, he was probably fishing to see if cancer had claimed my father, but I wasn't about to discuss Pop's decline like he'd been a lab specimen or something.

"Will you be able to get a leave of absence from your job?" he asked, getting the message and moving on. Five more points for his sense of decorum.

"They'll keep my job open for six months. It'll be inconvenient for them to have to hire someone on a temporary basis to fill in, but they were very nice about it." Before he could ask, I added, "I'm a P.A." Since he was a doctor, I figured he'd know that didn't mean public accountant.

"Oh! What's your specialty?"

"Family medicine."

"We have something in common, then. I'm an oncologist. I have offices in Manhattan, plus hospital privileges at Presbyterian and Sloan-Kettering."

I merely nodded as I took a spoonful of soup, hoping I looked unimpressed, like I was introduced to oncologists working at prestigious medical centers every week.

"Is everybody done?" Rosalind asked. At the nods of response she rose and began collecting soup bowls.

"Rosalind, why don't you let Emily and me help out?" Tanis offered.

I glared at her from across the table. *If you want to be helpful, fine. Don't bring me into it; I'm busy.*

"No, I've got it. You two stay put."

Rosalind disappeared into the kitchen, then emerged with a platter of golden brown Cornish hens atop a bed of yellow rice, followed by a bowl containing green beans with bacon pieces, and a basket of rolls.

After we passed the food around, I turned to Aaron. "What made you want to practice oncology?"

"How's Billy, Aaron?" Tanis asked on the heels of my query.

He glanced across the table at Tanis. "He's doing real good, thanks." Then Aaron caught my eye and explained, "My son. He goes to the same school as Tanis's daughter."

"Oh. How nice."

"To answer your question," he continued, "my grandmother died of cancer when she was younger than I am today. She suffered terribly, and being a kid, I wanted to find a cure when I grew up. But I didn't become a scientist. I'm merely a health provider." He shrugged, then took a sip of wine. His fingers around the stem of the glass were long and tapered.

"I'm sure you've saved many lives," I added sincerely.

"Yes, I suppose I have. Sometimes that's all my patients ask for, to live long enough to see their son's or daughter's wedding, or to hold their newborn grandchild, or to be able to attend high school or college graduations. It's rewarding if I can help them do that."

We smiled at each other, and I felt the connection as sure as if someone had handcuffed us together.

We were still grinning when Tanis interrupted again. "Are you all settled at your mom's, Emily?"

"Not yet. I have to go back to Indy and take care of some things."

"Has your husband gone back to Indiana already?" Tanis asked.

Rosalind choked on her wine. John blinked. Wayne looked taken aback. And Aaron's eyes narrowed into slits so narrow I couldn't tell what color they were.

I didn't buy Tanis's ignorance act. I'm sure her mother passed on the news of my divorce when it occurred, probably gleefully.

"Tanis, I've been divorced for about a dozen years," I said with a laugh. "I thought you knew."

"Oh, I don't remember hearing about it."

Damn, she was good. If I didn't know better I would have thought she really was embarrassed. But I wanted her to know she didn't fool me, so I met her gaze with a knowing smile until she looked away.

Wayne jumped into the awkward moment. "I was telling Tanis how great she looks."

"Yes, she does," I agreed. "There's something different about you, Tanis. I just can't put my finger on it." I tapped my cheek with my index finger, then discreetly bent my finger to rub my nose. She looked properly shocked at my bold gesture.

Then I turned back to Aaron, reasonably certain that Tanis would not break in again. "Now, what were we saying?"

After dinner John suggested we return to the living room. He waved us on, saying he wanted to help Rosalind bring out the dessert and coffee.

This time *I* was the one Aaron escorted as we returned to the living room. I caught a glimpse of Tanis glaring at me when Aaron and I sat together on the couch. She quickly covered her scowl with a smile and moved to sit in the chair closest to his end of the sofa, crossing her legs like they were on display at MoMA.

By the time John and Rosalind appeared with peach cobbler and cream we were having a spirited discussion about a prominent murder case in Rye. Aaron leaned in closer and spoke so only I could hear. "Did you say you'll be in the area for another few days?"

"Yes." The syllable came out matter-of-factly, but that wasn't how I felt. Those sexy eyes focused on me were almost more than I could bear.

"I hope you'll consider having dinner with me when you come back."

"I'd like that."

He leaned back, and I forced my attention back to the conversation going on around us. "I think it was the husband,"

John was saying. "He's overacting, if you ask me. Passing out when he identified the body, passing out again at the funeral . . ."

"You'd think if he'd wanted to get rid of her that bad he just would have left her," Wayne said.

"Marriages do fail every day," Rosalind remarked.

"I agree," Tanis said. She paused, then sighed theatrically. "I'm getting a divorce, myself."

The room suddenly became quiet, like she was about to give out hot stock tips or something, followed by murmurings of sympathy. Tanis accepted in a whispery voice, like she was fighting back tears. I felt like I was watching a performance of *The Little Foxes*. Tallulah had nothing on Tanis.

"It's always sad when a marriage ends, but I'm sure it'll be amiable," Tanis continued, after a pause to compose herself. "Rob and I waited for a lot of the bad blood to dry up before I filed. It'll be coming through in about sixty days." Then she looked at Aaron like she expected him to scoop her up and carry her away on a white horse.

Now I understood why she'd been on him all night like whipped cream on Jello. If I knew her, Tanis probably had Aaron all picked out to be her second husband before she decided to divorce the first one.

But *I* had Aaron's attention. And I was going to keep it. Tanis had beaten me out long enough. It was time to crown a new champ.

# Chapter 5

"Well, that was fun," I remarked to Wayne as he backed out of the driveway. I watched as Aaron climbed into a light-colored Jaguar and I couldn't help thinking how good I'd look riding beside him.

"Yeah. Tanis really looks good, doesn't she?"

"Fabulous," I said, feeling generous. Hell, I could afford to. Aaron had resisted Tanis's efforts to drum up sympathy and instead asked *me* out. She'd lost, and she knew it. She came up to him as we were saying good night and told him rather flatly that he had her blocked in, which prompted us to wrap it up. "Too bad about her and her husband." I had forced myself to sound compassionate, but in truth I couldn't wait to get home and tell my mother the scoop. It was a cinch this would come as news to her. I was sure Mavis Montgomery would much prefer to brag about all of Tanis's successes than mention anything less than sterling, like that nose job. I imagined Mavis would hold out for a reconciliation right up until the time the final decree came through . . . and then she wouldn't tell a soul about the divorce until she absolutely had to—like if Tanis married again.

"It looked like you and your dinner partner got on pretty well."

"He seemed nice," I said, proud of the blasé way it came

out. I knew damn well that if I was alone and not in the confines of Wayne's car I'd be doing cartwheels.

"Gonna see him again?"

"Yes, when I come back to town. At least if he hasn't met
anyone else by then." I decided to make a joke. "What about
you? Will you be seeing *Tanis* again?"

"I'd love to."

That's the last thing I expected to hear him say. I looked at
him sharply, but his eyes were focused on the road, his expression unrevealing. "Wayne, are you serious?"

"Why wouldn't I be? She's a good-looking girl. Always has
been. And she's about to be single again." He took his eyes
off the road for an instant to look at me. "Or do you think
it's a bad idea because she's a big-time actress and I'm just a
working stiff?"

I tried to come up with a response quickly but found my
thoughts couldn't get past his description of Tanis as a "big-
time actress." Did he really believe she was in the same league
as Angela Bassett or Halle Berry? You wouldn't see either of
*them* doing deodorant commercials. "It's not that. I seem a little
shocked because you caught me off guard. But in the end it's
what *Tanis* thinks that counts." I felt quite satisfied with my
diplomatic reply, but his next words burst my bubble.

"It's dark in this car, Emily, but I can see doubt all over
your face."

I didn't know what to say. I couldn't say I thought it was a
good idea, because I didn't. Of course, Tanis wouldn't look
twice at someone like Wayne. Was he so blind he hadn't noticed
how she had practically thrown herself at Aaron? Not only did
Wayne not hold a distinguished position, but he wasn't even
particularly good-looking. Money without looks was okay, and
looks without money might work, but neither looks nor money
wouldn't stand a chance, at least not with a woman like Tanis. *I*
didn't feel that way, of course. The fact that Aaron Merritt had
both looks *and* money was . . . well, purely coincidental.

"Did you ask her out?" I asked.

"No. I just told her it was good to see her, and to call if I could do anything to help her."

I kept quiet. If Tanis ever called Wayne it would be to ask him to wire her attic, not to light her pilot.

"Emmie, you have a phone call."

"Thanks, Mom." I yawned as I buttered an English muffin, then picked up the kitchen extension. "Hello."

"Hi, it's Rosalind."

"Well, good morning," I said cheerfully. "I was about to call you; you beat me to it. Nice party last night. Wayne and I both enjoyed ourselves." I considered sharing with her just how much Wayne enjoyed Tanis's company, then decided that wouldn't be right. Just because Wayne hadn't added a "just between us" clause didn't give me carte blanche to blab his private feelings to anyone.

"Glad to hear it. Now, I want to hear all about you and Aaron."

I bit into my muffin. "There's not a lot to tell. He asked if he could see me again, and I said yes. We'll get together when I come back from Indy." I gasped as I realized an oversight. "Oh, no! I'm just remembering that I never gave him my number, Rosalind." Then it occurred to me that maybe the oversight had been deliberate. "Damn. I hope that wasn't just a line he fed me about wanting to go out with me."

"It wasn't. He just called me and asked for your number. He said he'd forgotten to get it from you last night. If you ask me, he sounded a little panicked. I gave it to him. That's why I called, to tell you. Hope you don't mind."

"No, of course—" the beep of call waiting interrupted our conversation. "Oh, my. Someone's calling. Give me a minute to get rid of them." I depressed the flash button on the receiver. "Hello?"

"Hello, Emily. Aaron Merritt here."

I'd expected to hear the voice of one of Mom's friends. That he'd called so quickly showed real promise. "Well, hi! This is a surprise."

"I forgot to get your number, so I called Rosalind and asked her for it. I hope you don't mind."

"No. I'm glad to hear from you. Oh, there's the call waiting." There hadn't been any beep, but I didn't want to tell him I had Rosalind on the other line. "Can you hold just a minute?"

"Sure, go ahead."

"Be right back." I clicked back over to Rosalind. "It's Aaron. I'll call you back."

"I want to know what hap—," I could hear Rosalind saying as I clicked again.

"I'm sorry," I said to Aaron. "I know how annoying that can be."

"No problem. I enjoyed talking with you last night, Emily. I hate the idea of having to wait nearly two weeks to see you again." He'd asked about the timeline of my move as we said goodnight last night. "Would you consider having dinner with me tonight if you have no plans?"

"I'd love to." I gave him directions to Mom's apartment, and we agreed on seven-thirty.

Maybe coming back to Euliss wouldn't be so bad after all.

After I hung up I went to sit with Mom on the living room couch, where she sat perusing the newspaper with a cup of coffee and her morning roll. In this day and age when mugs had such popularity I didn't think I knew anyone who still drank coffee with a cup and saucer. She looked so lonely. She used to have breakfast at the small dinette table, but I think sitting there alone overwhelmed her with memories of Pop.

She smiled at me expectantly. "How was the party?"

"Very nice. Tanis was there. Did you know she and her husband are divorcing?"

"No! That Mavis never said a word. Not that I would expect her to bring it up at your daddy's funeral, but it's not like I haven't seen her lately."

After years of playing bid whist, all of Mom's old social circle now participated in bingo at the church on Thursday and Saturday nights, with only an occasional card party at someone's home. Increased crime and somewhat decreased mobility made the group of seventy-something-year-old women reluctant to visit each other's homes at night.

"Maybe she's waiting until it becomes final," I said.

"Maybe she just doesn't want to admit that her perfect daughter's marriage went down the tubes."

I choked on my orange juice and quickly took another sip to clear my throat. "That's a possibility." I never thought I'd hear Mom be critical of Tanis when she'd praised her for as long as I could remember. I rather liked it.

"Well, she does tend to brag, Emily. Helen Brown and I were talking about it a couple of weeks ago. We were all having lunch in Atlantic City when Helen told us her granddaughter is expecting. She's only seventeen and still in high school. We all tried to tell her that these things happen in this day and age, and that grandparents can't be responsible for their grandchildren, and Mavis made a comment along the lines that none of *her* grandkids had better get pregnant before they were married. I'm sure all of us privately had the same thought about our own grandkids, but Mavis actually said it. First of all, we grandmothers can talk all we want, but we have no control over what our grandchildren do. Second, her sounding so snooty didn't make poor Helen feel any better, that's for sure."

"Ah, so Mrs. Brown's going to be a great-grandmother, huh?"

"She already is. Her granddaughter had the baby last week.

The pregnancy was pretty far along when Helen told us."
She shrugged. "You know how it is."

"I understand. Did Winnie say anything about Valerie's
daughter being pregnant?"

"No. But that doesn't mean it's not true. She probably
feels that since Valerie lives on City Island no one will find
out. The only reason any of us go down there is to eat, and
those restaurants are expensive. The only reason Bea was
there was because her son took her for her birthday. Besides,
Winnie and Mavis are cut from the same sneaky cloth. They're
sisters, you know."

I remembered. Tanis made a big deal of both Wendy and
Valerie being her cousins from the time we were in grade
school, probably because they were both so cute while she'd
been saddled with her father's large nose.

I always thought it odd that both Winifred and Mavis Vin-
cent married men whose last names started with the same letter as their own first names. That was a heck of a coincidence.
I wondered if they'd planned it that way. That would explain
why they both married relatively late, at least for that time,
both of them in their late twenties. Mom always said that if
Mavis had married younger she might have had more children. She'd suffered three miscarriages before finally giving
birth to Tanis, her only child. I tried to tell her that was
nonsense, that Mavis had been young enough for her fertil-
ity problems not to be age-related, but like I said, Mom
gave the same credence to those old wives' tales as she
would to something she'd read in the World Book encyclo-
pedia.

But I had my own love life to worry about. "Mom, will
you be home tonight?"

"Well . . . I was thinking about going to bingo. But I can
stay home with you, dear."

I wolfed down the last of my English muffin, most of which
I'd consumed while still on the phone. "No, no," I said too

quickly. I hadn't even swallowed yet. Part of me expected Mom to admonish me fot talking with my mouth full.

She smiled. "You must have plans."

"I've got a date."

"With the doctor you met last night?"

"Yes, Mom," I said casually.

Her eyes narrowed suspiciously. "Is he white?"

I knew she asked this because she knew he was a friend of John Hunter. "No, Mom."

She sipped her coffee. "You know, I always liked that Rosalind. I knew she was the one to introduce you to some nice people."

Naturally, she didn't compliment Rosalind until she'd determined that her husband's doctor friend was black.

"Tell me about your new friend. What's his name? And how old is he?"

"Aaron Merritt. He's an oncologist at the Presbyterian Medical Center in the city. He's about my age, maybe a few years older."

"Has he ever been married?"

I picked up on a definite suspicious edge to her words, and I knew she was thinking that any man over forty who'd never been married had to have at least one foot in the closet.

"He's a widower, Mom. His wife died last year."

"Oh, that's too bad." Her tone held about as much sympathy as a pet rock. No doubt about it, my usually compassionate mother regarded Aaron's wife's premature death as an opportunity for me. At least she paused for decency before asking, "What does he look like?"

"Dreamy," I said without hesitation. "Mom, he's tall, slim, has beautiful skin and the sexiest bedroom eyes you've ever seen."

"He sounds wonderful. Uh . . . you know, I can always stay home tonight. I can open the door for your date."

I was glad to see Mom brighten, but the last thing I wanted was to have her gaping at Aaron. "I don't think that's necessary, Mom. I won't have a problem opening the door. You go on and play bingo. I've got a feeling you might hit the jackpot."

"No, dear," Mom said with a big smile, "*you're* the one who's hit the jackpot."

# Chapter 6

"You look lovely, Emily," Aaron said.

"Thank you." I wore the only other dress I'd brought with me, the black dress with the peplum. Something told me we wouldn't be going to the Burger Shack, so I wanted to look nice. One look at him and I knew I'd made the right move. He wore a navy suit with a light blue shirt and geometric tie and actually looked more formal than he had at Rosalind's last night. "Please have a seat."

He sat on the sofa and glanced around Mom's small but immaculate living room with its well-worn furniture that dated back twenty-five years. I guess I could understand the reluctance of people my parents' age to invest in furniture that would probably outlive them. I knew the room looked a little raggedy and I cast a sly glance at him to study his reaction, but his impassive expression gave nothing away. It made me wonder if he came from a background as modest as mine.

"Would you like a drink?" I offered.

"I should probably wait until we get to the restaurant. I don't think we have time now." He looked around the room. "So this is your mother's place?"

"Yes."

"It's very cozy."

I shrugged, thinking about my lack of a bedroom. "A little on the small side, at least for a mother and a daughter. My mother's out tonight. I've been encouraging her to start up her usual activities. She didn't have a lot of free time while my father's health was failing. She was afraid to leave him alone too long."

"How's she coping with the loss of your father?"

"Pretty good, actually. We were all worried about how she'd handle it, but Mom's a lot stronger than she lets on. Actually, I think it's easier on the family when there's a gradual decline in health; a sudden death can be devastating." I felt it would be immodest for me to add that I believed my presence helped her.

"I agree. There's no time to get affairs in order, and survivors often have to scramble to locate an insurance policy or a will to pay funeral expenses." Aaron fixated those sexy eyes on me. "Tell, me, Emily, do you plan on staying here with your mother permanently?"

Something in his voice suggested he hoped I'd reply affirmatively. As good as it felt to have him interested in me, I didn't want to lie to him. "I have to say I'm not planning on it. I like Indianapolis. There's so much going on there. It's a whole other world from Euliss . . . unless you count the bad roads, which are about the same."

"Do you have a room of your own here?"

"No. You're, uh, sitting on my bed," I said with a smile.

Instead of looking shocked or embarrassed, he patted the seat cushions with his palms. "It feels comfortable."

He certainly seemed quick on the draw. I wondered if Aaron ever found himself in a situation where he virtually didn't know what to say or do. "Actually, it pulls out to a bed. There is a two-bedroom apartment in this building, but I don't know if it makes sense for Mom to move to a place where the rent is higher when she'd only need it for a few months. Besides, people in this area tend to hold on to apartments like they're heirlooms. Sometimes they even arrange for family members to take over the leases when they die."

"Yes, space is at a premium here in New York. There are

so many co-op conversions that rentals have become scarce."
He glanced at his watch. "We should probably get going. We
have an eight o'clock reservation."

"Sure." I reached for my shawl casually, as if I had dinner
reservations every night.

In an instant he stood behind me. "Let me."

I glanced down at his long fingers as he arranged the shawl
around my shoulders. Those very fingers extended patients'
lives by carefully removing cancerous tumors. It made me
light-headed to think of what those fingers could do for me . . .
and I wasn't thinking about my health.

"What time is your flight tomorrow?" Aaron asked when
we were in his car. I'd never ridden in a Jaguar before. That
smooth ride was something I could get used to in a hurry.

I took a deep breath, not sure how he would react to my
news. "Actually, this afternoon I decided to stay for at least
another week."

"You did!"

He sounded happy, and that made me feel good. "Yes. My
mom suggested—and I had to agree with her—that it might
be a good idea to check the Sunday papers and see if I can
line up a job before I go back to Indy. My boss already
knows I'm taking an extended leave, although they won't be
happy when I call them Monday morning and tell them I'm
still in New York."

"I'm sure that under the circumstances they'll understand."

"I hope so. I'll need to use them as a reference." I looked
out through the windshield. I recognized the scenic road we
took, lined with old-money mansions, and wondered where
we were going.

Twenty minutes later we pulled up in front of a mansion
that looked like it had been built by one of those megabucks
families like the Rockefellers. The Hudson is lined with them—
mansions, that is. I didn't think this was the Rockefeller es-

tate open to the public; I was pretty sure some stray members of that large, wealthy family were still in residence.

"Nice," I said, feeling that I ought to give some kind of acknowledgment.

Aaron came around to the passenger side to help me out. "Believe this or not, this used to be someone's home. Someone bought it a couple of years ago and converted it into a restaurant."

I looked at the sizeable limestone building as I alighted. "It must be a hell of a large restaurant."

"It has a couple of private banquet rooms and one large hall upstairs. I chose this particular place because I'm not sure what you like and they have a varied menu," Aaron explained. "Beef, lamb, seafood, venison."

"Venison," I repeated. "Let's see, that would be . . . ostrich?"

"It's deer."

"Oh, that's right." I cursed myself for making a wrong guess. So much for giving Aaron the impression that I ate in settings like this all the time.

The maitre d' led us to a table by the window, which looked out over the Hudson River and the Palisades. The Palisades were nothing but tall cliffs on the New Jersey side of the river, but they were big in the world of real estate. Views of them commanded premium prices for homes, co-ops, and condos. You'd think they were the white cliffs of Dover from all the fuss, but I guess it was better to have a view of rock formations and the Hudson than another building.

Soft, piped-in violin music provided a perfect musical accompaniment to a room decorated in muted colors, with chandeliers hanging from the ceiling and fleur-de-lis wallpaper. "This is lovely," I said, seating myself in the cloth-upholstered chair the maitre d' pulled out for me.

"I hoped you would like it. They've got a fabulous veal scallopini."

"I'm afraid I'm not much for veal, but I'm sure I'll find something else on the menu I'll enjoy."

I ordered the chicken parmagiana from a menu that had no prices listed. Wow. I'd heard places like this existed, where only the man's menu listed the cost of each meal, but didn't ever expect to dine in one.

Aaron smiled at me from across the table after he gave the waiter our orders, his hand closed around a highball glass containing scotch and water. "I guess this is the time we exchange life stories."

"You already know most of mine. I'm from Euliss. I've been divorced about a dozen years. No kids. And I work as a P.A."

"Do you like kids?"

"I love kids. I just never had any. Maybe I would have if my marriage had gone differently." I left out the part about my miscarriage and how devastated I'd been to learn about my ex-husband's philandering. No sad tales for me tonight. Instead I merely shrugged. "Since I'll be forty-three in August, I think it's safe to say I won't be having any." I flashed a sunny smile. "Maybe in my next life."

"I'm glad to hear you like kids. I've got three. Two girls, twelve and fifteen, and a boy, eight."

"They're so young. It must have been—" I stopped abruptly. This wasn't the direction I wanted to go in. We'd already talked about how Mom was dealing with Pop's death. I didn't want the evening to turn morose.

He nodded. "It's all right; you can say it. It was very tough on them when their mother died. She had a brain tumor. It started with piercing headaches. She tried to treat them with over-the-counter migraine medication."

"But she was married to a doctor! Why didn't she just get medical attention instead of trying to treat herself?"

"I tried to get her to go, and she kept saying she would, but she didn't. Not until her right leg stopped working—she had to drag it—did she finally consult a neurologist. It was all downhill from there. The tumor was very aggressive. Eight months later she was dead."

"How do you manage taking care of three children?" Even as I spoke the words I felt confident that he had full-time household help, but I had to keep up my end of the conversation, didn't I?

"The kids' grandmother lives with us. She moved in when Diana was diagnosed. It's worked out very well. She's a real stabilizing influence on the kids."

I made a mental note of his late wife's name. Diana, like the late Princess of Wales. "How long has it been?"

"About eighteen months."

I wondered how many dates he'd gone on since his wife had passed.

"This is the first date I've had since she died."

I didn't expect him to say that, and I couldn't hide how much this startled me, first, because he said it just as I'd been wondering, and second, because I didn't know how to respond. It made me feel pretty good to know that I was the first woman he wanted to go out with after losing his wife, but somehow I didn't think telling him I felt honored would be appropriate.

Aaron looked a little embarrassed. "Maybe I shouldn't have told you that. You look a little uncomfortable. I'm afraid I'm not very good at concealing my feelings. I've lived with one woman for fifteen years, and there was no need for game playing."

I considered telling him how long it had been since I'd been on a date but decided against it. Instead, I gave him more points for being a no-bullshit type of guy and said, "I understand."

"Let me try to make it easier for you by telling you this: I'm enjoying your company tonight."

"Likewise."

We smiled at each other, and I felt confident that the intent behind his was as genuine as my own. I started to give him more points for sincerity, but realized that his points were already off the chart, and to continue giving him more was, well, pointless.

"It's your turn to tell me about you," I prompted.

"Well, I'm from Riverhead, Long Island."

"Suffolk County?"

He nodded. "It was just my mother, younger brother, and myself. I barely remember my father. Heck, if I saw him on the street I wouldn't know who he was. He cut out when I was seven."

"Sounds rough." I'd always considered myself blessed to have had both my parents.

"We didn't have much, but we managed. My mother worked for the phone company, plus she did extra work for the summer people. We all did, actually. As soon as my brother and I got our driver's licenses, we made extra money parking cars at parties."

"It sounds like you beat the odds when you became a doctor."

"My mother was determined that I be considered for every scholarship there was. It wasn't easy. A lot of these guidance counselors kind of dismiss single black mothers, but she persisted. She saw to it that my brother and I both got first-rate educations."

"Is he a doctor, too?"

"No, he's a chemical engineer. He works at DuPont. My mother lives near him in Delaware."

Now I knew that his comfort at Mom's simple apartment was more than good manners in play. Aaron hadn't come from money; he'd just made it. Better still, it sounded like he was aware of the great debt he owed to his mother for looking out for his future. It had to be tough, working all day, longer than that during the summer season, and still having energy to stay on your kids to keep their grades up for college. "Do you like working in oncology?" I asked.

He shrugged. "It has its ups and downs. I'm elated when I can prolong a patient's life, but it can be devastating when I can't. It's ultimately more interesting than being a general surgeon, which was what I originally considered. You know what they say: you've seen one appendix, you've seen them all."

We laughed again, and I thought, *I can have a lot of fun with this man.*

As our appetizers were delivered a thin, white-haired man wearing a tuxedo sat at the shiny black baby grand in the corner and began to play a series of standards, the type of music I heard in old black-and-white musicals. I almost expected to see the Nicholas Brothers come out from between the tables and do a tap dance routine. For a few minutes we sat in quiet companionship as we looked out at the twinkling lights of the George Washington Bridge in the distance, sipped wine poured from the bottle Aaron had ordered, and munched on breaded and fried vegetables, the background filled with piano music. I didn't know what his thoughts were, but mine were that this felt awfully good. Could it be that my reward for being a dutiful, concerned daughter was to capture the attentions of a handsome doctor? It would certainly make my time in Euliss a lot more pleasant.

My chicken was so tender I didn't need a knife to cut it, and it practically melted in my mouth. The restaurant's quiet, unhurried atmosphere suited us perfectly. By the time we consumed our appetizers, salads, entrees, and a scrumptious napoleon, a good two and a half hours had passed. The mood would have been ruined by anxious glances or throat-clearing hints from the staff, but no one here seemed to be in a hurry, just eager to please.

When we arrived back at my mother's apartment building, Aaron reached for my hand when he opened the car door for me, held on to it until I needed both hands to unlock the vestibule door. It seemed like such a natural thing to do, and Lord knew it felt good.

"I had a wonderful time, Aaron," I said as I reached inside my purse for my keys.

"So did I. Right now I'm thinking that I'd like to ask you what you're doing for dinner tomorrow night."

I beamed, grateful for his no-bullshit stance. He wanted to see me again!

"And the night after that and the night after that," he continued, his eyes on mine, "but something tells me that's not how it's supposed to be done, so I'll just tell you that I'm glad you're staying in town a little longer. But I don't mind you knowing how I really feel."

"I think it's a lovely thought."

When we were inside I held my index finger to my lips. "I'm just going to check on my mother. I'll be right back. Go ahead and sit down." I snapped on one of the lamps in the living room. In spite of the dark apartment, I knew Mom was home; I'd seen her car outside. I decided it would be best to warn her Aaron was here so she wouldn't come stumbling out to the bathroom in her rollers and nightgown.

She sat propped up in bed, dozing, an open book across her lap and the TV turned to a movie on the Lifetime network. One look at her and I knew that if it weren't for me she would have put the book away and turned out the light. Like she said, I was her baby. It didn't matter that I was forty-two years old.

"Mom, I'm home," I said softly.

Her body jerked. She looked like she'd been caught doing something illegal. I half expected her to hold her hands up, like a criminal who'd been suddenly apprehended.

"Emmie, hi," she said sleepily after recognizing me. How'd the date go?"

"It went fine. Aaron came in with me. I just wanted to let you know I invited him in, but I don't expect him to stay long."

"Doggone it. If I didn't have my hair set for church tomorrow I'd put on my clothes and come out and meet him."

"Another time. I'll see you in the morning. I don't want Aaron to think I forgot about him."

"Come back and tell me when he leaves. I'd like to get a peek at him, at least."

A thought occurred to me. "Mom . . . you haven't told your friends that I went out with Aaron, have you?"

"Of course I did. How often does my daughter date doctors?"

I sighed. What was it about my mother's generation, where so many of them thought doctors and lawyers walk on water?

"You should have seen the look on Mavis's face."

I couldn't help smiling at that. "I'll be back," I said as I closed her bedroom door behind me.

Aaron sat poised on the edge of the couch. He rose as I approached. How gallant, I thought.

"Is your mother okay?" he asked.

"She's fine. She was waiting up for me. Isn't that cute?"

"Very cute," he said, and from the way his eyes roamed over me I knew he wasn't thinking about my mother. My, he had sexy eyes. I loved the way they drooped downward slightly at the outer corners. His woodsy cologne fused with his skin and gave off an intoxicating personal scent. I knew the time had come for a good-night kiss. He took a step toward me and dipped his chin, and I raised mine. It was the quickest of kisses, feather soft . . . and a little bit disappointing. I should have known Aaron wasn't the type to French kiss on the first date. Any other dude would be teasing my tonsils by now.

Still, I thought of those healing hands of his, and I knew . . . Aaron Merritt would eventually become my lover.

# Chapter 7

Rosalind called the next morning to grill me about my date with Aaron, just as I was being grilled by Mom.

"All right," I said firmly, looking at Mom while holding the telephone receiver against my ear. "In the absence of a speakerphone, I'm going to talk to both of you at the same time so I won't have to repeat myself."

I cleared my throat and spoke slowly and clearly. "Aaron arrived on time. I wore a black dress, and he wore a navy suit." In hindsight, we both looked like we could have been going to a funeral. "His car rides like a dream. It's a Jaguar," I said to Mom, who stood gesturing for more information like her life depended on her winning a game of charades.

"Ooh," she said excitedly, sounding like she was all of eight years old.

I named the restaurant we went to. "It's in Dobbs Ferry. We had a table with a wonderful view of the river and the Palisades."

"I'll bet he tipped the maitre d' to get it," Rosalind said.

"What'd she say?" Mom asked.

I repeated Rosalind's statement for Mom's benefit.

"What's a maitre d'?" she wanted to know. "Is it like a hostess?"

Mom, bless her heart, was a woman best described as having simple tastes.

"Sort of, except it's a man," I explained. "Anyway, it was lovely."

"What'd you have to eat?" Mom asked.

"Chicken parmigiana." I knew that had nothing to do with the quality of my date, but I knew my mother, so I answered patiently. I think that being a child of the Depression lay behind her almost unhealthy curiosity about food.

"And what did Aaron have?"

"Veal scallopini, Mom." This time my voice came out sounding just a little sharp. Poor Rosalind, she must have thought my mother was a candidate for Bellevue. "Now, can I get back to my summary?"

"Go right ahead," she said indignantly.

"Anyway, it was lovely. He mentioned that I'm the first woman he's dated since his wife died."

Rosalind let out a whoop. "Go, Emily!"

Mom was impressed, too. "Emmie, that's wonderful!"

"So what happened when he brought you home?" Rosalind asked.

"Don't get personal," I said playfully. "Anyway, Rosalind, I told my mother I'd go with her to church this morning, so I've got to start getting dressed. I'll talk to you later."

"Can you call me when you get in? I'm trying to organize a twenty-five-year reunion for our graduating class, and I'd like to run some ideas past you."

"Uh . . . sure." I hesitated because it seemed like reunion plans should have started a year ago. This month marked twenty-five years since graduation. What could Rosalind possibly hope to organize between now and the six months left in the year?

The smile plastered on my face as we stood outside the church was sure to have my jaw aching by the end of the day. My mother's friends all told me how beautiful my hair looked. I got the distinct impression that none of them approved of nappy hair.

The kicker came from Helen Brown. "I'll bet your new boyfriend really likes your hair."

I raised an eyebrow. New boyfriend? Surely she didn't mean—

"Oh, yes, the doctor," Bea Pullman chimed in. "Your mother told us all about him."

"Well, I think it would be a tad premature to call him my boyfriend," I said politely. "We just met a few days ago." Our first meeting actually occurred less than forty-eight hours ago, but they didn't need to know that.

"Oh, but he's pursuing you, Emmie," Mom said. "He called as we were leaving the house. I still say you should have taken the call."

"Mom, maybe if it was Easter I would have, but the services today aren't going to last until dinnertime. He'll call back."

"Spoken like a woman who knows she's got a man's attentions," Mrs. Brown said with a knowing nod.

I smiled weakly and excused myself, moving on to chat with someone else.

Mom and I hadn't been home five minutes when Aaron called again. He made no mention of having tried to reach me, even though the call history showed two previous calls from an unidentified number. His name and number showed the first time, but, hey, if you're calling someone every hour on the hour, wouldn't you want to block your number from showing? Either he had a pretty good idea I'd be back by now, or he felt three hours was a long enough time to allow his number to show again.

"I was wondering if you might be interested in seeing the Jazz Score exhibit at the Museum of Modern Art." He chuckled. "Maybe seeing is the wrong word, although film clips are included. Hearing it is probably more accurate, but they're including exhibits and panel discussions. They're covering films with music scores written by Elmer Bernstein, Duke Ellington,

Quincy Jones, and that guy who wrote the theme to *Mission Impossible,* among others."

"Sounds like fun." I started humming the theme to *The Magnificent Seven.* "Were you planning on going this afternoon?"

"Yes. I figured I'd get in a little culture before heading back to work tomorrow."

"I just got back from church, but all I need is a few minutes to get changed." I'd promised to call Rosalind back, but she'd have to wait.

"Great. How about if I pick you up in half an hour?"

"That'll work. See you then."


Over the next week I talked to Aaron every day, often more than once, and saw him whenever I could. I thought it amusing how slowly the sexual side of our relationship was progressing. The day we went to the museum, which was the first time Aaron met my mother, he actually kissed my cheek upon returning me home. The next time we had dinner, during the week, he returned to kissing me on the mouth, but still no tongue. I wanted a real kiss so bad, complete with his arms around me, I feared I might lose it and thrust my tongue into his mouth.

When not daydreaming about how it would feel to be held in Aaron's arms, I spent the week putting in applications and went for an interview at a local practice. Dr. Wiley Norman had been practicing in Euliss for as long as I could remember. Two of his four sons had now taken over the practice. I didn't know any of the Norman offspring. Although they were in my general age group, they'd gone to parochial school.

Working at the Norman Family Practice would be more convenient than working at Euliss General, because it was closer. And employment at a private practice meant I wouldn't have to sit through one of those insufferable two-day orientations, complete with film shorts where the actors were picked up from Theater 101. They made Tanis's performances look Oscar worthy. And I swear, if I had to listen to just one more human resources associate whose blouse pulled because it was too tight across the chest and who tapped the floor with her ankle-strap shoes tell me how to dress appropriately for the office, I think I might lose it.

The Norman practice was located in what was laughingly referred to as "the plaza," a rather upscale euphemism for the town center that was downtown Euliss. The plaza consisted of a pharmacy, a liquor store, an outdoor newsstand, four banks, maybe three pizzerias, an electronics store that offered a layaway plan (naturally), a furniture store where the furniture's drawers were guaranteed to stick, a music store, a deli, a fish market, a cheap shoe store, and about eight discount stores. If you wanted jewelry or clothing or decent shoes or good furniture you had to go to the mall in the white section of town.

I arrived for my interview promptly at ten minutes of two. The patients in the waiting room were typical of a busy family practice, ranging from screaming babies, exasperated-looking young mothers, an obviously ill youngster whose whining was interrupted only by coughing fits, and a few elderly folks. The one thing that jumped out at me was that they were all black and Latino.

I found myself unable to conceal my shock when I was ushered into an office and greeted by none other than Wiley Norman himself.

"Dr. Norman," I said, surprise in my voice. "I didn't expect to see you here. Uh, are you still practicing?" I tried to keep the incredulity out of my voice, but the man was a contemporary of my mother. He had to be at least seventy-five years old. The only thing more ridiculous would be if he still used the suffix of "Junior."

He chuckled, a wheezy sound that itself sounded old. "Oh, I just come in a few days a month to see some of my longtime patients. My sons are good doctors, mind you, but some of the old-timers don't feel comfortable with anyone so young."

Having the old man in the office sure made for a hell of a lot of Dr. Normans, but his reasons did make sense. After all, the man's specialty was family medicine. His age wouldn't deter him from accurately diagnosing and treating everyday maladies. It wasn't like he used scalpels or other sharp instruments that could be dangerous in a less-than-steady hand.

"I'm so sorry to hear about your father, Emily," he said.

"Thank you. We appreciated you and Mrs. Norman stopping by the funeral home to pay your respects."

"And are you returning to Euliss?"

I began to relax. This seemed more like a conversation with an old friend than a job interview. "It's a rather uncertain set of circumstances. My brother and sister both live out of town. My mother is bound to have a hard time adjusting to life without my father. I decided to come back for an extended period of time to help her out." I wouldn't have been so honest about the possibility of not remaining in Euliss had I been talking to some anonymous hospital administrator— okay, I would have flat out lied—but I couldn't do that to Dr. Norman, who had been giving me checkups all through my school years. "I'm licensed to work in both New York and Indiana," I volunteered. "I'm going to make my condo in Indianapolis a short-term rental unit for business travelers. But I can't give you a guarantee that I'll be staying in New York indefinitely. I might be here six months. I might be here three years. Or I might not ever leave." That last sentence, for pure dramatic effect, came out with some difficulty. Stuck in Euliss for the rest of my life? Not a chance. Fortunately, Dr. Norman didn't seem to notice.

"I see," he said, nodding. "Well, it just so happens that Gina, our P.A., is having second thoughts about coming back to work after her baby is born. We can't guarantee her that her job will be available for her after the required maximum time for the Family Leave Act, but this might benefit both of you. It's not generally known, but . . ."

I recognized that to mean, *In other words, don't go blabbing this all over town.*

". . . we do plan to open a second office on Woodlawn Avenue."

The main drag stretched from the Bronx all the way to White Plains. Most of the shopping, restaurants, and multiplexes in the area were located along that fifteen-mile stretch of road. There would always be a need for a medical office in the plaza, which could be accessed easily by patients without cars. But Woodlawn Avenue would give the Norman practice more visibility.

I began to feel hopeful.

"I'm going to call in my sons. You can tell all of us about your work experience."

I felt pretty good when I left the office. My interview had gone well. The two younger Dr. Normans conveyed a polite but distant demeanor, in direct contrast to their father's warmth, which I read as "don't think that just because Dad knows your family the job is yours." I, of course, played it professional, sounding knowledgeable, not smiling too much, trying to convey by my body language that they didn't intimidate me.

I had an interview scheduled at Euliss General after my return from Indianapolis, and I had a feeling that I'd be able to pick which position I wanted. The benefits would probably be better at the hospital, but I'd have more freedom at the family practice. Then there was the consideration of money. Instinct told me that the only ones who did well in a family business were members of the family.

"Emily!"

Startled to hear my name, I stopped my stride and glanced around the waiting room for a familiar face. Something vaguely familiar about the pretty dark-skinned sister who sat comforting a cranky-looking little boy. Especially around the eyes . . .

She smiled knowingly. "You don't recognize me, do you?" I took a few halting steps in her direction. "Marsha?"

"Yes, it's me. How are you, Emily? I didn't think you still lived in Euliss."

"I don't. I mean, I haven't been living here, but I'm coming back."

"I heard about your father. I'm terribly sorry."

I took a seat in the vinyl-upholstered chair next to her. "Thank you." I realized I was staring, but I couldn't help it. "Marsha, you look fabulous."

She chuckled. "Thanks. I've made a few changes since high school."

I'll say. I'd known Marsha Cox since grammar school, but the chic woman sitting opposite me bore little resemblance to the child who stood five seven by the time she was ten years old and wore her mother's too big clothes to school and also pinned on her falls. I'll never forget the day Marsha and Tracy Turner got into a fight in sixth grade and Tracy pulled off Marsha's fake ponytail. Tracy had always been a mean bitch. My heart hurt for Marsha that day in the playground. She'd been so embarrassed, and naturally the kids watching thought it was the funniest thing they'd seen since Sammy Davis Jr. kissed Archie Bunker on *All in the Family*. I remember leading her away while I glared at Tracy.

Marsha, an only child, lived with her mother in a tenement on Dellwood Avenue that had since been torn down. I went over there with her a couple of times, and it was just awful, all musty smelling and creaky. They didn't even have their own bathroom; they had to share a hall bath with other tenants on the floor. To me, nothing says "poor" more vividly than two things: One is a street address that ends with "and a half," as in "15-1/2 Garver Street," which suggests to me that the residents were too poor to afford a whole apartment. The other is having to share a bathroom with your neighbors. I can't think of anything less sanitary. My ex-husband, bless his sloppy heart, couldn't even manage to hit the target half the time when he relieved himself. Whenever, in a moment of weakness, I found myself missing him in the period immediately following our separation, I would console myself with the thought that I would never again have to wipe up the floor behind him . . . or the seat, depending on whether or not he felt like lifting it up.

And what if you really had to go and Mr. Henderson from down the hall was in there, complete with newspaper and a fresh cigar? But it was probably all Mrs. Cox could afford. Marsha's mother worked as a cocktail waitress and couldn't have made much money, and in hindsight I realized that Marsha's thin frame might have had less to do with nature and more to do with not getting enough to eat. I knew from Marsha that her father had skipped out long ago. I don't know where he went, but wherever it was, I'll bet *his* ass didn't have to share a bathroom, like the family he'd abandoned.

"I love your hair," I told her now. Gone were the short strands that were barely long enough to smooth down close to her head so she could pin on one of her mother's hairpieces. Marsha now wore her hair in a stylish bob even with her chin on the left and with her earlobe on the right. Its texture was so straight it looked as shiny as patent leather, but a few strands of gray that the light hit told me it was all hers and not a weave.

"Thanks." She patted it with a hand I noticed had polished oval nails of uniform length and rings on both her index and ring fingers.

"Is this your son?"

"Yes. This is Cameron. He's not feeling so hot today, so I figured I'd bring him in to see Dr. Norman, now that I'm back in Euliss."

I directed my next statement toward Cameron. "I'm sorry you aren't feeling well," I said, rubbing his arm. "I'm sure Dr. Norman will give you something that will make you bounce right back."

"Thank you," he mumbled politely.

"So you left Euliss, too," I said to Marsha. "Where'd you go?"

"I wasn't far. I lived in New Jersey. I came back and moved in with my mother when my husband died."

"Oh, Marsha, I'm so sorry. I didn't know." Marsha seemed too young to be a widow, but I quickly realized that we weren't too young for anything anymore, even to die ourselves.

"Thanks. I've been back for two months."

The sliding frosted-glass window opened like a miniature shower door. "Cameron Hendricks," a woman called.

I quickly grabbed the notepad I always keep in my purse. "Marsha, we have to get together. Please give me your number, and I'll give you mine."

"Sure." She waited until I pulled the pen out of the loop that held it in place, and then she recited a number. "That's my cell phone. It's easiest to catch me on that."

"Okay." I took it down, then flipped a page and scribbled my mother's number. "This is mine. I have to make a quick trip to Indianapolis, but I'll be back the week after next. Let's plan to have lunch or even dinner together, okay?"

"Bet."

She stood next to Cameron, and we hugged briefly before I left and she disappeared into the inner office.

I walked back to my car with a spring in my step. Not only had the interview gone well, but I'd run into an old friend in the waiting room. Surely that was an omen.

I saw nothing but good things in my future.

# Chapter 8

I flew home on Tuesday to meet face-to-face with the property management service I'd chosen and to prepare my condo for rental. After speaking with the property manager, I'd come to the conclusion that it would be best if I made it a furnished rental. People relocated to Indy all the time, and businesses were always looking for furnished units for short-term rentals. This would mean that I could probably get back into my place the moment I was ready to come back and continue with my life.

The agent I worked with expressed admiration for my reasons for giving up my home. "Maybe one day one of my kids will do what you're doing for their mother and me," he'd remarked.

I was relieved at not having to move out my belongings, but I took the property manager's advice and rented a small storage unit to place my personal things, like my small collection of LPs, my large collection of CDs, and my photos, as well as clothing I couldn't bring with me to Mom's, given her limited storage space. I spent a few hours packing those up and driving them over to the storage place. I gave myself another day to take care of any loose ends, like making a key for the property manager, putting in a change of address at the post office, and stopping in at my bank, after which I would return to my condo and get to bed early. I'd promised the property manager I would leave my place ready for a renter, and that meant clean sheets and no dishes in the sink. As soon as I arose I would change the bed linens and freshen up the place before hitting the road for the long drive to New York.

I was about to load a box of clothes into my car to take to the post office when my cell phone rang, with its familiar theme from *Bonanza*. A quick glance at the caller ID window revealed Aaron's cell number, which made me smile. He'd called two or three times a day, every day, since I'd been gone. The insecure part of me feared he would move on to someone else—like Tanis, who would know from her mother that I'd flown home—the minute my plane took off, especially since his schedule didn't allow him to drive me to the airport. My niece took me to catch my plane, since my mother wouldn't consider driving anywhere within the five boroughs of New York City. Aaron apologized profusely for not being able to take me himself, and my last night in town he took me to the Ruth Chris's Steak House in Tarrytown.

"I wish you were back already, Emily," he confessed.

"That's sweet. But we'll be together again before you know it."

"Speaking of that, I had an idea I'd like your opinion on."

Immediately I started to feel squeamish. It always made me a little nervous when people asked me for my opinion. Often they were trying to justify something they knew damn well was wrong, or they wanted to be told that a too tight suit looked great on them. Either way, they were not going to like my answer, and then they'd end up getting mad at me. "And what's that?" I asked, my voice pitched low with caution.

"I can easily take a day off Friday. I thought it would be nice if I flew out to Indy and helped you drive your car back. You were planning on driving back on Saturday, weren't you?"

I was. I hesitated only because I hadn't expected such a generous gesture on his part. Aaron wasn't looking to have his ego stroked; he wanted to help me out. My heart filled with gratitude. The man was a physician with a busy and important practice, yet he was willing to take off from work for a boring drive across three and a half states. "I think that's a wonderful idea, Aaron. Are you sure you're not putting yourself out too much?"

"Not at all. My mother-in-law is here and can watch the kids. I'll have my secretary make my reservation and shuffle around a few appointments, and I'll be good to go. As long as I'm back by Monday, everything will be fine."

"I'm flattered that you want to help me," I said honestly.

"I guess I want to make sure you really do come back. I hate the idea of you being so far away from me."

"I'm definitely coming back. And now, thanks to you, I have something to look forward to."

After we said good-bye I smiled as I hung up the phone, and I suspected he did the same.


I stuffed as many clothes and shoes as I could into two tall dish cartons and took them with me to the post office, where I would ship them to my mother's apartment via parcel post. I left behind anything I felt I could absolutely, positively do without while I was in transition, knowing full well that the first thing I'd need for a special occasion would probably be something I'd left behind. I'd have to help Mom clean out Pop's closet when I got back, a task I wasn't anticipating happily. But even as I hoisted the cartons up onto the counter I wondered if there'd be enough room for it all in what was a very small closet.

Tonight I was to be the guest of honor at a farewell dinner hosted by my three closest friends, all of whom were shocked by my decision to return to Euliss. Sometimes I couldn't believe how quickly my life had changed, myself. Just a few weeks ago my friends and I went to a cookout on Memorial Day, and the Fourth of July would find me living in Euliss again. On my mother's sofa.

But at least I had Aaron. I couldn't wait to see him.

*  *  *

First thing in the morning, with a slight headache from the mango margaritas I'd consumed and feeling a little teary at the thought of leaving my friends in Indy, I washed all the bed linens and remade the bed, dusted and vacuumed the four rooms and the hall, mopped the floors of the kitchen and bathrooms, and polished the mirrors and TV screens. The management company would send in a cleaning service to spruce up the unit before rental, but I'd promised to do my part. Even though I knew I was making the best move for my unique situation, it felt a little weird, thinking about a stranger sleeping in my bed or putting his or her feet up on my coffee table. I felt very proprietary about my house, my most valuable asset. I even hummed the Diana Ross tune "It's My House" as I worked, a strangely upbeat song for my mood. I was leaving behind good friends who cared about me, plus the comfortable home I'd created, to sleep on my mother's sofa bed for the next few months.

If it weren't for Aaron, I'd probably throw myself across my bed and sob.

At eleven o'clock, after checking with the airline to make sure the flight from New York was on schedule, I headed out to the airport to meet his plane, my weekend bag sitting on the backseat and my desktop computer on the floor in front of it.

I started circling the drive outside the baggage claim carousels ten minutes after his flight landed. As I slowly drove through the second time I saw him sail out the doors, looking crisp and handsome in tan khakis and a short-sleeved collared cotton shirt. Pink plaid shirts aren't for every man, but Aaron pulled it off magnificently. He looked as refreshing as a bowl of raspberry sherbet . . . and just as tasty, I thought wickedly. Trying not to drool, I got out of the car and honked the horn so he'd see me.

As I watched him approach, his bedroom eyes hidden by aviator sunglasses, I suddenly realized that we wouldn't get to New York tonight. The only way to complete that seven-hundred-plus-mile, twelve-hour drive would be if we got on the road at dawn, but it was nearly noon. By eight-thirty it would start to get dark. We'd have to stop somewhere for the night.

And I hadn't packed the first thing to sleep in, or at least to wear to bed.

Shucks. I wanted our first time together to be special.

I got out of my Altima just before he reached it. He gave me a quick but forceful kiss with just a hint of tongue. Good thing he steadied me by putting an arm around my waist, or else I would have slithered to the ground like a garter snake. I used my remote to unlock the remaining doors, and he tossed the duffel that hung from his shoulder inside before turning to me once more.

"I missed you," he said earnestly.

"I missed you, too. Thought about you all the time." I gave him a quick peck on the lips. "Come on, let's get out of here so they can have the space."

I got behind the wheel, and he sat in the passenger seat. "Did you want to hit the road now, or maybe eat first?" I asked as I pulled away from the curb.

"You've gotten everything done?" He sounded surprised.

"Yes. I took my clothes—at least the ones I'll be needing—with me to the post office yesterday and shipped them to my mother's. I've got my computer on the floor in the back, and the condo is all clean." I shrugged. "So I'm good to go."

"It's been years since the last time I was out here. I attended an AMA convention here once. Tell you what. Since it's kind of late in the day to start a long drive, why don't we go get some lunch, and then you can give me a tour of the city. We'll get an early start tomorrow."

"Um . . . you do realize that my condo is all prepared for rental. I changed the linens and fluffed all the cushions this morning. I'd be afraid to as much as sit down in there."

He smiled at me. Even his mouth was sexy, I thought. "I

anticipated as much, and I certainly don't want to mess up all your preparations. I figured we'd get a room. Or, if you prefer, rooms."

I had a quick thought of my mother. Usually she sprouted lines like, "Why should he buy the cow when he can get the milk for free?" But when I told her that Aaron planned to fly out and drive back with me, she'd asked, "Will you be spending a night on the road?" with an eagerness that sounded to me like she was ready to make the hotel reservation herself, just to make sure we had no problems doing the deed. I knew she wouldn't be quite so receptive to the idea of my sleeping with Aaron if he were, say, a locksmith. What a difference an M.D. degree makes.

I decided to play with him a little. "You mean, you in one room and me in another? That doesn't sound very cozy, especially after us not seeing each other for nearly a week."

He grinned at me across the console. "I was hoping you'd say that. I just didn't want you to think I was rushing you," he said shyly. "You have to understand I'm a bit out of practice with this sort of thing."

I knew what he meant. One of the best things about being married is that you get all the sex you want.

"Do you feel like eating anything in particular?" I asked innocently.

He shrugged, my double entendre going right over his head. "What do you suggest?"

"There's a pub downtown I like. Burgers, chicken, ribs, pizza, sandwiches, stuff like that."

"Oh, I'm sure I can find something on that list that appeals to my taste buds."

I headed downtown and parked inside the Circle Center Garage. "It's just a short walk from here," I said.

At lunch he ordered the chicken-and-ribs platter and I had jambalaya. We both had beer. Then we walked back to the Circle Center, a collection of upscale shops that had been made into a mall via the contribution of a couple of smart architects. The department store anchors were still accessible for pedestrians on the streets of downtown, but somehow it all connected. We did a little window shopping, then went to the theater in the mall and caught a matinee showing of one of those innocent-man-accused-of-murder thrillers. Finally, we headed back to the car.

I drove around downtown, pointing out the State Capitol, the Convention Center, and Market Square Arena, even the Benjamin Harrison House.

Aaron looked at everything with what appeared to be genuine interest, although I knew he'd seen it all before. Maybe he was trying to figure out what was different. "Hey, there's the Hilton. Let's go by there and see if they have any availability."

They did, so Aaron registered us, or I guess he registered himself. I'd always presumed that men checking into hotels with women they weren't married to just listed themselves on the register.

He came outside waving a key card. We took our bags out of the car and got into the elevator. I tried not to look over at the registration desk. I'm sure the folks manning it were looking at me with that "*we* know what you're going to be doing in the next five minutes" look on their faces.

Actually, what happened in the next five minutes was that both of us fell asleep, me on the bed and him in the reclining easy chair. Travel on his part, cleaning and packing on mine, plus a heavy meal and all that sightseeing had done us in. I woke up before he did, and I was pleased to hear the sound of easy breathing and nothing else. I hugged myself in anticipation. Not only was he good-looking, not only was he rich, but he didn't snore. Mom was right: I'd really hit the jackpot.

I took a shower while he slept and put on a white cotton eyelet sundress in anticipation of dinner. It was rather casual, but it was all I had with me.

Aaron opened his eyes a little after six. "Wow, I was really knocked out."

"Not really. It was nearly four when we checked in."

"It's going on ten after six now. Would you like to get some dinner?"

The truth was, I was feeling a little peckish, but I didn't want him to think I was one of those women who ate like a horse when someone else was footing the bill and practically starved herself the rest of the time. Nor did I want to sound impressed by his casual invitation to go out to get another meal after that nice lunch we had. I could get used to eating out like this all the time.

"Something light," I said. "Maybe a salad. But this time it's on me." The man had flown all the way out from New York to help me drive seven hundred miles, plus he'd paid for an extremely comfortable hotel room. The least I could do was buy him dinner. Even if it set me back a hundred bucks.

He opened his mouth, presumably to object, but I stopped those kissable lips of his from forming the words by holding out my palm like a traffic cop. "I won't have it any other way, Aaron."

He gave me a lazy smile. "Something tells me its hopeless to argue with you. All right, Emily. There's a McCormick and Schmick's in the hotel. Good food, and I don't have to wear a jacket. How's that?"

"Perfect. I was hoping you wouldn't want to go far."

"I'm going to take a quick shower, and then I'll be ready."

I took advantage of his time in the shower by going downstairs to the restaurant and asking to see a menu. I was relieved to see it was a moderately priced restaurant specializing in seafood. Since Aaron assumed I was familiar with it, I figured they had locations in major cities.

It was still light out when we emerged from the restaurant into the hotel lobby, courtesy of it being close to the summer solstice. When we returned to our room Aaron remarked, "I probably should change and go down to the exercise room for a quick workout, but I'm going to take the loutish way out." He kicked off his shoes and stretched out on his back on one side of the king-sized bed, one arm folded behind his head, the other channel-surfing with the remote. I went to wash the make-up off my face and to take off those killer heels, which looked sexy but were hell to walk in. I saw no reason to stand on ceremony. In fact, this might be a good way for things to progress naturally. I'd eaten only a bowl of chowder and a Cobb salad with crabmeat, shrimp, and scallops, but my belly felt almost uncomfortably full. "You look awfully comfortable," I said. "Mind if I join you?"

He patted the empty space beside him. "There's plenty of room."

I climbed onto the bed and lay down close to him. His arm automatically went around my shoulder.

"Anything good on?" I asked.

"This spy thriller on pay-per-view doesn't look bad. I wanted to ask you about it. For all I know you've already seen it." He flicked to the title and description.

"I missed that one, but it sounds good."

For the next two hours, we lay companionably together watching the film. During the obligatory scene when the leading man bedded his love interest, Aaron turned to me for a kiss, and I was only too happy to comply. My body tingled when he squeezed my breast. Something had told me he wouldn't want to jump right into the nitty-gritty as soon as we returned from dinner. I liked the idea of cuddling together on the bed while watching a movie, playing footsie.

Aaron alternately stroked and squeezed my arm periodically. By the time the closing credits ran, I think both of us were ready to move to the next level. I can't remember the last time I felt so excited about the prospect of having sex.

He moved so excruciatingly slowly, it was almost maddening. He was a great kisser, though. When I reached out and touched the goods, I wanted to whoop for joy. Handsome, rich, successful, . . . and packing, too.

The way he stared at me after I was nude made me feel like

the most beautiful creature on earth, and that's quite a stretch, since I'm forty-two and I don't exercise.

Aaron, on the other hand, *does* work out. The sight of him naked left me breathless, and I'm not just talking about from the waist down. He had toned abs, muscled but not huge biceps, and a well-developed chest with tightly coiled curls in its center. He put on a condom and moved between my thighs, and the way he groaned the moment he got inside me brought tears to my eyes. I knew exactly how he felt. It had been a drought for me as well, although probably not as long as his. I squeezed the cheeks of his butt like they could save me from drowning and squeezed him with my vaginal muscles, welcoming him into my body.

I'm embarrassed to say this, but that first time went only about three minutes. I was just too excited, and so was he.

"My God, I think I lasted longer than that my very first time," he said ruefully, his face close to mine but to the side, where I couldn't actually see him. "I must apologize to you."

"Don't. I couldn't control myself, either." I had a memory of my own first time, and how quickly my partner had reached climax. It had taken all of thirty seconds. I giggled at the recollection. "Besides, we can always do it again."

"You can count on that."

Ten minutes later we did just that, and this time we acted more like experienced adults than horny teenagers with no control.

Afterward I reached down to finger his penis, now both limp and sticky. "I think it's dead," he joked. "But don't worry, it's not permanent." He kissed me firmly on the mouth. "You don't know how much I looked forward to tonight. I want you to know that making love to you was everything I thought it would be."

"I enjoyed it, too, Aaron."

We lay locked in each other's arms for a few minutes. When sleep began to overtake us we broke apart. I rolled over onto my stomach, fulfilled but with a nagging sense that something wasn't right.

Then, as I was falling asleep, it hit me.

The second time was exactly the same as the first. That was awfully unusual. I mean, I'm not saying I've been around the block more times than the mailman, but nothing like that had ever happened to me before. In my experience, the second time was always a little friskier, a little daring . . . a little less . . . traditional. It was like that "getting-to-know-you" phase giving way to "getting to know what you like." And it usually involved a different position.

I shrugged, a little sleepy, considering I had to get up in just a few hours and start on a long drive. Aaron was probably as tired as I was. Traveling always did that to a person. The next time he'd demonstrate that there's more than one way to skin a cat.

My arms went to the sides of my pillow and my eyes closed. The mattress rocked a bit as he changed position, lying on his side facing me. I smiled as his arm rested on the curve of my hip. His very touch excited me.

"I have a confession to make."

I opened my eyes. It seemed a little early to be making true confessions, but I was always ready to listen if someone wanted to spill his guts. I just hoped he didn't expect me to do the same.

"What's that?"

"You're just the second woman I've ever been with."

For a moment this rendered me speechless. I swallowed hard. Then I said the only thing I could say. "Really?"

"The only other woman I've been intimate with was the one I married."

My God. Was I lying in bed with a man who'd been a virgin when he got married? A man whose sexual experience paled in comparison with my own? I felt distinct twinges of discomfort at the center of my stomach.

"How old were you when you got married?" I asked.

"Twenty-seven. But we weren't virgins all that time. We'd known each other since freshman year in college."

Thank heavens for that. It gave a whole new dimension to the famous Jimi Hendrix question, Are You Experienced? Not that I was about to tell him how many guys I'd slept with. Even if I *could* remember them all. It's just not the type of thing one keeps track of, like a basketball score. With his chaste record, Aaron would likely think I was two steps removed from being a hooker.

If I was just the second woman he had known in the biblical sense, it was pretty easy to figure out that he hadn't had sex in quite some time. I was surprised he hadn't made a quick trip to Vegas or Rio or somewhere just to get laid anonymously, since he could afford it, with no one pulling on his M.D. strings, just to get release.

"It's like riding a bicycle," I murmured sleepily. But when I slept I had a strange dream. I was facing someone who was mostly unseen except for a slender arm and long, tapered fingers with polished nails. That told me it was a woman, and she was shaking her index finger at me.

My eyes flew open. The unseen woman had to be Aaron's late wife, and the gesture was clear. If I could see her face, she'd no doubt be mouthing the words, "Stay away from my husband!"

# Chapter 9

We didn't leave quite as early as we planned to. Last night's rigorous sex after such a long drought had worn both of us out. It was a little after eight by the time we got on the road for the seven-hundred-plus mile drive, which meant we wouldn't reach our destination before nine P.M.

I don't know which state is wider, Ohio or Pennsylvania. All I know is that both are boring in terms of scenery . . . and that the people of America consume a heck of a lot of corn. For years I thought all the corn came from true Midwest states like my adopted home of Indiana, which could be summed up as containing one large city at its center, the fringes of the Greater Chicago area in the northwest corner, a couple of college towns, and lots and lots of cornfields. Corn seemed to be a staple of the Ohio and Pennsylvania landscapes. One has to wonder how they're going to keep their young people down on the farm after they've seen Cleveland or Pittsburgh.

Speaking of Pittsburgh, my sister called my cell phone while we were riding through West Virginia to say she hoped Aaron and I would be able to stop by her house. We could even spend the night, she said. I knew that Mom hadn't been able to contain her excitement about Aaron's offer to fly out and drive back with me and blabbed, and that Cissy just wanted to get a look at him to see if he was really all that.

"I'm sorry, Cissy, but we can't," I told her. "Aaron has to

be back at work on Monday. We're going to drive straight through, and he'll be able to rest tomorrow."

As I spoke I realized something I hadn't thought of previously. So great was my fascination with all those farms we were passing that it hadn't occured to me that since we were driving my car, I would have to drop Aaron off. That meant I'd get to see where he lived.

We stopped at a Chinese buffet somewhere in Western Pennsylvania for a leisurely hour-long lunch. Aside from breaks to gas up and to use the bathroom, we kept driving.

The New York skyline lit up the twilight sky as we approached the George Washington Bridge. It had been many years since I'd seen the skyline in the evening, and I always found it breathtaking. I was grateful we hadn't taken the Lincoln or Holland tunnels across. The view from the approaches to either tunnel farther to the south would only emphasize the missing Twin Towers. The gap in the skyline isn't so obvious from this far north, where midtown giants like the Empire State Building and the Chrysler Building rule.

"I guess I'm home," I said softly. New York hadn't felt like home to me for a long time. My change in attitude had a lot to do with the man sitting next to me.

Aaron maneuvered to the shortest E-ZPass lane. "I've got my card with me," he explained. "I hope you don't mind having to drop me off, Emily. I don't know how else I can get your car to you." He paused. "You know, Tanis lives just a few blocks away from me. Maybe I could ask her to drive down behind me, and she can give me a lift home."

"No." It practically came out as a shout, and I quickly calmed myself and spoke more quietly. "No, I don't mind at all. Now that we're so close to Westchester I feel like I've gotten my second wind." We'd both napped during the long drive. "I can even take the wheel if you want. You've been driving since before we crossed into Jersey."

"No, I can make it from here. It's probably less than half an hour. Besides, I'd only have to tell you to turn here, turn there." He paused. "When we get to my house I'd like you to come in for a few minutes. My kids will be up. You can meet them."

"Uh . . . sure!" I said more cheerfully than I felt. I looked forward to seeing where he lived, but I had doubts about meeting his family. He'd met Mom, of course, but that was different. He could hardly come to pick me up without meeting her, since I was staying at her apartment. I couldn't help feeling a tad nervous at the prospect of meeting his kids. Isn't that supposed to be a good sign when a man invites you to meet his family? Unconsciously I brushed a hand over my chest, wiping away any lint. I felt something hard, like dried-up something.

Then I remembered that mustard I spilled on my T-shirt at the buffet. I'd immediately gone into the ladies' room and wiped it with a damp paper towel with liquid soap, but obviously I'd missed a spot. I looked down at my shirt and saw the offending spot, plus a faint yellow outline from my efforts to wash it away. It would be embarrassing to be presented to family with mustard stain on my shirt. And what about my hair? It came out a lot better than I thought it would after I washed it, but I'd been reclining and sleeping off and on all day, and I thought I'd thrown my brush into my suitcase.

"They've noticed I've been going out a lot lately, and I know they're curious about whom I've been spending my time with," he said with a chuckle.

"I suppose I can't blame them." If he didn't take me in and introduce me they'd probably be peeking out from behind the curtains, trying to catch a glimpse of me. I suddenly saw a way out, and I jumped on it. "Are you really sure your kids are ready for this? They've suffered a tremendous loss, and I can't imagine how difficult it would be for them to see you with someone other than their mother." At least until I had a chance to put on something without a mustard stain across the chest.

"I think they're more curious than anyone else. Their friends' mothers have been trying to set me up with their friends, their sisters, their in-laws. . . ."

I was human enough to be curious. "Do they know you've been with me for the last day and a half?"

"No, not really. To them it's just another quick business trip for a speaking engagement or something. I saw no point in telling them otherwise. They know they can always reach me on my cell phone, but they usually hear from me first."

"Do they at least know where you went?"

"Oh, sure. They know I was going to Indianapolis and would be gone two days. I couldn't give them a hotel name because I didn't know where I'd be staying." He chuckled. "My mother-in-law tried to press me for information, but I just told her I'd be back tonight, and if she needed to contact me, to call my cell. They don't know anything."

I wasn't sure how I felt about being kept a secret, like some backstreet mistress, even though the cat was about to be let out of the bag. I didn't understand why Aaron had been so hush-hush about seeing me. "Why didn't you just tell her the truth?"

"Because it's none of her business. I'm fond of my mother-in-law, Emily, and grateful to her as well, but Beverline will ask me questions my own mother wouldn't dare ask. I won't allow her carte blanche to my personal affairs."

That, I realized, was exactly what I'd become. A personal affair.

I managed to pull out my comb out of my purse and give my hair a going-over and catch it in a coated rubber band just above the nape of my neck. Before I knew it, Aaron was pulling into a private driveway that led to a Spanish-style stucco mansion. The iron gates swung open after he entered a password on the keypad. It was all I could do not to gasp audibly at the sight of the mansion. It's not like I expected him to live in a shack, but this place looked like it could be home to the King of Spain. It was a lot to take in after a long, boring drive through Middle America, where most people lived in ordinary ranch houses, Dutch Colonials, and old-fashioned A-frame farmhouses.

"Nice," I murmured.

"I wasn't sure what to do after Diana died," he said. "I thought buying a new place might help the kids cope better. I talked to them about it, and they all wanted to stay."

"Understandable." I looked around in awe. This wasn't just a house; it was an *estate.* Aaron stopped the car in front of one of the three single-car garages that attached to the main house, forming an L shape. The entire house had two stories, and I guessed at least a dozen rooms. There even appeared to be living space above the garage.

"Diana did a fabulous decorating job on it when we moved in when Billy—he's the youngest—was just two."

*Remember that,* I told myself, more nervous than ever. *His son's name is Billy.*

"Let's go in," he suggested.

I waited for him to come around and open the door for me, more out of stark terror than out of a desire for him to be chivalrous. I had barely alighted from the passenger seat when one of the massive oak front doors opened and a bunch of kids came running. "Daddy, you're back!" they exclaimed.

I stood back politely while Aaron embraced each of the youngsters, two teenage girls and a boy about eight or nine. Their happy reunion brought a smile to my face, and I kept it even after I became aware of a plump, white-haired woman wearing plaid Capri pants coming outside and staring at me apprehensively.

"Daddy's back," Aaron said jovially. "Everything okay here?"

"Fine," the children said in unison.

"We saw the lights," the woman said. "But I told the kids not to go outside until they saw it was you. We didn't recognize the car. At first I thought someone had managed to get through the gates."

My shoulders tightened up. Aaron's mother-in-law thought

my car belonged to *vandals?* All right, so I didn't drive a late-model foreign number, but my six-year-old, no-more-car-payments Nissan was, well, *reliable.*

"I rode with a friend. Beverline, kids, this is Emily Yancy. Emily, this is my mother-in-law, Beverline Wilson. . . ."

I smiled in response to her rather stiff nod.

"My daughter Kirsten . . ."

The older girl said a polite, if frigid, hello.

"My daughter Arden . . ."

A stare somewhere between shyness and hostility, with the edge toward the latter.

"And my son, Billy."

A friendly "Hi!"

Finally, a happy face. One out of four. Looked like I had some work to do. Instinct told me that Aaron had made a mistake by bringing me here tonight, although I saw no way to get out of it. I could understand a mother-in-law not wanting to see the widower of her deceased daughter show an interest in other women, just like I could see how two daughters would fear their father might be forgetting their mother. A little forewarning from Aaron might have been nice. From what he told me—and I knew it was the truth—he hadn't brought any women home since his wife passed. But, on the other hand, if they were that unhappy to see me, maybe they should have kept their asses in the house. Beverline had admitted to looking out at us through the window, so it wasn't like they didn't know I was here.

I noticed Aaron's mother-in-law looking at my license plate. "You're from Indiana," she said, sounding happy about the distance between Indiana and New York.

"I've lived there for quite a while now. But Euliss is my hometown, and I've moved back, at least temporarily."

"Oh. You're from *Euliss.*"

She said it like I'd just announced I was from Uranus. "Yes, I am," I said matter-of-factly. I'd long since been accustomed to well-to-do folks from White Plains or New Rochelle putting on airs. So what if Euliss was a poorer city overall? That didn't mean it was entirely populated by thugs.

"I *see,*" Beverline said, as if there was really something to see. "Uh . . . I'm confused. Did you two meet on the plane?"

I thought I actually saw Kirsten's and Arden's ears do little jumps, but I wasn't about to answer that one. I merely looked at Aaron.

"No, Beverline," he said. "As Emily just explained, she's back in Westchester for an extended stay."

I hated it when people said *Westchester* as a cover for *Euliss.* Apparently, many people felt there was little point in giving the name of a tacky city if you could get by naming a county that was home to many a wealthy suburb. Euliss is where I was from, and that was that.

"I flew out to help her drive her car here," Aaron concluded.

I sneaked a glance at all three females, all of whom looked distressed at this news that proved that Aaron and I hadn't just met, but had known each other previously. I could see the wheels of their respective brains turning as they recognized a connection between Aaron's frequent absences from home and the somewhat disheveled me.

"I *see,*" Beverline repeated. I decided that line was a favorite of hers, probably uttered when the situation called for something vocal and she had nothing else to say. I wondered if she always said it the exact same way, like that ring announcer on HBO who opened each boxing match with, "Let's get ready to rummmbllle!"

"Have you two eaten?" Beverline asked, graciously changing the subject. "Shirley made smothered pork chops."

Aaron made a "Mmmmm" while I wondered who Shirley was.

"We stopped for a good meal in Pennsylvania, but that was a while ago, and I think it's worn off for both of us. I know it has for me." He turned to me. "Emily, why don't you come in and have a little something?"

He was right; all those dishes I'd stuffed myself with at the buffet had long since been digested, even if part of the evidence lingered on my shirt. "An open pork chop sandwich sounds real good to me right about now."

The children and Beverline went inside. I followed them into an exquisitely designed house decorated in a Southwestern flair. Just beyond the entryway to the sunken living room hung a large portrait of a lovely young woman in a black scoop-necked top—maybe it was a dress—a large diamond gleaming at her throat, her manicured hand loosely holding a red rose. It had to be Diana. Now the finger-shaking figure from my dream had a face, and a pretty one at that, as well as an elegant-appearing hand.

I turned away, not wanting to make unflattering comparisons between her and myself. I did have one major factor going for me, one that Diana couldn't compete with: I was *alive.*

"I'd better give my mother a call," I said, "just to tell her that we got in safely, and that I'll be home shortly. I don't want her to worry."

"Emily, are you sure it's safe to drive home so late?" Aaron asked.

Beverline's smile relaxed to a bemused expression. Aaron had never said anything along the lines of Euliss being unsafe before. I knew he was just looking out for me, but I cursed his timing nevertheless.

"I'm sure," I said firmly, holding his gaze. "It's a quiet street, Aaron. And it's not exactly the middle of the night."

Billy came into the kitchen. "Daddy, guess what? I did a backflip this afternoon."

Aaron gave his son a high five. "Hey, good for you! I'm sorry I missed it."

"I'll do another one for you tomorrow. It was easy."

"There you are, Billy," Kirsten said accusingly, appearing from another room. "Don't you know not to bother Daddy when he's eating?"

"And who instituted that rule?" Aaron asked, obviously startled.

Kirsten's mouth quivered. "I just thought that . . ."

"She just wants to make sure that Billy behaves himself for Miss Yancy," Beverline said easily. A grateful Kirsten moved next to her grandmother, who put a reassuring arm around her shoulder.

"Oh, I think Emily can see us as we really are," Aaron said with a smile. He winked at me, an act I found so sexy that for an instant I considered staying. Maybe I'd get lucky and he'd sneak into my room. This house was probably big enough no one would even notice. We were overdue to get to know each other a little better, and we'd both sleep like the dead—no, that wasn't the right word—like *babies* afterward.

Beverline placed plates containing a pork chop smothered in gravy, a generous helping of macaroni and cheese, and a few spears of broccoli in front of each of us. "Oh, how wonderful it looks!" I exclaimed. Realizing that I probably sounded overly enthusiastic—God forbid Beverline think that all people from Euliss ate nothing but McDonald's—I hastily added, "I hadn't realized I was this hungry. I hope we didn't put you to too much trouble."

"Not at all. I enjoy rumbling around a little in the kitchen, even if the housekeeper does do most of the actual cooking."

My eyes darted toward the entry. I half expected to see a uniformed maid come in, ready to put the food back in the fridge. That must be the Shirley Beverline alluded to.

Obviously Kirsten noticed my action. "She left hours ago."

"Oh. Um . . . Mrs. Wilson, can I trouble you for a piece of bread?"

"No problem, Miss Yancy." Beverline turned to Kirsten. "Get Miss Yancy a piece of bread, Kirsten."

The teen obeyed, but her stiff movements told me she didn't want to get anything for me.

I lowered my head so no one would see me rolling my eyes.

*   *   *

"That was delicious," I said sincerely, wiping my mouth with my napkin.

"Oh . . . I think you might have spilled something on your shirt," Beverline said.

The mustard. "Actually, that happened at lunch." How had I known that wouldn't escape her eye and that she'd comment on it? She hadn't exactly made me feel welcome. Of course she wouldn't miss a chance to try to convince Aaron I was a slob or something.

I cleared my throat. "I hate to eat and run, but I really should be getting home."

"You know, Emily, you don't have to drive home tonight if you don't want to," Aaron said. "Maybe it would be better if you stayed here tonight. We've got an extra room for you." He glanced at his watch. "I know it's not the middle of the night, but it's going on ten."

One look at Beverline's face told me Aaron had gone too far. She hid it well, but that little smile she offered was tighter than last year's jeans. I felt kind of bad for her. She might have been able to absorb that her late daughter's husband had begun dating again, plus the possibility of having the woman in question sleep under the same roof, if she'd known Aaron was seeing someone. But it was an awful lot to swallow in one gulp. I suspected she'd rather I sleep under a bridge somewhere than under this roof.

"Oh, ten o'clock isn't that late," I replied breezily. "And parking isn't bad on my mother's street. It's a cul-de-sac," I explained to a relieved-looking Beverline, although I suspected she'd be thrilled to be rid of me if I were to meet with an unexpected case of death on my way home.

Aaron walked me to my car after I said good bye to the others, and when he kissed me good night I didn't care if anyone was watching or not. Aaron's kisses had that effect on me. His lips straddled the fine line of being both soft and insistent, and he always smelled so deliciously masculine. I burrowed as close to him as I could.

I kept rubbing my lips together as I drove. And I smiled, knowing that Aaron would be grilled about me like hot dogs on the Fourth of July by Beverline the minute he stepped back into the house.

Mom was sitting in the living room when I got in, watching CNN. "How did it go?" she asked, her eyes all lit up with the unasked questions, *Did you do the deed? Seal the deal?*

"Fine, Mom."

"I wish you'd had time to stop at Cissy's. She called me. She was so disappointed."

"Like I told you, Mom, it was a quick trip with a purpose, not a leisurely drive across a third of the country. I'm exhausted. We drove all day, for nearly thirteen hours. Aaron did most of the driving. I can only imagine how he must be feeling. And he's got to go to work Monday. All I have to do is sit and wait for the phone to ring to see if Dr. Norman was able to talk those snotty sons of his into hiring me." I'd decided I'd rather work at the Norman Family Practice than at the hospital. I sighed. "I just hope they come up with an offer before the hospital does."

"I'm sure you won't be waiting long. Where is Aaron, anyway?"

"He's home. We were driving my car, remember?"

"Oh, that's right." Her eyes flashed with excitement. "So you got to see his house. Tell me all about it."

"Better than that. I met his entire family, his kids and his mother-in-law."

Worry instantly clouded my mother's features. "I wish he'd given you a chance to clean up a little. Isn't that a stain on your shirt?"

Go figure. Mom couldn't thread a needle two inches from her face, but she could see a slight spot from five feet away. "A little mustard sauce from the spareribs I had for lunch. I'm sure they weren't expecting me to look like Miss America, especially once they learned we'd been on the road since early this morning."

"What were they like?"

"Oh, his daughters and his mother-in-law were a little apprehensive, but that's to be expected. Aaron told me he's never brought a woman home. And they didn't know he's been with me; all he told them was that he was flying to Indianapolis and would be back the following evening. Naturally, they assumed it was a business trip. I think seeing him pull up with me, in my car, came as somewhat of a shock. As for his son, he's a sweetie. But he's a lot younger than his sisters and probably doesn't see the implications."

"I'm sure you'll charm them." Mom chuckled. "You know, Mavis must have asked me three times if you were back yet."

I made a face. "Tanis must have put her up to that. She probably learned Aaron had gone to Indy and put two and two together."

"I'll just bet she did. If you ask me, she needs to forget about Aaron and look for somebody else. He's smitten with you, Emmie."

My expression changed to a scowl to a faraway look as my thoughts went from Tanis to Aaron. I wanted to be alone with my thoughts, to savor the memory of our making love and to daydream about all the wonderful things the future might hold. "Mom, I'm going to go to bed now. I'm awfully tired."

"I understand. Sweet dreams, sweetheart."

# Chapter 10

The job offer came Monday morning. Dr. Norman asked if I could start right away, and I was only too happy to oblige. It looked like this new chapter of my life was all falling into place.

We agreed that I would come in for at least a few hours on Thursday and Friday to get oriented and see a few patients with Gina, the pregnant P.A. I knew that meant that Gina would be observing me and report her observations and recommendation to Dr. Norman and his sons, and on Friday I'd either be asked to return after the Fourth or told that it wouldn't work out, but I wasn't worried. I was good at what I did, and patients liked me.

I shared my good news with Aaron, who immediately suggested we have a celebratory dinner Wednesday at Euliss's new—and only—five-star restaurant. I thought it might be better to do that on Friday, but I guess a table was easier to get without a reservation midweek. I'd barely known Aaron a month, and already I was getting the hang of this reservations thing.

Besides, as it turned out, he had other plans for us for Friday. As we watched the sun set over the Palisades while we enjoyed a melt-in-your-mouth T-bone cut, he explained to me that intimacy was impossible at his home, as it was at mine, because of his kids and mother-in-law. "How do you feel about joining my family and me at my place in Sag Harbor for the Fourth?"

That sounded great to me except for that part about his family.

He must have noticed my hesitation. "I'm sending Beverline and the kids out on the train Friday. I hope you'll consider spending Friday night at my house. We can drive out Saturday morning and come back late Sunday, after the traffic jams clear up. Uh . . . you'll have to sleep in the guest room at Sag Harbor, of course, but at least we'll have Friday."

My disappointment must have shown on my face.

"The kids and their grandmother spend the summer at the house there. I usually go out on Friday or Saturday mornings for the weekends, but I've got a feeling that I'm going to be busier than usual this summer, if you know what I mean."

My apprehension turned into a wide, slow smile. I'd been wondering precisely how we'd conduct our newly established sex life, and I happily told him that was fine.

My thoughts were filled with memories of last night's dinner as I alighted from my car and walked toward the entrance of the medical building for my first day at work. Suddenly I realized that someone held the door for me. I quickened my steps, tossing out the memory of the coconut and mango and pineapple dessert I'd consumed last night, as well as Aaron's good-night kiss, something he's truly talented at. "Thank you," I said to the man who held the door. Then I looked at the light brown face more closely, realizing I had seen it before. It came to me in a flash. "Teddy, is that you?" I'd known Teddy Simms since we were in the same third-grade class.

He broke into a grin. "Yeah, it's me. Where you been hidin' yourself, Emily? I ain't seen you in years. You look great, by the way."

"I've actually been in the Midwest for a long time, but I'm back in Euliss now, at least for the time being."

"I did hear your father passed. I'm sorry."

"Thanks." I noticed he carried a white lab coat on a hanger, covered with plastic. "You work in the building?"

"Yeah, I work for Dr. Jensen three days a week. I'm a denture technician."

I nodded. It was a small building, and I'd seen the dentist's name on the directory. "I guess you stay pretty busy."

"Yeah, I do. I work Mondays, Wednesdays, and Thursdays for Dr. Jensen, and Tuesdays and Fridays for another dentist in Mount Vernon. All that stuff they told us about taking care of our teeth when we were kids was right on."

I instantly looked at his teeth, which appeared to be in pretty good condition. In fact, Teddy Simms looked pretty good all over. Most of the boys I'd gone to school with became better looking as they got older, Teddy included.

Despite a forehead that was a little flat, Teddy had turned into a real cutie by the eighth grade, and that's when I decided I wanted him to be my boyfriend. He'd even looked cool with glasses. He kind of gravitated toward me for about five minutes, but then he decided he liked Tanis better. It must have been the hair. Tanis had what was politely known as "a good grade," thick with a natural wave, which back in the day she often wore loose. My hair was almost as long as hers, but too nappy to be worn loose. Anyway, being Tanis, she promptly forbade him to talk to me.

God, I hated her even back then.

"Have you moved back here?" he asked as we got into the elevator.

"Well, not permanently." I immediately thought of my blossoming relationship with Aaron and wondered, as I always did, just where it would take me. "A few months, at least. My mother shouldn't be alone right now. So I'm filling in for Dr. Norman's P.A. while she's on maternity leave."

"What's a P.A., an accountant or something?"

Of course. I hadn't been fair to expect him to know what it meant. The man was a dental professional, not a medical one, and there were light-years between the two. I knew next to nothing myself about dental work. I still couldn't understand why there were so many fields of dental medicine: general dentistry, orthodontics, endodontics, oral surgery, pedodontics, periodontics. "A physician assistant," I explained.

He nodded. "Hey, didn't I hear something about you marrying somebody from Chicago or something? How's your husband feel about your spending an extended time in Euliss?"

"Actually, it was Indianapolis, not Chicago. And I haven't been married for years." When Al and I got married Mom insisted on putting a wedding announcement in the *Dispatch,* so everyone would know I'd managed to snag a husband. They also ran birth announcements, but there was nothing broadcast when someone got divorced. "I stayed there after the divorce because I liked the city and I'd made friends there."

Teddy laughed. "Anyplace is probably better than Euliss."

I couldn't help being curious. "What about you, Teddy? Are you married?"

He shrugged. "I guess I'm destined to be a lifelong bachelor. Besides, who'd have me?" His eyes traveled approvingly down the length of my body, eliminating any automatic suspicions that arise about never married men over forty. No question about it, Teddy Simms was heterosexual, through and through.

Who'd have him, indeed. He wasn't particularly tall, only about five-nine, and not classically handsome, but he had undeniable sex appeal, with a neatly trimmed beard and full head of close-cropped hair. I'd jump on him in a minute . . . if Aaron wasn't in my life, of course.

The elevator stopped on the third floor, and he paused in the entryway, his palm preventing the door from closing on him. "You and I will have to have lunch sometime. Catch up."

"Sounds great. Anytime next week will be fine, assuming I pass my orientation, which is today and tomorrow."

"I'll stop by. Good luck."

"Thanks, I'll need it."

He stepped out of the elevator, and I continued on to Dr. Norman's sixth-floor office, free to let my mind return to how great this weekend's sex with Aaron would be.

Aaron made light breathing sounds—no way could they be called snores—as he slept beside me, his arm extended so that his wrist rested in the crook of my waist, his palm against my abdomen. But I was wide awake.

I had called him as I left work this afternoon and insisted he let me take him to dinner. I was in a celebratory mood, for all three Dr. Normans told me that I'd done a wonderful job in my two-day trial and that they wanted me to come back after the holiday as a full-time employee.

Of course, I took him to an ordinary place, a bar in Riverdale where they have live entertainment and great burgers. We didn't hang around after eating. I think he was as eager as I to get to his house. We held hands as we walked toward his front door, and I could feel my heart racing.

We made love again, twice. But it was the same, the *exact same* as it had been last weekend in Indy. Now, there's practically some kind of rule that says that the first time a man and woman have sex, he should be the one on top. But in my experience, the second time—which usually occurs very shortly after the first—was done differently. When this didn't happen last weekend I merely chalked it up to exhaustion after a plane trip followed by sightseeing. Now, every instinct in me warned that something was terribly wrong. I'd never had sex four consecutive times with no variation. Either I'd get on top, or we'd do it doggie style, or something. Surely in all those years Aaron spent with Diana, they'd done some experimentation. Not for one minute did I believe that people who married young remained sexually naïve. Like everybody else, they learned what their partners liked, played dress-up, shared fantasies. . . .

I'd already felt my excitement diminish a bit when Aaron positioned himself between my thighs. He always got me so excited with his skill at foreplay, and just when I started to think that this was the time we'd do it in a different position and really go at each other, it turned into the same old, same old.

Don't get me wrong. The sex was good. Aaron's been blessed with a penis that can please any woman, and it's a nice, tight fit. But it would be truly out of sight if we mixed it up a little.

Therein laid my dilemma. I lay awake wondering how I could possibly make the suggestion that we try a little variety. I didn't want to scare the man off by boldly lying him back and mounting him like Lady Godiva. He'd already confided that Diana had been his only sexual partner. I didn't want him to think that I was some kind of slut.

Something about Aaron's breathing and his arm wrapped around my waist soothed me, and my eyelids began to feel heavy. I fell asleep thinking, *The key is not to rush him. He's such a good match for me. If I concentrate hard enough I'll be able to figure something out, make him think it was his own idea.*

We were on the road by eight A.M. and arrived in Sag Harbor at ten-thirty. Aside from an occasional firecracker, the street where Aaron's house was located was quiet, with houses set back from the street, most of them fenced in with white picket or log fences. Aaron's house had the former.

Beverline sat in a white wicker rocker on the front porch reading a newspaper. I was sure she sat there so she'd be sure to see us arrive, although I wasn't sure why. Maybe she hoped there'd be a change in plans and I wouldn't make it, because her face still bore that constipated look.

"Where're the kids?" Aaron inquired after we greeted one another.

"Oh, they took off on their bikes right after breakfast. They're around the neighborhood somewhere."

How nice, I thought, to live in a place where you didn't have to worry about harm coming to your children while they were riding their bicycles. In Euliss, many parents forbade their children to go outside unless accompanied by an adult.

A *whole new lifestyle,* I reminded myself.

"How was the drive out?" Beverline asked.

"Not bad. I think most people came out last night if they weren't here already." Aaron held the screen door open for me. "Come inside, Emily, and I'll show you around."

I admit to being a little surprised at Aaron's summerhouse. For some reason I was expecting something along the lines of his New Rochelle house, large and imposing and elegant. The house in Sag Harbor was probably sixty years old or older, more like a cottage, like most of the other homes in the area, small and cozy.

After thinking about it for a bit, I realized how silly I'd been. Aaron was wealthy, but he wasn't a movie director or a star musician who could afford the upkeep on multiple homes, each one a mansion.

The house, dark green shingled with white trim, was actually quite handsome. It had a front porch across its width, a relatively small living room with attached dining area, a nice kitchen that had obviously been remodeled, two bedrooms, and a remodeled bath on the main floor. When he showed me a bright corner bedroom with a double bed I looked at him quizzically, wondering if this was where I would sleep. "That's Beverline's room," he said. "Diana and I used to sleep here, and the kids next door. I thought it would be better to let Beverline have this room after . . ."

*After Diana died,* I thought. I had to get him off the subject of his late wife.

"But surely there's more than these two bedrooms."

"Yes. Kirsten and Arden sleep next door, and Billy and I sleep downstairs. There's also a guest room down there. That'll be your room." He added in a sexy whisper, even though no one was around, "Right across the hall from me."

Well away from Beverline's prying eyes. I started to feel better about the weekend.

We traipsed down to the basement through an attractive open staircase, which gave the house more of a two-level feel rather than one level and a basement. Aside from the two bedrooms with a bathroom in between, it had a laundry room tucked into a corner, and a great room with a microwave and mini-fridge. Aaron explained to me that the great room was where Kirsten, Arden, and Billy entertained themselves and their friends.

The nicest feature of the house was the backyard. It was spacious, with a large whirlpool tub, a detached garage, and grounds as beautifully manicured as in the front. Because I was a city girl, botany was not my area of expertise. I could identify only a rose, a daisy, and a black-eyed Susan, although if I had to guess the type of pink, white, and yellow flowers that had been planted in neat multilevel brick-bordered beds and gave a wonderful burst of color to the yard, I'd say they were lilies.

I stood at the kitchen window, transfixed by the pretty scene. "Let's go out and chat with Beverline," Aaron suggested.

I sat in the second rocker on the other side of a matching glass-top table, while Aaron perched on the railing. In an attempt to be pleasant, I said, "It's so lovely here," unwittingly opening the door for Beverline to go after me the way a rabid dog would tear up anyone it could sink its jaws into.

"I suppose you've never been here before, Miss Yancy."

Aaron spared me from having to answer. "Now, considering Emily has lived in Indianapolis for the past twenty years, that would be an awful long way to travel for the weekend, wouldn't it?"

"I knew that. I just thought she might have friends who summer here."

What she actually thought, and what she wanted to hear me say, was that I *didn't* have friends with summerhouses in the Hamptons. "First of all, Mrs. Wilson, please call me Emily. And in answer to your question, no, I believe the people I know spend the summer on the Vineyard, or at least they used to."

I loved it when she was caught off guard, and she clearly hadn't expected to hear me say that. The look on her face was priceless.

"I *see*," she said, resorting to her old standby.

"I know Tanis has a place up there," Aaron added.

Having Tanis's name come up had to be my punishment for feeling so smug about besting Beverline. "Yes, she does," I said. Naturally Mavis had told Mom when Tanis and Rob had bought a summer home.

"Emily, do you know Tanis Montgomery?" Beverline asked, her voice pitched a little higher than usual.

"All my life. She and I went to school together." I added pointedly, "In Euliss."

"Oh, is she from Euliss? Somehow I thought she was from New Rochelle."

"She was born and raised in Euliss," I said, almost crankily. "Her mother and mine have played cards every week for as long as I can remember. Some people like to hide where they're from if their hometowns are a little on the shabby side." I paused for effect. "As if a person is automatically grungy just because he or she comes from a grungy place. That makes as much sense as always voting for a white male, regardless of his politics."

Beverline shrugged. "It hardly matters. Tanis is just an actress, and a not terribly successful one at that. She's hardly of the caliber of Ruby Dee," she said, naming one of New Rochelle's more famous residents. "It's probably just as well that she goes up to the Cape. She probably wouldn't fit in well here. Businesspeople find more acceptance in the Hamptons."

I didn't bother to hide my contempt for that way of thinking. "Having an MBA or a PhD doesn't make one person better than anyone else."

"That's technically true, Emily, but people's attitudes aren't necessarily fair and equitable. Sometimes they feel that certain people just aren't in the same class as they are." She turned to Aaron. "Like those friends of yours. What are their names again?"

"Ballard. Thais and Lucien Ballard. You'll meet them later tomorrow, Emily. They're having a barbecue, and I told them we'd be by."

"Ah, yes," Beverline said with a nod. "That soap opera actress and her husband, the gardener."

Aaron's features hardened. "Soap opera work is perfectly respectable, and so is gardening, but it so happens that Lucien Ballard is not a gardener. His family owns the service that did my landscaping, and that of a whole lot of our neighbors. They've lived here for generations. You're starting to sound like a real snob, Beverline, and you and I both know you haven't a leg to stand on when it comes to that."

He sounded really angry. I'd never seen this side of him before. And what was that about Beverline not having a leg to stand on?

"That was uncalled for, Aaron," she said, trying her best to sound dignified as she stood. "It isn't right for you to speak to me this way . . . especially in front of a stranger."

I lowered my chin to my chest. *I might be a stranger to you, but your son-in-law and I know each other* real *well.*

Beverline was opening the front door to the house when Aaron spoke to me. "Come on, Emily, let's see if we can find the kids."

I obediently got up and walked down the driveway with him to the street. "Are you okay?" I asked. "It seems like your mother-in-law kind of got to you there."

"Sometimes she really pisses me off. Putting on all those airs, and baiting you the way she does. Don't think I don't plan to speak to her about it."

"I can just imagine her reaction when you told her you were bringing me with you for the weekend," I said grimly.

"She didn't like it much. Kept telling me I could do better than 'a Euliss girl.' " He blew out his breath loudly. "Sometimes I think she forgets *I* come from Riverhead."

"I wonder if she would act the same if you brought home a nice woman doctor from White Plains, rather than a P.A. from Euliss."

"That might have something to do with it, but I also think she feels a little threatened. She sold her house and got rid of her furniture. She plans on living with me and the kids for the rest of her life, and she's having a wonderful time acting like she was born with a silver spoon in her mouth, both in New Rochelle and out here."

"Wasn't she?" *She certainly acts like it.*

"Hell, no. She's from Camden, New Jersey." He chuckled. "Of course, the so-called friends she's made would drop her like a hot rock if they knew she came from a city officially ranked as one of the most dangerous in America."

I knew next to nothing about New Jersey. "Really? Is it that bad?"

"Unfortunately, crime stems from poverty, and many of the people there are poor. The Wilsons were more like lower middle class. Beverline worked as an admissions clerk, and Mr. Wilson worked on the docks. They owned their own home, but I wouldn't have paid twenty grand for the house and everything in it. He had already died of a heart attack when she moved in with us after Diana got sick. She actually wanted to come way before that, but Diana said no.

"I'd hoped she'd go back home after Diana passed. I'd already spoken to my mother about coming to stay with us to help with the kids. We were ready to put her condo up for sale. But then Beverline started bawling, saying that my mother has a son and grandchildren in Delaware, but that she just lost her only child and wanted to be close to her grandchildren."

I began to soften toward Aaron's mother-in-law. "Well, that's understandable."

"I thought so at the time. What she neglected to tell me was that she'd already sold her house and donated her furniture to charity. She had no intention of returning to Camden."

"Oh, that's sneaky, Aaron."

"I know. The funny thing is, I would have had no problem if she'd asked me outright if she could stay. But going behind my back like that . . ." He shook his head. "I was tempted to throw her out, but I couldn't bring myself to do it. I let her stay, for Diana's sake, as well as for that of my kids."

"And now you're stuck with her."

"Probably for the rest of her life. And I have to listen as she tells everyone she's from Philly and looks down on people who don't have the things she didn't have herself until she came to live with me."

"Like she looks down on me," I said flatly.

"Exactly. And my friends. Lucien Ballard is a great guy. I knew him slightly in high school. We both played basketball, me for Riverhead and him for Westhampton Beach. I ran into him at a party there my buddy Zack took me to last year." He chuckled. "Naturally, Beverline hates for me to have contact with anyone from my days in Riverhead."

"Do you ever go back there?"

"Every now and then, like to bring the kids to the water park. But I don't look up people I used to know, if that's what you mean. It's been a very long time since I lived there, Emily. Sometimes I feel a little funny spending my summers just a short distance away from my hometown like I've never been there in my life. But there's nothing for me in Riverhead anymore."

"Sometimes you just outgrow a place. I know I'd never go to Euliss if my par—if my mother didn't still live there. You've worked hard to get where you are, Aaron. You should never let anyone make you feel guilty about it."

He grunted. "Maybe I've got the same hang-up as Beverline except mine is in reverse. Sometimes I like to hide my success. But my esteemed mother-in-law likes to forget that just a few years ago she was living in a crummy house in Camden, New Jersey, and that's not right."

I took his arm. "Don't let her ruin your holiday, Aaron." Even as I tried to soothe him, I couldn't help thinking of the irony. The woman who turned up her nose at me for being from Euliss was just as working class as my parents were.

I knew that information would come in handy eventually.

# Chapter 11

We found the kids, but I'm not sure it was such a good thing.

Billy Merritt had been happy to see me, but Kirsten and Arden stopped just short of giving me what's known as the cold shoulder. They clearly felt as threatened by me as their grandmother, seeing me as some monster who was slowly moving in on their father and who planned on erasing every reminder of their mother. I'd thought things would be different once they all had a chance to accept the idea of Aaron dating again. Did they really think it would never happen?

That afternoon we went to a barbecue at someone's home, another shingled cottage with a pool out back. Our hosts, married dentists, had the event catered, and the meats were prepared on a grill by two black men wearing immaculate white aprons and tall white chef hats. Waiters passed a variety of blended drinks around, and a tended bar was set up in a corner of the yard. They even had live music. Being around all these well-off black folks made me feel like I'd died and fallen into an episode of the old *Cosby Show.*

Unfortunately, my bliss didn't last long. I soon became uncomfortably aware of being the focal point of everyone's interest. Small groups of people talked among themselves with less than discreet glances in my direction and even some pointing fingers, proving that money doesn't buy class.

Aaron tried to shield me from the gossip, but a person would have to be missing a couple of senses not to recognize what was going on. In addition to Beverline sitting with some of her contemporaries, whose glances my way told me I was the subject of their conversation, a number of women in their thirties showed up, their hair, skin, and make-up looking like they were fresh from the beautician's chair, dressed in sexy outfits that showed lots of skin, every one of them approaching Aaron for a few friendly words and perhaps an invitation or two. It was like it was open season on the handsome widower, and every single woman wanted him.

Aaron was gracious, but he quickly introduced me by only my name and not adding any type of description, like that old reliable one "my friend." I could see the blend of surprise and curiosity in those women's eyes. One woman actually asked, "Are you staying nearby, Emily?" to which Aaron and I exchanged amused glances and I explained, "I'm Aaron's house guest." Smiles promptly lost their luster like hair on a day with 90 percent humidity.

Despite my feelings of triumph at having succeeded where so many others had failed, I didn't enjoy my time on Long Island. I was elated when Aaron walked me around to the front—under dozens of watchful eyes—and said, "I'm afraid this hasn't been a pleasant experience for you, Emily. Do you think we should go back to Westchester?"

I'd been trying to put on a brave face, but at his suggestion I crumpled, falling against his chest. "Oh, Aaron, how did you know?" In the relatively brief time we'd been seeing each other, Aaron already recognized my needs . . . and he responded to them.

He held me close. "I'm not blind, Emily. You're getting it from all sides. I'm so sorry. Tell you what—a friend of mine lives on the North Shore and had invited me to stop by. We'll head toward the city, hang out there until the traffic dies down, and then we'll spend the rest of the weekend at my place."

"Didn't you promise your friends in Westhampton you'd come over?"

"They'll understand. They can meet you another time."

I still felt badly about him cutting his weekend short. "Your kids will be disappointed to see you leave so soon."

He nodded. "But only Billy had nothing to do with our leaving so early. I know what a pain Beverline can be, but I can't tell you how disappointed I am in my daughters, Emily."

I didn't know what to say. I could point out that his family's dislike of me would make it difficult for us, but I certainly didn't want to sound as if I was giving him an ultimatum, something like, *Fix your family's attitude . . . or else!* I settled for murmuring, "It's an unfortunate situation."

It took about an hour to drive to his friend's house in Sound-view. Dr. Elias Ansara lived in a quaint two-story home two blocks from the beach. The house, about seventy years old and completely modernized, was small, but charming.

Elias was very charismatic, and he had the looks for it. He was taller than Aaron, with a cleft in his chin, chiseled features, and dark curly hair. I put his age in the midforties. His two adolescent sons were present, both handsome, with light brown hair. Although Elias's blond companion had the right coloring to be their mother, her young age, maybe thirty or even younger, pretty much ruled that out.

We settled around the oblong table for six on the patio with our plastic dinner plates and matching glasses. "Elias, what's your specialty?" I asked, curious about this handsome doctor.

"G.I."

"Emily's a P.A.," Aaron offered.

"I always think it's good when health-care professionals get with other health-care professionals," Melissa, Elias's girlfriend, said.

"What do you do, Melissa?" I asked.

"I'm a phlebotomist. That means I—"

"I *know* what it means," I said so testily that everyone at the table looked taken aback. Everyone except Aaron, who looked concerned. Maybe I should have toned down the vehence, but I just wasn't in the mood to deal with white people who thought I didn't know a damn thing. Would she have felt it necessary to explain that she draws blood from patients if I'd been white? Hadn't Aaron just said I was a P.A.?

Melissa shot a "Help me!" look at Elias, who calmly cut his steak and said, "You're forgetting that Emily isn't a layperson, darling. She's a physician assistant." He smiled my way. "I think Melissa is just accustomed to having to tell people what 'phlebotomist' means, darling. No insult intended."

His calling me "darling"—in a faint accent reminiscent of both his boyhood spent in Syria and his education in London—enamored me, even if he'd directed the same term toward Melissa two seconds earlier. "I didn't mean to sound so snippy," I said graciously, directing my words to Elias, not to Melissa, who hadn't apologized or even agreed with Elias's explanation. I knew I needed to calm down, but it'd been a bad day. First Beverline resented me out of fear that Aaron was going to move me in and throw her out on the street. Then his daughters acted like they were afraid I was going to erase their mother from Aaron's memory by coating her portrait with black paint. Then every single woman—not *every* single woman: every *single* woman—in Sag Harbor was whispering about me because I was dating Aaron. And now this heifer thought she had to explain a medical profession to me? Enough already.

"I hope you two plan on staying for the fireworks," Elias said easily, with his faint accent.

"Yeah, Mr. Aaron, we can see them right here from the backyard," one of the boys said. I'd picked up that both boys knew Aaron and his family well. I'd heard one of them ask where Billy was, showing visible disappointment when Aaron said he was out in Sag Harbor.

"Oh, I don't know, Elias," Aaron replied. "It's been a long day for us."

"You can chill out here." Again Elias turned to me. "I've only got two bedrooms, darling, one for me and one for my boys, but my basement is furnished. You and Aaron can always go down there if you'd like to, uh, rest a bit. No one will bother you."

Instinctively I knew Elias meant if we wanted to fool around. The man radiated sex.

And it was a cinch *his* sex life wasn't dull.

In the end we left at seven-thirty, after more guests had arrived. Elias was calling all the women "darling." I wondered if he actually knew any of their names. Not that anyone seemed to mind.

Traffic conditions were favorable, probably because we traveled before people started hitting the road for the nearest fireworks show. It was still light out when we got to Aaron's.

This was only the third time I'd been to the imposing mansion, but it still impressed me. Aaron had opened up a whole new world to me. I was still a little bit in awe of it all.

The first thing I saw when I stepped inside was Diana's portrait. It had made me uneasy last night—I'd actually imagined I saw her eyes move and watch Aaron and I ascend the stairs to the bedroom she once shared with him. Tonight it just annoyed me.

"Do you want to lie down?" Aaron asked. Before I could answer he made a suggestion. "I was thinking you could use a little TLC. How about a nice Jacuzzi?"

"That sounds perfect."

We practically ran up the stairs. Already my mind was going ahead to what would happen afterward. I prayed that tonight the sex would be a little different. I wanted to . . . well, I couldn't say I never felt the earth move with him, but I wanted to explode, like those fireworks that would be lighting up over Long Island Sound in just about forty-five minutes.

He disappeared inside the master bath while I stretched out across the bed, remote control in hand, half watching some documentary about street gangs, because in July there's no fresh network programming.

When Aaron poked his head out and said my bath was ready I eagerly stripped and stuck the ends of my hair into the same coated rubber band at the root of my ponytail so it wouldn't get wet. Since getting my hair relaxed, I was much more conscious of weather and other conditions that affected my hair. I still scoffed at those women who, when an unexpected summer storm caught them without an umbrella, were willing to wait for twenty minutes for the storm to pass before going out to their cars, and, even worse, the women who pulled out those old-lady plastic rain scarves from their purses, letting the elements mess up their clothes but not their hair.

I entered the bathroom, enjoying Aaron's lingering glance at me.

"Ooh, you're naked," he said lecherously.

"That I am." I looked around. Instead of turning on the light Aaron had lit about ten fat candles, including one that burned a few inches below a dish of scented vanilla oil, making the room smell heavenly. He'd also brought out a bottle of wine and a glass. "All this for me?" I squealed.

"It was no trouble. Come on, get in."

I stepped into the sunken, bubble-filled tub, feeling that Cleopatra had nothing on me. As soon as I sat down, Aaron depressed the button that turned on the whirlpool jets, then handed me the filled glass.

"I can't figure out how you did this," I said. "You never left the bathroom."

"Everything's in the vanity cabinet," he explained. "I enjoy relaxing in the Jacuzzi myself. Without the bubbles, of course. Sometimes I listen to music, sometimes I watch TV." A small television was positioned on one of those wall mounts. "That's why there's only one glass."

Because he'd never invited anyone into his Jacuzzi before.

That was enough to make me forget that the bubble bath and beads I soaked in had belonged to Diana.

"This is wonderful," I said. The warm water felt wonderfully soothing luxurious. "But what will you do, just sit and watch me? That doesn't sound like much fun."

"Actually, I had something else in mind." He undid the buttons of his polo shirt and pulled it over his head. Within seconds he had stripped naked and had joined me. Only with masterful self-control did I keep from reaching out for his erect penis and feasting on it, but I believe my mouth fell open and I made the motions of doing just that, imagining how it would fill my mouth.

Because I was already in the tub, Aaron could position himself only leaning against me, but the water served to make him almost weightless. The back of his head rested against my left upper collarbone. I felt his hand on my thigh. "You feel good." His fingers began to move toward my inner thighs like my body was the Yellow Pages.

"Mmmm. Keep that up, and we'll be making a beeline for the bed and leave a wet mess for your housekeeper to clean up." I was enjoying this new type of intimacy for us.

"All right." He returned his hand to my outer thigh and let it rest there. "I've got a confession to make, Emily."

"Oh? What's that?"

"When I told you that you were only the second woman I'd made love to, I wasn't being quite honest."

"Go on."

"When Diana was failing she wasn't able to make love."

"That's understandable." *The woman had a brain tumor. What did you expect?*

"I still found that I had certain . . . well, needs."

"So you saw a . . ." I trailed off, not wanting to say *hooker.*

"A call girl. Elias put me in touch with a service."

"Elias? He doesn't seem to have any trouble finding women."

"Sometimes a man just wants release. He doesn't want to have to wine and dine a woman, or risk having her try to ingratiate herself into his life, especially once she learns he's an M.D."

"So you docs like professionals." Damn, I was learning something every day about how the other half lives.

"Right. It might sound callous, but sometimes you just don't want an emotional attachment."

"I understand."

"I hoped you would. You're a practical-minded girl, Emily. Anyway . . . I saw the same girl every time, just to burn off all my sexual energy. I kept doing it for a little while after Diana passed, until even that gave me no relief." He took my hand and traced invisible circles on my palm. "So while you technically weren't just the second one, you *are* the second one who counted for anything."

"Thanks for telling me. Uh . . . what'd you think of sex with a professional?"

"I think they really earn their money. That girl did things to me that I would never have asked Diana to do."

A warning shot through me like Robin Hood's arrow.

"Let me rephrase that. It's not *what* she did, it's *how* she did it."

I wondered if he was talking about different sexual positions or about oral sex. That seemed like an awfully old-fashioned point of view. Maybe lying flat on your back was more lady-like than on all fours with your ass in the air, but that's why sex is done in private.

"That reminds me. I've got a question for you."

I smiled. "In that case, I've got an answer for *you*."

Instead of spilling his question, Aaron seemed hesitant, and it occurred to me that something might be troubling him. "Is something wrong?"

"No, no. It's just that I feel a little awkward. It's, uh, a sexual question."

My ears perked up. I couldn't imagine what was on his mind, but oh, the possibilities. "Okay, shoot."

"I wanted to ask you . . . how do you feel about oral sex?"

I answered without hesitation. "Gosh, I'm crazy about it."
I felt him stiffen, and I realized I should have toned down my
enthusiasm a bit. I wouldn't want him to think . . .

"I haven't been satisfying you, Emily?"

Oh, fine. Why didn't I think before I opened my big trap?
"Well, of course you have!" That was partially true, at least
in the very broadest sense. I wasn't unsatisfied, merely a little
bored. "It's just that . . . we're still new, Aaron. We're still
learning how to please each other." I felt rather satisfied with
my own explanation. It sounded so hopeful.

Which was exactly how I felt.

After we relaxed a while longer in the tub we stepped into
the huge stall shower to rinse off. The shower was bigger than
any closet in Mom's house and could probably hold a family
of four. I thought that after we finished soaking we'd go
straight to bed and, given his question about oral sex and my
affirmative reply, devour each other. So it came as a complete
surprise when he said, "It's almost nine. Let's go out back
and watch the fireworks."

I was speechless. I'd put on a new sexy sheer nightgown
that fell just above my knees, with nothing underneath, and
he was bare chested, wearing only a pair of plaid drawstring
pants.

He pressed his lips against mine. "We can put the double
lounger in a reclining position and maybe create a few fireworks of our own while we watch."

"But won't we have to get dressed?"

"No. My property is private. Let's take the wine with us.
I'll get another glass from the kitchen."

The show had just started when we went out onto the patio,
which Aaron lit with just enough white light for us not to
bump into the furniture. I relaxed on the double-wide lounge
chair and took a sip of wine. Aaron's hand rested on my thigh,
but it soon moved and urged my legs apart. I closed my eyes

and enjoyed his touch, feeling myself become damp as my excitement mounted along with the sound of the explosions above.

"You're missing the fireworks," he murmured.

I opened my eyes and watched the technicians' handiwork, which was quite spectacular. Silently I chided myself for not being more amenable to Aaron's suggestion. I should have known I could trust him.

I liked being fingered by him under the stars and the fireworks. But when he climbed on top of me I got nervous. "Aaron . . . out here?"

"Live a little, Emily. No one can see us."

*My missionary man,* I thought, but with fondness rather than frustration. I put my arms around his neck, and for once I didn't mind making love in the same old position. It was exciting seeing the night sky light up as we moved together until we, like the lights in the sky above us, exploded.

The position might have been the same, but the sense of making love outdoors was a new kind of bliss altogether.

We brought it inside for Act Two, but there was a long delay between acts. When we got into bed we both drifted off. I opened my eyes a little past midnight, frowning at the unfamiliar surroundings.

Aaron lay on his back next to me, and I thought I saw a telltale lump in the linens in the area of his groin. My impulse came as swiftly as it did urgently.

I first lifted the covers to confirm his erection, and then I did what most red-blooded women would do.

He reacted with a grunt. I looked downward and saw that his big toes were bent backward. Then Aaron pushed the covers away. Good thing, too. It was getting a little hard for me to breathe down there.

"Emily," he said in a half groan.

I couldn't respond; my mouth was full.

For the next few minutes we both communicated with our

mouths, but without intelligible words. Aaron grunted and moaned. I used my lips and tongue. When the first stream came from the tip of his penis, I sat up. My work here was done.

Aaron was busy enjoying his orgasm, so I decided to continue with my bold streak. Leaning in so that my face was just inches from his, I asked as tantalizingly as I could, "Did you like it?"

"God, yes." He opened his eyes then, looking at me through sexy slits. "Whatever took me so long to tell you how much I like that?"

"I don't know, but I'm glad you did," I said angelically.

"I was a little apprehensive. You see, Diana, she didn't . . . wouldn't . . ."

"She wouldn't give you head?"

"She had some sexual hang-ups. She felt so guilty when I gave it to her, in spite of how much she enjoyed it. It got so bad that I only did it . . . well, she always had an increase in her sex drive in the days before her period started, and I took advantage of that." He shrugged. "Then she had a whole week to stop feeling remorseful."

"She never warmed up to it?"

Aaron shrugged. "Like I said, she had some hang-ups. She felt that there was something morally wrong with oral sex, that it was something a lady didn't indulge in. And I never could get her to do the same for me."

So Diana had been too prudish to be bored. The reasons for my dull sex life were starting to make more sense to me now.

"I guess you must think I'm a slowpoke or something," he said sheepishly.

"There's nothing wrong with being cautious, Aaron."

"I'm still getting used to this," he said apologetically. "This whole thing with STDs . . . I never had to worry about that. Not that I think that you—"

I pressed my index finger to his lips. I took no offense. "We have to consider all the possibilities, Aaron. Not doing that would be foolish, and reckless, too. We're both medical professionals, and we know more than anyone about the consequences of being sexually irresponsible."

He grinned, obviously feeling relieved that he hadn't hurt my feelings. "So I guess this means we're no longer practicing safe sex, huh?"

"Well . . . I guess so. Are you all right with that?"

"Of course. Emily, I never believed that you carried any STDs."

Even before he said his next words, I found myself wishing we could talk about something else.

"And I'm sure you're not out there messing around with anybody else." He chuckled. "Again, I do apologize for moving so slowly on this." He stretched lazily, a sexy sight. "Wow. What a great way to wake up in the middle of the night." He rolled over and lowered his head to mine, giving me a light kiss. As his face slid lower and lower down my body, finally settling between my thighs, it was suddenly my turn to squeal and moan with excitement and rapidly increasing pleasure . . . and then, finally, sigh with contentment.

"Aaron, can I ask you something?" I said as we cuddled in the center of his large bed. "Aside from what you just told me, did you ever step out on Diana?" Maybe I was jumping the gun, but I had to know if Aaron viewed cheating the way Al had. I never wanted to feel that devastation again, doctor or no doctor.

"Never," he said without hesitation. "And I still believe that I should have been stronger then. I still feel guilty about having sex with a stranger while she lay deteriorating, requiring massive doses of Demerol to ward off seizures. But it really didn't feel like cheating. That call girl meant nothing to me. I was so stressed out. . . . Diana's doctors told me her case was terminal, and I didn't know what I was going to do without her."

I could hear the pain in his voice and knew he was telling

the truth. "The role of caregiver is a difficult one, Aaron. There's nothing wrong with needing release. You really shouldn't beat yourself up. It's not like you cheated on her before she became ill."

I felt happy as I fell asleep in Aaron's arms. His king-sized bed was swathed in the softest linens I'd ever slept on, and an abundance of oversized, fluffy pillows and a thick, feather-stuffed white quilt ensured a good night's rest. I'd stayed at a Four Seasons once, and being in Aaron's bed I felt like I'd gone back there. How marvelous to have this opulence at one's disposal on a daily basis.

Most sofa beds were designed for occasional use by overnight guests, not to be slept on every night, and Mom's was no exception. I'd forgotten how good it felt to sleep on a really comfortable mattress.

I spent the rest of the weekend at Aaron's, just hanging out with him, exchanging thoughts and ideas about politics, economics, just about anything we thought of. At mealtimes we cooked together in the large gourmet kitchen, with its six-burner cooktop, double oven, Sub-Zero refrigerator with French doors, and work island with the pans hanging over it. The LCD television in the kitchen allowed us to keep up with the movie we were watching on cable while we created meals together. Aaron was an excellent cook. He made great scrambled eggs with smoked sausage, onion, and green pepper mixed in, plus shredded cheese on top.

We were getting really close emotionally and physically, and the lavishness of the surroundings was a bonus. I didn't realize I could be this happy. Would six months in Euliss be enough time for me to see this thing with Aaron through all the way? I wasn't sure just how serious this was.

I was prepared to go home Sunday night, but Aaron asked me to stay over. I figured Mom could do without me for another night, even though I was supposed to start showing her how to balance her checkbook. I'd been too busy with Aaron to have taken the first step toward preparing Mom to live on her own, which had been the reason for my coming back to Euliss in the first place.

But what if I ended up staying here in New York? What if Aaron turned out not to be just someone to pass the time with?

# Chapter 12

Aaron still slept soundly when I awoke Monday morning. I quietly slipped into the adjoining bathroom to dress.

This house still amazed me. I'd always known there were rich people in the world, of course. But it was difficult for me to grasp that people actually lived like this. I ran my fingertips over the cool marble countertop, with his and hers sinks made of the same material. His comb and brush, razor, deodorant, and toothbrush were neatly inside a small wicker basket by one of the sinks. I couldn't help imagining my toiletries in a basket on the counter by the second sink, which currently looked so forlorn and empty.

I had coffee going by the time Aaron came downstairs, showered and fully dressed for work. He gave me a luscious, lingering good-morning kiss that was all the breakfast I needed, but when he made me his favorite breakfast—a toasted sesame seed bagel topped with cream cheese, bits of smoked salmon, and red onion—I became an instant devotee. I'd spent the first eighteen years of my life in New York and never once had bagels and lox. It was delicious.

"This is nice, isn't it," he said, smiling from his stool next to mine in the breakfast nook.

I nodded, smiling broadly. Aaron's face glowed with contentment, and why wouldn't it? He was able to entertain me in his home, and we were getting to know one another in a *real* way. There was more to our relationship than just sex . . . even though there was still room for improvement in that department. Last night had been a return to the same routine as before.

But I was still optimistic. I suspected that if our connection continued to bloom, Aaron would eventually offer me the lifelong position of his queen. He definitely was the marrying type.

I also knew that my little queendom wouldn't necessarily be a happy place, not with Beverline's open disdain, the resentment of Arden and Kirsten, and that damn portrait of Diana, which had been the first thing I saw when I came downstairs. That damn painting was fucking with me. I felt like her eyes were following me like a crazed stalker. Silly, I know.

Regardless of my semihallucinatory state when it came to Diana's portrait, my gut told me Aaron wasn't the type to shop around a lot. He'd already made the decision that he was ready to start dating again. If he met someone he cared about and who shared his feelings, chances were excellent that woman would become his second wife. Of course, we were a long way from anything like that happening . . . but the possibility that it could happen was nearly overwhelming.

And, considering our unfulfilling sex life, more than a little frightening.

"Emmie, you're looking wonderful these days," Mom said. "Your skin is just glowing. You ought to be in one of those Noxzema commercials."

Heat rushed to my cheeks. My skin looked so great because I'd swallowed a healthy dose of Aaron's semen over the weekend. They say it's loaded with protein.

"What's your secret?" she pressed.

"Oh, I don't know. Maybe it's those new vitamins I've been taking."

Teddy stopped in at Dr. Norman's office the following Thursday. "Emily, are you doing anything for lunch today? I was hoping we could grab a bite downstairs. It'd be fun to catch up."

"Sure. Twelve-thirty okay?"

Someone ran a café in the building's lobby. It was actually quite nice; I'd eaten there with Gina, whom I'd replaced, last Friday. It had gotten her out of the office while the nurses set up the cake, coffee, and punch for her farewell party. The café served salads, burgers, chicken, and sandwiches, including a very tasty one made of rib-eye steak.

I arrived ahead of Teddy by about five minutes.

"Sorry I'm late," he said, slipping into the chair opposite me. "I had to do a repair job of someone's cap. They cracked it on a date-nut cookie."

"That's all right. We're closed for an hour and a half, until two o'clock."

"Old Dr. Norman never took that long for lunch. Must have been his sons' idea."

"Do you know them, Teddy?"

He shrugged. "Only to say hello. I see Dr. Norman whenever I need medical care. Most of the doctors in the building trade services for each other's staff. But if you ask me, they seem a little uppity, like they can't be bothered giving the time of day to anyone who doesn't have an M.D."

That was the vibe I'd gotten from them as well.

"Wait till one of them cracks a tooth. I'll fix the bastard."

I pictured Teddy deliberately not adjusting the doctor's bite properly and having him come back in a day or two holding his painful jaw. It was a picture that, employers or not, made me smile. I hate uppity types.

"I know what you mean," I said. "But I do like working

there." I'd expected him to pull out a pair of reading glasses to see the menu, but he didn't seem to be having a problem. "Teddy, what happened to your glasses?"

"One word: LASIK."

"Oh." I waited as he perused the menu. Then I remembered Rosalind and the planned reunion. "Hey, Teddy, Rosalind and I are planning a twenty-fifth class reunion."

"Planning? You'd better hurry up, or it'll be a twenty-*sixth* reunion. Are you sure you can even find a place at this late date? I think most of the halls are booked way in advance for weddings, anniversary parties, things like that."

"That's true, but we won't be holding it at a hall. That takes too much organizing, too much money up front. Rosalind and I thought we'd hold a picnic at her and John's house and just invite people and have whoever shows up pay a nominal fee at the door, to help recover the food costs. At least this way we can send somebody to the store if we need more hamburgers. We can try asking people to RSVP, but you know how that goes. People don't bother to respond; they just show up at the last minute."

Teddy made a snorting sound. "Yeah, and if somebody ends up not getting a piece of chicken, they'll talk about y'all like dogs. Lots of luck with *that* plan, Emily. Besides, do you really think John Hunter is going to allow a bunch of Euliss people in his house? Do you have any idea how many kids we graduated with have criminal records?"

He sounded just like Aaron's mother-in-law, I thought with annoyance. Since when was it such a terrible thing to be from Euliss? "I don't see why not, Teddy. We won't be in the house, we'll be in the yard. Besides, John is from Euliss himself, and so is Rosalind, even though they live in New Rochelle now."

"Think about this, Emily. Most of the people who would come to a class reunion that's held anywhere in this vicinity are going to be people from Euliss, meaning they'll be black.

Most of the white kids have moved to Connecticut or Jersey or Florida, and their parents have left town, too, so they have no reason to come back. Hell, a lot of the black kids are long gone, too. When's the last time you saw Wendy Woods?"

"A long time. She's in Baltimore someplace." I giggled. "I'm sorry, but I never thought she would have the smarts to leave town. Sometimes I think the only one dumber than Wendy was Bitsy Mason."

"Well, I haven't seen Wendy lately, but I have seen Bitsy."

"Really?" I leaned forward, interested in a bit of gossip. "How does she look?"

"Let me put it this way. They ought to start calling her Hefty."

I laughed so loudly that other diners turned to look at me, but I couldn't help it. "Stop making me laugh," I said in a choked voice between giggles.

"Sorry. Listen, Emily, I hate to sound like a snob, but if I had a house, I sure wouldn't invite our classmates over. A lot of them will bring guests, so you won't know half the people who are there. Even at an outside function, people will find an excuse to go inside, like to use the bathroom. And what happens if it rains?"

My shoulders drooped. He had made valid points. "We did talk about renting Port-A-Sans, but the rain thing might be a problem."

"Have it at a bar," Teddy suggested. "You can probably negotiate a deal with the owners. They can get the bar business, they can split the admission profits with you, and a lot of bars have kitchens, so you might even be able to fix the food there."

"You know, Teddy, you might have something there," I said.

We spent the rest of our lunch reminiscing about old classmates. Teddy had a line on just about everybody and made many humorous references, even if some of them were in questionable taste, like the crack he made about Bitsy. I laughed so hard over his comments that I became short of breath.

"I suppose you know about Marsha Cox," he said after giving me the lowdown on a classmate who'd been jailed for operating an identity-theft ring.

"No. I just saw her last week, when I was in for my interview with Dr. Norman. We exchanged numbers, but I haven't had a chance to call her yet. She looks magnificent. What about her?"

"Hell, she *should* look good. She was married to a big-time drug dealer. Whatever she wanted to do to herself, he had the money to pay for it."

"She was married to a *drug* dealer?" I repeated incredulously.

He shrugged. "Well, she was until somebody shot his ass last year. It was big news. He was the biggest dealer to come out of Harlem since Nicky Barnes. I heard the government confiscated everything they had and she had to move back in with her mother, in Sherwood Forest."

"No, Teddy. Not Marsha." I couldn't imagine the woman with the elegant carriage I'd talked to in Dr. Norman's waiting room living in a notoriously bad housing project. Forest, my butt. *Jungle* was more like it. But I couldn't picture her living large off of drug money, either. The Marsha I'd known was a basically moral person. She wasn't like Tracy Turner, who I felt positive had taken my lunch money that day in seventh grade when I received a restroom pass during science class and left my change purse at my desk.

Then again, a person could change a lot in twenty-five years.

"She did mention her husband had died," I recalled. "Of course, she didn't mention what he did for a living, but I guess that's hard to admit."

"She wanted to get out of the ghetto, Emily. So she had a

chance to live the good life. I don't think she realized it probably wouldn't last."

When the check arrived I reached for my wallet. "Here, let me give you something toward that."

"Put your wallet away. This was my idea, remember? Save it for the reunion, since you and Rosalind insist on feeding half of Euliss. I can just see people stuffing food in their pockets."

Laughing, I wiped my eyes with a corner of my cloth napkin. I couldn't remember the last time I laughed so hard.

"We'll have to do it again."

Teddy didn't miss a beat. "How about next week? Make it dinner."

I stopped laughing. Lunch was one thing; dinner was something else. "Um . . . Teddy, I'm, um, kind of seeing someone. So dinner might be awkward."

The corners of his mouth turned up in amusement. " 'Kind of' seeing someone? That doesn't sound very firm."

He had a point. Aaron had said nothing about our relationship being exclusive. Well, he *had* said he was sure I carried no STDs, and that I wasn't out there messing around with anyone else, but that wasn't an *official* declaration, just a reassurance.

In my heart, I knew that was a sneaky way of sidestepping the issue or using the technical meaning to whitewash it, along the lines of the famous "I did not have sexual relations with that woman" because it had been just a blow job. Aaron had been married for a long time, and prior to that his girlfriend/future wife had been the only woman in his life. He probably assumed we were a couple, simply because that was what he was accustomed to.

"I guess it won't be a problem," I heard myself saying. "Let's make it during the week, though." At least that way it wouldn't interfere with any weekend plans Aaron might make. I knew he'd be spending at least part of the weekend with his family in Sag Harbor.

Teddy shrugged, like he didn't get what all the fuss was about. "Next Thursday, then?"

"Thursday would be fine."

We passed on getting on the first elevator after six adults and two children got inside. "I'm curious about something, Teddy," I said as we waited for the other elevator to arrive. "When's the last time you saw Tanis?"

"I just saw her on TV the other day. A household product commercial, I think."

I felt certain he knew that wasn't what I meant. "I mean in person."

"Oh. Hell. Years. Last time I saw her she had her original nose."

I laughed. "I noticed that change, too."

"It's definitely an improvement. You could eat lunch on that old honker she had."

Indignant, I lowered my chin to my chest. "So why'd you dump me for her in the eighth grade?"

He didn't hesitate. "I was a typical junior high school kid, Emily."

"And what's that mean?"

"It means she had bigger boobs."

I laughed. This made for just another time when I'd been bested by Tanis. I could laugh about it easily, though, because that was then. This was now.

And *I* had Aaron.

We parted ways and headed for our respective offices without so much as a peck on the cheek. It had been a completely chaste meal, but Aaron would certainly be disappointed if he learned about the date I'd just made. Not that he'd ever find out about it. Nor was there any need for him to worry. It would be completely harmless, just two old friends catching up on twenty-five years.

There I went again, evading the truth about what might

come of dinner. Who was I kidding? I mean, just how much catching up could two people do? Teddy Simms looked at me like he wanted to put me on a plate and suck me like a barbecued chicken wing.

And I couldn't deny that I didn't mind being the appetizer if he'd be the entrée.

# Chapter 13

I shared the news of my running into Teddy and lunching with him with Rosalind, as well as his thoughts on what we were planning for our class reunion. She admitted that John had vetoed the idea of the reunion being held on their property. Her sheepish expression suggested to me that there were a few expletives involved, but I couldn't blame him.

At her suggestion, she and I stopped in at Cleo's, a bar on North Avenue, to see if it could work for our reunion. The bar wasn't the most elegant place in the world, but in dim lighting it didn't look too shabby. You couldn't see that the tears in the vinyl seats of some of the bar stools had been covered with black masking tape. Besides, if we had it at the bar we wouldn't have to deal with RSVPs or with collecting payments in advance. They also had a kitchen that the owner said we could use provided we clean up after ourselves. We took a good look around, and Rosalind turned on the oven and all the burners in the kitchen. I opened the ancient refrigerator, the inside of which was both clean and cold, which was all that mattered.

"I think we've got our site," I said to Rosalind.

"I think so, too. All we need is somebody to man the door and collect the cover charge as people come in. I can probably get John to do it." Once again she looked slightly embarrassed. "You know, he keeps asking me why I even want to bother getting our class together in the first place, but I think it'll be fun."

"Especially since you're not inviting them to your home," I said. "Teddy Simms told me that he wouldn't want anyone to even know his address, much less invite them over. Rosalind, you have to face the fact that some of our old classmates are up to no good." I thought of some of the people he'd told me about, like the quiet, soft-spoken girl who'd been convicted of grand theft for taking Social Security numbers from the reputable tax-filing service she worked for and then establishing credit with it and buying furs and jewelry, and the guy who'd been in and out of jail on various drug charges.

We had to give the bar owner a date. We both thought Thanksgiving weekend would be the best time to hold it, since a lot of people who'd left Euliss came to spend the holiday with family still living there. Rosalind wanted to hold the reunion on Saturday night, but I liked Friday.

"Sunday is such a huge travel day for people going home," I explained. "I think a lot of people leave on Saturday to get ahead of the traffic. If we hold the reunion Saturday night, they won't be able to attend."

Rosalind relented. "Now, we need to get the word out."

"That's easy," I said. "Flyers. We'll put them up all over Euliss. I'm sure if we ring enough bells we can get somebody to let us in the major apartment buildings. There's always a bulletin board up in the laundry room. The supermarkets always have bulletin boards, too."

"So do barbershops," Rosalind said. "They're so junky to begin with, with those two-year-old magazines lying around, another piece of paper will hardly make a difference. And all the black beauty salons."

"Don't forget Classmates e-mail," I said.

When we finished making arrangements, we went to Applebee's for lunch. By the time our food arrived we'd moved on to the reunion menu. I was grinding pepper over my steak fajitas when Rosalind said, "I must tell you, Emily, Tanis called me last week and asked if I thought things were serious between you and Aaron. I mean, she worked it into the conversation."

"Oh, yeah? What'd you tell her?"

"I asked her what would make her ask that out of the blue. She said she talked to Aaron's daughter Arden at the dance studio. Her daughter goes to the same one as his girls, you know, even though she's a lot younger than they are."

"I didn't know."

"Anyway, when she asked about Aaron, Arden told her he was in Indianapolis for a few days. She said she knew you'd gone out there to close out your condo."

No doubt Tanis knew my travel plans from her mother. Mom had reported that Mavis continually inquired when I was returning home, obviously put up to it by Tanis, who was eager for me to leave town. "Rosalind, I sure hope you asked her why she felt my relationship with Aaron is any of her business."

"What I told her," Rosalind managed to say with remark-able dignity, considering she spoke between chews of a grilled portabello sandwich, "is that I certainly hoped so, since it was my idea to set the two of you up in the first place."

"Good answer. I bet that shut her up."

"It did."

"I wish Tanis would mind her business and stay out of mine. Isn't she supposed to be getting divorced?"

"Oh, I'm pretty sure that Tanis had Aaron all picked out to replace Rob. She didn't count on you showing up and putting the eighty-six on her plans."

"I wouldn't be surprised. But it looks like this is one time Tanis won't get what she wants. Look, I'm tired of talking about her."

"Fine," Rosalind shrugged. "Tell me what Teddy's up to these days."

"He works for one of the dentists in the same building I work in."

Rosalind nodded. "That's right; it's a medical building. Is he a dentist? Somehow he doesn't seem like the type."

"He's a denture technician. He creates bridges and crowns, and even full sets."

"Definitely a viable skill, but it can't compare to Aaron." Rosalind flashed a devilish smile. "So how was it, breaking in a widower?"

"Now, now, Rosalind. You're getting a little personal, don't you think?"

"Hey, I've been with the same man so long, I get a kick out of living vicariously through you."

I'd practically forgotten that Rosalind and John had such a long history together. Immediately I went to work trying to figure how I could pry without it seeming like I was prying.

"You and John didn't have a lot of sexual experience when you got married, did you?" I asked, praying it sounded casual and not like I was conducting a survey. Which, of course, I was.

"Of course we did. We went to different colleges, remember?"

I'd forgotten. Neither the Gills nor the Hunters were thrilled with their childrens' interracial relationship, so they steered them to different colleges. Rosalind and John both chose colleges in Virginia, but their parents were satisfied because Hampton University was on the Atlantic Coast and Virginia Tech was in the western part of the state. The distance made it impossible to maintain a steady relationship, but they hooked up again shortly before graduation, and it soon became clear that it wasn't mere puppy love. Their families had no choice but to accept the inevitable.

So much for my hopes of getting a better understanding of my predicament with Aaron. And I also had another problem to deal with. Rosalind was sharp, and I knew she'd find my question strange.

"What on earth makes you ask that, anyway?" Then she asked a question that really put me on the spot. "Does it have anything to do with Aaron? I know he married his college sweetheart."

I did what any self-respecting woman would do. I lied. "Oh, I guess I was just curious about where people who've only had one partner learn their technique."

"Oh, everybody learns," Rosalind said with a smile. "The important thing isn't where Aaron picked up his skill; it's that he did pick it up."

I grinned. "You can say that again."

And that was no lie.

My heart sank in what was becoming a familiar Friday night routine. I couldn't understand it. Every time Aaron and I made love, after exciting foreplay, he'd climb on top of me in the same position. Hadn't he learned anything about variety in all those years of marriage? I mean, what was the problem here? A lot of sexually inexperienced childhood sweethearts got married and lived happily ever after. I didn't believe for one minute that sex was so ordinary for all of them.

The whole thing struck me as implausible. Women who married young might have had only one sexual partner, but didn't all guys have *some* experience? I mean, didn't there exist in every town the slut who fucked like the Energizer bunny, as well as those sexually aggressive older women who liked their partners young, like those notorious schoolteachers who have made headlines? And if neither of those was available, what about that old sex-ed standby, the porn movie?

I wasn't sure how to handle the situation. I was afraid that if I should suddenly start riding him or kneel seductively on the edge of the bed I'd scare him off. Maybe I shouldn't do anything at all. I mean, it wasn't that he didn't have what it took to get the job done. He'd been gifted with more than healing hands. It was just that I'd like some variety and spontaneity, so that the initial excitement that made my heart pound would continue and, yes, even increase.

By Saturday morning, when Aaron left for the Hamptons, I doubted that doing nothing was the answer. Sex with Aaron was as mechanically organized as a Detroit assembly line. I merely lay back expectantly and told myself diversity wasn't everything. At least I *tried* to convince myself of that.

It might not have been so bad if I could have had my misery in peace, but everyone around me assumed I was the luckiest woman on earth. My own mother repeatedly told me how overjoyed she was for me. Rosalind ribbed me about standing up for me at the wedding. My friends from Indy, all of them looking for Mr. Right, wanted to hear every detail of our courtship, their listening interrupted by an occasional romantic sigh.

And then there was Marsha Cox, whom I caught up with on the phone. At the end of our lengthy conversation we agreed to get together for an early dinner at the Outback on Saturday night, which I had free because Aaron was in Sag Harbor.

"You don't know how lucky you are, Em," Marsha said wistfully when our fried shrimp was delivered to our table. "You snagged a doctor."

"I haven't snagged anybody, yet," I said, just a teensy bit envious. Everyone telling me how fortunate I was was starting to get tiresome, especially since I didn't see it as a complete gift. God certainly had a sense of humor. Aaron was a prize in every way but one.

"Trust me, he's as good as got. The man's wife died. He's probably been really lonesome, and along you come. Pretty, charming, witty . . ."

I started to feel better. There's nothing like a load of compliments to perk up a person's ego.

Marsha's next words quickly made me realize it wasn't just about me. "You know, the only job I could get after Roger got killed was as a bank teller, which was what I did before I met him. Me and my kids are living with my mother in Sherwood Forest, and at this rate I'll never get out of there."

Sherwood Forest was probably the only public-housing project in Euliss that wasn't named after some long-deceased public official no one's ever heard of.

Marsha sighed. "I guess I should have taken advantage of Roger's money and gone to school, learned how to do something."

That was my thought as well, but of course it wouldn't be appropriate for me to point that out. "Does the bank offer any type of tuition reimbursement?" I asked instead.

"Yeah, the key word being *reimbursement*. It'll probably take forever for me to get the money together just to pay for one course. I'm forty-three, Emily. Getting a degree will take too long."

"Lots of people go back to school and get their degrees when they're in their forties. Remember our old English teacher in high school? She was past fifty when she got her bachelor's, and she was one of the best teachers we ever had."

"Sure. She was a nice, cozy, stay-at-home mother whose kids had grown up and left home and her husband was at work all day. She wasn't a widow with no money and two kids to support. Teaching was more of a hobby for her, not a necessity."

I hesitated only a moment before proceeding with a slightly prying question. "Didn't you get any cash at all after Roger was killed?"

"Not a cent. He was barely cold when the FBI showed up. They attached everything: the house, the furniture, the cars, the bank accounts. We were only allowed to take our clothes. And of course I didn't get to keep any of my furs." She grunted. "I'm all right for the time being, but eventually everything I've got is going to go out of style."

I felt she was safe for a while. Marsha wore a cap-sleeved knit sweater and plain tan Capri pants. Somewhere along the line she'd learned that classics worked best. It would prolong the stylishness of her wardrobe. "This isn't any of my business, Marsha, but didn't it ever occur to you that one day something like this might happen? Roger's profession isn't exactly known for career longevity."

She sighed. "You know, Roger never told me how he made his money, other than he was a hardworking entrepreneur. He had a couple of businesses set up that were pretty much bogus, as fronts to launder his money."

"You wouldn't be the first wife who got duped into thinking her husband was an honest businessman."

"He did an excellent job concealing it from me. In fifteen years there were no calls in the middle of the night or things you might expect from a drug kingpin."

"You really had no idea, Marsha?" I hated to sound so doubtful, but come on. "Not in all that time?"

She shrugged. "All right. I did start to get suspicious once I realized how he always kept his cell phone on. He kept it on vibrate and slept with it under his pillow. And how some of the stores he owned didn't seem to carry much merchandise. But, Emily, by then I was so caught up in the lifestyle. If there was anything I wanted, I could just go out and buy it. He never complained about the bills or anything. Our kids went to the best private schools." She chuckled. "Of course, some of their classmates were kids of mobsters, and some porn king had his kids enrolled at those schools, too. Then again, Eddie Murphy used to live in Englewood Cliffs, so there were residents who made their money without breaking the law." A wistful smile formed on her lips. "Emily, there's nothing like being able to buy anything you want without having to ask the price. It's a whole new . . ." She trailed off, perhaps overcome with emotion for what she once had had and lost.

I'd had a taste of what she described just from my brief time with Aaron. I understood why it left her speechless. It was a whole new kind of bliss, one that poor girls from Euliss could only dream about.

"Of course, once you marry Aaron you'll probably experience that," Marsha stated matter-of-factly.

I could only shrug at that.

She continued sharing her memories. "Roger never complained about the bills. Plus, I was able to give my mother money."

My forehead wrinkled. Money was nice, but so was having a decent place to live. "I'm surprised she didn't ask you to get her out of Sherwood Forest."

"She probably has the nicest furnished apartment in the place."

"Why didn't she want to leave?"

"She kept telling me Roger had to be doing something illegal, and if he got caught, the government would confiscate everything, including any co-op apartment or condo we bought her. And, of course, that's exactly what happened."

"Gee, I'm sorry, Marsha. I wish there was something I could do to help."

She chuckled. "I guess we're a pair, aren't we? Living with our mothers like two old maids, except we've been married. And, of course, *you've* got a shot at getting married again. I've got no prospects."

I hated seeing Marsha look so sad. But she was right. Her future did look bleak, both for herself and for her children. Heaven knew what type of kids they were coming into contact with over there in crime-ridden Sherwood Forest.

Then I thought of something, courtesy of Elias Ansara's blond companion. "You know, there are some medical fields you can get into that require only a two-year course, like phlebotomy."

"Fla-what?"

"Phlebotomy. Phlebotomists are the people in labs and hospitals who take blood."

Marsha made a face. "Well, that sounds pretty disgusting. Giving people needles? Filling up those vials with blood? I'm way too squeamish for that, Emily. Plus . . . well, I'm not as smart as you."

I guess everybody wasn't up to handling patients who sometimes faint during blood draws or trying to find the tiny, mobile veins of babies, but I hated to hear her call herself stupid. "That's no way to think about yourself, Marsha. Do you think every practicing physician and attorney in the country today finished at the top of their class? Who knows how many times they failed their medical boards or the bar exam. The fact is that the great majority of us possess average or just above average intelligence. But we can still make a living."

She shook her head. "I really think the best way out for me is to find another husband, one who'll take care of me and my children."

Her attitude was straight out of 1950, but I realized that while my parents had always told me that I would go to college and have a profession, Marsha's mother had probably instilled in her that the best thing she could do as an adult would be to find a good man. I was sure some mothers were still telling their daughters that, even in the twenty-first century. If those were the circumstances behind her attitude, I really couldn't blame Marsha for thinking the way she did—we were all products of what we learned at home to a certain extent—but my heart ached for her just the same. She was about to find out the world didn't work that way.

# Chapter 14

I was almost sorry when the waitress discreetly laid the dinner check near Teddy's elbow. It had been a fun evening spent at this out-of-the-way bistro near Euliss's business park. Teddy had turned into a charming man, very different from the kid who wore a perpetual scowl back in the day. The scowl had disappeared after he'd gotten eyeglasses, and now I knew there'd been a connection between his poor vision and his continual grimacing, which had disguised his squinting. He had a wicked sense of humor that reminded me of someone, except I couldn't recall whom. He had me in stitches as we trashed our hometown.

I'd been updating him about the latest on our class reunion when the waitress had appeared with the check. "What a nice time I had tonight, Teddy," I said, almost shyly.

"How about stopping by my place for a nightcap?"

*Nightcap, my ass.* I knew exactly what Teddy was getting at. There'd been an undercurrent of sexual tension flowing between us all evening. I'd felt it, and I'm sure he had, too.

And I didn't hesitate. "Sure!"

I knew it was a little wrong to set foot in Teddy's house, especially when I knew what could happen. But a part of me that hadn't been satisfied in a long time made it impossible to say no.

Teddy lived in the Trevor Tower—in Euliss, most of the

apartment buildings have names—a thirty-story building on the banks of the Hudson with fabulous views, including of the George Washington Bridge, in the distance. I still wasn't impressed with the Palisades, but I guess looking at the steep cliffs beat the alternative view, which would be the cityscape of Euliss, including a long-abandoned, onetime luxury mid-rise Tudor-style apartment house.

Londontowne was a boarded-up symbol of white flight that had taken over when the surrounding garden apartments and mid-rises had become increasingly occupied by blacks. The rumor was that Londontowne's owners refused to rent to black tenants, and they chose to abandon it as their residents left for greener—no, make that *whiter*—pastures. The owners did, however, have no problem renting out parking spaces to blacks at somewhat inflated rates. Anything to pay those pesky property taxes, I suppose.

Teddy's apartment was on the seventeenth floor, and he had a small terrace—the city dweller's answer to a backyard. A compact gas grill and a side table maybe a foot in diameter flanking two beach chairs took up most of the space. Still, it was comfortable, and the green outdoor carpet he'd put down allowed him and his guests to go outside barefoot.

By New York standards it was a top-of-the-line apartment, with beautiful parquet floors throughout, and long vertical windows, to make the most of the view. "Teddy, this is lovely."

"Thanks," he said from the kitchen, where he poured white wine into stemmed glasses. "I've lived here almost fifteen years, and they keep going up and up and up on the rent."

I nodded understandingly. The builder of Trevor Tower had the misfortune of completing construction just before white tenants began moving out of Londontowne across the street thirty years ago. Initially the tower had been occupied by mostly whites, with a smattering of blacks. Located just steps away from a Metro-North station, it was a popular choice for Manhattan commuters. But the racial make-up of the neighborhood became too uncomfortable for the new tenants, and when their leases expired they moved farther up the river to neighbor-hoods not yet infiltrated by blacks. The gym and the club room on the lobby floor closed, and the building became one of those income-restricted properties where tenants had to provide management with their W-2s every February. Of course, anyone with a computer was able to doctor his or her W-2s to reflect incomes much lower than what they actually earned.

I remember being shocked when I moved to Indianapolis and learned that Al and I could rent an apartment that came with carpet and our choice of either blinds or curtains. In New York, renters get four walls and not another damn thing. Of course, rising rents are a fact of life no matter where you live. That was the biggest benefit I'd realized in the years since buying my house: my mortgage payment stayed the same, but my income rose. For Teddy and other tenants of Trevor Tower, it was hard to get ahead when your rent ate up your salary increase every year.

"And the kiss of death came last year," he said, handing me a glass and joining me on the couch. "Apparently, the rul-ing class decided that these apartments are too nice for us work-ing slobs. A resolution was passed to start charging rates more in keeping with the market. So starting October first, I have either to cough up seventeen-fifty a month or move out."

"Seventeen hundred a month!"

"Well, it could be worse." He chuckled. "I could be living in midtown Manhattan, in which case the rent on a one-bed-room with terrace would be more like twenty-five hundred a month."

"Still, seventeen hundred seems like a lot of money for Eu-liss." The mortgage on my town house was only six-fifty, something I didn't have the heart to tell him.

"Haven't you heard, Emily? They're redoing the entire wa-terfront. They opened a beautiful new library by the train station. They've got a new water taxi that takes people down to the Wall Street area that stops here. One of the celebrity chefs opened a new restaurant on the pier. A hundred dollars a person for dinner, and forty-dollar brunches."

I'd eaten there with Aaron to celebrate my new job, but Teddy sounded so disdainful, I chose to keep that quiet, too.

"And apartments in those brand-new mid-rises right on the waterfront are going for about two grand a month. I predict that in five years this entire area will be all, or at least mostly, white."

I was dumbfounded by this. "But now it's all black, and a lot of them can't afford those rents. Where's everybody going to go?"

Teddy shrugged. "A lot of them are talking about downsizing into studios, which they can get for fourteen hundred. Others are talking about becoming roommates and splitting half of a two-bedroom, which will go up to two grand, two thousand seventy-five if there's a terrace. And most of the people who have balconies are trying to get into apartments without them, since that adds seventy-five bucks every month to what they're paying." He took a slug of wine, downing half the glass. "It's a damn shame, if you ask me. Black people have lived in this part of Euliss for the last sixty, seventy years. Now we're being run out of town like bandits in the Old West. The only ones who are safe are senior citizens."

"I don't remember seeing any senior citizens in this building."

"No, not really. But this building isn't the only one with the problem. They're going to run everybody out of River Road and Hillside Avenue before they're done."

"But there are private homes on those streets, Teddy. They can't force home owners out."

"No, but they can offer them a ton of money. Most of those home owners are old people with old houses with no mortgages. I guarantee they'll take it and move to Delaware or North Carolina."

He had a point. I found myself glad that the five-family house my mother lived in was a full half mile from the river.

"The buyers will bulldoze those old homes and build modern ones in their place," Teddy continued. "They'll modernize those older apartment buildings and rent each one for thousands. Now, the folks who won those new-house lotteries, *they're* the ones who'll benefit. The values of their homes are going to skyrocket."

I remembered Mom telling me about the ten new homes they built on a block of River Road that had been affordably priced and awarded by lottery in an effort to get working-class people into homes of their own.

"What're you going to do?"

"I'm not sure," he said. "I've still got a couple of months to make up my mind. But I know this much: I don't want to worry about it right now." He moved closer to me and gently lowered the hand that held my wineglass down. I let go of the glass when my hand was level with the table, but Teddy didn't release my hand. "I've got a better idea." His breath felt warm against my skin, and while I didn't meet his face halfway as it moved closer and closer to mine, I didn't pull away, either.

I'm embarrassed to admit this, but I was a pushover. I wasn't in Teddy's apartment fifteen minutes before I was stark naked. The only time I'd undressed faster was in the gynecologist's office, because I was always afraid that the doctor would show up before I'd pulled off my drawers and hopped up on the exam table with that oversized napkin covering my lower body.

Teddy was a completely satisfying lover. Like Aaron, he had the gift, but unlike Aaron, he really knew how to use it. Making love was an art, and there wasn't a single Crayola missing from his box.

"So you're seeing somebody, huh?" he said to me after Round Two, propping himself up on one elbow while I lay beside him on my back, gasping for breath.

"Um . . . sort of. We're having a rough spot right now. It can really go either way." At least that sounded like it could justify my behavior. Even if I knew better.

"He must not be too much on the ball if he's not doing everything he can to keep you."

"I really don't want to talk about it, Teddy."

"Oh, you don't have to talk." He pulled me to him, cupping my breast and squeezing my nipple as he rolled on top of me and reached between my legs. "You don't have to talk at all, Emily."

And I didn't say a word. Unless moans count as words.

My guilt started the moment I drove off. It was after midnight when I left his apartment. He walked me to my car, opened the door for me, and before I could get in, pulled me close for a good-night kiss. "Let's do it again soon."

I felt my body stiffen and quickly moved out of his embrace. The sex had been electrifying. I'd given myself to him with an abandon that surprised me, jumping his bones like he was the last barbecued spare rib on earth. Of *course* he wanted to do it again; what did I expect?

Good Lord, what had I done?

It took me less than five minutes to drive home, and by the time I crept into the apartment my stomach was knotted tightly enough to anchor a boat.

I'd hoped Mom would be asleep, but she called out to me in a weak voice, "Emily, is that you?"

I went into her room. "I'm home, Mom. Go to sleep. It's late."

"I'll say it is. Aaron called."

*Shit.* I'd told him that I was having dinner with an old school friend—the truth, of course—and that we'd probably sit up and gab till late; I'd considered the possibility of being out late, but with an activity other than talking. I'd hoped Aaron would take the veiled hint that he shouldn't bother calling because I wouldn't be there, but obviously he hadn't. "What time did he call?"

"Just before nine. He said he thought you'd be out late, but he just thought he'd try you anyway. He said he'd talk to you tomorrow."

He'd waited until as late as he could; nine o'clock was regarded as the cutoff time for calling the home of anyone who didn't live alone. That was fine. I could tell him I'd gotten in by ten.

The thought of covering up what I'd done with Teddy with a lie made me feel physically ill. I told Mom good night and headed straight for the shower. Scrubbing away all traces of Teddy's touch didn't make me feel any better. Yes, I was completely satisfied, sexually speaking, but emotionally, I felt lower than the average savings interest rate.

I worried that I'd lie awake half the night, but I fell asleep right away.

By late Friday morning I realized the underlying reason for my stomach cramps and fatigue. My period had started.

There were times in my younger days, long before I knew that conception would be so difficult for me, when "seeing red" was reason for rejoicing, and this was a late addition to that list. Not because of any pregnancy fears, for of course Teddy had used a condom. All three times. But Mother Nature had just given me a reprieve, the best reason in the world for not being intimate with Aaron tonight.

Fortunately, he took the news well. "I figured it would happen sooner or later," he said when I gave him the news. "Why don't I pick up some food, bring it over, and we'll curl up on the couch and watch TV?"

"That sounds wonderful," I replied, relieved. I didn't feel like facing the world, but suddenly I felt very eager to face Aaron. I wanted to see him. The very prospect excited me. He'd been so easygoing about not having sex this weekend. It appeared we were moving into an old-folks-at-home stage of our relationship, where it wasn't about expensive restaurants, but just the two of us spending a quiet evening at home, talking and maybe necking a bit.

I greeted him at the door with an enthusiastically wet kiss, enjoying how it caught him off guard. He mouthed the words, "Your mother?"

"She took a bus ride to Atlantic City. She'll probably be home in an hour." When I told Mom that Aaron would probably be there when she returned, she'd broken into a wide grin. Although she hadn't come out and said anything, I knew she'd been worried about my staying out so late last night with a school chum I dodged identifying by confidently saying, "You don't know her." Mom knew the great majority of my friends, and I thought she might have figured out I was with another man. Fortunately, I caught myself before I said, "You don't know *him*."

"Did you have fun last night?" Aaron asked as we munched on the steak-and-cheese calzone pie he'd brought. He'd also brought some black-and-white cookies, a New York classic that I'd never been able to find in the Midwest, because he knew I loved them.

His thoughtfulness made me feel all the more guilty about last night with Teddy.

"Oh, yes. I've got close friends in Indy, but I'm enjoying getting reacquainted with the people I grew up with. I didn't get home until nearly ten."

"I tried to call you. I'd hoped I'd be able to reach you, even though you said you probably wouldn't be in until late. I guess I just wanted to hear your voice." He nibbled at my neck. "Could it be I'm getting accustomed to having you in my life?"

"Would that be such a bad thing if you were? Especially if I feel the same way."

Aaron held my gaze for a few moments before giving me one of his delicious kisses. The man could teach a course on how to kiss. Even now, with me totally unable to act upon it, he made my pulse race. I felt his hand slip beneath my T-shirt and settle on my breast, gently squeezing and teasing my already hardened nipple.

My breathing became audible, and my eyes remained closed after the kiss ended. I *had* to find a way to make this work. Aaron was so perfect for me. This could be the beginning of a whole new life for me.

# Chapter 15

Aaron told me that Beverline and the kids were back at home for the weekend, because Kirsten was attending a classmate's *quinceanera*. He asked me to join them in seeing her off to her first dress-up affair. I didn't want to, but remorse for sleeping with Teddy got the better of me, and I accepted. I was still unsure about the wisdom of spending an evening around people who hadn't exactly welcomed me, even if one daughter wouldn't be present.

Then again, maybe things would be different, now that Aaron's mother-in-law and daughters had had time to adjust to the idea of there being a woman in his life.

As it turned out, I should have stuck to my original hunch. Beverline seemed shocked to see me, and Kirsten's sunny smile became a scowl when she saw me standing by as Aaron filmed her descending the stairs, looking lovely in an orange gown with spaghetti straps that made her skin look beautifully bronzed.

Billy greeted me cheerfully, and Arden with polite caution. Beverline managed to convey that I'd come at an inappropriate time. "Emily, I hope you won't be bored, since we're all so preoccupied with my granddaughter. This is her first grownup party, and our whole family is excited about it."

What she didn't say, but I just knew she was thinking, was, *And only the family should be here tonight.*

Ignoring the slight, I gave her a hundred-watt smile. "I think it's wonderful. I remember my first dress-up party."

Kirsten looked at me, obviously startled. "*You* went to a *quinceanera?*"

"No. It was my prom, so I was a little older than you are now. But I had a beautiful dress, and I still felt like a princess out of a fairy tale."

"Kirsten has to be home by midnight," Arden said with a giggle. "Or else she'll turn into a pumpkin."

"You look real pretty, Kirsten," Billy said, sounding awestruck in the way only kid brothers can.

"Yes, you do," Beverline added as Kirsten thanked her brother with a warm hug. "Although I do think that fifteen is a little young to be going to a formal party," she fretted. "In my day it was put off until sixteen."

"It's not your day anymore, Beverline. It's Kirsten's," Aaron pointed out.

Her face took on a pinched look. "Thank you for pointing that out," she said in a tone as dry as hay.

"It's the truth, Beverline," he said gently. "Your day, and mine as well, have passed."

She gave him a meaningful stare, then moved her eyes to me for a few moments, then back to his, as if to say, *If your day has passed, then what's* she *doing here?*

He ignored her. "Kirsten, walk into the living room and stop in front of Mom's picture."

Aaron looked just like a movie director as he followed Kirsten with his video camera.

As Kirsten stood in front of that large painting of her late mother that continued to give me an uneasy feeling, I was struck by the strong resemblance between the two. I felt a little teary eyed when the teen smiled at the camera her father held, then spontaneously turned to blow a kiss toward her mother's likeness. Then, in an instant, she crumpled. Aaron quickly put the camera down and ran to embrace his daughter, reaching her a few steps before Beverline. "It's all right, sweetheart," he said as she fought back tears. "Don't cry. Mom would want you to be happy tonight."

Suddenly feeling like an intruder, I discreetly slipped into the foyer and sat in a wing chair. Perhaps Beverline had been right and tonight should have been just for their family.

But surely if Aaron hadn't wanted me to be here he wouldn't have invited me.

I tried to settle my discomfort by studying my surroundings. There was enough room in this white-tiled foyer to hold a dance, like in all those old movies Mom used to watch. The ornate, large, painted Bombay chest that my chair and its twin flanked must have set Aaron back two or three grand. My eyes went to the gently curving staircase, which probably had twenty steps, due to the high ceilings on the first floor.

I wasn't in the foyer for long. Aaron soon came looking for me. "I'm sorry about that, Emily."

"Nothing to apologize for. I just felt I shouldn't be witnessing such a personal moment between father and daughter, so I came in here. Is Kirsten better now?"

"Yes, she's fine. She teared up a little, but she didn't break down. Her ride will be here any moment. I want to film her and her friends driving off, and then I thought we'd order some Chinese food. Billy wants to bowl downstairs later, so how about you and Arden teaming up against him and me?"

I looked down at my brown leather Earth Shoe sandals. "I don't have bowling shoes."

"You don't need them. I happen to be a very close friend of the lane owner." He winked as he helped me up, a sight so sexy my knees almost gave out. "Come on. Let's go back. I want to take some still photos."

Aaron held my hand as we returned to the living room, a fact that wasn't lost on Beverline, who openly stared at our clasped hands.

My back normally went up when people tried to make me uncomfortable, but this time my opposition was winning. I'd seen the emotion on Beverline's face as she'd watched her granddaughter posing under the painting of her deceased mother. For a moment she, too, looked as if she were about to cry. I'd known all along about why she'd moved in with Aaron and the kids, but suddenly her grief had a face. Her daughter had died tragically young, leaving behind three children who needed a mother. Kirsten was trying to cope with her mother's permanent absence during an important event in her young life. A loving grandmother was a wonderful thing . . . but there was no one quite like mom.

I thought of my own mother. Lord knew that Ruby Yancy could try my patience at times, but she'd always been there in the audience beside my father at school functions and dance recitals, applauding wildly whether I had a featured part or not. She'd been at all my graduations, even the one from fifth grade. She'd taken me shopping for new school clothes and shoes at the beginning of each school year. She'd helped me pick out a prom dress and, later, my wedding gown. Kirsten and Arden, despite having all the advantages money brought, would have to grow up without that.

That had to be tough.

Still, I couldn't let Beverline make me feel like I had no business in the house. I squared my shoulders and said, "Aaron, why don't I take some pictures with you in them?"

He handed me his digital camera, and I took various shots of him with Kirsten and then a few that included Arden and Billy as well.

Kirsten was riding with five other girls in a seven-passenger minivan, courtesy of someone's parents. I hung back, not sure if Aaron wanted the couple who were driving to know he'd rejoined the dating world, but he gestured for me to come out and casually introduced me to Kirsten's classmate's parents. If they were surprised to see a woman with Aaron, they kept it under wraps.

Aaron draped an arm around me as Kirsten joined her friends in the backseat. "She's beautiful, isn't she?" he said to me proudly.

"She certainly is."

"Diana would be so proud. Kirsten's the spitting image of her, you know." He sucked in his breath. "I'm sorry, Emily. I guess that was a thoughtless thing to say."

"It's all right. I think I understand."

He moved his hand down to squeeze mine while waving good-bye to Kirsten as the van took off. When we broke apart to go inside, there was Beverline glaring at me before she went inside ahead of us, letting the front door close.

I was surprised she didn't lock it.

I tried not to look envious of the couple who sat across from Aaron and me.

Dr. Elias Ansara continually whispered sweet nothings into the ear of his companion, another attractive blonde, this one named Kara.

When Kara excused herself from the table to go to the ladies' room, I asked Elias, "So what happened to Melissa?"

He winked. "She got tired of me, I guess."

"Don't believe it, Emily," Aaron said with a laugh, his warm palm resting easily on the bare skin of my shoulder. "The reality is, I've yet to see Elias go out with the same woman twice. He loves 'em and leaves 'em."

"Don't be lyin' on me, Aaron. Emily will think I'm some kind of lothario," Elias said in an unconvincing manner I found captivating.

"I can see you're all broken up about it," I said with amusement. "Took you forever to find someone new."

"What can I say, darling? I've always believed that the best way to get over someone is to get under someone."

That broke us up. I'd learned that Elias was probably Aaron's closest friend. I found it fascinating to be in the company of a man who oozed sex appeal, but it also made me feel a little sad to think of my own predicament. I felt pretty damn sure there was no boring sex going on in *Elias's* bedroom. Get under someone, he'd said. I could picture some blonde riding him like she was at the rodeo. Not like my missionary man, who always had to be on top.

Aaron had been especially attentive tonight. His conservative displays of affection toward me—squeezing my shoulder, holding my hand, even giving me a quick kiss—in the restaurant made me feel terribly guilty. It had been just over a week since I'd slept with Teddy.

This week there'd be no reprieve, and I felt like someone had taken my nerves and shaken them like an improperly mixed martini. Teddy had stopped by the Norman practice several times after our encounter and tried to schedule another one.

"I can't," I'd told him when he last dropped by. "My friend and I are trying to patch things up."

He hadn't been convinced. "Come on, Emily, there's no boyfriend. You're putting me off, for some reason."

"I never said he was a *boyfriend*," I'd clarified. "He's a friend I've been seeing romantically here and there."

"Yeah, and all this happened in just a few weeks. You haven't been in Euliss long enough to develop a relationship that's already hit the skids. If a couple has problems that early on in a relationship, y'all would have just called it quits."

*He had a point,* I realized with annoyance. Then I'd decided to capitalize on it. "Maybe that's the problem. Maybe it happened too fast."

Teddy had flashed his most irresistible smile. "What're you doing Wednesday?"

"No, Teddy."

I couldn't say I regretted having slept with him. I just had to prove to myself that sex was every bit as exciting as I'd remembered and that I was right to feel cheated. Still, one time was all it took for me to know that. I wasn't about to do it again.

I really wanted to make it work with Aaron.

* * *

"Oh, my God," I moaned into Teddy's mouth. "I can't *believe* I'm doing this."

"Come on, baby. Let's get it on."

I felt powerless to resist. I only came here to tell Teddy I couldn't see him anymore. I'd finally gotten him to stop his visits to the office, but then he started calling my cell phone. He insisted I have a drink with him before I left. I wondered if he'd slipped something in it, because the next thing I knew we were kissing, my shirt was pushed up to my collarbone, and my breasts were exposed.

He yanked my arm, pulling me toward the bedroom, tearing off his shirt with his other hand.

Completely nude, I pulled back the sheets and lay down, and once he stepped out of his jeans he dove between my legs. I wiggled my hips toward his face while he reached up with one hand to squeeze my breast. My heart was thumping with pleasure and anticipation.

Teddy moved his body up the length of the bed, his leg brushing mine, and rummaged around in the drawer of his nightstand.

"Uh-oh."

I didn't like the sound of *that*. "What's wrong?"

"I'm out of condoms."

I groaned. "*Now* you tell me." Nothing kills passion faster than those four dreaded words *I'm out of condoms.*

"You don't happen to have any on you, do you?"

"No." I'd never seen the point in buying condoms "just in case." Every man likes his own special brand. Me buying condoms was kind of like a man picking out a box of tampons for me.

"Don't panic. We can go to the store; they're still open."

"It's ten to ten, Teddy."

"Then we'd better hurry the hell up if we don't want to go across town." No merchants stayed open around the clock on this side of town; you had to go to the white section if you wanted a Tylenol at midnight.

Never before had two people put their clothes on so fast. I had no time to do anything to my hair, including look at it. I imagined that after the combination of my stretching out on the bed and Teddy messing with it, it must have resembled one of those strawlike witch-hair wigs they sell at Halloween. I pulled my brush out of my purse as we rode down to the lobby in the elevator and wished I had a coated rubber band on me.

Once outside, we raced to his car, and Teddy gunned up the hill. The steel curtain in front of the store was partially pulled down, but the store was still open. From the haphazard way a car was parked in front of ours, Hardy's had at least one customer.

"I'll wait here," I said. The mom-and-pop grocery store was located on Burns Boulevard, a major thoroughfare just a few blocks away from my mother's place, not that she'd be driving anywhere after dark. But there were plenty of other folks driving down the street, and while I couldn't say I was exactly hiding from the public, nor did I want to flaunt the fact that I was out with Teddy.

Now that we'd managed to make it to the store before it closed, I was able to chuckle at the silliness of it all. This kind of thing hadn't happened to me in years, and I thought those days were behind me.

I glanced in the sideview mirror on the outside of the passenger seat just as Teddy emerged, talking to a woman who'd also been inside, probably the owner of the car in front of us. They stood outside for a minute, while the store owner pulled down the steel curtain and disappeared inside.

My jaw dropped when I realized the woman talking to Teddy wasn't just someone he knew from the neighborhood, but someone we *both* knew.

Tanis.

What in heaven's name was she doing down in Euliss at ten o'clock at night?

My head darted about, as I tried to think how I could

make myself invisible. Throwing myself flat across the bucket seat wouldn't work; no way could I wedge my body in that tiny space between the gear and CD storage box. Besides, Tanis had to walk past Teddy's car to get to her own and would surely notice me stretched out. Damn. Why couldn't Teddy have parked in *front* of her?

I had nowhere to hide. How could I possibly explain being out with Teddy at this hour? She might even have seen him purchasing the condoms!

My ass was toast.

They started moving toward me, and I did the only thing I could. I turned my body away from the window and scrunched forward, pretending to be adjusting the radio. Teddy knew that Tanis and I knew each other, of course, but I felt fairly positive he wouldn't feel it necessary to point out to her that I was his passenger. He knew discretion was the name of the game.

With one hand I quickly gathered up my hair and pushed it over my left shoulder. A lot of women had long hair, but the less Tanis saw of it, the better. I wanted to be as anonymous as possible. I wished to God I had thought to grab the baseball cap Teddy kept on a table near his apartment door; I could have stuffed my hair inside it.

The driver's door opened, and I heard Teddy's voice. "Good seeing you, Tanis. I hope your father feels better."

"Good to see you, too, Teddy. And thanks."

My God, her voice sounded like it came from barely a foot away from where I sat. Did I imagine it, or did she linger a few seconds before moving on?

I didn't dare look up for confirmation when I sensed she had finally moved on. I might have been wrong and looked dead at her.

"Okay, you can straighten up now," Teddy said as he made a right turn onto Hillside Avenue. "She went straight."

I sighed as I straightened. "Well, that was a close one. The last thing I need is Tanis Montgomery in my business."

"I think she's in your business already."

I looked at him suspiciously. "What's that mean?"

"She recognized you, Emily."

"Whattaya mean, she recognized me? All she saw was the back of my head."

"Yes, and your gray streak. The light from the street lamp shone dead on it."

I exhaled like a slowly deflating balloon. That damn streak. It had made me a marked woman. I might as well have a port-wine birthmark across my cheek.

"Oh, God," I moaned, my shoulders slumping.

"Come on, cheer up." He leaned as close as he could while driving. "I got the condoms."

At the moment that was my least concern. "Did she see you buying them?"

"I really don't know. If I had to guess, I'd say no, but I can't say for sure."

"What was that you said about her father?"

"Apparently Mr. Montgomery was having some abdominal pain tonight, and they took him to the ER. Tanis drove over to check on him. They didn't admit him, so it looks like he'll be okay."

Doggone it. Why couldn't George Montgomery have waited an hour or two to develop a bellyache? A little bit of a timing shift, and I wouldn't have been found out. The worst part was I hadn't even done anything wrong—at least not yet.

For a crazy moment I thought about telling Teddy I'd changed my mind but decided against it. If I was about to be reported to Aaron, I might as well do what Tanis would *say* I'd been doing.

When the door of Teddy's apartment closed behind us, the mood returned, and in the blissful feeling of making love to Teddy I forgot all about Tanis and what she may or may not have seen. At least for the moment.

The wheels of my mind started spinning as soon as I got in

the car to drive home. I had to come up with a legitimate reason for being out with Teddy.

As it turned out, I had to invent that reason sooner than I planned. Rosalind called me the next morning on my cell phone.

"Good news," she said cheerfully. "Tanis called me and offered to assist with the reunion planning. I suggested that we get together at my house tomorrow after work. Will that work for you? I know you usually spend Friday nights with Aaron, but John and I are taking the kids to Ocean City for the weekend and we're leaving first thing Saturday morning." I'd confided in Rosalind that Beverline's attitude made me choose to sit out summer weekends in Sag Harbor in favor of waiting until the fall, when the kids were back in school and Aaron and I could go out there alone.

"Sure," I replied, forcing myself to sound eager. "I'll just let Aaron know I'll be a little late. Uh . . . I wonder what made Tanis want to help out." I knew *exactly* what had brought on the offer, but I wanted to know if she'd given Rosalind a reason.

"I don't know. All I know is that when I spoke to her about it before she said she didn't have time. I know that's an hour-long show she's filming, but I doubt she's in every scene."

"Amen to that." The reason behind Tanis's change of heart was as clear to me as glass.

"She said she'd even contribute to the food," Rosalind added. "That means she'll probably get her housekeeper to make something and will pass it off as her own, but what do I care? We need all the help we can get."

"You know, I think Valerie might be interested in helping, too," I said, an idea forming in my head. I needed an ally, preferably one far removed from Euliss, and I was running out of friends close enough to cover for me. Valerie, whom I'd known just as long as Tanis, would probably consent to help me. She and Tanis might share blood—they were first cousins through their mothers being sisters—but they'd never been close. Tanis had always been a little jealous of Valerie, who had both good looks and good grades while growing up. That was probably why Tanis was closer to Valerie's sister, Wendy, who had the nonthreatening qualities of being cute as a button and dumb as a doughnut. The sisters weren't twins, but we were all in the same grade because they'd both been born within the same year, Valerie in February and Wendy in December. "I'll give her a call."

"Sure. The more hands we have, the better. Can you come over around six? I'll order pizza. And bring Valerie if she wants to come."

# Chapter 16

It didn't take long for Teddy's name to come up at our meeting Friday night. The four of us had been sitting around the table in Rosalind's dining room for about ten minutes, eating pizza and planning the reunion menu, when Valerie asked Tanis, "How's Uncle George?"

"Oh, he's doing fine. He gave us a scare the other night. The doctor said it was probably just something he'd eaten." Tanis's gaze settled on me as she casually said, "I ran into Teddy Simms when I stopped at Hardy's convenience store on my way home."

"Does old Mr. Hardy still run that store?" Rosalind asked, incredulous, and with good reason. The grocer had been just a few years removed from social security back when we were in high school.

"No, some Spanish dude owns it now, but he kept the name."

"Emily told me Teddy's doing well," Valerie offered.

The surprised look on Tanis's face told me she didn't expect to hear my name come up in conjunction with Teddy's. She didn't know I'd cued Valerie in on what had transpired and pleaded for her help. "Have you seen him lately, Emily?" Tanis asked innocently.

"All the time. We work in the same building, at least a few days a week. He's a denture technician, and he has two clients in different locations. As a matter of fact, we got together just the other week for dinner to catch up."

"Emily says that Teddy knows what just about everybody from our graduating class is up to these days," Rosalind remarked.

God, was I glad I'd told her that. That was a completely unrehearsed statement, and considering Rosalind had no clue about what had transpired Wednesday night, one that came right on time.

Tanis looked at Rosalind blankly, then at me. "Well, he had some chick in the car with him Wednesday night," she said slyly. "I didn't see her face, but it was pretty obvious she was trying to hide it from me."

Rosalind shrugged. "Is he married?"

"No," Tanis replied.

"Then unless he was with someone who is, I don't see the big deal."

I was saying a silent prayer of thanks for Rosalind's support when she added, "I'm just glad he's getting some from *somebody*."

My face froze. That remark gave just the image I wanted to avoid. Tanis looked at me with an expression similar to that of someone who'd just found a fifty lying on the sidewalk.

"Not necessarily," Valerie said. "Why don't you tell them, Emily?"

Rosalind, sensing a secret about to be revealed, instantly perked up. "Tell us what?"

"That I was the one in the car with Teddy," I said. "I was out with Valerie Wednesday night down at City Island, and I'd just gotten off the parkway in Euliss when my engine gave out. I didn't have any of my nephews' phone numbers with me, but Teddy's number was still in my cell phone from when we met for dinner the other week, so I called and asked him to give me a jump. The car didn't make it all the way to my mother's, so we managed to park it and he drove me home."

I shrugged. "It was all perfectly innocent. I tried to keep out of sight because people tend to jump to conclusions, and the next thing you know there's this huge, totally untrue rumor going on." I gave Tanis a pointed stare.

She took a sip of her Sprite, her eyes meeting mine over the rim of her glass. "I'm surprised you didn't just call Aaron," she said after she swallowed.

"Aaron does his surgeries in the mornings, and I preferred not to bother him that late unless it was a real emergency."

"Did you get your car started, Emily?" Rosalind asked.

"Yes. Yesterday morning it started up just like that, and Mr. Norris didn't find anything wrong with it."

"That happens sometimes," Valerie said with a nod.

"Maybe Teddy's jumper cables were weak." This smart-assed comment came from Tanis. I had a little trouble digesting her statement and had to press my lips together to keep them from twitching. Teddy had a tiger in his tank, and the idea of any of his equipment not functioning at capacity made me want to roar with mirth. But of course the object here was to prove Tanis wrong, preferably with some quiet dignity.

"I have no need to get any from Teddy, Rosalind," I said. "I have Aaron, remember?" I smiled sweetly. "When I leave here I'm going straight over to his place."

"You lucky girl, you," Rosalind said.

Now Tanis wore an expression that looked like she'd eaten some bad pepperoni. She let the matter drop like the grease off the slice she was eating, and we returned to menu planning between bites. At least Rosalind, Valerie and I did. I wasn't surprised when Tanis seemed to lose interest in the reunion after that. She even made an excuse for leaving early, something about a promise she'd made to her kids.

Valerie and I walked out together to our cars, both of which were parked in the street. "Thanks again for covering for me, Valerie. I really owe you one."

"Tanis is such a pain sometimes. I can't tell you how sick I am of having her and Wendy and their husbands shoved down my throat."

"But Tanis is getting divorced."

"My mother isn't giving me any reprieve. Already she's predicting that Tanis will probably be remarried within a year, the implication that everyone can find a husband except me." Valerie's upper lip curled. "I hope her new show flops."

I chuckled at her hope for the failure of Tanis's new gig, but I felt for Valerie. I'd been hearing about Tanis's accomplishments all my life. Poor Valerie had to hear about both Tanis *and* Wendy.

"I really appreciate it," I repeated. "I don't know what I would've done if you hadn't helped me cover."

"No problem. So tell me, how was he?"

I'd never actually come out and expressed that I'd been to bed with Teddy; I'd only said that Aaron was bound to misunderstand if word got back to him through a vengeful Tanis that I'd been riding with Teddy at night. But Valerie was no fool. What other conclusion could she come to?

"Valerie! You're embarrassing me."

"Listen. I always thought Teddy Simms was cute. He always struck me as the type who'd want to settle down, so I'm surprised he never got married."

I saw an opening and took it. "Valerie, haven't you ever wanted to get married?"

"Of course I have. Both of my parents were worried when I started getting promotions that if I became too successful, I'd never get a husband. My father said *he* certainly wouldn't want a woman who made more money than he did. My mother actually tried to get me to turn down a promotion. When Wendy got married and had her son, got divorced, and was remarried within a year and started having more babies and I *still* couldn't find anybody to go out with, I started to wonder if maybe they'd been right."

I could understand how she felt. Wendy Woods was a nice enough person, but her brain was as absorbent as a cheap paper towel. I was amazed she managed to get through high school. Nobody would want to finish behind her at anything.

"So I decided not to let that get in the way of having babies. Since I made enough money I'd find someone to sleep with and raise my baby on my own. Then when Melanie started school, I found I missed having a little one around, so I did it again. And again." She looked at me and smiled. "You probably think I'm nuts, Emily, but I love kids. I always have."

I remembered Valerie as a little girl with her collection of dolls. When we got older and got into the Barbie phase, Valerie still preferred her baby dolls. "When I grow up I'm going to get married and have a house full of kids," she used to say.

"You look happy," I ventured.

"Life's good. I've attained more success than in my wildest dreams, Em. I've got three wonderful children. And it looks like I'm going to have another baby in the house. Melanie's pregnant."

Her oldest daughter. So Bea Pullman hadn't been imagining things. "But she's so young, Valerie!"

"Sixteen." She sighed wearily. "At least I was a woman in my midtwenties before I got pregnant, and it was planned. But Melanie is tough. She knows that having a baby doesn't mean she can't achieve her goals. I'll help her, of course. It'll be kind of nice to have a baby around again. Only six more weeks to go."

She sounded only vaguely disheartened at her teenage daughter's pregnancy. I'd say her leading emotion right now was excitement, and I didn't know what to say. All I could think of was, *If you're happy, I'm happy.*

In the end I said nothing, and Valerie kept talking.

"I know what you're thinking, Emily, but Melanie will be fine."

"Haven't you ever met a special man, Valerie?"

A wistful smile formed on her lips, and her eyes took on a faraway look. "Only twice. Once when I was in college—we broke up my junior year. Then again just a couple of years ago. He was an attorney. For a couple of months everything was perfect, but then he started to change. He'd start complaining about the way I did this or that. I felt like he was trying to mold me, and I'm nobody's clay. We ultimately decided it would be best if we went our separate ways."

"I'm sorry, Valerie."

"No need for that. I've done pretty well for myself, Emily. I wanted the whole package, but since I couldn't get it, I took the parts of it I could get." She chuckled. "Too bad I didn't meet someone like your doctor friend. *He* wouldn't have a problem with my income."

The weight of my burden descended over me in a manner that was becoming familiar. Marsha wanted someone like Aaron. Valerie wanted someone like Aaron. And Tanis just plain wanted Aaron. I had him, but I didn't feel like celebrating. What was wrong with me? Why couldn't I appreciate what I had? "Gee, Valerie, I don't know what to say."

"Just promise me something. If you decide you'd rather have Teddy than the doctor, make me the first to know so I can get to him before Tanis does." She opened the door to her maroon Saab SUV and climbed in. "See you later!"

The next afternoon I shared with Mom what Valerie had told me. I sat in the La-Z-Boy in the living room, and she at the table in the adjoining dining area with her latest bank statement. "Well, I think it's a shame when a young girl in her twenties feels her situation is so hopeless that she has to choose between having a husband and having children."

"Her parents certainly didn't encourage her. In fact, Winnie tried to discourage her from becoming too successful."

"In a way you can't blame them. It can be damaging to a man's ego when his wife has a higher salary. I know David had some problems accepting Cissy's promotion."

I choked on my bottled water. Euliss tap water tasted nasty with a capital N, so bottled water was an extravagance I refused to give up. "He did?"

"They came close to separating. She asked me not to tell anyone, and I didn't. Just like you asked me not to say anything to anyone when *your* marriage was in trouble," she reminded me. "But it's been such a long time, and he's gotten over it, so L don't think Cissy would mind my telling you about it now. Men and women from Winnie's and my generation look at these things differently from you young folks, Emmie. In our time, the man was the breadwinner. Professional women worked as either nurses or schoolteachers or social workers. There was no such thing as a woman making the money you girls make now." She sipped her water. "Sometimes I look at you and Cissy and I wonder what I could have been if I'd been born a generation later."

Her statement shocked me. Never once had it occurred to me that my mother, who hadn't worked outside the home since she got pregnant with Sonny, ever wanted to do anything with her life besides care for her family. The knowledge was fascinating . . . and a little bit sad, for the answer to her musings would forever be unknown.

"Back to Valerie," Mom said. "Does Aaron have any nice doctor friends you can introduce her to?"

"Unfortunately, they're all married. And the one who isn't, he seems to have a thing for blondes."

"Well, if you ask me, instead of getting pregnant with that first baby she should have been out looking for a nice doctor or lawyer once she started moving up the career ladder. Even if he was still in school at the time. She wasn't doing nearly as well then as she is now. They could have built a beautiful life together."

"Well, Mom, it's not like there's a place women can go to pick out a nice med or law student, it's not like buying a new car." Although the idea of it was rather pleasant. Imagine going into a showroom with men on display instead of cars and picking the one you wanted.

"I'm just glad you met Aaron." Mom sighed.

"You okay over there?"

"I'm trying to find this fifty cents I'm off by."

"You'll find it. Try re-adding your outstanding checks."

"Why bother? It's only fifty cents, Emmie."

"Today it's fifty cents. Tomorrow it'll be fifty dollars. That's why it's so important for you to balance your checkbook every single month to the penny. That's the only real way you can keep up with your money."

"Yes, 'Mother,' " she said with playful meekness.

I glanced at her as she worked on the Case of the Missing Fifty Cents. She muttered to herself as she worked her pencil. Mom was nearly eighty, but I envisioned her at eight, sitting at her wood desk at school, all hunched over with her legs fidgeting, struggling with a sum.

Then I concentrated on the television movie I was watching, and for the next few minutes the only voices came from the television. Finally, Mom said, "I found it! It was a nine, and I wrote it down as a four."

"Well, congratulations! You've balanced your checkbook."

She let out a sigh. "And I have to do this every single month?"

"Don't worry; it'll get easier as you go along." I didn't have the heart to tell her that I never balanced my own checkbook; paying bills electronically and using a debit card had pretty much eliminated the need for checks. All I had to do was make sure I had the money to cover what I paid out. Even I felt it would be too much for Mom to learn to operate a computer at this point in her life.

"Emmie, I've been a little worried about something," Mom said as she gathered her statement and other papers.

"Oh, yeah? What's that?"

"I can't help noticing that you've been going out during the week and staying out really late, and I know you're not with Aaron. Is everything all right between you two?"

"Everything's fine," I said easily. "So don't you worry about anything. I'm just catching up with some of my old friends, and the best time to do it is during the week because on the weekends I'm with Aaron."

"Oh! Well, yes, that makes sense. I, uh, thought you might be upset with him for leaving you alone on Saturday nights."

"I'm not upset with him, Mom. I understand that his family has to come before me. Who am I to complain if he spends a day and a half each week with them? Besides, I *could* go with him if I wanted. I just chose not to. I don't feel like being bothered with the attitude of his mother-in-law and his daughters."

"Why are you letting them run you out of Sag Harbor? That's not how I taught you, Emmie. You have a perfect right to be there."

"I know I do, Mom. Maybe I should have stuck it out. It just didn't seem worth the aggravation."

"I hope you won't mind my saying this," she began.

That was a sure sign she was about to say something I'd mind.

"I don't think Aaron is handling this very well. He should have talked to them, told them he won't tolerate their being rude to you."

"Technically, Mom, they haven't been rude. They've just been . . . unwelcoming."

"Oh, is *that* all," she said with a snort.

"Mom, Aaron and I enjoy spending time together, but we're not married, we're not engaged, we're not even in love." *Or exclusive,* I thought, a picture of Teddy looming over me. I could almost feel his sweat dropping on me, and I bit the inside of my lower lip to force the image from my mind. "I don't believe he should have to go through a lot of changes with his family to accommodate me."

"All right, so it's not serious between you two, which I can understand. You've only known each other two months. But what happens if you two *do* get serious? His family's attitude can nip it before it even starts. If you ask me, he needs to take

a more definitive stand than splitting his weekends in half."
She added, "Besides, I was in love with your father by our
third date."

When Mom threw out a hint, she didn't mess around. But
I did give her points for not saying, "What's taking you and
Aaron so damn long?"

"Doesn't your stomach flutter when you see him, or your
heart skip a beat?" she pressed.

It usually did, but I had concerns about Aaron that I wasn't
about to confide to anyone. Instead I said, "It's too soon for
all that. And I'm perfectly content just to spend Friday nights
with him."

The look on Mom's face told me she didn't believe one
word of that. "Well, if you say so."

# Chapter 17

I went to the movies Saturday night with Marsha, and seeing all those couples holding hands or with their arms around each other made me lonesome for Aaron, who was away in Sag Harbor. I considered that maybe Mom was right. Aaron splitting his weekends, spending Friday nights with me and then driving out to the island after we had breakfast together Saturday morning, was nothing but a compromise and no more effective than the Missouri Compromise nearly two centuries ago. It did nothing to solve the long-term problem. Tensions among his daughters, mother-in-law, and me were going to keep rising until war broke out, just like those shots fired at Fort Sumter.

Aaron called Sunday night, like he usually did. He would always wish me good night and tell me he missed me. But this time he had a surprise for me. "I'm approaching the Whitestone Bridge."

"Already? It's only Sunday night." Usually he left Sag Harbor at sunrise Monday morning and went straight to work.

"I decided to come in earlier. I know it's late, but I was hoping you'd agree to meet me at the house. I really need to see you."

My breath caught in my throat. Could Tanis have told him about seeing me with Teddy? I didn't know if she had something else up her sleeve, and the possibility remained that she could have seen Teddy purchasing condoms at Hardy's.

I decided it didn't play out. First of all, Tanis was two states away in Oak Bluffs. Second of all, Aaron sounded eager to see me, not angry. "Is everything all right?" I asked.

"It will be once I see you. I want to tell you something, and I'd rather do it in person than on the phone. Plan on staying the night, huh?"

Curiosity won out. "Give me a minute to throw my clothes for tomorrow into a bag, and I'll see you soon."

Aaron's Jag was in his driveway when I arrived, along with his seven-passenger SUV. He kept an older but good condition sedan in the garage of the house in Sag Harbor for Beverline to use while there, disconnecting the battery at the end of the summer.

I rang the doorbell and he answered it quickly, scooping me off my feet to give me a deep kiss. I let my overnight bag slide to the ground and wrapped my arms around his neck and my legs around his waist, holding on as he backed into the house and kicking my right foot out to slam the door shut behind us. A second later my back was against that same door.

"Wow!" I said breathily when he broke the kiss but continued to hold me upright by my hips. "What was that all about? Not that I'm complaining."

"I missed you, Emily."

"I missed you, too. I miss you every week when you go out to Long Island," I said softly.

He leaned me against the wall where I could see Diana's portrait through the arched doorway to the living room. Her eyes appeared to be fixated on me. I quickly looked away.

"That's what I wanted to tell you," Aaron said. "In a few weeks it'll be our turn to spend the weekends out there."

"What?"

"I put my foot down, Emily. I told Beverline and the girls that I didn't like the way they were treating you. I wasn't happy with the way they responded, so I told them I'm cutting their summer short."

I drew in my breath. "You told them that?" Then I paused. "So what'd they say that you didn't like?"

"Probably every nasty thing you can imagine them saying. 'I don't like her, Daddy.' 'She's going to try to make you forget Mom.' 'She's only with you because you're rich.' "

"Hold up." The first two statements fell under the umbrella of what I'd expected Beverline and the girls to say, but that third one made me see scarlet. My back straightened against the wall, and if I hadn't needed to keep my arms around Aaron to keep my balance, I would have let go. But I did loosen my grip. "They think I'm a *gold digger?*"

He sighed. "Arden's the one who said that. Trust me, Beverline put that idea in her head. She told me the night we got back from Indy that maybe bringing you to the house wasn't such a good idea, because it might give you 'ideas,' as she put it."

"Why, that—"

"I'm sorry, Emily. Maybe I shouldn't have told you. I was really trying to give them time to get used to the idea of us seeing each other. But it doesn't seem to be getting any better. A friend of mine asked if he could rent my house for the latter part of the season, the first of August through Labor Day weekend. At first I told him no, but I changed my mind. Fortunately, he's still interested, so he and his family are going to live upstairs, and you and I will be downstairs."

"In the *basement?*" What the hell was happening? I was sleeping on my mother's couch at home, and now I'd be going out to Sag Harbor without Aaron's family being there, and I'd have to sleep in the *basement?* Why did I always get the bag of potato chips with the crumbs? This had to be my punishment for losing my head with Teddy. On two separate occasions.

"The basement isn't bad. I've made arrangements to have a kitchenette put in down there, with cabinets, cooktop, and a sink. And if you're able to get some time off during the week we'll stay upstairs, since Zach and his family will be out only from Friday through Sunday."

I started to feel better. Aaron was spending a nice sum on a home improvement. Why shouldn't he make some of it back by renting part of it?

I still couldn't believe he'd actually taken this drastic step. "Aaron, you're actually going to leave Beverline and the kids here at home while you and I go out to Sag Harbor every weekend?"

"Beverline, yes, and without a second thought. My kids, no. They're going to spend the rest of the summer in Delaware with my mother. She lives fairly close to the beach."

"That sounds nice, but something tells me they like the Hamptons better."

"Billy can have fun wherever he is, but the girls do prefer Long Island. That's Beverline's doing. I'm sorry to say she's turning Kirsten and Arden into little snobs. I used to have them split their summers, half in Sag Harbor, half in Dover. Then Kirsten said she didn't want to leave her friends, so I changed it to a two-week visit to Dover in early August, then brought them back out to the island for the last weeks of the season."

"Your house in Sag Harbor has four bedrooms. Isn't there room for both grandmothers?"

"Unfortunately, my mother can't stand Beverline."

I could only shrug at that. *That makes two of us.*

Still, I felt overjoyed that Aaron had taken a stand to be with me. Wait til I told Mom.

But not now. Aaron, still holding me up against the wall, began gyrating his groin toward mine. "Aren't you proud of me?"

"I can do better than that," I said, loving the feel of his hardened penis against the thin crotch of my shorts. "I'm . . . *aroused.*"

"We'll take care of that right now."

It wasn't until an hour later that I remembered my overnight bag, still sitting outside the front door where I'd dropped it.

I drove to work the next day with a smile on my face. I didn't even feel embarrassed when I ran into Teddy at work.

"You're looking happy," he remarked.

"I am. My boyfriend and I are back together," I said. I was happy to share my good news with Teddy. It could only help get him off my back . . . and keep me out of his bedroom.

He scowled. "Glad to hear it."

He sure didn't *look* happy. For a moment I saw him as a ten-year-old who needed glasses. His expression was more in keeping with the appearance of the sky, which was darkening with some morning showers.

But I couldn't worry about it. It had been a mistake to sleep with Teddy. I just wanted to put it behind me.

The rest of the summer breezed by. As Aaron stated, staying in the basement wasn't half bad. These surroundings were much plainer than those in New Rochelle—it was, after all, a vacation house—but still quite comfortable, like a really nice hotel room. The microwave and mini-fridge that had been in the living room area were replaced by a full-size refrigerator, a stove with a microwave over it, a sink, and a small countertop with two burners, and oak cabinets.

We spent a minimum amount of time indoors anyway. I enjoyed spending afternoons lying on the sand at the beach, and we loved to relax in the hot tub at night with a bottle of wine. Sometimes we were joined by Aaron's friends who rented the upstairs, Zach and Vivian Warner, after their kids went to sleep.

I really liked Zach and Vivian, but I still felt a little uncomfortable with some of the other neighbors, many of whom I suspected were gossiping about me and wondering about how I'd managed to snare the most eligible bachelor over age forty-five in the entire state, as well as Aaron's having banished his children and mother-in-law to the hot city so he could spend weekends with me. Fortunately, Aaron introduced me to some pleasant people who seemed to accept me at face value without particular interest in the progression of our relationship. He invited an intimate group over to celebrate my forty-third birthday. Even Elias drove out with his latest squeeze, a Beyoncé blonde with a booty to match.

I felt a little guilty about leaving Mom, the one I'd come to Euliss to be with, all alone on the weekends, although she encouraged me to go. I knew she was hoping I'd marry Aaron, which would put me in Westchester permanently. If I knew her, she was expecting an engagement by Labor Day. I knew it would be useless for me to try to explain to her that things move more slowly nowadays than they did in the fifties, when she and Pop were courting, and that in the case of Aaron and me there was more to consider than the feelings of just two people. And she'd never understand that our sex life, oral sex or not, still left a lot to be desired.

Aaron and I planned an extra-long Labor Day weekend, and I asked him if it would be all right for Mom to join us. I wanted to make up my absence to her somehow. He agreed readily, giving me a rush of exhilaration when he took advantage of the opportunity to give me a kiss and squeeze my butt. I made yet another vow to make it work between us.

It seemed as if everybody Aaron knew was giving a barbecue or a party that weekend—we gave a party ourselves Saturday night—and Mom had the time of her life. Her visit was capped when she met the wife of Aaron's friend Lucien Ballard. Thais Ballard had a leading part on one of the soap operas Mom never missed, under her maiden name, Thais Parker. My normally levelheaded mother just about lost it when Thais and Lucien walked into Aaron's backyard.

I teased her about it after we got home Tuesday. Aaron dropped us off at noon and rushed right out, as his kids were returning from Delaware and he had to meet their train. I fixed lunch while Mom, sitting at the table, went through the few days' mail that had accumulated. I don't know what it is about older people never wanting to miss a day's mail delivery. I usually only checked mine twice a week.

"Honestly, Mom, I half expected you to ask for Thais's autograph," I said as I moved the grilled cheese sandwiches I'd made from the skillet onto plates.

"Don't be silly. What am I, some starstruck kid from Des Moines? What would I do with her autograph?" Her expression became serious as she read the letter in her hand.

"Is something wrong?" I asked as I set her plate in front of her, then sat down.

"We've got a problem, Emily."

"What's wrong?"

"My lease isn't getting renewed. The building has been sold, and the new owners are going to convert the building back into a single-family house."

"Oh, no! When's your lease up, Mom?"

"January thirty-first."

She wasn't exaggerating. It was already September. February was just a few months away.

"I'm a little scared," she continued. "Rents are so expensive. and I can't get into senior citizen's housing with you living with me."

"Well, Mom, I'll probably be back home by February."

"Emmie, you can't leave Aaron."

"We both knew it was going to happen eventually." I tried to sound matter-of-fact about it, but I suddenly found myself feeling nauseous.

"But if you leave now you'll never get to find out what might have happened with you two. His wife, God rest her soul, has been gone long enough for him to fall in love with another woman. Why shouldn't it be you?"

*Why shouldn't it?* "My biggest concern right now is you, Mom."

"That's sweet, but I'm not going to let you give up your future just so I can get into senior housing." She twisted her bottom lip. "Not that I know what to do about it. It'll cost a fortune for you and me to take out a lease on just a one-bedroom apartment."

I felt her pain. The thought of packing up and moving to a new apartment where I still wouldn't get to have a room of my own didn't sit too well with me, either. And what about the cost? Mom had insisted I was not to help with the rent, saying that she'd paid it before I moved in with her and she'd continue to pay it after I left. Of course, she knew I still had a mortgage, utilities, and a storage unit to pay for each month. The proceeds from the short-term rentals of my condo helped with that. But the condo was empty more than it was occupied, and the management service took a commission.

Mom's rent was pretty low, because she'd lived in this building for so many years, and the landlord could raise your rent only by so much each year. But the difference between what she paid now and the cost of a market-rate apartment would have to come out of my pocket.

I recalled Teddy saying his rent was going up to seventeen hundred dollars a month. I didn't see how I could possibly swing that. Sonny and Cissy had already put out a total of fifteen hundred dollars to help me transition from Indy to Euliss, and while I doubted it caused either of them hardship, I also knew they would be glad when those three months were up. I only saw one possible solution.

"Mom . . . have you thought about moving in with Sonny or with Cissy? You know you're always welcome at either one of their homes."

"I don't want to leave Euliss, Emmie," she said in a near whine that sounded painful to my ears. "All my friends are here. I don't want to go and die upstate or in Pittsburgh."

If the situation wasn't so frightening I would've giggled at her last remark. I wouldn't want to live in Pittsburgh or New Paltz, much less take my last breath there, myself. Instead I concentrated on trying to make the best of the situation. "Would joining a new church, meeting new people, really be such a bad thing? You know, Mom, I was apprehensive about moving to Indianapolis all those years ago. The only one I knew was Al and his family. But I've made very good friends there."

"It's not the same. You were a lot younger than I am."

"I understand that, Mom." I sighed. She clearly didn't want to leave Euliss, and I really couldn't blame her. As miserable a town as it might be, it was all she knew. "In that case we'll have to see what we can do. But I can't make you any promises. Apartments don't come cheap."

# Chapter 18

That simple letter in the mail threw my plans in a tizzy. I'd been considering extending my time in Euliss, perhaps applying for another job if Gina, the new mother, decided to return to her job at the end of six months, but now I didn't know what to do. I did go down to the department of housing and put my mother's name on the waiting list for senior housing. They might not have an apartment for her in four months' time, but these were elderly people. Surely death made for more vacancies than your ordinary apartment complex.

I was ready to throw myself into plans for the class reunion to help reduce the stress, but now that the date, the place, and the menu had been decided upon, there really wasn't much left to do.

The one thing I didn't do was confide in Aaron. I knew he'd try to help, but I saw nothing he could possibly do in this situation. I didn't want to burden him. Sonny, Cissy, and my nieces and nephews were aware of the problem, and no one had been able to come up with a solution that didn't involve Mom leaving the area.

I ran into Teddy one day in the elevator on my way down to the snack bar, and we ended up having coffee together.

"You're right about the housing situation," I said after I told him about Mom's predicament. "I doubt it was black people who bought her building."

"I'm sorry, Emily. I hope you can work it out."

"Thanks. Have you decided what you're going to do?" I figured as a dental technician he probably made decent money.

"I'm going to bite the bullet and stay. It won't break me, but it'll take some economizing and a sharp drop in recreational activity." Teddy grunted. "It'll mean take-out pizza instead of going out to dinner and waiting for the DVD instead of going to the movies."

"I wish there were places to be had with lower rent that aren't dumps."

"Oh, there are places out there. Leon Murphy's grandfather had an apartment in that nice walk-up building on James Street. He lived there for years."

"His *grand*father!" I exclaimed. "Leon was only a year behind us. His grandfather's still alive?" I knew that everyone's parents weren't as old as mine had been, but having living grandparents at our age still seemed like a stretch to me.

"No, Emily, he's dead. That's my point. Leon moved to North Carolina years ago. I figured he wouldn't want the apartment, and his parents own a home, so I went over and talked to the super to see about taking it over."

"And?"

"He absolutely refused to show it to me or even discuss it. Carried on something awful about it being downright indecent of me to inquire about taking over the apartment when the old man wasn't even cold yet."

I broke out into laughter.

Teddy joined me. "I guess it is funny, but it wasn't at the time, Emily. He practically accused me of knocking grandpa off, just so I could get his apartment. Of course, he looked like a candidate for the Grim Reaper himself."

"Only in New York," I managed to say when I stopped laughing. "That's the nice thing about Indianapolis. It's affordable, much more than, say, Chicago. You can get a really nice apartment for not a lot of money. And, of course, you can actually save enough to buy a house or a condo."

"Speaking of Indiana, do you see yourself going back, or are you going to stay here in Euliss permanently?"

"I honestly don't know, Teddy," I said with a shake of my head. "I'm in a relationship, and I don't know where it's heading." Lord knew I didn't want to stay in Euliss any longer than I had to, but Aaron and I had had such a lovely summer together. I couldn't remember when I'd been happier. True, the sex could still be better—okay, a whole *lot* better—but they say everything comes with a price tag. Could that be the price that had to be paid for all this happiness? Would there always be one thing that prevented men and women from being true soul mates? And why did it have to be something so important? Why couldn't Aaron just be a snorer or something?

He glanced at his watch. "I've got someone coming in at ten for a fitting. Why don't we get together for dinner one night this week? We can talk about the apartment situation some more."

"Lunch would be better."

He looked properly insulted at my insinuation, then said, "Twelve-thirty today?"

"Sure."

I enjoyed lunch, but it didn't yield any new information . . . other than that I still found Teddy desirable. I could barely look at him without visualizing him naked. What the heck was wrong with me? There should be no contest between Aaron and Teddy when it came to the title of Dream Man. I mean, Aaron's delicate fingers and medical know-how extended people's lives. Teddy's gift allowed old folks to be able to chew. Aaron lived in a graceful mansion overlooking Long Island Sound with a full-time housekeeper, plus he had a vacation home. Teddy admitted it'd be a struggle for him when his rent increase went into effect in November. Even if I were eighty and toothless, Aaron would win hands down.

Of course, before we returned to work to complete the afternoon, Teddy tried to convince me to go out with him that night, but I held my own. I had no desire—no, that's the wrong word—I had no *intention* of getting into bed with him again. Our two-night stand was a mistake that came close to costing my blooming relationship with Aaron because of our running into Tanis that night.

I had Aaron now. Wonderful Aaron, who treated me with respect and consideration, who told his family that if they didn't like me they could put a sock in it, who adored my mother, and who was as successful as he was good-looking.

Teddy and I had the elevator to ourselves when it stopped on the Normans' floor. "I guess I'll be seeing you," he said reluctantly.

"Thanks for having lunch with me, Teddy. I'm not any closer to a solution than I was before, but sometimes it makes it better just to talk things out with someone. I appreciate your listening."

"Glad I could help."

I was stepping out of the elevator when I felt a pull on my arm. In an instant I was in his arms, and the tension poured out of me as I kissed him back like a woman starved.

That kiss pretty much guaranteed that I was about to go back on my word. Teddy got off work at four-thirty, me at five. We agreed to meet at his place that afternoon.

After what seemed like an excruciatingly long afternoon seeing patients, including the teenage daughter of Mom's upstairs neighbors, who had a case of crabs, I headed straight for Teddy's apartment. During that five o'clock drive I found myself cursing slow-moving drivers, drumming my fingers impatiently against the steering wheel while stopped at a red light, and honking when the car in front of me hadn't moved within three seconds of the light changing to green.

He opened the door for me, wearing nothing but boxer shorts, and promptly picked me up. Instead of taking me to his bedroom he went into the kitchen just to the left of the entry. He deposited me on the counter and started stripping my clothes off. Once he'd removed my panties he bent to give me head, leaving me to hold on to the overhead cabinets.

I kept telling him we needed to get on the bed, but he didn't seem interested in waiting. Instead, once he had me dripping wet, he put on a condom in record time and we did it right there in his kitchen. It was a scene straight out of *Fatal Attraction.*

I'm not sure how we managed to get to his bedroom afterward, but we literally fell on the bed on our backs at different levels. Teddy's head was on one of his pillows, while I fell lower, with my head resting on his lap and my hand resting on my heart, which was still thumping wildly. He'd loosened my hair from its bun while we were still kissing in the kitchen, and now he alternated between twirling it around his fingers and threading his fingers through it. The man was a hair freak.

"Emily, I know you and your man have been going through some hard times, but I hope you realize how easy it's always been with you and me. Maybe you should just forget about that other guy."

I sat up and looked at him incredulously.

"Seriously, Emily," he said. "I think you and I have what it takes to make it in this world. I think we'd make a good team. Together we could have a good life. Plus, your mother can get into senior housing and still have you close by."

I quickly gathered my wits. A team? A *life,* for crying out loud? He had to be kidding. I broke into a knowing smile. "C'mon, Teddy. You're just looking for someone to pay half your rent."

He looked so genuinely hurt that I regretted my words. But surely he couldn't be serious about the idea of us becoming a couple. Didn't he realize what our relationship was built on?

"What we have together is great sex, Teddy. You can't build a relationship on that."

"You make it sound like we never talk to each other. That's not true, and you know it."

No, it wasn't true. Conversation came easy for Teddy and me. Sex between us was undeniably combustible. But I was with him for all the wrong reasons, and it was supposed to be just once, to prove to myself that Aaron wasn't delivering for me in the bedroom. My life was complicated enough from my own inability to stay away from Teddy. The last thing I needed was for him to start falling for me.

After I went home, I thought about what Teddy wanted me to consider. Would I be willing to stay here in New York for love? And was I being too picky?

Aaron and I were so well suited. All right, so the sex wasn't as exciting as it should be. I had to consider everything he had to offer. I liked Aaron. I could easily love him. Our relationship as it was would not work in the long run. Therefore, the key was for me to change it.

Teddy, on the other hand, had such a derisive way of looking at things. His down-to-earth manner almost bordered on the slick. He was entirely too practical. He reminded me . . .

My mouth fell open as I realized who Teddy reminded me of. Myself.

All throughout my shower, and even as I climbed between the cool sheets of Mom's sofa bed for the night, I kept seeing Teddy's eyes with that wounded expression when I dismissed his suggestion that the two of us would make a good team as nothing more than a carefully calculated attempt to get a roommate. He had recovered quickly, but it bothered me to think that I'd hurt his feelings. I had to do something nice to apologize to him. Something nonsexual, of course.

Oh, no. *Oh, no!* "Oh, *noooooooo!*"

"I don't know where that's coming from," Teddy managed to say between grunts as he thrust his hips up and filled me what used to be known in romance novels as his "throbbing member." "Your lips may be saying no, but your hips are saying, 'Give it to me, baby.' "

I couldn't believe I'd ended up in bed with Teddy yet again. I'd stopped by his apartment merely to apologize for what I'd said, and he'd kissed me, and I was lost. What a mess I had made of things. What a miserable excuse for a human being I was—

"Oh, God, I'm coming. . . ."

# Chapter 19

"What's wrong, Emily? I know there's something on your mind. You've been distracted lately. I want you to talk to me."

Aaron and I were lying in bed on a Friday night at the motel in the town of Mamaroneck, where we spent most Friday and Saturday nights since returning from the Hamptons. Since we'd just made love, right now the main thought on my mind was how unfulfilled I felt, something I could hardly tell him. That was just a temporary feeling that would go away once the joy of simply being with him took over. The thought that wouldn't go away was where Mom and I would live after January, since it was now mid-October and I was no closer to finding a place for us than I'd been a month and a half ago.

I took a deep breath and told him about the situation.

He listened intently. "What about senior citizen housing?"

I became tongue-tied. I didn't know how to explain to him that I'd decided to stay in Euliss indefinitely, largely because of him. "She does have an application in. They haven't called her yet, and besides . . . I won't be able to live with her in that setting; I'm too young." *That* was an expression I never thought I'd use. Under any other circumstances it would be worth a good chuckle.

"You mean . . . you're going to stay in Euliss beyond six months?"

I gave a weak smile. "I know I was adamant about not doing that, but I guess I've changed my mind."

"Do you mind if I ask why?"

He wasn't going to let up until he knew the exact reason for my change of heart.

I met his eyes, feeling almost shy. "Because I'm feeling very happy these days, and because my condo is rented through the holidays." I'd eagerly accepted the offer of a relocating couple who didn't mind house hunting during the holiday season but did not want to physically move again until after all the halls had been undecked. They'd be in residence through mid-January.

Aaron laughed. "You're nothing if not practical, Emily."

"I'd also miss you if I left."

He replied with one of his delicious kisses, slow and dreamy, leaving me breathless. If only he made love with the same skill.

"I can't tell you how happy that makes me. I've been coping with a feeling of dread recently. Every weekend I've been afraid that you're going to tell me the date you're leaving to return to Indianapolis, and I didn't want to hear it."

"I'm sorry, Aaron, both for not telling you and for making you worry. I'm embarrassed to tell you I've been too consumed by this apartment business to even notice anything amiss with you. And I guess I was too shy to tell you I'd changed my plans."

"It's all right. You know, I have a guest house above my garage."

All I could do was blink. Was he going where I *thought* he was going?

"It's actually a nice size," Aaron continued. "I think you and your mother could be comfortable there."

I had to ask. "How much is the rent?"

"Well, it's not like I'm a landlord or anything. It's been empty since I bought the house. I want to be fair. . . . How do you feel about five hundred a month plus your own utilities?"

I gasped. That was less than what Mom paid now. "Aaron. You're actually going to offer my mother and me a place to stay on your property?"

"Sure, why not?"

"Well . . . it's a lifesaver, but don't you feel a little uncomfortable with the thought of you and I living so near each other?" My inner voice started wailing, *What if I want to see Teddy?* I'm ashamed to say that I'd let my urges get the better of me several times since the day Teddy and I had had lunch, but at least now we got together right after work and I was home by eight o'clock, which I covered by telling both Mom and Aaron that I went out for drinks with coworkers after work. I couldn't risk Mom becoming suspicious again.

He kissed my lips lightly. "I happen to like the idea of being close to you. So you can just throw your arms around me and call me your hero."

I was only too happy to oblige, and my disappointment at the motel that night wasn't as acute as it usually was. I guess I was truly happy to have this tremendous load off my shoulders. Then again, maybe it just had to do with the fact that Teddy had been taking care of curling my toes.

Aaron took me to dinner the next night, to the same restaurant in Dobbs Ferry overlooking the Hudson where we'd had our first date. "I thought it was appropriate," he said after we were seated, "since from that first evening I knew I wouldn't want you to leave, and now you aren't."

"How wonderfully sentimental, Aaron."

He kissed the back of my hand. "These past months have been wonderful. You've brought hope back into my life, Emily."

His words stunned me. Just as a mind was a terrible thing to waste, hope was a terrible thing to lose. It was the one thing we had left when everything else was gone. "Had you actually lost hope?"

"Maybe that's not the right word. As long as I have my children I'll have hope. But I felt I'd never truly be happy again.

Being with you has changed all that." He covered my hand with both of his, and his eyes never left my face. He took a deep breath. "I know it took a lot for you to tell me why you decided to stay in Euliss, so I want to be truthful with you as well."

I held my breath.

"I want you to know," he said as he gently massaged my hand, "I'm not telling you this to elicit any type of response from you, so don't feel obligated. I didn't think this could ever happen again, but I've fallen in love with you, Emily." He added hastily, "Now, I don't expect you to feel the same, but I do sense you care for me, and that's enough, at least for now."

I felt all warm and tingly inside. Aaron loved me. He loved me. He never thought he'd feel this way about anyone again, and I was the one.

I also had to marvel at his consideration at letting me off the hook. Here was a man who'd married his only serious girlfriend. Although he was too refined to come out and say it, he understood that sexually speaking I had more experience than he did. I think that's difficult for any man to admit, not that a whole lot of them are in that predicament. He was astute enough to know that I didn't fall so easily. Of course, I'd have beaten him to the finish line if it wasn't for our sex life.

I'd be throwing myself into that with everything I had, for in my heart I knew I could never sleep with Teddy again. It was true that neither myself nor Aaron had ever said anything about exclusivity in our relationship, but when a man tells you he loves you, he clearly expects to have you all to himself. How understanding of Aaron to allow me to accept his feelings without pressure or obligation to reciprocate. And he was right; I did care about him. Maybe I even loved him a little.

My mouth fell open. Yes, I *did* love him, and not just because he was wealthy and had shown me a lifestyle that I'd only seen in the movies. I loved him because he was a good man. As I'd predicted on our first date, we had a lot of fun together, whether we were cooking, washing the car, watching the news, or just talking.

I intended to tell Mom about Aaron's offer as soon as I returned home Sunday afternoon, but I heard her talking and quickly realized she was on the phone. Now, I was no eavesdropper, but when I heard my name mentioned I naturally stood outside the bedroom door to hear what she was saying about me. "Oh, he's just wonderful. He has such elegance about him. He reminds me of a black Cary Grant."

I rolled my eyes but couldn't keep the corners of my mouth from turning up. Obviously Mom was talking about Aaron.

"And I tell you, he's just crazy about Emily. . . . Oh, of course it's serious. I mean, it's too early to talk about *marriage,* of course, but Aaron does seem to be the type who likes to be settled." A pause, then, "Isn't that just like my daughter. She met him just a few days after she got into town, you know. Who else but my Emily could snag the most eligible bachelor in the county so quickly?"

I moved into the doorway and discreetly cleared my throat. Mom looked up guiltily. "Dear, I really have to go. Emily just came in. Why don't I call you back?" She paused, then laughed at something the other party said. "Yes, I'll be sure to let you know if Aaron proposes. Bye-bye, now!"

I groaned as she hung up the phone. "Proposes? Mom!"

"Well, can I help it if my friends enjoy hearing about your romance? It reminds all of us of our first love. So what if we're living vicariously through you."

"Mom, I'm past forty and divorced. Aaron is hardly my first love."

"Love is love, Emily. It doesn't matter how old you are."

"And what's all this talk about love, anyway?" I said

rather testily. "Just because Aaron says he loves me doesn't mean I automatically feel the same way." In my annoyance I'd spoken without thinking.

Mom lit up like a theater marquee on opening night, and I knew what she was about to say before she even opened her mouth.

"Emily! He's in love with you? Oh, how wonderful!"

I held my hand palm out. "Hold everything. Do not mail the wedding invitations yet. As I said, the feeling isn't necessarily mutual."

"But Emmie, I don't understand. Now, I know I taught you to have high standards, but, my dear, don't you realize Barack Obama is taken? Besides, Aaron's much better looking than he is."

My mind quickly searched for a way to express my thoughts. I could hardly tell my mother the real reason for rejecting Aaron. I just wouldn't feel comfortable, yet my instincts told me it would be a good thing to keep her talking as long as possible. The minute I left she'd probably pick up the phone, call another one of her friends, and this time fill them in on Aaron's very private feelings.

Which raised a question in my mind. "Who were you talking to on the phone just now, anyway?"

"Helen Brown."

My jaw dropped. "Mom! Didn't you say Mrs. Brown's teenage granddaughter is having a baby? And isn't that Joanne's daughter?"

"Well, yes. But what does that have to do with you and Aaron?"

"For one thing, Joanne Brown's marriage broke up years ago, and her ex has moved to another state and hardly ever sees their daughter. Two, everybody knows that Joanne does nothing but chase men. It's no wonder her daughter got knocked up, if her behavior is any example. And you're bragging to Helen about how your daughter snagged a doctor the moment she got back into town?" The tone of my voice stretched upward in incredulity. "Mom, not only is it inconsiderate for you to say that, it's . . . not right," I concluded after being unable to think of a stronger phrase. "How's Mrs. Brown supposed to feel?"

"Like she wishes that could have been *her* daughter. And trust me, if it were, I would be hearing about it at every card game plus at every conversation."

I shook my head. Mrs. Brown was the sub at the bid whist games, filling in when one of the regulars couldn't play. I just didn't understand the strange way my mother and her so-called friends treated each other. I thought that type of cattiness was reserved for society ladies.

"There hasn't been this much gossip since Valerie Woods was dating that criminal attorney a few years back," Mom continued. "Usually Winnie never talks about Valerie, but she certainly had a lot to say when it looked like they were getting serious. She went on and on about it. When she stopped all of a sudden we all knew that meant it was over. Of course, it was Mavis who told the rest of us on the sly that they'd broken up, so Winnie wouldn't have to address the matter."

Feeling defeated, I shrugged my shoulders. "All right, Mom. Have it your way. But there's something I must insist on."

"What's that?"

"You have to promise me that you won't say a word to any of your friends about Aaron's feelings for me. I shouldn't have told you. It just slipped out, but it was something he said to me, not to me and you, and certainly not to me, you, and your girlfriends. The last thing I need is for Tanis to get wind of it. She's after him, you know, and she's like a dirty politician. She'll use any means necessary to cause problems between Aaron and me so she can take over."

"Well, Emmie, you have to consider the possibility. I mean, if you don't want him . . . It's no fun being in love all by yourself."

"Point taken, Mom."

"You're a sweet girl. You really deserve to be with someone special, have someone to share your life with." She sighed. "Sometimes I really worry about you girls. Not just you, but girls Sasha's age," she said, referring to Sonny's youngest. "Even that sweet little Jasmine upstairs."

I averted my eyes. I knew all about little Jasmine. She'd come into Dr. Norman's office a couple of weeks ago, and I'd treated her for crabs. I can still hear her gasping in shock when I came into the room, immediately bursting into tears and begging me not to tell her parents. I explained that I was bound by practitioner-patient privilege, and that anything she said to me could not and would not be repeated to anyone.

I did issue a strong warning to her regarding her sexual behavior and recklessness in not practicing safe sex, which I suspected she would ignore. When you're sixteen, you think that all the bad stuff happens to other people, not to you, and that the little incident that happens to you will be cured. But Mom thought she was the sweetest young thing. I hoped I wouldn't be so easily fooled when I was Mom's age.

"I know Tanis would love to take Aaron from you," Mom said now. "You should see Mavis at our card games. When I drop little tidbits about you and Aaron, I'm waiting for her to pull out a notebook and take notes so she can tell Tanis all about it."

"Really?" My eyes narrowed. "You aren't telling her anything she shouldn't know, are you?"

"No, just bits and pieces, like where Aaron has taken you, the name of the restaurant you ate at, the name of the Broadway show you saw, things like that. Her eyes bug out. You should see her. She looks like she's got a thyroid condition."

As much as I enjoyed visualizing the amusing picture Mom just painted, I held off telling Mom about the apartment. I didn't want her calling all her friends with the news before it was decided upon, and we hadn't even seen the place yet. I'd take her for a ride tomorrow after church, and I'd tell her about it on the way.

Mom was using the bathroom when the phone rang, so I answered it. My sister was calling. "Oh, hi, Cissy."

"How's it going? I heard your big news."

I blinked. "My big news?"

"That you landed the big dog."

"Cissy, what the hell are you talking about?"

"Aaron, silly. Mom told me he's made a declaration."

I sighed. "Oh, for heaven's sake. I told her to keep that quiet. It wasn't intended to be broadcast."

"I haven't said anything to anyone about it. But Mom was concerned. She said you're holding back. What's up?"

"Quite frankly, Cissy, that's none of your business."

The silence that followed reflected my sister's hurt feelings.

"I'm sorry," I said gently. "It's just that I need to keep some details of my private life private."

"Yes, of course you do. Is Mom around? I forgot to tell her something when we talked earlier."

# Chapter 20

I drove Mom over to see the apartment that afternoon. She'd never been to Aaron's house before, and she gaped at the impressive tan stucco-and-stone mansion behind the tall locking gates. "My God! He really has money, doesn't he, Emmie?"

"Oh, I'd say he's done pretty well for himself." In spite of my amusement, I understood her awe. It was one thing to know in the back of one's mind that a person had money. It was another to actually *see* it. Visualizing Aaron's house was just as good as seeing his latest bank statement.

I felt a little uneasy as I rang the doorbell. I hadn't seen Beverline Wilson since the Fourth of July weekend in Sag Harbor. She'd disliked me from the time of our very first encounter, and time had likely done nothing to change her opinion. I wish I could have been the proverbial fly on the wall to see her reaction when Aaron told her he planned to rent the guest house to my mother and me.

I cheered up when the housekeeper answered the door. I'd met Shirley Whitman when she came to work one day before I left Aaron's. Shirley was a sweet woman, but she would make a lousy poker player. She hadn't been able to conceal her shock at seeing me. I was fully dressed at the time, but there is only one conclusion one could come to when a man has female company at eight in the morning.

I was happy to see her. Maybe Mom and I could tour the

apartment without having to see Beverline or the kids at all.
"Hello, Shirley."

"Hello, Miss Yancy. The doctor said he was expecting you
and your mother." Shirley was an attractive brown-skinned
woman in her late fifties who always wore khaki pants and a
white blouse—maybe the twenty-first-century version of a
housekeeper's uniform? She smiled at Mom. "You must be
Mrs. Yancy. Welcome."

Shirley was her usual pleasant self, but I always felt a little
. . . well, overprivileged at having her address me so formally.
The woman was, after all, older than I, probably by a good
fifteen years. It made me uncomfortably aware of class differ-
ences. Not that I considered myself better than anyone else.
The cold, hard fact was that Shirley worked for Aaron, while
I claimed the status of being a friend and lover to him. This
was the way protocol declared things should be.

"If you'll make yourselves comfortable, I'll let Dr. Merritt
know you're here," Shirley said.

I glanced at Mom, and the way she held her own made me
proud. She managed to look like she was accustomed to
being in such elegant households. She whispered to me as we
walked inside, "I thought his house would be like Cissy's or
Sonny's. But this is like a *castle*. Look at the size of this foyer!"

Mom tended to make presumptions that everyone's expe-
riences matched hers, which translates to the rather narrow
belief that everyone's house must be like those of her children. I knew better, although I haven't gotten so jaded that
I've forgotten my own astonishment the first time I saw Aaron's
home. An image of Marsha's wistful expression flashed through
my mind. Is this how she'd felt when she'd left Sherwood
Forest so many years ago to marry that drug dealer? Her
house across the Hudson in Englewood Cliffs was probably
even more grand than Aaron's abode. God, it must have killed
her to have to return to the projects, even if her mother's
apartment had beautiful furnishings and a plasma TV within
its cinder-block walls, courtesy of Marsha's late husband.

I'd been holding Mom's arm, and I almost tripped when she stopped dead in her tracks in front of the portrait of Aaron's late wife. "Who's that?"

"That's my daughter."

I knew who the proud voice belonged to before I turned around. I did turn, and there she stood, about six steps from the landing, wearing a black sweater and black pants, her hands clasped in front of her and her gray hair brushed back, looking creepily like a black version of Mrs. Danvers from the movie *Rebecca*. Not a bad analogy, considering I felt as welcome here as the second Mrs. de Winter.

"Hello, Mrs. Wilson," I said with as much pleasantness as I could muster. "This is my mother, Ruby Yancy. Mom, this is Aaron's mother-in-law, Beverline Wilson."

"I'm glad to know you, Mrs. Wilson," my mother said in a tone she would use to teach Sunday school.

"Likewise, Mrs. Yancy." Beverline's eyes returned to the portrait. "That's my daughter, Diana. Aaron's wife." She spoke in an offhand manner that suggested Diana was at the hair-dresser and would be back momentarily.

Mom didn't let me down. "Well, that would certainly make you his mother-in-law," she said brightly.

Beverline's smile faded like a once vivid memory. She walked down the remaining stairs and said, "Aaron tells me you may be renting our guest house."

She said "our" like her name was on the deed to Aaron's property, which I sincerely doubted.

"That's right," Mom replied.

She responded with a weak smile as Aaron entered the room and rushed toward me. "I was downstairs bowling with Billy. Shirley just told me you were here." He kissed me on the mouth, and I could have sworn I saw Beverline flinch out of the corner of my eye.

Aaron moved from me to Mom. "Mrs. Yancy, good to see you," he said, wrapping her in a warm hug.

"Aaron, you have a beautiful home. Did I hear you say you have a bowling alley in your basement?"

"Well, thank you. And yes, I do. Just two lanes, though."

Mom flashed me a "whatever-you-do-don't-let-this-man-get-away" look.

"Diana decorated it," Beverline said proudly. "She did it alone, too. No help from a decorator."

"That's right, she did," Aaron said in a matter-of-fact tone.

"Well, she certainly has . . . er, had excellent taste." Mom looked distressed at her gaffe, then said sheepishly, "I'm sorry. I seem to be tripping over my tongue today."

I couldn't fault her for her mistake, not with Beverline making it sound like Diana would come strolling through the front door at any moment.

We heard footsteps running down the Southwestern motif–tiled hall, and Billy appeared. He ran over to me and greeted me with a hug. "Hi, Emily!"

"Hi, Billy. It's good to see you. It's been quite some time, hasn't it?"

"Yeah, it has. Daddy and I were bowling. You gonna play with us?"

"I'm afraid Emily came for something else, Billy," Aaron said.

The disappointment in Billy's eyes was genuine, much to my delight.

"Billy, we have another guest," Aaron continued. "Emily's mother is here. Her name is Mrs. Yancy. Mrs. Yancy, this is my son, Billy."

"Hi!" Billy said.

"Hello, Billy."

"Billy, you have better manners than that," Beverline chided. "It's 'Hello, *Mrs. Yancy.*' "

"Hello, Mrs. Yancy," Billy said so obediently that I couldn't suppress a chuckle. He turned to Aaron. "I guess y'all are gonna be talkin' about grown-up stuff."

"Yes, Billy. Why don't you go down and finish the game? We'll pick it up later, okay?"

"Okay. But I'm gonna go upstairs for a minute first." He bounded up the stairs.

"What a charming boy," Mom remarked. "By the time junior high rolls around, the girls will be calling for him all the time."

"Are you kidding? He's getting calls now, and he's only in third grade," Aaron said.

"He's the spitting image of Diana," Beverline piped up, confirming my belief that she would mention her deceased daughter at every opportunity. It had already gotten old. Especially since Billy looked more like Aaron.

Mom was cool about it. "Yes, I see the resemblance."

Aaron draped one arm around my shoulders, the other around Mom. "Well, why don't we take a look at the apartment?" he suggested.

I hoped Beverline would find something else to do, but the next thing I knew, she had her coat on and was trailing us like a suspicious store detective.

We crossed the driveway to the garage, which had an enclosed staircase at the far end.

"I hope the stairs won't be a detriment for you, Mrs. Yancy," he said apologetically.

"Oh, I'm sure I can manage."

Beverline spoke up. "You do realize it has only one bedroom. So I'm sure it's smaller than what you have now."

I felt pretty sure she already knew my mother had a one-bedroom apartment. "Actually, my mother's apartment has just one bedroom," I said politely.

"Good heavens, Emily, where do you sleep?"

"Beverline," Aaron said, caution in his tone.

Mom jumped into the breach. "You see, Mrs. Wilson, I'm fortunate to have devoted children. None of them live in Westchester, but my son and older daughter both wanted me to come live with them. My Emmie had a life of her own in Indiana, including owning a lovely townhome, but she put everything on hold to make sure I was taken care of after my husband passed away. But then again, that's what families do in times of loss."

"We understand perfectly, Mrs. Yancy," Aaron said. "Beverline was good enough to come and live with the kids and me while Diana was ill, and she stayed on to help out."

"Well, that was a little different, dear," Beverline pointed out. "*I* came to live with *you,* not the other way around."

Only with supreme self-control did I not say that it wouldn't have been practical for Aaron and his children to move to Camden.

"Who moved in with whom isn't the point," Aaron said calmly. "Mrs. Yancy was making the point that families stick together in times of need." He turned and inserted his key in the door. "Let's go in." He held the door open for us to walk through.

"Oh, how very nice!" Mom exclaimed, and I had to agree. The rooms were bright, courtesy of two windows in the dining area and three more in the living room. The floors were covered with a tan carpet that looked like it had never been stepped on, and the walls were painted a stark but crisp-looking white.

"It looks like it's never been lived in," I remarked.

"It hasn't," Beverline said. "Not since Aaron and Diana bought the house. I understand that the previous owner had a live-in housekeeper. Shirley goes home when her work is done."

Aaron shrugged. "I suppose I could have rented it for extra income, but it never occurred to me."

Mom met my eyes. *Because he doesn't need the money,* she silently conveyed.

She walked to inspect the kitchen, which was compact, but well equipped. She opened the door to what looked like the pantry and let out a delighted squeal. I quickly moved behind her to see what had her so excited. Inside the pantry was a small washer and dryer.

"Oh, Emmie, look at this!" she said, obviously forgetting herself. "I never had a washer and dryer before."

"You mean you have to take your clothes to the Laundromat?" Beverline asked incredulously.

"You don't have to make it sound like not having a washer and dryer is comparable to holding up a 7-Eleven," I said. "Even some luxury apartments on the East Side of Manhattan don't always have the proper hookups."

"I've never lived on the East Side. I've only lived in the suburbs."

"I don't think too many people would call Camden suburbia, Mrs. Wilson."

Her mouth dropped open, and she looked accusingly at Aaron.

"Yes, I told Emily where you used to live," he said quietly. "You and I have had this discussion about your pretending to be something you're not, haven't we?"

"Excuse me." She headed for the door, and a moment later we all heard it slam shut.

"I'm sorry, Aaron," I said. "But I couldn't bear listening to her sound like she held court at Buckingham Palace another minute."

He came up behind me and massaged my shoulders through my jacket. "Don't worry about it. If she doesn't like it, she can always move out."

I knew my chances of winning that Powerball jackpot they have in Connecticut were higher than the odds of Beverline ever leaving Aaron's house.

"So Mom, what'd you think about the apartment?"

"Are you kidding? It's much nicer than the place I've lived the last twenty-five years. And it's less money. What's to think about?"

I chuckled. "And you don't think New Rochelle is too far from Euliss?"

"Well, I'll probably join a church there, just so I can find out about their social functions. But I'll still drive to service in Euliss, maybe once a month or so. Getting there on Sunday mornings won't be a problem for me."

Like many a woman her age, Mom drove during daytime hours but avoided driving after dark.

"But, Emmie, Aaron will have to give us a lease, and it has to specify that either one of us can keep the apartment. If anything should happen to me—"

"Mom!"

"Listen to me, now; I'm serious. I don't trust that mother-in-law of his. At the first sign of a loophole, she'll try to get him to throw us out. Not that I think Aaron would ever do that . . ."

I had a vision of me having sex with Teddy and furiously blinked it away. But it did make for one hell of a violation, *if* Aaron should ever find out about it.

". . . but if something should happen to him, even. Not that I think it will."

I shrugged. Mom was certainly being a Gloomy Gertie this afternoon. If she *had* to kill someone off, couldn't it be Beverline?

"I take it Beverline left you with the same charming impression she left on me."

"What a bitch!"

My eyes widened. The only questionable language I'd ever heard my mother use was, "Damn it!" and then only when she spilled or broke something. "I can't believe you said that."

"Well, she is one. Going on and on about her daughter like that. 'Not since Aaron and Diana bought this house,' " she mimicked. "The only thing her daughter did in terms of helping buy that house was marry Aaron. I know she wasn't a doctor, too. Otherwise Beverline would have made sure I knew it." She grunted. "I'll bet she wasn't anything else but a housewife."

"Yes, she was. She did teach for a few years, but Aaron said not since they had their first child."

"The nerve of that woman, looking down on us just because we come from Euliss!" Mom continued. "Especially considering that cabbage patch *she* came out of." Then she sighed. "But I do feel a little sorry for her."

I took my eyes off the road long enough to give her a dubious look across the console. "Whatever for?"

"Because she lost her child. I can't imagine how difficult that must be, whether you had one or ten, or whether they were a baby, five years old, or fifty, for that matter. It takes a tremendous amount of strength to be able to bury your child and go on."

"Yes, I suppose it does," I conceded. "And Diana was Beverline's only child. She'd already lost her husband."

"And if that weren't bad enough, now she has to watch her son-in-law get involved with another woman."

As the other woman in question, I felt compelled to defend myself. "Well, Mom, it's not like Aaron's cheating on Diana. She's dead, remember?"

"Of course I remember. And it's not reasonable for her to expect a healthy man like Aaron to go without . . . female companionship."

I rolled my eyes. She meant that as a euphemism for sex. I knew there were some things mothers just couldn't accept from their unmarried daughters, even if they were over forty.

"I suppose that if I were in her shoes I'd be resentful of any woman whom I perceived as trying to take over my late daughter's life," Mom concluded.

"I did consider that myself," I admitted. "But the way she acts makes it awfully hard for me to be sympathetic."

"You do realize it's going to be a challenge living so close and probably seeing her often. But do try to be patient. She acts that way because she feels threatened." Mom paused. "I noticed Aaron's daughters didn't come downstairs, and I'm sure little Billy told them you were there. I suppose they feel a little threatened themselves."

I sighed. "They're teenagers, and they miss their mother terribly. Besides, they probably feel Aaron is too old for things like se— female companionship." Hmph. Maybe there were things this unmarried daughter felt uncomfortable discussing with her mother, as well.

I had plenty on my mind that I didn't want to discuss with Mom. Aaron's revelation made me want to work out the sex angle even more. But it had to be deftly handled, and five months into our relationship I still wasn't sure how to do that.

# Chapter 21

Teddy looked like he didn't believe me. "I don't get why you felt you had to meet me for coffee and announce we won't be seeing each other anymore. You've said that before, Emily, under far less dramatic conditions."

"I know I have." I cursed myself for being such a weakling. "But things are truly different now, and I can say with absolute certainty that it's over between us."

He studied me, and I knew my unyielding expression showed I meant business. "There's something different about you, Emily."

"Yes. I'm in love." My smile was as bright as the day was gloomy.

"Hmph. So I guess I'm out of the running, huh?"

I didn't have the heart to tell him he'd never really been *in* the running.

I was about to excuse myself when Teddy's cell phone rang. He answered it right away. "Okay. I'll get my jacket and be right out." He flipped his phone shut. "I wish you well, Emily."

I took that as a dismissal, and I scraped my chair as I pushed back from the table. We rode up in the elevator together to our respective offices.

As glad as I was to have the unpleasantness of breaking it off with Teddy over, I was curious about whom he was meeting outside.

My small office faced the north side of the building, which was lined with parking spaces, including the one Teddy usually parked in. I picked up the chart of my next patient and brought it over to the window, looking outside under the pretext of pretending to study the chart.

A brunette with full, straight, shoulder-length hair stood leaning against a sleek red sports car that was parked directly next to Teddy's Santa Fe, driver side to driver side, smoking a cigarette. Something about her belted trench coat and the way her asymmetrical bangs covered part of her face gave her a mysterious air, like something out of a film noir. My curiosity grew as Teddy appeared, ambling over to her and kissing her cheek. Who was this chick, anyway?

I stood watching for the next few minutes. They talked for about three or four minutes before she stubbed out her cigarette. They embraced briefly, and then they got into her car, him behind the wheel, and drove off.

I actually felt a little jealous. It hadn't occurred to me that Teddy might be seeing someone else. He'd obviously been balancing her along with me.

But whatever was going on between Teddy and this woman, it clearly wasn't any of my business.

Our class reunion was approaching fast, and preparations were right on time. Rosalind, Valerie, Tanis, and I split the cost of food, and we would share whatever profits the cover charge brought. I brought in a fifth participant as well—Marsha. While she couldn't contribute financially, she offered to assist with the preparation. Even if we got stuck with a lot of leftovers, at least it was food we all liked: chicken drummettes, scallops wrapped in bacon, meatballs. Casualties would likely be things like the large tubs of potato and macaroni salads or the sheet cake.

By the time Marsha and I arrived at noon, Rosalind was already busy, stirring a lobster pot full of pasta and chopping onion and green pepper. Valerie, whose daughter had given birth to a baby girl, was doing her preparations at home and would bring the food with her to the party tonight.

"You're the early bird," I said after we greeted each other.

"I knew it would take this water forever to boil. I wanted to get the pasta cooked for the baked spaghetti first."

Marsha glanced around the kitchen. "Are you going to bake it now? I don't see a microwave here for heating, not that you could fit that huge dish into one anyway."

"No, I'll mix it up, cover it, and put it in the fridge. I'll put it in the oven tonight, and it'll go straight to the table. I think everything else can be heated up."

Marsha nodded. "Yeah, like the mini chicken wings I'm gonna do."

"Where's Tanis?" I asked.

"She's cooking at home."

Marsha rolled her eyes. "She can't come here and work with the rest of us? What, she thinks she's too good to work in the kitchen of a bar? Sounds like a position she'd take. She always did think she was cute."

Marsha had never really liked Tanis. I think it was because she was jealous of Tanis's long, wavy hair and nice wardrobe. If I'd been in Marsha's too big shoes I'd probably feel the same way. Marsha had always been prettier, but her looks were hidden by ill-fitting clothes and raggedy hair.

Rosalind may have had the same thought, for she tried to cover. "It kind of makes sense, Marsha. She makes her meatballs from scratch, and she said it's messy, plus her daughter likes to help. She's doing half barbecue and half Swedish. I brought my Crock-Pot so she could use it to keep them warm, since she has only one."

Personally, I believed what Rosalind had told me on the phone a few months ago, that the task of making meatballs would probably be assigned to Tanis's housekeeper.

Rosalind's explanation seemed to mollify Marsha, who asked, "Rosalind, do you think a lot of people will show?"

"I think so. It's only ten dollars a head, and we put up fly-ers all over Euliss. We even got them to announce it on the local news. So a lot of people know about it."

"If not, we're going to have a whole lot of food to take home and we won't be getting any of our money back," I re-marked.

"Hey, Emily, is Teddy coming?" Rosalind asked.

Marsha perked up like someone was talking about large sums of money. "Teddy Simms? Will he be here? What's he up to? Is he married?"

"He's a denture technician," I said. "He works in a den-tist's office in the same building as me, at least a few days a week. The rest of the time he's at another dental office."

Marsha nodded thoughtfully. I knew she was trying to fig-ure out how much a denture technician made. The thought of her making a move on Teddy made my throat constrict. I wasn't being fair, and I knew it. But I also knew that Marsha was about to be disappointed if she saw Teddy as the answer to all her problems. With that rent increase that had just gone into effect this month, he'd barely be able to afford to take her to dinner.

It soon became apparent that the reunion would be a suc-cess. People started coming in so fast that Wayne joined John on door duty to help out. Rosalind and John had both brought their old yearbooks, and people were looking at our pictures and cracking up. It was rather funny. So many of the white girls looked like Marcia Brady, with long center-parted straight hair. Most of the black kids had Jheri curls, which really looked ridiculous through twenty-first-century eyes. The music was playing, the bartenders were mixing drinks, and we were about to put the food out. By "we," I mean Marsha, Rosalind, Valerie, and myself. I felt rather guilty for having recruited Valerie to join the reunion committee just to lie for me about having dinner with her the night I was with Teddy. She had a lot to do, what with having a newborn baby in the house and the traveling her lucrative career required of her.

Tanis, on the other hand, had volunteered to help out but hadn't even arrived yet. I couldn't say I was surprised, given that her offer came out of trying to be nosy. The rest of us poured the hot foods into big foil pans and put them over lit disposable chafing dishes. The cold foods were placed in foil pans over slightly larger, ice-filled foil pans. The Crock-Pot Rosalind had brought for Tanis's meatballs sat empty.

I recognized most of the attendees on sight; no one had changed all that much in twenty-five years. Tracy Turner showed up in a simple scoop-necked black dress. Always a big girl, about Rosalind's height but heavier, like most of us, she'd put on weight since graduation, but her dress had a slimming effect. Her thick hair had been texturized with waves and styled in a sculpted updo that I'd seen on many a fashion model. On the models it looked fashionable, but Tracy had too much hair to carry it off. The result made her look like a cross between the Bride of Frankenstein and Marge Simpson.

I had to look twice at James Hardy, who wore striking Marine dress blues. James had moved to Euliss when we were in the fourth grade and was put in our class, even though he was eleven years old at the time, more in line with a sixth grader. He struggled through school with barely passing grades and disappeared after graduation.

Valerie's sister, Wendy, was in town as well with her husband, an average-looking brother who, like many of the men present, wore a sports coat and a mock turtleneck. Wendy barely said five words to Valerie. Their lack of interaction made it hard to believe they shared the same parents.

A small number of white classmates attended as well, all of them now living here in New Rochelle or in nearby towns like Larchmont and Mamaroneck. I was surprised to see how many former brunettes had gone blond. Elias Ansara would have a field day.

One dark-haired woman who looked vaguely familiar said,

"Hi!" with so much enthusiasm that I was certain she spoke to someone else.

I turned around, but when I saw no one there I turned back. "I'm sorry, were you talking to me?"

"Yes! Emily, isn't it?"

I was embarrassed to not know her identity, even though I felt certain I'd seen her somewhere. "Yes?"

"I'm Shelly. My last name was Muldoon in high school."

Recognition slowly dawned on me. This was Shelly Muldoon? She looked so different from what I remembered.

"Yes, it's me." She laughed. "I know I've changed some since then."

I'll say she had. The Shelly Muldoon I remembered had been a big, strapping girl, second only to Tracy Turner. This woman, in her long-sleeved red dress with a skirt that molded to her hips, was slim enough to be a fashion model. But the light brown hair, the dark eyes . . . they hadn't changed, other than the hair being a lot shinier.

"You look great," I said in a restrained voice.

"Thanks. You, too. Do you still live in Euliss?"

Already I was weary of being asked the same questions over and over again. Fortunately, something caught Shelly's eye, and she didn't appear to be paying much attention to me. Out of curiosity I turned to see what she was looking at, and in doing so it came to me where I'd seen her.

She was looking at Teddy.

She was the woman in the trench coat with the sports car. Uh-*huh*.

I kept waiting for Aaron to arrive, but I saw everyone but him. I had hugged yet another former classmate, and after she moved on I finally saw him . . . with Tanis. Instinct told me they'd come together. He carried something wrapped in a brown paper bag, holding it lengthwise in front of him. No doubt it was a dish of meatballs.

Tanis wore a cream-colored silk pantsuit with no blouse.

She didn't wear her hair as long as she had as a girl, but it still fell just past her shoulders. She looked quite lovely . . . and that's what bothered me.

Contrary to Valerie's hopes, Tanis's new TV show had turned out to be successful, one of a handful of new offerings that was a bona fide hit with the public and critics alike. Everyone knew she was on the show, and she happily stopped every few steps to accept congratulations and answer questions about the show's leading cast members.

Aaron approached me and carefully leaned in to give me a kiss. "I'm so sorry to be late," he said. "Tanis called and asked if I could help her carry the food." Tanis carried a padded bag with rounded sides that looked like it held a Crock-Pot. "When I got to her house she wasn't quite ready."

"Why am I not surprised," I said dryly. I could just hear her appealing to Aaron for help, like she couldn't make two trips to the car to put the covered dishes in the trunk. I made a mental note to ask Wayne if he'd offer to drop her off. I had come in my own car and brought Marsha with me, but no way was I going to let Aaron drive Tanis home at the end of the evening.

The party was on. Our class might be over age forty, but we were hardly over the hill. The bar was doing a brisk business, which would please the owner.

I kept a close watch on Teddy and Shelly, who didn't give any signs that they were anything more than old classmates. They barely spent time together, although I did pick up on a few discreet meaningful glances between them. The person who was frequently at Teddy's side was, to my dismay, Tanis. I thought she still had lingering doubts about that night last summer and wanted to see what she could get out of Teddy, something that she could go to Aaron with when he took her home. I made it a point to get over to Teddy as quickly as I could.

I counted to twenty after Tanis went to talk to someone else, made sure Aaron was occupied—he was talking to John Hunter—and then walked over. "Teddy, I have to ask you something. Has Tanis asked you anything about me?"

"Yeah. She did ask if you and I were still seeing each other."

My throat went dry. *Still* seeing each other? Tanis was setting a trap. Had Teddy fallen into it and brought me with him? "And what did *you* say?" I held my breath.

"I told her you and I were never involved, other than being friends, and we see each other fairly often because we work in the same building."

I let out my breath. "Thanks, Teddy."

"I saw your boyfriend come in. So that's my competition, huh?"

I went stiff. "So?"

"Tanis said he's a doctor. That explains a couple of things."

"Explains what?"

"Why you tried so hard to make your relationship work instead of telling him to get lost. When a black woman gets to choose between a dental technician and an M.D., the M.D. will win hands down."

My spine straightened in indignation. "*Black* women? So white women are totally unimpressed by summer homes and elegant restaurants? Don't kid yourself, Teddy. Every woman is.

"And I'll tell you something else," I added, watching Shelly Muldoon chatting with Aaron and Wayne. "White women who date black men are more interested in thumbing their noses at the establishment than anything else. Especially if they're from Euliss." I watched as Shelly said something, and all three of them laughed heartily. It was probably perfectly innocent, but it annoyed me nonetheless.

"I'm not trying to start something, Emily. All I know is that black women are more hung up on occupation than anyone I know, at least the ones who aren't doing much themselves. That rules you out, but look at Marsha. She talked to me for one minute and in that time managed to ask what I do. She's been flirting with me ever since."

I decided I'd rather see Teddy with Marsha than Shelly. He was a good catch. A sistah should get him. "Is that such a bad thing? You have to agree that Marsha's looking pretty good these days."

"She went and got herself some new teeth, just like Tanis has a new nose. I say let her flash her choppers at somebody else. I watch the news, Emily. I know all about that guy she married. The drug czar who got his head blown off."

"So what?" I bristled. "She married a criminal, one who took her nice places, really courted her, and misrepresented to her how he made his money. That doesn't mean she isn't a nice girl, Teddy."

He gave me a playful poke in the side. "I'll tell you a secret, Emily. There's a whole bunch of nice girls out there looking for nice men, and there're more than enough females for men to choose from. With all those available women out there, a man would have to be crazy to get involved with somebody like Marsha. Talk about baggage. She might be sitting on all kinds of knowledge that might be of interest to her husband's business associates. The phrase 'knowing where the bodies are buried' takes on a whole new meaning. What she may know about his business puts not only her, but everyone close to her, in danger."

"You've been reading too much James Patterson," I said, rolling my eyes.

"Hey. You're her friend, right? Do us all a favor and tell her to forget about me. I'm not interested." Hands in pockets, he sauntered off. Moments later I saw him dancing with Valerie.

I cornered Marsha the first chance I got. "Listen . . . Teddy's been getting your signals, but I'm sorry to say he's not interested. He thought I should be the one to tell you."

Her shoulders drooped, and I tried to soothe her. "Hey,

nothing ventured, nothing gained. He's not the last man on earth, you know." I scanned the room. "What about Wayne? He's unattached."

"He's ugly."

"He is not," I said indignantly. "He's just . . . not particularly handsome, that's all."

"Besides, he's got eyes for Tanis. Not that he'll ever get anywhere with her, that's for sure."

I watched Wayne and Tanis dancing. So Marsha, too, had figured out that Wayne's heart burned for Tanis. I wondered if Tanis knew about his admiration.

"What about James Hardy?"

"Are you kidding? He's even uglier than Wayne. And he's dumb, to boot. He got left back twice, for God's sake."

"No, he didn't. They put him in our grade when he moved to Euliss. I guess that's the level he tested at. His family were migrant workers, Marsha. It's not unusual for kids from those circumstances to be behind in school." We'd all giggled behind James's back about how ugly and stupid he was, but this wasn't fourth grade anymore. "If those bars on his sleeve are any indication, he's done pretty well for himself in the Marines." Then I played my trump card. "Besides, I don't see a wedding ring on his finger."

The deejay announced he was slowing it down, and Tanis appeared to excuse herself, leaving Wayne looking dejected. James Hardy, who back in the day was a not too bright tough guy with a flat head, small eyes, overly thick lips, and a swift right hook for anyone who dared make fun of him, approached Marsha with an outstretched hand, and they began dancing. With the typical heartlessness of a child, I used to make fun of James myself . . . privately, of course. It was nice to see that he'd done well. He had apparently made a career out of the military, and he looked almost handsome in his uniform . . . at least from a distance.

Now Aaron was chatting with Teddy, which made me uncomfortable. I rushed over to join them, but I was stopped by someone who told me what a nice party it was. In the few seconds it took for me to acknowledge the compliment, Tanis beat me to it, and she and Aaron fell into step just seconds before I reached them.

"Come on, let's dance," Teddy offered.

I was annoyed at having missed Aaron but decided to have a little fun with Teddy. "That Shelly Muldoon looks fabulous, doesn't she?"

"Yeah, not bad."

"Have you seen her since graduation?"

"Here and there."

*Yeah, right.* "What's she up to these days?"

"She sells medical equipment. I hear she's really good at it, too. Looks like she's trying to interest your boyfriend in some."

My head jerked at his phrasing. Anyone who didn't know better would interpret Teddy's words as meaning Shelly was trying to interest Aaron in something *else.*

Teddy turned his head so that his lips were close enough to my ear to kiss it without leaning. "I was just talking to your boyfriend."

"You can tell me that normally." He was entirely too close, and I didn't like the way that looked, even though the floor was crowded with couples. If Tanis saw she'd be sure to say something to Aaron about it.

"Lighten up, Emily. I'm not gonna start nothing. Why do you think I told Tanis she's barking up the wrong tree? You think I want him coming after me if he finds out you've been sharpening my pencil?"

I spoke in a murderous whisper. "Teddy."

"That wouldn't be the problem, would it? Am I able to give you something you can't get from him?"

I decided that Shelly must have been praising his bedroom skills and given him a swelled head. "No. It's just like what I told you before. We were going through a rough time, and now everything's fine between us."

"That's not enough for you to end up in bed with me. Remember what I told you. We're compatible, in bed and out of it." He tightened his grip around my waist.

Considering the words that came out of his mouth, now I was glad he spoke so close to my ear, lest anyone overhear. But we were dancing too close. I tried to wiggle free.

Teddy kept his grip on me. "Relax. Tanis isn't watching. She's too busy dancing with your doc. She's got her eye on him, you know."

I perked up immediately. "What makes you say that?"

"Because she's a little too interested in what went on that night she saw us at Hardy's. Plus she's been in his face tonight every chance she's had." He'd continued to speak softly into my ear, but now he straightened up. "Just don't say I told you. I don't believe in getting in the middle of shit."

"No, actually I knew about it. I'm just kind of surprised that you noticed as well."

"Yeah, well, I'm an observant type of guy."

By two-thirty in the morning most of the attendees had left, including, thank God, Teddy. It didn't surprise me to see Wayne still hanging around—he probably hoped to have another shot at Tanis—but I didn't expect James Hardy to be one of the last ones out the door.

Rosalind, Valerie, Marsha, Tanis, and myself surveyed the leftover food. To our relief, the great bulk of it had been consumed. We decided that everyone could just take home what she had prepared. We'd given the kitchen a thorough cleaning earlier, in the afternoon, right down to mopping the floor, so all that remained to do was a quick wipe down and then simply cover the dishes with foil and put them in our respective vehicles.

I soon saw why James had lingered. When Marsha said good night to me, she added, "James was kind enough to offer me a lift home. This way I won't have to trouble Valerie for a ride. I'm sure she wants to get back to City Island."

"That was nice of him. Thanks for everything, Marsha. You were a tremendous help."

"I just wish I could have contributed more," she said wistfully.

"You can't put a price tag on time," I pointed out, giving her a hug. "Now, run along, and be a good girl. No hanky-panky with James."

There was no way was I letting Tanis cozy up to Aaron for a ride home. *I* was leaving out of here with him, even if I had to leave my car parked here overnight. But it really wasn't fair for me to ask him to drive me all the way to Euliss when I had my car.

I was pondering how to handle this when Aaron came up behind me, putting his arms around my waist. "I've got a suggestion."

"Aaron, I really don't want to go to that motel." I'd never warmed up to the idea of spending nights there. It was the type of place where you'd see Acuras and BMWs parked outside at noon . . . a time when the occupants clearly were supposed to be at work, which was likely where their spouses believed them to be. I felt out of place with all those adulterers and the other group that constituted the majority of the motel's clientele: twenty-something live-at-homes who had their sex on the weekends.

"I know. I don't, either. Why don't you come home with me? Everybody's asleep."

"Isn't that a little brazen, my spending the night? I know Beverline is a big girl, but what about your kids?"

"I'll sneak downstairs and lie down on the couch in my office before anyone gets up. I'll just tell them we were out too late for you to go home."

Before I could answer Tanis approached us. "Well, it looks like that's that," she said briskly. "Aaron, can I get a lift with you?"

"We'd be happy to drop you off."

She looked startled. "We?"

"Emily and I."

"Oh. Emily, didn't you drive over from Euliss?"

"Yes, I did." I refused to give her any more information. It was none of her damn business.

Wayne came to my rescue, carrying Tanis's coat. "Tanis, can I take you home?"

"Well, I hate to take you out of your way. . . ."

"Not a problem." He looked at Aaron and me. "I think Emily and Aaron have plans."

Even in the dim lighting I could see the disappointment on Tanis's face. "Um . . . all right." Wayne moved behind her and slipped her coat on her shoulders.

After Aaron seated me in the Jag, I turned to look at Wayne and Tanis crossing the street to Wayne's car.

I wasn't surprised when Tanis turned to look at Aaron and me.

"I think you girls did a good job," Aaron said.

"Thanks. It was a real success. I hope you didn't mind being around a whole bunch of people from Euliss."

"Emily, I hope you don't think I'm such a snob that I would judge someone strictly by where they're from."

"No, of course not." What I'd been doing was trying to work the conversation so I could find out what he and Teddy were talking about, but of course this had to be deftly handled. "I guess I'm saying I hope you weren't too bored. I'm not sure you have anything in common with Wayne, or Teddy, or anybody."

His forehead wrinkled. "Now, I know Wayne, but I'm not sure who Teddy is."

I had scored the perfect opening. I offered a brief physical description of Teddy. "You were talking with him. I don't know if it came up, but he's a denture technician."

"Oh, yeah. Nice fellow. He certainly thinks very highly of you, Emily."

"What did he say?"

"Just that he'd known you since grammar school and what a sweetheart you are." Aaron grinned. "Of course, I had to agree with his assessment."

"Of course," I teased back. I was dying to know what else Teddy had said, but my instincts told me to leave it alone. Aaron didn't seem disturbed by anything Teddy might have told him, and if I pressed it would only make him suspicious.

# Chapter 22

"What are your plans for Christmas, Emily?"

"We usually drop in at my oldest niece's place in the afternoon. She assigns a dish for everyone to bring, and we have a wonderful family dinner. What about you?" I imagined the holiday had to be rough for Aaron's family since Diana died.

"We spend it at our summerhouse in Sag Harbor. It makes it easier, since . . ."

I understood. Changing the location of their holiday celebration probably went a long way toward their being able to enjoy it without guilt. Of course, it helps when you have a summerhouse.

"We usually drive out Christmas Eve and put up the tree," Aaron continued. "I usually stay out there for two or three days, and Beverline brings the kids back New Year's Day. I just hate the idea of not seeing you over the holiday."

I tensed. There was no polite way to say that I wasn't ready for a family get-together that would run longer than ten minutes—not with *his* family.

"What about the night before Christmas Eve? You know, Emily, if we're going to live so close to each other, we probably need to spend a little time together socially."

"Yes, I suppose you have a point." I'd hoped to avoid this. Thanksgiving had given me a reprieve, for the Merritts had gone to Delaware to spend the holiday with Aaron's side of the family, coming back on Friday so Aaron would make my class reunion.

"Why don't I bring Beverline and the kids down for a quick visit, maybe an hour? I think it'll do the kids good to see you at home, in your own environment. They need to understand that you have a life outside of coming by our place."

I noticed he didn't say anything about his mother-in-law. That told me he felt his kids would warm up to me, but he had no such hopes for Beverline.

"All right," I said with more enthusiasm than I felt. "Y'all come over."

I answered the door to see two smiling faces and three unsmiling ones. I joined the former camp, pasting a big smile on my face that wasn't entirely false. As with every year, the holiday spirit had enveloped me like a warm blanket. One couldn't help but get the spirit, what with the airwaves full of the familiar holiday tunes and the streets and apartment windows all lit up with colorful decorations. The streets of Euliss actually looked pretty. "Welcome, everyone!"

Billy greeted me with his usual enthusiasm. "Merry Christmas, Miss Emily!"

"Hello, Billy! Merry Christmas to you!" I gave him an affectionate hug, then gestured to Mom, standing a few feet behind me. "Billy, do you remember my mother, Mrs. Yancy?"

"Yes. Hi," he said to her, punctuating his words with a friendly wave. "Merry Christmas!"

"Merry Christmas, Billy. You know, I think Santa Claus left something for you here."

He made an all-knowing face. "Santa Claus? Come on, Miz Yancy."

"Billy," Aaron admonished.

"Oh, that's all right," Mom said. "Emmie never believed in Santa Claus, either. It's because her sister and brother are so much older than she is." She turned to Billy. "You come with me."

"Everyone, take off your coats," I urged.

Although it was a bit on the warm side for late December, Beverline had worn a full-length mink and matching hat, no doubt to accentuate her membership in the Other Half. "What a lovely little tree," she remarked in a condescending tone as she handed me the dark fur.

"Thank you, Mrs. Wilson. My goodness, you must have melted in this."

"I was actually quite comfortable. I often get chilled in the winter." Her tone had an unmistakable tinge of indignation, which told me I'd hit my mark by pointing out that it wasn't cold enough for mink.

I moved on to Arden and Kirsten, figuring Mom could hold her own with Beverline. "Hello, girls. I haven't seen you in ages. I, uh, missed you when my mother and I were over a few weeks ago."

"Yes," Arden said. She was clearly The Voice out of the two of them. Her younger sister just nodded. "We were up in our room that day . . . watching a really good movie on TV."

"I see. Well, go and sit down. I'll just put these coats away." I went into the bedroom and put the coats on Mom's bed.

When I returned I heard laughter coming from the kitchen. Apparently Aaron was helping Mom bring out the refreshments she'd prepared.

Beverline was telling Billy to take his gift home with him and open it Christmas morning with the rest of his presents. Arden and Kirsten were standing awkwardly.

"Please, sit down," I said.

The girls sat together on the sofa. Billy sat on one of the floor pillows. I wondered if Aaron had told him ahead of time to sit there, because there wouldn't be enough room for everyone to sit on the furniture. Beverline chose the single chair that matched the loveseat and sofa. Out of the corner of my eye I saw Mom and Aaron coming toward us, Mom carrying a tray of pinwheel sandwiches and an ice bucket, and Aaron holding a tray with two small glass pitchers, one of eggnog and the other of Sprite, plus highball glasses.

Then two things happened. "Can we watch TV?" young Billy inquired as Beverline paused mid-descent. When her right hand swung behind her, I gasped. Was she going to do what I *thought* she was going to do?

Then Beverline brushed the cushion of the chair with her palm before sitting down.

I was rendered speechless, something that rarely happens. But the cat didn't get Mom's tongue.

She bent to place the tray down on the coffee table, then stood straight up and faced Beverline. "I may not have a house-keeper, Mrs. Wilson, but I keep a clean house. There's no need for you to brush away imaginary dust."

"Beverline? Did you do that?" Aaron sounded astounded.

She shrugged guiltily. "It's a reflex action. I do it every-place. I didn't mean to imply your apartment isn't clean, Mrs. Yancy."

Mom gave a tight little smile that told me she didn't be-lieve that for a second. She then focused on Arden and Kirsten. "Girls, help yourselves to eggnog, or soda if you prefer."

"What are these?" Kirsten asked, pointing to the sand-wiches.

"Dear, you've had those before," Beverline said quickly. "They're sandwiches, made on that Middle Eastern bread, then rolled into wheels and sliced."

"Oh, yes." Kirsten took a sandwich and a napkin.

I quickly turned on the television for Billy, thinking it might provide a welcome distraction. I handed him the remote con-trol.

Aaron poured Beverline an eggnog and sprinkled it with nutmeg. I wished it was strychnine instead.

"Where's the HBO?" Billy asked as he flipped from chan-nel to channel.

"I'm sorry, dear, I don't have HBO," Mom replied.

"All you have is news stations," he complained as he passed through a series of channels.

"Billy, you know better than that," Aaron admonished.

"If you flip around some more you'll find the Cartoon Network," I offered. I glanced over at Mom, who had taken a seat on the loveseat next to Aaron. Her eyes had narrowed into slits so small I was amazed she could see anything through them.

I sat in the only vacant seat left, the opening on the sofa between Arden and Kirsten. The eggnog I'd poured for myself just before they arrived still sat on a coaster on the coffee table. "Are you all ready for the holidays, girls?" I asked pleasantly

"Yes," Arden and Kirsten responded simultaneously.

In a legal setting, this would be considered a question asked and answered. And the answer was delivered with as much personality as someone on the witness stand.

I tried again. "Are you looking forward to spending your holiday out of town?"

"Yes."

Oh, fine. I hadn't fared so badly since I interviewed a recent certified nursing assistant graduate for an opening my employer had. The girl had excellent grades, but Calvin Coolidge would have viewed her as a conversational challenge.

I tried for what I told myself would be the final time. "Are there many people out in the Hamptons this time of year?"

"Yes," Arden said.

I took a gulp of my eggnog, glad that I'd spiked it with some of Pop's old bourbon. I silently acknowledged defeat, but Arden surprised me by continuing to speak. "Lots of people spend the holidays out there."

"It'll be nice to get out there and see our friends whom we haven't seen since *July*," Kirsten said, accenting her last word.

Beverline made a sighing sound just before taking a demure sip of her eggnog. I knew it was directed at me, just as

Kirsten's remark had been, but I let it slide. The bourbon was making me mellow.

Aaron spoke up. "Keep that up, Kirsten, and you won't see them until *next* Christmas."

My eyes immediately went to Beverline to check her reaction. She pretended to be studying her eggnog . . . maybe for poison.

"Aaron, I'm so sorry you and Emily won't see each other over the holiday," Mom said.

"Actually, Mrs. Yancy, I'll be out on the island for only a few days. I'll be driving back at home on the twenty-seventh. I've got a few loose ends to clear up before the first, and of course I want to spend some time with Emily."

"Will you be going back to Long Island for New Year's?"

I reached for a sandwich. I knew what Mom was up to. She'd already asked me about Aaron's plans. She knew Beverline didn't like the idea of Aaron spending a special occasion with me and wanted to hear him state his plans aloud just to irritate her.

"No. I'm going to spend New Year's with Emily at home."

Beverline suddenly perked up. "Aaron's arranged for a limousine service to drive us back New Year's Day."

Mom beamed. "Well, I'm glad you two will get to ring the New Year in together, since you'll be separated on Christmas."

I flashed her a look that I hoped she would interpret as a warning not to go overboard.

"I understand you're going out of town yourself, Mrs. Yancy," Aaron said, deftly changing the subject.

"Yes. My other daughter lives outside of Pittsburgh. Her children live here, but they always go out after Christmas and spend a week or so. She and her husband give a large New Year's bash every year. It's really quite lovely."

"When are you leaving?"

"The twenty-seventh. The same day you'll be driving back to New York."

Arden, who'd been eyeing the tray on the coffee table in front of her, said, "Those sandwiches are good. Is it all right if I have another one?"

"Of course, dear. You go right ahead," Mom said.

"Now, Arden, you don't want to eat up all of Mrs. Yancy's food," Beverline cautioned, effectively giving her grandchildren the impression that Mom and I were starving.

Aaron tried to defuse the potentially explosive situation. "Beverline, I'm sure Mrs. Yancy's cupboards are full," he said easily. He nodded at his uncertain daughter to go ahead.

"Thank you, Aaron," Mom said. "You know, I've always hated it when people put out food and liquor for guests and then turn around and complain about how much they ate or drank. That's definitely not me." She looked directly at Beverline as she said the last sentence, as if defying her to make another implication. I could swear that Beverline's complexion darkened a shade at Mom's insinuation.

Aaron got up. "I'm going to have another one of those sandwiches myself, and then I'm afraid we'll have to run. I want to hit the road early tomorrow, by six-thirty."

Just minutes later I was handing out coats. The visit Aaron estimated would run about an hour had lasted barely half that long.

Mom said good night to everyone and promptly made herself scarce, disappearing inside her bedroom, knowing that Aaron and I would want a few minutes alone. Beverline, on the other hand, showed no such consideration. She waited expectantly in the doorway after the kids had already left the apartment. "Aaron, aren't you coming?"

"Why don't you start the car up? I'll be out in a minute."

She flashed an expression that looked like he'd just slapped her, nodded curtly to me, and left.

I turned to Aaron. "Well, *that* went well," I said brightly. His hangdog expression made me giggle.

"Kirsten and Arden don't dislike you, Emily. They're just having a little difficulty with the idea of there being another woman in my life. I've talked to them about it and assured them that I won't ever forget their mother. But it's hard for them nonetheless."

"Billy doesn't seem to have a problem," I pointed out.

"No, but he's younger. He doesn't have the memories of Diana that his sisters do. I was hoping they would open up to you a little bit. You know, talk to you about things teenage girls worry about. I hoped they would see you as someone who's a little more in touch with their generation than their grandmother."

"I guess we have to give it more time. They've only seen me a handful of times, and it's clear Kirsten blames me for kicking them out of the Sag Harbor house. Things might change for the better once Mom and I move into your guesthouse."

"You're right. Of course, there's also the possibility that Beverline is influencing them in a negative way."

"She really hates me, doesn't she?"

"I think she's just scared. Arden asked me just the other day if I would put Nana out if I were to remarry."

"Does your own daughter really think you'd do something so cold, Aaron?"

"Not on her own. At least I hope not. But I think Beverline is trying to get her to think that. The truth is, my house probably wouldn't be big enough for Beverline and any other woman."

"Did she honestly think you would never start seeing women again?"

"Well, I was pretty broken up when Diana passed . . . but someone of Beverline's generation probably should know that widowed spouses have to move on . . . eventually."

Part of me understood Beverline's fear. But didn't she realize that by being so unpleasant she was setting the stage for Aaron's next wife to throw her ass out?

"I guess I'd better get going," he said reluctantly.

I suddenly felt an almost overwhelming sadness. Tomorrow was Christmas Eve, and my boyfriend was going out of town. Yes, that's what he was now, my boyfriend. He was handsome, successful, rich . . . and he was in love with me. When he pulled me to him I threw my arms around his neck and kissed him fervently. Aaron pressed his cheek to mine and squeezed me. "I know how you feel, but I'll only be gone three days, Emily. We'll have dinner the night I come back and celebrate Christmas then. Plan on staying at my house the rest of the week. How's that sound?"

"Sounds great." How nice it would be to be able to lounge around a private residence, rather than rush to vacate that motel before eleven.

He kissed me once more before leaving. "I'll call you tomorrow."

"Okay."

While watching him from the kitchen window, a squeal escaped from my lips that would have made Al Green proud. Aaron turned around before getting behind the wheel to wave at me. I blew him a kiss.

Even though I could have waited until after the holiday to take advantage of all those post-Christmas sales, I chose to shop for Aaron's gift on Christmas Eve. I enjoyed the revelry of the mall atmosphere as people good-naturedly purchased last-minute gifts.

I went to a men's specialty store, which sold everything from underwear and socks to overcoats. The store aisles were packed with special displays of holiday gifts, some of them ludicrous. I mean, did people actually buy those ear and nose hair trimmers? I couldn't think of a more insulting gift. There was just no nice way to say, "You need to cut the hair that's growing out of your nostrils." That was like me giving Beverline a nice jar of Porcelana for her liver spots.

After much looking at all the goodies, I chose a snazzy brown and white tie with matching hanky and a gold love-knot tie clip for Aaron. He preferred to wear plain white shirts to work—they went with the white smock he wore—but the tie would give some pizzazz to his everyday wear.

It would be hard to go without seeing him over the holiday. I had to be satisfied with knowing he was thinking about me . . . and with wondering about what he'd gotten for me.

I took a day off on the day Aaron came home. That morning I took Mom to the airport to catch her flight to Pittsburgh. She was happy about her trip, and so was I. I could spend the next five days at Aaron's and not feel guilty about leaving her alone in the apartment at the most festive time of year.

I figured Aaron would want to take me to dinner his first night back, but I thought it would be a nice surprise if I cooked for him. I called Shirley, who was freshening up the house for Aaron's return, and arranged for her to let me in.

"You know, Miss Yancy, we have plenty of food here in the house," she said as she took one of the grocery bags I held in my arms. "You really didn't have to go to the store and buy all this."

"I wanted to be responsible for the entire dinner," I said. "You know how it is."

"I think that's very sweet. Are there more bags?"

"No, just my suitcase. Um . . . I'll be staying here through New Year's Day."

"Just let me know if there's anything you need, Miss Yancy."

That familiar guilt came over me, and I decided to put a stop to it. "Shirley, won't you please call me Emily?" I saw no reason to give an explanation for my request; instinct told me she knew where I was coming from.

"The doctor might not like it," she protested.

I didn't think she truly believed that. "He won't mind," I said. I looked at the kitchen clock. "I'd better get started. Aaron said he was leaving after lunch. He'll probably be here soon."

"I'm about to leave myself. Do you need me to take out any pans or cooking tools for you? It can be hard when you're not familiar with where everything's kept."

"Good idea. All I need is a saucepan, a broiler pan, a cutting board, and a salad bowl." I was making a simple surf 'n' turf: steak, boiled shrimp, loaded baked potatoes, and salad.

Shirley left soon after taking out the utensils I requested. It made me feel good to know that she felt she didn't have to stay and keep an eye on me until Aaron arrived. I was glad she left, for that allowed me to carry through a part of my plan that I didn't think I'd be able to.

After six months and two sexual positions—missionary and spooning—it occurred to me to shake things up under the guise of spontaneity.

I was all set when I heard Aaron's key in the lock. "Emily!" he called out, sounding excited. "Where are you?"

"In the kitchen."

He rushed into the room. "I saw your car in the driveway. That was real smart of you, to get here before I—" he broke off at the sight of my French maid outfit. "Wow."

"Shirley went home for the day, so it's just you and me," I said in a throaty voice a half octave lower than I normally spoke in, playfully twirling the hem of my short skirt. The three-and-a-half-inch heels I wore were hurting the hell out of my feet, but the enchanted look on his face made it worth the pain.

"Oh, yeah." He jerked his jacket off and threw it toward a stool, not even turning at the sound of it hitting the floor instead. "C'mere, baby."

I wrapped my legs around his waist when he picked me up. Aaron leaned me against the refrigerator for balance as he kissed me, allowing his hands to roam over my body, including my bare upper thighs where my elasticized thigh-high stockings ended. "I don't think we'll make it upstairs," he said between gasps. "Let's go to my office."

"I don't think I can wait that long," I whispered back. "I say we do it right here." I wriggled against his erection and moved his hand to my conveniently crotchless panties. He caught on quickly, moving to unzip his jeans.

I held on for the ride of my life.

\* \* \*

"I thought it would be nice to invite a few people over for New Year's," Aaron said as we ate the dinner we ended up preparing together. "Nothing too big. What do you think?"

I was still reeling from the exciting sex we'd had before dinner. Wow. First I came to stay for a few days, and next we were entertaining as a pair. I could hear Mom saying, "You'll be married by this time next year."

"I think it'll be fun," I said. "I just wish people would dress up more for casual parties. It seems so less festive when people throw on a pair of jeans and a sweater, like they're going to the mall or to wash the car or something."

"So we can tell people to dress up."

"We can?"

"Sure. I think that'll be nicer, anyway. More festive, like you said."

I found myself starting to get excited. "Who should we invite?"

"Elias and his latest flame, of course."

I shook my head. "He really gets around, doesn't he?"

"He's gone buck wild since his divorce. Sometimes I don't think he'll be satisfied until he's bedded every single woman over twenty-five in New York."

"And no doubt he calls every one of them 'dahling.' " I giggled.

"I'm sure. Let's see. My other close friends are all out of town until after New Year's. But there's Rosalind and John, Tanis, your friend Wayne, Tanis's cousin . . ."

"Valerie."

"Yes, that's the one. And your other friend, Marsha." Aaron frowned. "That does make it a little female heavy, doesn't it?"

"Do you know any single doctors, Aaron?" Marsha would certainly love that.

"Not a one, I'm afraid. Everyone I know who isn't married is dating someone. Do you think Wayne has any friends he'd like to bring? Not that I want word to get out that there's a party going on here and have fifty people show up."

"I'd rather not vouch for any friends Wayne might have. I've always known him to be pretty much a loner, anyway."

"You can always ask your other old schoolmate from the reunion. Teddy. He seems to go way back with you girls."

The last person I wanted around, especially if Tanis was present. "Uh . . . I think he's away for the holiday. He mentioned something about going upstate."

"Oh. Too bad. Nice guy."

"What about food?" I asked, eager to change the subject.

"I'll give you the number to my caterer. She won't appreciate the late notice, but since it's a small gathering I'm sure she can squeeze us in. That's another reason to keep it at about a dozen people. All the best caterers are booked."

"I wouldn't know anything about that," I remarked. "But there is something I do know that I'd like to share with you, Aaron."

"What's that?"

I smiled at him with all the warmth in my heart. "I love you."

# Chapter 23

I dreaded calling Tanis with an invitation to the party. If I thought I could get away with telling Aaron that she simply wasn't able to make it I would have, but the likelihood of them running into each other at their kids' school or at the dance school their daughters attended was too high. I had no choice.

I forced myself to think of good things, like the joy on Aaron's face when I told him I loved him. It had been a long time since I'd been this happy. I couldn't let Tanis ruin it for me.

To my surprise, a man answered the phone. I was more surprised when he called me by name. "Wayne? Did I dial the wrong number?"

He laughed. "No, I'm at Tanis's. I normally wouldn't answer the telephone, but your name and number—I mean Aaron's—showed up on the TV screen, so I figured I would."

I knew what he meant. Caller ID showed up on Aaron's TV screen, too. I also understood why he picked it up. He thought Aaron was calling and wanted to know why.

"Tanis went to the store. She'll be back any minute."

I felt happy for him. "So how long has this been going on?"

"We've been seeing each other since the night of the reunion."

The night he took her home. Wayne was probably a poor

substitute for Aaron in Tanis's eyes, but he was a kind and caring man, and those kind of men were always hard to find. It didn't hurt that he obviously adored her.

"I'll tell you why I'm calling," I said. "It's awfully last minute, but Aaron and I thought it would be fun if we had a small group over to ring in the new year here at his place. We'd love to have both you and Tanis."

"That sounds great. We really didn't have any plans. Tanis's kids are with her ex until New Year's Day. Why don't I ask her to call you at Aaron's?"

That thought made me smile. "You do that. I'll see you New Year's Eve."

I called Rosalind next, inviting her to the party as well as sharing the gossip about Tanis's involvement with Wayne. "Wayne sounds so happy, Rosalind."

"I hope he enjoys it while it lasts, because it won't."

"Why do you say that?"

"Tanis told me that she won't ever marry another man in the entertainment industry, but that she wanted someone who made a good living. I don't think that's Wayne, do you?"

"No." *It sounds more like Aaron.*

"I know she'd planned to make a play for Aaron until you showed up and put a butcher knife in her plans. Aaron's friend Elias is single now, and heaven knows he's handsome, but he likes blondes."

If I'd been surprised when Wayne answered Tanis's phone, I was astounded when Marsha asked if she could bring James, when I called her next. I couldn't even form an intelligible response.

She laughed. "I know you're surprised. But we've been in pretty constant touch since the night of the reunion, and he's driving up from Beaufort the day after tomorrow to spend New Year's with me."

"That actually makes it easier," I noted, "since my guest list is short on men. But Tanis is coming with Wayne, and you're coming with James—"

"Wait a minute. Tanis and *Wayne?*"

"I know it seems unlikely," I said with a smile. "Apparently you and James aren't the only ones who hooked up at the reunion."

"He doesn't seem her type."

"You said the same thing about James," I reminded her.

"I know, but he's so nice, Emily. I admit I made a mistake. I can't tell you how excited I am about him coming up. We've talked just about every day since Thanksgiving weekend. I've learned so much about him. But seeing him in person again . . ."

"You mean you'll be sleeping with him."

Marsha giggled. "I'm so excited. It's been a while."

I felt her excitement over the wire. Silently I expressed my hopes that she wouldn't be disappointed.

Tanis called a few minutes later. "I see you're playing house with Aaron while his family is away."

"Yes, just like you and Wayne."

"Touché," she said easily. "He told me about your invitation. We'd love to come. Can I bring anything?"

"No, but thanks. I've spoken to the caterer, and she's taking care of everything."

"Oh. Can I ask who else is coming?"

My instinct told me she wanted to know if anyone from Euliss was coming, which meant word could get out about her and Wayne. "It'll be small. A friend of Aaron's and his date, plus Rosalind and John, you and Wayne, and Marsha and James Hardy. I haven't spoken to Valerie yet."

"James Hardy is coming with Marsha? I thought he was a drill instructor down in South Carolina. Did he retire or something since last month?"

"He's still working, but apparently he'll be in town."

"That might create a problem for my cousin," Tanis said, not sounding particularly concerned. "I don't think she's seeing anyone, and it'll be awkward for her not to have anyone to kiss at midnight. Her life might revolve around her family, but her son and grandson are both too young to escort her."

"I'll leave that up to her." Tanis made it sound like Valerie should be pitied for not having a man in her life, but I knew better. Valerie seemed perfectly content with her life around her children, her new grandchild, her career, and, undoubtedly, her vibrator.

"You don't know any unattached men you can invite just to even things out?"

"Truthfully, Tanis, I don't know if she'd really care about being the only one without a date."

"Hold on a minute, Emily. Let me ask Wayne." I could hear her as she spoke to him. "Do you know a nice man we can invite to the party so Valerie will have someone to pair off with?"

I laughed at his response. "Tanis, I don't be runnin' with a pack of dudes like that."

"Well, I tried," Tanis said to me through the receiver.

I'd gone shopping and found a simple navy knit dress with a tight-fitting bodice, three-quarter sleeves, a belted waist, a scooped back, and a full skirt that fell to just above my ankles. I wore navy high-heeled sandals and skipped the hose— the straps around my big toes made stockings impossible anyway—and showed off my freshly pedicured toes. Aaron whistled appreciatively when I came downstairs, and I felt like a fairy princess.

That is, until Tanis arrived.

She and Wayne showed up a little after eleven, after Rosalind and John and Elias and his latest squeeze, a pretty Latino whose honey blond hair came from a bottle and whose name was, of all things, Eliana. I watched, steaming like a lobster pot, as Tanis gave Aaron a hug much warmer than the phony air kiss she'd given me.

Tanis wore a dark mink. She was wearing her hair longer

these days, in a cascade of curls with a center part. It looked quite nice. She removed her coat to reveal a green rayon dress with two clear halves to its bodice, each cut all the way down to the wide belt, revealing the swell of firm, C-cup boobs. The cinched waistline also showed off the great shape she was in. I looked down at my modest chest, which looked grossly underdeveloped next to Tanis's bold display.

Rosalind came up beside me. "Double-sided tape," she whispered. "There's nothing like being the center of attention, is there?"

"I hope she gets a chest cold," I muttered. I turned to see how Aaron had reacted to Tanis's plunging neckline, and was dismayed to see his eyes glued to it. Elias, too, couldn't seem to control his stare, which went down to her cleavage even while he greeted her. I even noticed John Hunter's gaze lingering on Tanis's chest, at least until Rosalind gave him a firm poke in the ribs.

Aaron glanced up at me, embarrassed at having been caught. He leaned toward me for a kiss and I relented. So he'd been caught looking. He was a man, after all. What did I expect?

I was refilling the ice bucket and didn't hear the doorbell ring, but when I returned I was happy to see Valerie, wearing a black velvet pantsuit with red satin trim, handing her coat to Aaron.

Tanis rushed forward to greet her cousin. "Valerie, I'm so glad you made it," she said, her voice dripping sugar.

Valerie's response brought a chuckle to my lips. "I don't know why you're so surprised to see me, Tanis. You called me yesterday to see if I was coming."

"That's because I arranged for a surprise for you, and in order for it to work out you had to be here."

Valerie responded the same way most people do when being informed of an impending surprise. "What is it?"

"You'll find out soon enough." Tanis stretched the last word out to three syllables over two octaves. Then she turned to freshen her drink with the ice cubes I'd just replaced. She leaned forward slightly, and I could have sworn Elias craned his neck to see if he could get a glimpse of tit.

"You know, I've always loved this painting of Diana," Tanis said, pausing in front of the picture that I was finally learning to ignore. "It's in such a nice place, too. It's the first thing people see when they step inside the house."

I deliberately offered to fix Valerie a drink, which she accepted. As I took Valerie's arm and led her to the bar, I saw Tanis shift position out of the corner of my eye, like she was turning around to give me a triumphant little smile.

"I like it, too. But I'm thinking of moving it to the girls' room," I heard Aaron say, and instinctively I knew his eyes were on me. "None of us will ever forget Diana, and I wouldn't want us to. But she's no longer mistress of the house."

Tanis seemed to shrivel before my eyes.

The doorbell rang at ten minutes to twelve. Both Aaron and I went to answer it, laughing and clasping our hands. I closed one eye for a look through the peephole.

"It's Marsha," I said as I stepped back, gesturing for him to open the door.

The first thing I noticed was the happy expression on Marsha's face. James had arrived in town yesterday. I guessed he'd pushed all the right buttons. No wonder they'd barely made it before midnight.

The second thing I noticed was that someone stood behind them. Had they brought someone with them? Why hadn't Marsha mentioned it?

When they moved inside I got a better look at the third wheel.

Teddy.

"Hey, man. I didn't think you'd be able to make it," Aaron said jovially.

"Thanks, Aaron." Teddy shook his hand, then turned to me. "You seem surprised to see me, Emily. Didn't Tanis tell you I accepted your invitation?"

*Tanis!* "I guess it must have slipped her mind, but we're happy to see you, Teddy. Come in; you're just in time."

"Everybody, let me take your coats," Aaron urged.

"Aaron, what a lovely home you have," Marsha said with admiration.

"Thanks. It's comfortable."

"I'll say," James said with a chuckle. As he had at the reunion, he wore his dress blues and looked quite dashing.

I faced Teddy while Aaron took Marsha's and James's coats. "She didn't tell you, did she?" he guessed.

"No. She's up to something, and I think I know what it is."

"I'll talk to her."

"No, let me. Just give your coat to Aaron, Teddy."

I sought Tanis, who stood next to a stunned Valerie saying, "There's your surprise! You have a partner, so you won't have to sit alone while the rest of us are dancing. Wasn't that thoughtful of me?"

"Extremely solicitous," Valerie said drolly.

I quickly stepped in. "I've only got five minutes to get the champagne. C'mon Tanis, give me a hand in the kitchen." I grabbed her arm before she could protest. Tanis was the type of guest who never offered to help.

I started in on Tanis the minute we were alone. "All right, what gives? Why did you invite Teddy to come and not say anything to me about it?"

"Because we both said we wished we knew someone who could prevent Valerie from feeling left out around all these couples. Teddy was the perfect choice. We're all old friends, aren't we? I can't imagine why you'd be upset."

Too late, I realized my mistake. If there'd been nothing between Teddy and me, I wouldn't have been upset by his unexpected appearance. I'd just given myself away, and that syrupy sweet way Tanis spoke proved it.

She gave me a knowing smile. "So what's the deal, Emily? Why *are* you so upset to see Teddy here?"

"Listen, Tanis, I don't know what you think you're up to—"

"Cut the crap, Emily. You and I both know you were boning Teddy while you were supposed to be seeing Aaron. Don't you think I know why you were trying to hide from me, and why Teddy stopped at the store? What happened? Did you run out of protection?"

The kitchen door swung open. "Hey, it's almost twelve," Aaron announced. "There're only a few minutes left to pour the champagne. Do you need help with the cork?"

"Oh, we're just gossiping," Tanis said lightly. "You know how we women are. The time got away from us."

I sprung into action, removing two chilled bottles of Freixenet Cordon Negro—actually a bubbling sparkling wine— from the refrigerator and arranging flutes on two round trays. Aaron removed the cork from the first bottle and started to pour.

Tanis seemed only too eager to hang around now that Aaron had appeared. She pulled and tugged at her dress until she achieved the desired wardrobe malfunction.

Aaron noticed before I did. "Um . . . Tanis." I looked up to see him patting his chest, then saw Tanis's uncovered tit.

"Oh, look at me." She giggled.

"We've seen it," I snapped. "Now, fix your tape and cover it up."

She promptly began to fiddle with the inside of her bodice, standing where she was.

"For God's sake, Tanis, turn around!" I said, disgusted.

"I'll take this batch out," Aaron said hastily, turning away from Tanis and her tit. "You two can take in the rest. Don't take too long; you only have about two minutes."

I poured champagne into the remaining glasses and found a tray to place them on. I sensed Tanis a few steps behind me, but I let the door swing shut in her face.

"Three . . . two . . . one . . . *Happy New Year!*"

Aaron and I shared a chaste but prolonged kiss, plus an

embrace that neither of us seemed to want to end. "I love you," he said softly against my ear. It meant all the more to me because we stood not three feet from Diana's portrait, and Aaron actually faced it. In my heart I knew that painting would never bother me again. It was just a likeness of someone who had passed on, and it couldn't watch me or curse me or have any effect on me whatsoever. I clutched him tightly and savored the moment, momentarily forgetting we were in a room full of people. When I opened my eyes, knowing we had guests to entertain, I was reminded of the threat to my happiness. Tanis slipped out of Wayne's embrace. He caught her hand, and she smiled at him but pulled away, her eyes fixated on Aaron.

Everyone was making rounds, wishing each other a happy new year. Teddy and Valerie embraced like the old friends they were, and when Teddy moved on Elias quickly stepped in and kissed Valerie full on the mouth, very different from the innocent peck on the cheek he'd just given Rosalind and then gave me.

Aaron and I wished Rosalind and John a happy new year, and out of the corner of my eye I could see Tanis still trying to get to Aaron. But Teddy intercepted her before she could reach him. To my surprise, he held her cheeks and kissed her full on the mouth, then said something to her meant for her ears only, something that made her face turn to stone. It reminded me of the kiss of death Michael gave Fredo in *The Godfather, Part II*. The scene so captivated me that I was distracted only when Marsha put her arms around me and said, "Happy New Year, Emily!"

When Teddy embraced me there were too many people around for me to ask him what was going on, so I managed a terse, "Is everything all right?" to which he merely nodded.

Once the new year had arrived we simply made merry. I unveiled the spread the caterers had made, and everyone ate. Then we danced to old-school music like we were all twenty years younger.

Valerie left just before two, saying she wanted to check on her kids.

Elias's date, Eliana, was clearly a party girl. She was on her toes most of the night, shaking her bony booty like she thought it looked good or something, and showing the guys salsa steps, obviously her specialty. Elias was pretty good at it, although he'd probably danced with her before. James Hardy picked up on the steps with remarkable ease. "He's got some nice moves," I said admiringly to Marsha as we cheered him on.

"Yes, and the dance floor isn't the *only* place where he's got good moves."

"So that's the reason for that ear-to-ear grin you've been wearing all night." I squeezed her arm affectionately, but inside I felt that familiar twisting of my gut. Everything was perfect in every other respect between Aaron and me, but sexually speaking, there'd been nothing out of the ordinary since our kitchen sexcapade of a few days ago. Was everybody but me having great sex?

Tanis didn't look too happy and actually hadn't since the clock struck twelve. I wanted to corner Teddy and ask him what he'd said to her, but my intuition warned me against spending any time alone with him, even if it was in a corner. Tanis waited like the Wicked Witch of the West, ready to pounce anytime she could to discredit me, and in the process claim the prize that was Aaron for herself. By being so upset to see Teddy, I'd just handed her what she needed to know, and who knew what she might try to do with that information.

Tanis put away quite a few drinks, and by three A.M. she was wobbly and slurring her words.

Elias announced that he and Eliana should probably start heading home. Eliana was dancing with John, which was rather a funny sight. Eliana knew her way around the dance floor, but John was best left tapping his feet in a chair. Beside them were Rosalind and Teddy.

"I don't envy you that long drive," Aaron remarked to Elias.

"Traffic shouldn't be too bad at this hour." Elias glanced over at the still dancing Eliana as she and Rosalind switched partners. "You know, I think it's really nice that so many of you have known each other such a long time."

"We went all through school together," I said.

"Thas right," Tanis added. "Iz kinda funny the way we all hooked up. Rozzalin an' John, Marsha an' James . . ."

"You and me," Wayne lovingly prompted.

"You and me," Tanis repeated, "Val'rie and nobody . . ."

I rolled my eyes, glad Valerie had already left.

"Em'ly and Teddy."

I drew in my breath, and Aaron's already small eyes got even smaller.

"Emily and *Teddy?*" Wayne repeated incredulously. He reached out for the highball glass Tanis held, which was practically empty anyway. "That's it; no more liquor for you." He chuckled. "Do you even realize what you just said?"

"Oh!" Tanis exclaimed, slapping a palm to her mouth. "I'm sorry. I guess I'm just not used to seeing Em'ly with Aaron. The las' time I saw her she wazout wit' Teddy."

"Out with Teddy?" Aaron repeated calmly, but with an unmistakable edge. "When was this?"

I laughed nervously, covering my thought of *I'm gonna kill that bitch*. "Oh, you mean this past summer, when Teddy picked me up after I had car trouble." I looked at Aaron, whose dubious expression made me nervous. "Remember, Aaron? It was a weeknight. I'd gone down to City Island to have dinner with Valerie, and my car stopped on the way home right after I got off the parkway. I told you about it the next day."

"Oh, yeah." Aaron nodded, covering nicely, but I knew he didn't recall. Because I'd never mentioned it to him. Because no such incident had ever happened. I wished Valerie were still here to back me up. I felt fairly certain I could count on Teddy to support my story as well, but he was still dancing with Eliana, unaware anything was wrong.

I could practically feel the tension in the air, and something in Aaron's eyes told me we'd be talking about this some more after the guests left. My eyes met Tanis's, and the way she unabashedly stared at me told me this was no accidental outburst. The heifer was acting, using intoxication as an excuse to rat me out and create static between Aaron and me.

Just as everyone started to relax, Tanis opened up her damn mouth again. "My fahder got sick that night, and I drove down to meet my mudder at the ER. On my way home I stopped at da store furra bottled water." She shrugged. "There was Teddy at da counter, and Em'ly in his car." Then she threw back her head and laughed. "Ya know, I never did see what Teddy bought that night. Whatever it was, it was too small to put in a bag."

At that Aaron's eyebrows shot up, and everyone else looked startled. There are two common purchases that come to most people's minds when thinking about items too small to be bagged, and the shocked expressions on everyone's faces left no secrets what they were thinking. Especially since it was pretty obvious that Teddy didn't smoke.

I frantically tried to paint another picture to replace the one everyone was clearly thinking of. "I think he said he needed some gum."

"Oh, I rememba now," Tanis said, ignoring Wayne's restrained nudge and for-her-ears only statement. "When I asked you why you were tryin' ta keep me from seeing your face when I went to my car, you said it wuz 'cause you didden wanna be gossiped about. And here I am, gossipin'." She giggled.

*And starting rumors,* I thought wryly. "What I *said* was that sometimes people make something out of nothing, and then unfounded rumors get started," I clarified, my tone more than a little sharp.

"Oh, sure, things like that happen all the time," Marsha said quickly.

"Yes, all the time," James added. "Parris Island is so full of gossip about who's doing what with whom, it's just unbelievable sometimes."

Tanis laughed loudly. "I know if *I'd* been in a man's car at ten o'clock at night and I wuzn't seeing him socially, I wouldn't want anyone ta see me, either."

This time we all heard Wayne's response to her. "Tanis, shh!"

Elias cleared his throat. "I'm going to get my coat and Eliana's. We've got a long drive home."

Wayne quickly picked up on the vibe. "Tanis, I think we should call it a night as well."

She responded with a loud burp and an embarrassed "*Excuse* me!" that made us all laugh and helped relax some of the anxiety in the air.

Marsha and James said they would go as well, and when Rosalind, John and Teddy stopped dancing, they made it unanimous. Tanis had successfully brought on the end of the party.

Aaron and I saw everyone out, but it was too cold to stand in the doorway until they all drove off, so we closed the door, even then shivering from our few minutes in the cold.

"It was a wonderful party, don't you think?" I said chattily, dreading the inevitable.

"Yeah, it was."

"I'm just going to put the leftover food away. I'll clean the kitchen and wash the dishes in the morning."

"I'll help."

I thought I'd have a few minutes to plot a strategy, but with him offering to help I had to think quickly. I was torn between raising Tanis's allegedly drunken revelations or letting the matter lie. I decided to address it; if I didn't it would suggest I had something to hide. Righteous indignation was the way to go.

"How about that Tanis?" I began as I covered dishes with plastic wrap. "Trying to make it sound like Teddy and I had something going on when we've never been nothing but friends who work in the same building."

Aaron bent to place plates in the dishwasher. "She certainly got *my* curiosity revving."

"Oh, come on," I said in my very best "don't be silly" voice.

"Emily, you never told me about having car trouble. Why didn't you call me?"

"Aaron, Valerie and I were at dinner for over two hours. It was about nine-thirty when my car died on me. I didn't want to call you that late to come to Euliss, especially if you were performing a procedure in the morning. I had Teddy's cell number in my phone; we'd exchanged numbers before we had lunch. Friday is usually just a half day for him. So it made sense for me to call him."

He walked over to me and placed his hands on my shoulders. "Look at me, Emily."

I tried not to look nervous.

Aaron spoke softly. "From the way Tanis was talking, it sounded like he was buying condoms. I know that's what everybody thought."

"That's why everyone made such a hasty exit. She really cast a pall over the mood, didn't she?"

"I don't really care how it sounded; I just care about the truth. Did you sleep with Teddy, Emily?"

There was only one answer I could possibly give. "No, Aaron." I lied, waiting for God to strike me down dead.

What I felt was Aaron's fingertips on my chin. He raised it, leaned in, and kissed me tenderly. "That's all I wanted to know. Now, let's get this food put away and go to bed."

I swallowed the breath I'd been holding so he wouldn't feel me letting it out. I felt lower than a damn limbo stick.

Wayne called me the next morning. "Is everything all right with you and Aaron?"

"Of course," I said breezily. "Why wouldn't it be?"

"Because of that ridiculous story Tanis told. She feels really bad about it."

*I'll just bet she does.* "Like you said, Wayne, it was a ridiculous story. Aaron recognized that. Besides, he remembered that night. We had a good laugh over it. So be sure to tell Tanis there's no harm done."

"Oh, that's great. I'll let her know. I'm about to go home. She wants to pick up her kids." He sounded a little sad, like he wished he could stay, but apparently Tanis didn't want her kids to know he existed. I had a feeling she planned to keep it that way.

# Chapter 24

Beverline managed to come outside as Sonny and the boys were unloading the U-Haul, under the guise of picking up the mail, which was pretty transparent, considering the mailman didn't deliver until about noon and it was barely ten A.M.

No one but me was around when she came out. When she returned, holding a sale circular I was pretty sure she'd deliberately left in the box from yesterday, the fellows had come out to bring in more boxes and furniture, with Mom looking on. I watched as my brother and nephews greeted her respectfully. Sonny even tipped the rim of his baseball cap, a gesture that reminded me of just how old he was.

Beverline nodded acknowledgment and remarked to me, "My, my, you certainly have a lot of help. All these people aren't moving in with you, are they?"

"Mrs. Wilson," Mom said in a weary tone before I could stop her, "my family has been very fortunate. We never had to live in overcrowded conditions, like many people were forced to do because most landlords charged blacks higher rents. We're not about to start living like locusts at this late date."

"I *see*."

"The great majority of black people weren't born with silver spoons in their mouths. Where did you live before you moved into Aaron's beautiful home, Mrs. Wilson?"

Beverline's mouth went flatline. "In Philadelphia," she replied haughtily.

"Funny. I could have sworn my daughter mentioned something about Camden, New Jersey."

Sonny overheard and exclaimed, "Whoa! Camden? That's a rough town. It's sure a long way from a mansion in New Rochelle. You're from Camden, ma'am?"

Beverline turned on her heel and disappeared inside the house, leaving the three of us to watch her retreating back. "What'd I say?" a bewildered Sonny asked.

Mom and I didn't bother to restrain our laughter.

Aaron invited Mom and me to join his family for dinner on Monday. Mom told me she didn't want to accept, but she didn't think it would be right not to, so we went. Shirley had made place cards for us. Aaron sat at one head of the table, and Beverline at the other. I sat on Aaron's right at the table, next to Billy. Mom sat across from me, next to Kirsten and Arden. I blessed Shirley for keeping Mom and me close to Aaron and as far from Beverline as we could get.

Beverline didn't disappoint us. "Are you getting settled?" she asked as she spooned some mashed potatoes onto her plate.

"Yes, we are," I said, trying to be amiable.

"We do hope you'll be comfortable," Aaron said. "If there's anything you need, just holler."

"I hope the apartment isn't too small for you," Beverline added. "It is, after all, the servants' quarters."

Arden giggled, while Aaron, his gaze hardened, said, "It's also referred to as a guesthouse, Beverline, and that's the description I want used."

After that, Mom refused to go back, even though Aaron invited us for dinner at least once a week. I had no problem telling him that Mom simply couldn't deal with Beverline's attempts at putting us down.

"I'm sorry, Emily. I've talked to her about it. I can't say I blame your mother for not wanting to join us. Beverline is deliberately being difficult."

"Personally, I think it's a lost cause."

"I'm still hoping there's a chance for the girls."

I grunted. I didn't see how.

We settled into our new home in the next weeks. Mom found a church, and I attended services with her the first time she went and then occasionally afterward.

My living so close to Aaron made both of us reluctant to go to the motel on the weekends, so we worked out a system. After we'd come back from wherever we'd been for the night, we'd go to the guesthouse and have a nightcap, chat, and ultimately, after Mom had fallen asleep, we'd neck. He'd go home, then call me when the coast was clear, and I'd dash in through the side door off the laundry room and up the back stairs to his bedroom. We'd fall out laughing—quietly, of course—at having pulled a fast one, and then we'd spend the night together. I'd get up at seven and leave the same way I'd come before anyone else woke up. Making like a tiptoe burglar wasn't the most satisfying way to have a love life, and of course the sex itself wasn't overly satisfying either, but I told myself to concentrate on how good life was. If it wasn't for Aaron, Mom and I wouldn't have a place to live. And he seemed satisfied. He had a healthy sexual appetite. If only he realized how much he was missing.

At Aaron's urging I took to going to The Big House, as Mom and I dubbed it, nightly during the week to have a drink and some conversation with Aaron. "I want Kirsten and Arden to get used to you being around, maybe get to know you better," he'd said. "If they get to know you on their own, they won't be so influenced by what their grandmother says."

I still felt more at home chatting with Shirley in the kitchen than I did trying to make conversation with Aaron's daughters. I was sliding rings on the cloth napkins as she cooked a roast for dinner one Thursday night when the phone rang. Shirley answered it in her usual professional manner. "Yes, Doctor," she said. "Everything's almost ready. And Emily is here." A pause. "Yes, she's in her room."

Obviously that part wasn't about me. I watched as Shirley pressed a button on the intercom. "Kirsten, your daddy wants to talk to you."

I felt a twinge of jealousy, which I immediately told myself was wrong. Aaron had every right to want to speak with his daughter.

A few minutes later a sullen-looking Kirsten entered the kitchen and handed me the receiver to her cordless phone. "Daddy wants to talk to you."

I took it, wondering why she looked so upset. "Hi, Aaron! What's up?"

"Hi," Aaron said. "I just wanted to let you know I'm going to be late tonight. I'm at the Rye Town Hilton. There's a demonstration of a new scan, and I decided at the last minute to check it out. Between the demonstration, the questions, and all the networking going on here, I probably won't get out of here for another hour. They've got food and drinks here, so y'all go ahead and eat. Don't worry about holding dinner for me."

"Oh! All right." I was wondering how I could get out of dinner with the family, since Aaron wouldn't be there. "Uh, Kirsten looks very unhappy about you being late."

"That's because I promised her I'd take her out for a driving lesson. Like I said, this came up at the last minute. She might sulk for a while, but she'll live."

"All right." Then I heard him talking to someone in the background. "Tell Elias I said hello."

"That wasn't Elias. That was your old friend Shelly."

I frowned. I had no friends named Shelly. The only one I knew was . . . "Shelly Muldoon?"

"Yeah. She's giving the demonstration."

"Oh." Suddenly I remembered Teddy telling me that Shelly sold medical equipment. "I wouldn't exactly call her a friend, Aaron. She's just someone I went to school with."

"Okay. Listen, they're about to start. I'll see you when I get home, huh?"

"Yes. Bye."

I clicked the OFF button on the phone. "Shirley, Aaron says not to hold dinner for him. He's at a demonstration in Rye."

"All right. Will you be staying for dinner?"

I sighed. Shirley was aware of the tension that existed between Beverline and myself. "I'll let you know." I had an idea that might make for warmer relations between myself and Aaron's daughters.

I found Kirsten in the family room, her arms crossed stiffly over her chest and her lower lip slightly protruding.

I handed her the receiver. "Your dad won't be able to take you out for your driving lesson, since it'll probably be dark by the time he gets home. I can understand why you look so blue."

I was being kind in my choice of words. Between her arms and her lip she looked like a spoiled brat. Still, I remembered how it felt to be sixteen and have your learner's permit. At that age I'd wanted to practice driving at every opportunity, too.

"Yeah," she said. "I don't know why he had to go to that dumb seminar."

"Well, I have to go to Walgreen's to pick up some things for my mother. Would you like to be my chauffeur?"

She brightened cautiously. "Really, Emily?"

"Sure. You do promise not to total my car, right?" I added with a chuckle. "And not kill me."

Her back straightened as she sat up expectantly. "Neither of you will get a scratch. When will we go?"

"I think we should go now. I want to be back before the sun even starts to set."

Kirsten was on her feet in a second. "Let's go!"

"Well, I have to get my purse, and so should you. Having your learner's permit with you is the only way you can prove you're authorized to drive, remember?" I watched as she made a run for the stairs, taking them two at a time in her youthful exuberance.

I started to head for the back door when I heard voices and recognized Arden's voice. "What are you in such a tearing hurry for?"

"Emily says I can drive her to the store so I can get some practice in, since Daddy's going to be late tonight."

"Ooh, can I come?"

"Sure, but you'd better hurry up. We're leaving *right now*."

I quickly headed for the guesthouse, not wanting Kirsten to have to wait for me and possibly get jumpy. A nervous driver could be hazardous to the health of my car.

Both girls stood by my car in the driveway when I emerged from the guesthouse with my purse and keys, and to my surprise, so was Beverline.

*What does* she *want?*

She walked forward to meet me as I approached. "I know Kirsten's excited," she began, speaking in a low voice, "but are you sure this is a good idea, Emily? She's not even licensed yet."

"It's not like she asked me for the keys, Mrs. Wilson," I pointed out. "I'm going to be sitting right beside her in the passenger seat, supervising every move she makes. That's how she'll learn."

"It's just that Aaron was very stern with her and told her she's not to operate a vehicle in which anyone outside the family is a passenger."

I got it now. Beverline wanted to drive home the point that I was an outsider.

"I think that's a very good rule," I said. I wasn't about to dispute Aaron's word. Wouldn't Beverline just love to tell him how I'd gone against the rules he'd set for his children.

"But Kirsten has promised not to damage my car or cause any injuries to me, so I'm sure it'll be okay."

She didn't even crack a smile. "That's precisely Aaron's concern. Lawsuits."

"Mrs. Wilson," I said, my patience gone, "I'm not going to sue, so you can stop worrying."

Kirsten called out just in time. "C'mon, Grandma. Can't you talk with Emily later?"

I brushed past Beverline, saying over my shoulder, "Excuse me, I've got an impatient driver waiting."

During our outing I gave Kirsten a few tips, like, "Try to hug the curb closer," when she made a wide right turn, and "Don't put on your blinker quite so soon before your turn. A half block is sufficient." Arden sat transfixed in the backseat, as if preparing for her own lessons, which wouldn't be for another three years.

When Kirsten pulled up into the driveway she said, "Thanks a lot, Emily. You're . . . you're almost as good a teacher as Daddy."

"What about your grandma?"

Kirsten made a face. "Grandma hollers at me. That's why I stopped going out with her."

"Emily, are you going to have dinner with us?" Arden asked shyly when we got out of the car.

I couldn't tell if she really wanted me to join them or if she was just being polite. At any rate, I felt I'd been around enough for the day, and I didn't feel like hearing any of Beverline's negative comments about my allowing Kirsten to drive. "I think I'll eat with my mother tonight," I said. "I'll be over later, after your father gets home."

It didn't come as a surprise to me when Kirsten knocked on the guesthouse door the next afternoon, just as Mom and I were sitting down to dinner. "Hi, Emily!"

"Well, hello there." I waited expectantly.

Kirsten looked almost embarrassed, as she should have, if she was about to say what I thought she would. "Um . . . Daddy's home, but he's kinda tired tonight. I was wondering if you'd take me driving again."

"That's fine with me as long as it's okay with your father. But Mom and I are about to have dinner."

"We're going to eat in a few minutes, too. Can I come back when I'm done?"

"That'll work."

Kirsten turned to go, then turned around. "Thanks a lot, Emily."

I smiled as I closed the door. Could it be I was winning her over? Or would she forget about my help once she got her driver's license?

I went to The Big House with Kirsten after our spin. Aaron was sitting in his office, reviewing some notes. He smiled at me and removed his reading glasses when I tapped on the door, then came around from the back of the desk. "You look as good as a chocolate sundae," he said as his arms went around me.

I hadn't expected this action. The door to his office was open, and Aaron rarely indulged in public displays of affection. I closed my eyes and enjoyed the moment.

"I'm glad you came over early. I'm going to go upstairs to bed in a few minutes," he said as we walked across the hall to the living room, arms around each other.

"I guess you're tired from last night."

"Yeah, it was a long day. But it was worth it. That scanner is fantastic." He bent to open the top of the round globe, which revealed wine and liquor bottles and glassware. He poured Sauvignon Blanc for me and a Johnnie Walker for himself, then excused himself to get some water and ice cubes for his drink.

When he returned he rejoined me on the couch. "I want to thank you for taking Kirsten out for driving practice these last two nights."

"She mentioned you were tired. Are you sure you didn't steer her in my direction tonight?"

"Trust me, I'm really bushed. But I did think it would be a good opportunity for you two to bond. And Arden, too, since she wants to do everything her sister does." He sipped his drink, then looked at Diana's portrait, which faced us. "You know, I think I'm going to move that picture to the girls' room this weekend."

"Lots of luck with *that* move. You know it won't go over big with Beverline."

I was just falling asleep when the phone rang. I frantically groped for the extension on the end table, hoping the ringing wouldn't wake Mom up, since she'd always had difficulty staying asleep once she got there.

It was my nephew Michael. He'd cut his ankle on the bottom edge of the door to the terrace of his studio apartment. "Emmie, I really don't want to go to the ER," he said. "My insurance charges a high co-pay for ER visits, probably because people use them as primary doctors. But it's bleeding a lot. Is there any way you can come and look at it? I'll give you forty bucks."

I heard the anxiety in his voice. "I'll be there in about a half hour."

Once I was at Michael's I examined the cut. "It's pretty deep."

"Am I gonna need stitches?"

"It could probably stand to be sutured, but I wouldn't recommend it. The bottom of that door is probably filthy. Suturing it will only seal in the dirt, and that might lead to infection later on. I'm going to irrigate it with saline and bandage it for you."

"Um . . . I don't have any saline, Emmie." My sister's and my brother's older children simply called me by my first name, since I wasn't all that much older than they were.

"That's all right. I brought some with me. Bandages, too. When's the last time you had a tetanus shot?"

"I had a booster about two years ago." Michael chuckled. "Don't tell me you brought that along, too?"

I knew his joking was an effort to cover his obvious fear of just a few minutes before. I was glad to see he was feeling better. Even grown-ups got scared sometimes, and as he said, there'd been a lot of blood.

"I think you'll be fine," I said as I taped the bandage in place over the cleaned-out wound. "Just make sure to watch out for any of those signs I told you about. And try to stay off it. At least tomorrow's Friday. Take the day off if you can."

He kissed me as he pressed two twenties in my palm. "Thanks a lot, Emmie. You're a lifesaver."

"So, where'd you rush off to last night?" Aaron asked.

I put down my fork and stared at him. The light tone he used did nothing to disguise the fact that he was prying. And, since I hadn't yet mentioned to him my nephew's emergency, that meant he'd been spying on me. "You keeping tabs on me or something?"

"No, of course not. I just wanted to make sure everything was okay, especially with your mother."

"Aaron, I would have called you if there'd been any type of emergency with my mother. I mean, you are a doctor." I tried to hide my annoyance. We were in a public place, a local seafood restaurant. I fought back the urge to tell him that I'd gone out and made forty dollars and see how'd he react. "It just so happens my nephew in Euliss cut his ankle on his terrace door. It was a deep cut, and there was a lot of blood. He wanted to avoid an ER visit, so he called me." I stopped to take a deep breath. "Now, would you like to tell me how you knew I'd gone out, Mr. I'm Going Upstairs to Bed Now?"

He appeared speechless for a few moments. "Wow."

"Wow, right. I'm very upset, Aaron." It wasn't like him to

monitor my movements. I remembered that I'd worried about that momentarily as I was considering his offer for Mom and me to rent his guesthouse. Granted, that was because I was concerned with how I'd continue to see Teddy, an activity I'd since abandoned like a sinking ship. But I still didn't like it. Aaron and I were supposed to be in love. That meant he wasn't supposed to check up on me.

"Calm down. I'd woken up and decided to put on the ten o'clock news when I saw headlights in the driveway. I got up and saw you pulling out." He paused. "You know, Emily, I don't ever want you to hesitate to call me if you need my help for anything, no matter what time it is, no matter where you are."

Maybe that was supposed to be reassuring, but to me he was recalling the incident—okay, the *fabricated* incident—with Teddy that Tanis so sneakily brought up New Year's Eve. I'd thought I'd reassured Aaron when I'd looked him dead in the eye and lied to him about being involved with Teddy, but had he been thinking about that all these months? Did he lie awake last night waiting to see what time I came home and wondering if I'd gone to Euliss to meet Teddy because of lingering doubts?

Damn Tanis.

"Aaron, I want to go home," I said.

"Emily, I think you're over—"

I tossed my cloth napkin onto the table. "Maybe it's best that you stay. I'll get a cab." I grabbed my purse and left.

# Chapter 25

I still steamed as I unlocked the door to the guesthouse. I hadn't had to answer to anyone for anything I'd done for many years. I'd be damned if I'd begin now. Who was Aaron to start acting like he was my father? Was he confusing me with Kirsten or Arden? I was forty-three years old, not some damn teenager.

I heard the sound of voices as soon as I swung open the door, voices that sounded too real to be coming from the television set. The scent of collard greens filled the air. Perhaps Mom was contributing a dish for a church potluck or something.

The voices came from the kitchen. I closed the door quietly and headed in that direction, stopping in my tracks at the sight of my mother wearing an apron and one of her prettiest blouses—the kind she took off immediately after returning home—standing over a pot, a tall, heavyset gentleman spoon-feeding her. Mom was giggling like a fourteen-year-old. And neither of them even noticed me.

I quickly stepped back into the living room, then said loudly, "Mom, I'm home!"

Seconds later she appeared in the doorway, her guest close behind. "Oh, hello, Emily. I wasn't expecting you."

"I know. Aaron and I had a fight. There didn't seem much point in continuing the evening." I turned my gaze on her companion. "I didn't know you were having company," I stated innocently, trying not to smile at Mom's visible nervousness, the way she kept rubbing her palms up and down a five-inch span of her thighs.

"Emily, this is Henry Johnson. Henry, this is my daughter Emily."

We met each other halfway, our arms extended. Henry Johnson was a big bear of a man who dwarfed my mother. He'd lost most of his white hair, but the wide sideburns and big belly reminded me of Santa Claus. "Nice to meet you, Mr. Johnson."

"Likewise, Emily. Your mother's told me quite a bit about you."

I didn't point out the obvious, that she hadn't said a word about him. Instead, I sniffed the leafy pork tinted air. "Are you two cooking?"

"Yes," Mom said, a little louder than necessary. "You see, Henry and I met at church, and one day we were discussing cooking. Henry said he makes the best collards in New Rochelle, and I told him I make the best collards in Euliss, and well . . . we thought it would be fun to have sort of a cook-off."

"Actually, Emily, now that you're here you can serve as a judge," Henry suggested.

I still couldn't believe it. My nearly eighty-year-old mother had a gentleman friend? A friend she'd invited over when she thought I'd be gone for the evening? That sounded like something I would have done when I was seventeen. Had we changed places? "Uh . . . sure."

Mom retreated back into the kitchen, with Henry following. "Now, Ruby, she can't see which greens came out of which pot, or she'll know which ones are yours."

"All right. I'll just spoon some from each into a bowl." Mom turned to me. "Emily, you go sit in the living room so you can't see."

When we saw each other in the kitchen Sunday morning, Mom wore an expression of a kid who'd been caught munching on potato chips when she'd been told not to snack before dinner. "Well, what'd you think of Henry?"

"He seemed very nice. But why didn't you tell me you had a date?"

"It wasn't a *date*, Emmie. We were cooking, that's all. And I'm still mad at you for saying his greens were better than mine."

I knew she'd have something to say about that. "I can't help it, Mom. Those were the best greens I've ever tasted in my life. What *does* he put in them?"

"He won't tell me," she said, obviously sulking. Then she changed the subject. "So what happened with you and Aaron?"

My jaws immediately tightened as I bit into my English muffin. "Oh, he made me so *mad!*" I recounted the events of the previous evening.

Mom listened intently. "Emmie, I know you treasure your independence, but do you think you might have overreacted a bit?"

"No, I don't. I know cheating is a serious offense, Mom." My ex-husband's duplicity still hurt, even after all these years. "But if I let him off the hook too easily he'd think he could start questioning me at any time. And I can't have that."

Teddy showed up at the Norman medical offices the next morning. "It's April, Emily, and I've seen you maybe five times since New Year's, with not many more words than that be-tween us in all that time. How about lunch today?"

"Sure," I said without hesitation. It was true that I'd al-ways managed to be in a rush to get somewhere whenever we saw each other in the building or parking lot. He brought back too many memories of lustful nights of abandon so dif-ferent from the orderly sex Aaron and I had, and I still didn't trust myself around him. But it was time to stop ducking him. He deserved better.

The timing of his invitation had an undeniable irony to it. I had used the excuse of being on the outs with Aaron for sleeping with Teddy, and Aaron and I had just had our first real fight last night. Regardless of my dissatisfaction with Aaron's performance in the bedroom, my dalliance with Teddy had come dangerously close to ending it all, and thanks to Tanis, the seeds of doubt had been planted in Aaron's head. I knew myself well enough to know I wasn't going to chance that happening again. I was a woman in love, even if I was still pissed off at the object of my affection at the moment . . . and at myself for previously being unable to stay out of Teddy's bed. I'd known Teddy most of my life. The sexual side of our relationship was behind us. We were too much alike to ever be able to carry off a romantic relationship, but we were still friends, and hopefully would always be.

We went to the café on the street level. We'd barely put in our orders when Wayne came in, wearing his work uniform. We waved him over. The look of surprise on his face at seeing us together told me that he, too, recalled Tanis's so-called drunken outbursts of nearly four months ago.

"What a coincidence," I said. "This is the first time Teddy and I have spent any time together all year, and who do we see but you, Wayne."

"Yeah, how 'bout that. I had a doctor's appointment to get my blood pressure checked. I figured I'd pick up one of their steak sandwiches and take it back to work with me." He flagged a waitress and placed his take-out order. "I'll be sitting here with my friends. Can you bring it here when it's ready?"

"Certainly, sir."

"So," Teddy said after the waitress left, "what's new with you, Wayne? Are you still seeing Tanis?"

I averted my eyes. I knew from Rosalind, who talked to Tanis regularly, that Tanis was no longer seeing Wayne. According to Rosalind, Tanis had decided Wayne was getting too serious and she'd dumped him. She'd since found a new boy toy, a twenty-nine-year-old technician who worked on her show.

"No, not for a while now," Wayne was saying. "Not since the middle of January. You know, ever since I saw Tanis at Rosalind's dinner party last spring I was just . . ." his voice trailed off as he remembered with a rueful little smile.

"Yeah, I know *that* feeling," Teddy said, his eyes on me.

I frantically shook my head, not wanting Wayne to notice.

Wayne grunted. "We started seeing each other the night of our class reunion. But it didn't take too long before I started to notice, shall we say, flaws in her personality. For one, she always had an excuse to keep from introducing me to her kids. She also seemed a little inconsiderate. I mean, she knows I work for Con Ed. She wanted to go out to dinner two or three times a week, and I'm not talking Applebee's, either." He shook his head. "I must have put over a thousand dollars on my Visa card. But when I figured out that she really wanted some other dude, I let her go."

I blinked. "Wayne, are you saying you broke it off?"

"Yeah. A man can take only so much. I felt like shit—excuse my French, Emily—when I realized she was just with me until she could get who she really wanted. And that's someone who can afford to drop a couple of hundred dollars a week on dinner." He paused. "Maybe I shouldn't tell you this, Emily, but it's Aaron."

I shrugged. "She's never made a secret of wanting him, ever since Rosalind's dinner party when she announced she and her husband were divorcing. And then there was her 'accidental' "—I held up my hands and made quotation marks with my index fingers—"outburst New Year's Eve." I didn't add that that outburst was presently causing static between Aaron and me.

"What outburst?" Teddy wanted to know.

"That's right, you were dancing with Elias's date," Wayne said. "We were talking about how so many of us at the party had known each other since childhood, and how neat it was that we'd formed couples as adults. Tanis had been drinking almost nonstop, and she blurted out that you and Emily were a couple, Teddy."

"Son of a—"

"When I asked what she meant by that, she said she'd seen Emily out with you last summer at a convenience store in Euliss. It sounded kind of convoluted. She said something about Emily trying to hide from her, and then she said that whatever you'd bought, Teddy, it was too small to go into a bag."

"She said *that?*"

"I told her you stopped to get some gum," I said quickly.

"I got her out of there quick," Wayne said, "but I'm afraid she left a vivid impression on everyone's mind on what might have happened that night."

"Well, as I told you New Year's Day, Wayne, there was no harm done," I said. "Aaron said he remembered my telling him about my car breaking down and how I'd called Teddy to bring me home."

"Tanis said she felt awful about it when she woke up, and I believed her, but I've since learned what a little schemer she can be," Wayne continued. "You know, I'm tired of all the plots black women have run on me. I think I might find me a white girl."

I lowered my chin to my chest. "I know how Tanis can be, but don't judge all black women by her." I must say I was getting a bit tired of seeing black women portrayed by black men as evil, scheming creatures.

"First there was Tracy, getting pregnant on me like that."

I raised an eyebrow. "And she did this by herself?"

"No, but she took advantage of me one morning, and I ended up operating without my gloves. She knew exactly what she was doing. Then she got an attitude when I told her I wasn't marrying her. Hell, I didn't even *like* her all that much. I sure as hell didn't want to get stuck with her forever. I think part of the reason she wanted to hold on to me was because I had a steady job. I'm sorry to say, Emily, that it's been that way for me in every relationship I've had except with my ex-wife—and that relationship had a *different* set of problems. I'm tired of being viewed as a security blanket."

Maybe he had a point. I knew from myself and my friends that the older we got and still remained single, the more fearful we tended to become, and one had to work at not appearing desperate. Nonetheless, hearing it expressed made me cranky. I was tired of seeing good black men run to the other side. Who the hell were black women like my friends supposed to hook up with? In my annoyance I glared at Wayne. *At least you've got something that makes you desirable to women. Your looks alone sure as hell aren't going to attract anybody.*

"I don't know, Wayne," Teddy said. "White women can be just as bad. I don't think it's a color thing as much as it's just a female thing."

The waitress brought our food and handed Wayne a bag and a check. "I'm gonna pay for this and get going," he said. "It's good to see you both. Take care."

"At least he found out about Tanis in time," I said to Teddy after Wayne had gone.

"That bitch. I still can't believe I fell for her telling me that you knew she was inviting me to your party. I told her when the clock struck twelve that she'd better not be up to anything to try to make trouble for you or else I'd see she regretted it."

"Teddy! You *threatened* her?"

"Damn right. I knew she was up to something. I guess she didn't believe me."

"She knows you wouldn't do her any harm. But it doesn't really matter now, Teddy. Wayne dumped her—" I believed his version of the breakup more than I believed the one Tanis had told Rosalind—"and she hasn't been heard from since Aaron backed me up at the party."

"Yeah, I guess."

As Teddy and I ate, I inquired innocently, "So you've revised your opinion of black women as being gold diggers?"

He rolled his eyes. "Why am I not surprised that you still remembered that? All right, you got me. I told you that I'd have to cut back on my social activities once my rent went up."

"And that didn't sit too well with the woman you were seeing."

"No. I bought a co-op on Maynard Street. I decided that if I was going to pay all that rent I might as well get some equity in something."

"Congratulations, Teddy!"

"Thanks. I just moved a month ago. It's a nice place. Garden style, with a big patio and views of the river. It's got hardwood floors and granite countertops in the kitchen, and there's a pool and a gym."

"It sounds wonderful."

"I'm pretty happy with it. The previous owner made some nice improvements, like mirrors on the bedroom closet doors and a step-in shower with glass door instead of a bathtub. But the lady I was seeing already had a house that went to her in her divorce settlement. To her, buying a one-bedroom apartment is no big deal. She just wants a man who'll spend money on her."

I hesitated, not sure if I should ask what I wanted to know. "Teddy, . . . it was Shelly, wasn't it?"

The startled look on his face made confirmation unnecessary. "How did you know?"

"Because I saw the two of you in the parking lot here last year. I guess I wasn't the only one who was seeing someone else simultaneously, huh?"

"I told her she needs to take up with one of those doctors she comes in contact with. She's a leading salesperson at her company. Easily makes six figures." He smiled. "So how have things been going for you these past months? How do you like living on Aaron's property?"

"It's not bad, but it's not perfect, either."

*   *   *

Teddy was a perfect gentleman at lunch, making only one reference to our affair. "I missed you," he said as we were pulling bills from our respective wallets to pay the check. "But you seem happy, and I'm not going to interfere with that. I want you to be happy, Emily." He sounded sincere, and I believed he really meant it.

It was nice to be cared about.

I looked at Arden's neat cornrows quizzically as she got out of the backseat after tagging along on Kirsten's driving practice, which we now did once or twice a week, with me staying for dinner afterward. "Your hair wasn't like that yesterday, was it?"

She giggled. "No, a friend of mine did it at school today at lunchtime."

"Oh. Well, it looks very nice."

"You really like it, Emily?" she said, obviously pleased.

"Yes, I do. Do you plan on keeping it in long?"

"That's going to depend," Kirsten said a tad ominously as we walked into the house.

I thought I might be missing something, or walking into a trap, but I asked anyway. "Depends upon what?"

Before either girl could answer, Beverline appeared. "Arden? Is that you?"

"Hi, Grandma!" Arden patted her hair. "I had my hair braided at school today."

"So I see."

Had I imagined it, or was there disapproval in Beverline's tone?

"Emily just told me how nice it looks," Arden said proudly.

I understood what was going on here even before Beverline gave me a stare that could put out a forest fire. "Oh, she did?"

"I seem to have stumbled into the middle of a family disagreement," I said quickly. "Arden, maybe it's best that we forget about what I said."

"Arden is well aware of my feelings about those hairstyles," Beverline said in her snootiest tone. "Young lady, I want you to know that it doesn't matter in the least to me whose opinion you solicit. *I'm* your grandmother. And no grandchild of mine is going to walk around looking like . . . a field hand."

Every fiber of my being wanted to jump to Arden's defense. Even though I didn't appreciate her setting me up, I also felt that Beverline was overreacting to a ridiculous extent. Arden's hair couldn't have been braided neater. Her parts were straight and even, and the coated rubber bands that kept her hair from unraveling were all black and blended nicely with her hair.

Beverline brushed past us in a manner that suggested she wanted nothing more to do with Arden until she took out her braids.

I expected to see a chastened Arden come to the dinner table with her hair brushed out. I was surprised when, in an obvious show of defiance, she appeared with her hair unchanged. Aaron, unaware of the tension between his daughter and mother-in-law, remarked, "Arden, you got your hair braided."

"Yes. Do you like it, Daddy?"

I averted my eyes downward. Sometimes it was nice to know that even parents got used as pawns.

Beverline cut off Aaron's response. "I was telling Arden that no granddaughter of mine would wear her hair that way."

Aaron's eyes narrowed. "Beverline, stop acting like Mrs. Astor."

She recoiled as if Aaron had slapped her.

I silently told myself over and over that the best thing I could do was stay out of their business, but I heard myself speaking, "So Aaron, what do you think of Arden's hair?"

"I think it looks really cute," he said without hesitation. "Whoever did it did a good job."

"I'm surprised there's anyone at that school who even knows how to braid *that way*," Beverline said. She pronounced "that way" like she was talking about something illegal, like hot-wiring a car. "Who did it, Arden?" she demanded.

I couldn't help thinking that Beverline's agitation was more in keeping with the reaction of a parent upon learning her unmarried daughter was pregnant.

Aaron ignored her, instead asking me, "Do you like it, Emily?"

"Yes, I do. Cornrows are always so nice and neat."

"Can I keep them in, then?" Arden asked Aaron, hope in her eyes.

"It'll probably be just a few days before strands start coming loose, but it's all right with me if you keep them." His eyes on Beverline, he added, "Don't worry about your grandmother. She and I will talk after dinner."

"Thank you, Daddy." Arden gave me a shy smile. "Thank you, too, Emily."

"You asked me if I liked them," I explained, "and I do, so I told you as much. Just for future reference, I won't lie to either of you girls, so you might not want to ask for my opinion unless you really, really want to know the answer."

"Thanks for sticking up for Arden," Aaron said to me later, while we enjoyed our after-dinner cocktails—actually wine for me—in the living room.

"It's like I said. If I didn't like the way her hair looked, I would have said so." My voice had a deliberate coolness to it.

He reached for my hand. "I have to ask you, Emily, are we all right?"

I sighed. By nature I disliked confrontations, but we had to talk this out. "Aaron, if you and I are going to work, you have to trust me. I'm not sure you do."

"Of course I do. I never said I didn't trust you, Emily."

"No, but can you honestly tell me you didn't think about what Tanis said on New Year's?"

"All right, I did, but just for a second. Come on, Emily. Maybe I came off sounding like a jerk when I asked for an explanation, but you told me what happened, and that ends it. We can't let this interfere with what we have. Especially not now that the girls are really warming up to you." He held my gaze. "I love you, Emily."

How could I resist? "I love you, too."

He leaned in for a kiss, which made me forget about everything else.

Aaron might be a bore in the bedroom, but the man could kiss me senseless.

# Chapter 26

I just about choked on the tapioca balls on the bottom of my iced tea at the Asian restaurant when I saw the glistening diamond in the box Aaron had just presented to me. It brought tears to my eyes. "Aaron . . . I don't know what to say."

"You could say yes."

I laughed nervously. For the first time I understood the meaning of the clichéd expression, "This is so sudden!" But it truly was.

Aaron and I had been getting along great, and he never failed to defend me against Beverline's criticisms, which had diminished in recent weeks. A fed-up Aaron had told her that if she couldn't be pleasant to my mother and me, she would have to go. Of course, she still resented my presence, although Kirsten and Arden had lightened up considerably, and Billy was a doll, like always.

Mom was doing well also, having adjusted completely to our new home. I giggled at the crazy thought that if Aaron and I did get married, both Mom and I could move into the house and put Beverline in the guesthouse. Or, as she liked to think of it, "the servants' quarters."

"What's so funny?"

"Nothing really. Just a nervous reaction," I answered

semihonestly. "I've got to tell you, Aaron, I really didn't expect this."

"Emily, I get the distinct impression that you're avoiding giving me an answer."

He was right, of course. Our relationship had actually headed down that primrose path my mother so badly wanted it to, but I knew that sex with little to no spontaneity for the rest of my life would be a hard sell. Yes, I'd get to live in a luxurious house and have maid service, take fabulous vacations and buy pretty much whatever I wanted, but would that really be enough to fill that void?

"I don't want to pressure you," he continued. "But everything's been going so well the last couple of months, since you and your mother moved into the guesthouse. We're in love, and I don't want it to ever end. I want you close to me always."

I caught my breath. Aaron spoke so simply, yet eloquently. His words came from the heart. He spoke the truth. I did love him, and he loved me. The sex wasn't quite there, and I had to consider that it might not ever be. In nearly a year's time we'd made love in two positions, with just two out-of-the-ordinary sessions. But I did love him; I truly did. I reminded myself that it was up to me to get more juice in our sex life. In the meantime, in asking me to marry him, Aaron was practically placing a kingdom at my feet. I'd be crazy to turn it down.

My lips curled up in a smile. "The answer," I said softly, "is yes."

The next thing I knew we were kissing, and then I heard the sound of applause from the other restaurant patrons. We had an audience.

He slipped the ring on my finger. "I took a guess about the size." He twirled it, and it was a nice fit, not too snug. "Looks like I was right on the money."

"Oh, Aaron, it's a beautiful ring."

"If you'd like something different we can always exchange it."

"No, it's perfect." The ring, a gleaming solitaire, made my fingers look long and tapering and my entire hand look pretty . . . as well as in need of a manicure. "My mother's crazy about you, so I know she'll be thrilled. But what about your family? Things have gotten better between Kirsten and Arden and me, and of course I've never had any problems with Billy, but even he might feel differently when he learns we're getting married. And we both know how Beverline will feel."

He delivered his words with steely determination. "I love my children, Emily, and Beverline held us together during a very difficult time for our family, but none of them has the right to determine what I do with my life."

I appreciated his firmness, but I was worried just the same. "You can't blame me for being a little concerned, Aaron. I mean, although Kirsten and Arden and I have been getting along a little better these days, a shock like this is likely to wipe out all that progress. Do they have any idea you were going to propose to me?"

"None. I figured it would be best if you and I told them together. Why don't we all have dinner Friday night? I'll get Shirley to fix something special. I'd like your mother to join us as well. But I have to ask that she not give anything away before that."

That wasn't the same as asking me not to tell her the news. How sweet of Aaron not to ask me to keep my big news away from Mom. No wonder I was so crazy about him.

A little voice spoke to me. *Emily, you just agreed to marry the man. You have to be in love with him, not just crazy about him, and if you're not, you need to give him his ring back.*

My inner voice started having a conversation with itself, right there in the restaurant.

*It'll be fine. I do love him . . . a little bit. The rest will come*
*in time. You wait and see.*
*Yeah, fool yourself. But you can't fool me.*

My mother grabbed my wrist. "Emily! Oh, my goodness.
Is that a diamond?"

"Ouch! Lighten up on your grip, will you, Mom?" I doubted
police handcuffs hurt that much. "Yes, Aaron gave it to me
last night."

"You did it!" Mom cried out joyously. "You're going to be
Mrs. Aaron Merritt. Oh, I'm so happy." Her voice cracked a
little, and she quickly wiped the outer corners of her eyes
with her fingers.

"Mom, try to control yourself."

"Oh, you don't know how I prayed this would happen.
Your father would be so happy."

I had to admit, I felt a little giddy myself.

"I always knew you'd get married again one day," Mom
said. "But I had no idea it would be to someone as good as
Aaron. Now, don't misunderstand me. . . ."

I chuckled. This was the part where Mom was going to say
that his being a doctor didn't have anything to do with it,
that she would love him equally as much had he been a bus
driver, just because he made me happy. Such a line of shit.

"Now, the fact that he's a rich, successful doctor is more of
a bonus. He's still a good catch for you, Emily, even if he dug
ditches for a living, because he treats you well."

I couldn't dispute that, but she had to be kidding with that
example. What mother in her right mind wouldn't object to
her daughter marrying a ditchdigger?

"Ooh, and just wait til I tell Mavis. She'll turn green as a
peapod."

"Mom, you can't do that. Aaron's kids don't even know
about it yet. This is really important, okay? You can't tell
anyone until after his family knows."

"Of course, dear. I won't do anything to give it away. But when do you plan on telling them?"

"We're having dinner over there tomorrow night."

"So Beverline doesn't know yet, either."

"No."

Mom smiled in a manner that suggested she should be holding a pitchfork in one hand. "Oh, I wish I could save the expression on her face when she finds out for posterity. Wouldn't it be great if she picked up and left rather than live there with you, the mistress of the house?"

"It would be wonderful, but I think she'd rather stay on and stay in my hair."

I was careful to remove my ring before leaving the house the next morning. I hated to put it away, but it really wouldn't be fair for anyone at work or any of my friends to learn about my engagement before Aaron's family knew about it. As Mom said, I'd be mistress of the house.

That gave me an idea. If I was going to be the lady of the house, I might as well claim my position now.

Friday morning I dialed Aaron's home to put my plan in motion. I hoped Shirley would answer. I didn't want to speak with Beverline.

"Good morning; Merritt residence."

"Hello . . . Shirley?"

"Yes."

"This is Emily."

"Hello, Emily. How are you this morning?"

"I'm good. I suppose Dr. Merritt has told you my mother and I are coming for dinner tonight."

"Yes, he did. I just made up place cards, as a matter of fact. I always do them when the doctor has extra guests for dinner."

I laughed nervously. "That's exactly why I was calling. I

know this is going to sound like a strange question, but where do you plan to have me sit?"

"I put you to the right of the doctor, like I usually do. Is that all right?"

"Actually, I'd like you to put me at the opposite head of the table."

Shirley's uncertainty came through as loud as a sonic boom. "That's where Mrs. Wilson usually sits."

"Go ahead and place *her* on Aaron's right. And I'd like my mother to be on my left. Billy can be between my mother and his grandmother. And of course, Kirsten and Arden will sit next to each other on the other side."

Shirley didn't respond, and I realized she was concerned about taking orders from me. "If you're worried about any repercussions, don't be. I'll clear it with the doctor."

"I'd appreciate that, Emily."

"I know this seems a little strange to you, but you'll understand after dinner."

"Oh!" she exclaimed, sounding as if she'd put two and two together and gotten an engagement. "Very well, Emily. Please let me know if there's anything else I can do."

Already she sounded as if she was ready to take instructions from me. It felt rather good.

I reached Aaron afterward and told him about my request. In the few minutes in between conversations I became nervous. Had I really done the right thing, or was I being too eager to move into my new role?

Aaron was busy, as usual, but he did take time to listen to my concern. "Sure, I don't have a problem. It'll probably be a little difficult for Beverline, but she's going to have to get used to it sooner or later . . . so why not sooner?"

I sighed in relief.

When we went to sit at the table, Aaron escorted Beverline, leading her directly to her new position.

"What's this?" I heard her say as I led Mom to her seat. "I don't normally—Aaron, what's going on? Why am I sitting here?" She looked at the opposite head of the table just in time to see me stand behind the chair. "And why is *she* standing *there?*"

"Humor me, Beverline," he said calmly as he pulled out her chair and seated her.

She cast a tight-lipped stare at me. Aaron then darted over to the opposite end of the table and pulled out my chair. I couldn't actually hear what she said, but from the movement of her lips it looked like her familiar, "I *see.*"

Beverline pretty much guessed something out of the ordinary was going on. "Well, this is certainly nice, Aaron, having Shirley make us this wonderful dinner, and having company to share it with." She nodded at Mom and me.

It was all I could do not to blurt out our engagement. I was getting tired of Beverline and her continued efforts to make me feel like I didn't belong. Maybe Mom could be considered company, but I'd eaten at this table on a semiregular basis for months now.

"Yes, Aaron," Mom spoke up. "What's happening in your life? Have you been promoted at work?"

I made a mental note to tell her when we were alone what a wonderful performance she was giving.

"No, Mrs. Yancy, something even better than that."

"What happened, Daddy?" Arden asked.

"I know. We're going to Orlando," Billy said hopefully.

"All right, all right. There's no easy quick way to say this." Aaron paused dramatically. "Emily has consented to be my wife. This dinner is to formally announce to all of you that we're engaged."

Ten seconds wasn't a long time, but it certainly could seem that way when a room containing seven people suddenly became completely graveyard quiet.

Billy was the first one to recover. "Emily, you're going to be our new mother?"

Nothing like starting in first with the tough questions. "Actually, I'm going to be your friend. But if you want the technical term, I guess stepmother fits as good as any. I'll never take the place of your own mom. No one can do that. And no one should. But as a part of the family—as your stepmother—I'll help your father take care of you. And I hope that we can all learn to love each other." I glanced at Aaron to see how he reacted to my explanation. His beaming face told me he approved.

Then I looked Beverline's way. She was putting up a good front, but it didn't quite reach her eyes, which clearly showed fear and anxiety.

Mom clapped her hands, looking almost childlike. "Well, I must say that I'm thrilled to hear this. I just know you two will be very happy together."

Maybe Aaron's kids believed that our engagement came as news to Mom, but I knew her performance didn't fool Beverline.

Billy piped up again. "Does this mean I'm going to have a little brother or sister?"

I chuckled, joined by Aaron and my mother. Beverline still looked shell-shocked. "Probably not, Billy," I said. "I'm not a young woman anymore."

"So why are you getting married?" Arden asked.

"Let me put it this way," Aaron began. "It's always a good idea to be married when you have kids. I'm certainly expecting that from all of you. But you don't get married just because you want to have children. Emily and I love each other, and we want to share our lives together."

I felt I needed to say something. "Arden, I hope you don't think I'm trying to take your mother's place," I added.

"I think it'll be nice to have a lady around all the time again," Billy said cheerfully.

Kirsten turned on him. "Have you forgotten Mom already?" Her voice broke.

Aaron held out a hand. "Kirsten, you have to realize that

Billy doesn't have the memories of your mother that you have. You and Arden are older. You have a lot more to remember."

"Of *course* I remember Mommy," Billy said indignantly. "But she's in Heaven, and she can't come back. All my friends have mothers. I'd like to have one again, too."

I got out of my chair to give Billy a hug. He seemed comforted as he embraced me. I returned to my seat.

Beverline cleared her throat and spoke for the first time. "Well, this explains a few things, Aaron. Like why you took down Diana's portrait."

"I didn't take it down, Beverline; I moved it to the girls' room. Don't make it sound like I stuck it in the garage or something."

"This certainly is a surprise," she replied, ignoring his remark. "I suppose I should have seen it coming. When do you plan to get married?"

Mom and I exchanged glances. No doubt Beverline wanted to know how much time she had to bust us up.

"We're not really in a hurry," Aaron replied. "We both feel it would probably be best to wait a while and give everyone a chance to get accustomed to the idea."

Beverline openly checked out my bare left hand. "Aaron! Did you actually propose to Emily without a ring?"

"Of course not, Beverline. But that's not the way we wanted to tell you our plans. It wouldn't be right for you to learn about our engagement by noticing her wearing it, would it?"

"It's at home in my jewelry box," I explained. "I'll start wearing it tomorrow. It's certainly too beautiful to be sitting inside a dark box."

At Aaron's suggestion, I took to joining him and the family for dinner just about every night after we got engaged. "It'll help the kids get used to the idea of you and me being married," he explained. "Plus, it'll also help Beverline get accustomed to sitting someplace other than the opposite head of the table. I'd like you to get involved more in the household, Emily. It should be your job to approve Shirley's menus, for instance."

"Do you do that now?"

"No, Beverline does it."

I hid my wicked smile. "I'd love to take it over."

I also started spending the night in Aaron's luxurious master suite, instead of in the guesthouse, on Friday and Saturday nights without the discretion we used to employ. No more tiptoeing down the stairs and across the driveway. I respected Aaron's wishes to shield the kids from our sex life, but I always hated the sneakiness involved in my slipping in and out of The Big House. Now that we were officially engaged, he saw no reason for us to hide. He pointed out that we'd be going to Sag Harbor soon, and we'd be sharing a bedroom there as well. So now I woke up when I woke up, not at the crack of dawn with assistance from an alarm clock, and instead of returning to the guesthouse I usually went downstairs to have breakfast. Like I belonged here.

Which I did.

"I do wish you wouldn't be so brazen about sleeping with my son-in-law," Beverline said to me one morning. Neither Aaron nor the kids were up yet. "This puts me in a very embarrassing position. What am I supposed to tell his children?"

My bagel popped up out of the toaster, and I calmly began spreading cream cheese on it. "I would hope that Kirsten and Arden, at thirteen and sixteen, are old enough not to have to ask, or else you've got a much bigger problem on your hands. As for Billy, if he asks you why I'm sleeping in his daddy's room on the weekends, I suggest you refer him to Aaron." I added sweetly, "After all, it was Aaron's idea that I stay with him. There's no reason for you to feel like you're in a tight spot."

She let out her breath loudly and left the room with her coffee in a huff.

I giggled as I added lox to my bagel.

*    *    *

"Good morning, Teddy," I said cheerfully as I took my place behind him on line at the lobby coffee shop.

"Hey! I haven't seen you in a while." His eyes narrowed slightly. "Have you been avoiding me again?"

"I was never avoiding you before," I lied. "It's just that we've both been busy. How's the new place coming along?"

"I'm enjoying it," he said with enthusiasm. "Of course, it's not like that palace Aaron has, but it's all mine." In response to the face I made, he said, "What?"

"Nothing." I hated it when Teddy compared himself to Aaron. Teddy had done pretty well for himself. "I'm glad you're liking your place."

"It makes a difference when those four walls belong to you permanently, not just for the next thirty days. So why haven't I seen you?"

"We've probably been getting in at different times in the morning." The truth was that since our last lunch I'd deliberately been parking in the back, and the times I did see him pull in I hung back for five minutes, giving him a chance to get his breakfast at the snack shop in the lobby, so I wouldn't run into him. The man simply radiated sex appeal, a fact that despite my best intentions I simply couldn't ignore. I'd made a commitment to Aaron, and I was going to keep it. Of course, the very fact that I felt I couldn't trust myself in Teddy's company didn't say too much for me, but I chose not to probe further into that little detail. My future was with Aaron. I *loved* Aaron.

I was saved from further interrogation by an impeccably dressed man wielding a briefcase who dashed into the elevator just as the doors were closing. He had the look of a salesman who was late for an appointment.

"What floor are you going to?" I asked politely while he straightened his tie and ran his fingers through his windblown thinning hair. Normally I didn't volunteer to be the elevator operator, but I felt kind of sorry for the guy. We've all been there. Important appointment, everything goes wrong, and you show up late. Even five minutes can make or break you when you're trying to sell products or services to busy doctors.

"Six, please."

I reached out and pressed the button and was startled when Teddy suddenly grabbed my hand. Too late, I realized he'd seen my diamond. This wasn't the way I wanted him to learn of my engagement.

"What's this?"

"What does it look like?" I countered.

He frowned, then set a determined stare on me. "Lunch. You and me. Today. Twelve-thirty. I'll call for you," he said as the elevator doors opened on my floor.

I yanked my hand away and stepped out. He had a hell of a lot of nerve, practically ordering me to have lunch with him. Who did he think he was?

Even as I tried to be indignant, I knew Teddy did deserve an explanation. Sure, it was true I'd never made him any promises, but I had slept with him, and he did demonstrate that he had feelings for me, albeit unrequited.

I didn't relish spending an hour listening to him try to talk me out of my engagement.

We'd barely sat down when Teddy started in on me. "I just want to know one thing. Why are you marrying Aaron?"

"Because I love him," I replied, my voice strong and sure. "And I want to spend the rest of my life with him."

Teddy seemed taken aback by my unwavering confidence. "So where does that leave me?"

"Where it's always left you, Teddy. An eligible bachelor, and a catch for just about any woman. But not for me."

"All right, so tell me this. If you're so much in love with him, why did you end up in bed with me?"

I wanted to remind him that he'd asked me that question before, but I decided to share more details with Teddy instead of singing the same old song. "Like I told you before, we were having a little . . . friction. Aaron has a home life that isn't particularly conducive to his dating anyone. He has three children, including two teenage daughters who were very close to their mother and were devastated when she died, plus he has his wife's mother living with them as well. As you can imagine, none of them is happy with having me in the picture."

"He's a widower?"

"Yes, for a few years now."

"I didn't know."

"It's not the type of thing you mention to people during a casual conversation," I pointed out. "Teddy, the last time we had lunch you said you just wanted me to be happy. If you really meant it, I need for you to stop trying to create something between us that never really existed." I saw pain flash in his eyes, and I suddenly realized how difficult this was for him.

I felt like crap.

# Chapter 27

Islowly began to feel comfortable with the idea of being
Mrs. Merritt and living in The Big House . . . and being a
mom to Billy. I was determined to forge a good relationship
with Aaron's youngest child, the one who made no secret
that he wanted a mother. It was May, and we were on the
fringes of summer. When it was warm enough we used the
pool. When Kirsten and Arden chided him for splashing them,
I came to the rescue, and we swam laps in a race, sometimes
beating the girls. He and I frequently bowled together in the
basement, and we went bicycling as well. I understood Billy. I
remembered what it was like when I was young, being in an
entirely different age group from my siblings. Kirsten and
Arden saw him as a nuisance, and that sometimes hurt his
feelings. I knew all about that, too.

Aaron loved his children, but the wealthy lifestyle he provided took up quite a bit of his time. I tried to fill in.

Kirsten earned her driver's license, and Aaron gifted her
with a used Volkswagen Bug.

There was something else I wanted to do, but I kept putting
it off, not wanting to appear too forward. But one night I
found my nerve.

"Aaron, I was wondering if it would be all right if I invited
a few of my girlfriends over for lunch on Saturday."

"I think that's a great idea. This is going to be your home,

Emily, and I want you to be comfortable here. Sure, go ahead and do a little entertaining. Ask Shirley if she can come in that day so she can prepare the food."

"Really? Do you think she'd do it?"

"Well, you might have to change your date if she's got plans, but sure, she'll do it. All you have to do is tell her what you'd like to serve and she'll take care of it. If you want something that's out of her range of expertise, just call a caterer."

It floored me to think that all I had to do was hand the housekeeper a list of menu items, and if it contained something she couldn't make, I could call for more outside help. I felt like I'd stumbled into a whole other world—a world where the streets were paved with dollar bills.

Only great sex felt better. But this would last longer.

I spoke with Shirley first, and after she confirmed her willingness to work the following Saturday, I began making calls. I invited Rosalind, Valerie, Marsha, and grudgingly, Tanis, only because I knew it wouldn't be right to leave her out. I didn't want to put the stress of letting something about the luncheon slip on Rosalind, who saw her fairly often.

After confirming that none of my guests had shellfish allergies, I decided to serve a meal heavy on seafood: bruschetta, crab bisque, shrimp and lobster salad, chicken salad finger sandwiches, and parmesan cheese drop biscuits. It would be my first time entertaining at what would become my new home, and I wanted everything to be perfect.

"All right, guys," Aaron announced Wednesday night at dinner, after my plans were firmly in placed. "Saturday afternoon I need you to be on your best behavior. Emily's entertaining some of her friends for luncheon. They'll be out on the patio."

Kirsten didn't hide her disappointment. "Does that mean Arden and I can't go swimming?"

"I want to swim, too," Billy added.

"Oh, of course not," I assured them. "Do what you normally do. The yard is certainly big enough for all of us."

"Yeah, kids, that's right," Aaron agreed. "But I would ask that you don't have any company that day, all right? We'll have enough guests."

Beverline, who'd been ominously silent, spoke up. "Well, Aaron, I don't know if that's fair. Saturday comes only once a week."

"Beverline, summer is just beginning. After next week the kids will be out of school and can have friends over any day of the week as long as you're here to supervise them in the pool. If they want to invite their friends over this particular weekend, they can do it on Friday or they can do it on Sunday. You're right. Saturday does come only once a week. And since Emily works Monday through Friday, this is the best time for her to entertain. No one's being shortchanged here."

"It just seems odd to me that Emily is having her friends here. I mean, it's not like—"

Aaron defended me as I steamed at the insinuation that I had no right to have friends over and disrupt the family's routine. "As I told Emily, this is going to be her home, and I want her to start acting like it."

"Hmph. From where I sit, she already has." She stared at me, or rather at the position of my chair at the head of the table.

I broke in before Aaron could respond. "Mrs. Wilson, I understand that this is a difficult situation for you. I'd like to make it as easy as possible. Maybe you and I could get together after dinner and talk about how we each envision things will be around here after Aaron and I are married."

All eyes at the table jockeyed back and forth between Beverline and me like tennis balls. I could see she was torn. If she refused my earnest plea, she'd come off looking uncooperative and surly. On the other hand, neither was she willing to accept me. I had her by the nipple, and she knew it.

"Maybe that would be a good idea," she said haltingly.

Aaron beamed at me from across the table. I felt pretty proud of myself. Someone had to make a move to put an end to the tension between us. It always felt good when you take the high road.

After dinner, Beverline and I adjourned to Aaron's office, which I'd already ascertained he would not be using. "Wish me luck," I'd said to him beforehand, giving him a quick kiss.

"For whatever it's worth, I think you're doing the right thing," he'd said.

"Thanks. That means a lot," I'd replied.

Beverline cautiously sat on one end of the brown Chesterfield sofa, and I on the other. Nothing in her demeanor suggested she wished to speak first, or even at all. I took charge of the conversation.

"I think you and I are overdue for a sit-down," I began. "Mrs. Wilson, you've made it very clear that you disapprove of me. Ever since that first day last summer when Aaron invited me to meet all of you."

"That isn't true, Emily."

"Maybe you honestly feel it isn't, but you've never made me feel welcome. Maybe I shouldn't say this, but I get the distinct feeling that you've also encouraged Kirsten and Arden to dislike me as well." I plunged on before she could interrupt to protest. "What I'd like to know is this: is your aversion to me because of me in particular, or because you just don't want to see anyone take your daughter's place?"

"No one is going to take Diana's place," she said harshly. "She will always be the mother of Aaron's children, and she lives on through them. Kirsten, especially, is in her very image."

"So is there something about me specifically that you dislike?" I asked as gently as I could.

"Emily, you're a nice girl."

Well, that was *something*.

Beverline sighed. "I guess I always knew that Aaron would eventually want female . . . companionship."

Mom had used that same expression, but at least she didn't make it sound dirty. What did Beverline think I was, a twenty-dollar ho?

"Frankly, I just pictured him with a different type of woman, and I was a little disappointed."

She didn't seem even remotely aware that she'd just said something insulting. "And just what kind of woman were you anticipating Aaron would become involved with?" I asked sweetly. I decided to throw out a few hints. "More educated? A different physical type, maybe?" Beverline was light-skinned, and Diana had been the same. I wouldn't put it past her to feel that those of us whose complexions were too rich to pass the brown paper bag test didn't belong in her family. Not counting Aaron, of course. Or his money.

Then another possibility occurred to me. "Or maybe someone who hails from a different place?"

"Well, Emily, you have to admit that Euliss . . ." This time Beverline appeared to realize how that sounded and tried again. "Don't get me wrong. Some very fine people have come out of Euliss. People like Tanis Montgomery, for instance."

The mention of Tanis's name was enough to make me see red. *Not again,* I said to myself.

My mother had finally stopped mentioning Tanis's accomplishments, other than saying how much she enjoyed her show, even if Tanis didn't get a whole lot of screen time. Now here was Beverline talking about Tanis like she was the best thing to come along since *The Weather Channel.* I was willing to bet Beverline knew nothing about the Montgomerys in general. All she knew was that Tanis had achieved some minor level of success with her acting and had become a local celebrity. Of course, even with the show being declared a bona fide hit, it would be unlikely, given her age, that she would ever be much more than a character actress, but as far as Beverline was concerned, money talked.

"I might not be in show business, Mrs. Wilson, and I might not collect a hefty check, but I work steadily, and I have a rewarding career that allows me to live reasonably well," I said stiffly. "Actually, my work is not dissimilar from Aaron's. I just do it on a more limited scale, and I don't operate on people. But I treat more cases than he does." It wasn't everyone who could relocate and get a new job right away, I reminded myself.

While my being from Euliss might have something to do with Beverline's dislike of me, I also believed that she would resent any woman who threatened to take Diana's place and just didn't want to admit it. I decided to make a little comparison between Diana and me. "Helping my patients is as important to me as I'm sure helping students was to your daughter."

When we emerged from the room, having said all there was to say to each other, I felt no more optimistic about getting along with Beverline than I had before. We'd solved nothing.

I went up to the master bedroom, where I knew Aaron waited. "How'd it go?" he asked, handing me a glass of wine.

I sank into the double-wide chaise longue. "Not particularly well. If anything, she just reiterated that she doesn't feel I'm good enough for you. Now, if I were a successful actress, like *Tanis* . . ."

He groaned. "Not that again."

"You've heard it before?"

"Ever since her show became top rated, Beverline's been trying to steer me toward Tanis. Even if I was attracted to her, I wouldn't do anything about it."

I looked at him curiously. "You're not attracted to her?"

"No. Tanis has made it clear that she'd like to get close to me, but I'm not interested. For one, Rob Renfroe is a friend of mine, even if not a particularly close one. I won't take up with a friend's ex-wife. Second, Tanis has a great figure, dresses well, and always makes a good appearance. She's attractive in a Natalie Cole type of way. But she's not *pretty*, at least not to me." He moved in close to me. "You, on the other hand, are beautiful." He kissed my mouth, and I put my arms around his neck.

"Say it again."

"You're beautiful, Emily. I never felt the remotest attraction toward Tanis. To me she's just the mother of Billy's friend."

I threw my head back and chuckled deep within my throat. Tanis had never posed any threat to me. Aaron just said so. Lord, I wish I had a tape recorder. I could listen to Aaron saying Tanis wasn't his type over and over again.

Marsha called Thursday morning. "Emily, I just realized since you guys have a pool, is it okay if I bring Cameron and Cheyenne along on Saturday?"

I really wasn't particularly keen on having a couple of kids other than Aaron's splashing around during my luncheon, but on the other hand, I could understand Marsha wanting to get them out of Sherwood Forest, even if just for an afternoon. I hastily tried to come up with an excuse.

"I don't see why not," I said slowly, "although I don't think my menu is particularly kid friendly."

"Oh, I hadn't thought of that." Marsha went silent. I knew she was thinking.

"You know, I could always just pack them some sandwiches," she finally said.

I should have known she'd come up with a solution, but that didn't seem right to me. She and her children were my guests. I should provide food for them.

"I'll tell you what, Marsha. I'll get the housekeeper to make some hot dogs and Tater Tots just for them. How's that?"

"That would be perfect. They love hot dogs."

I called Shirley Friday morning and asked her to make the additions to the menu, and she cheerfully agreed. Just as I was priding myself on a situation well handled, I had a call from Valerie.

"Hey, I just heard that Marsha's bringing her kids. Is it all right if I bring mine, too?"

I swallowed hard. I understood why Marsha wanted to bring her children, but Valerie's situation was different. She didn't live in a project; she lived on a quiet block on City Island. Couldn't she get her housekeeper to watch them? Now I was faced with having three more children plus a baby at my luncheon, in addition to Marsha's two. The sophisticated meal I'd planned was turning into a children's hour. Aaron's backyard was going to look like a playground—a playground that he'd specifically asked his own children to refrain from inviting playmates to on Saturday afternoon.

Unfortunately, I saw no way out. The smart thing would have been for me to tell Marsha not to mention our arrangement to anyone, but since I'd already told Marsha she could bring her kids, I certainly couldn't tell Valerie she had to leave hers at home. Besides, I owed Valerie a favor for the way she lied to protect me against Tanis's deviousness.

I tried to sound positive as I told my friend that would be fine. My palm was sweating as I hung up the receiver, but nonetheless I promptly picked it up and dialed Aaron's home once more.

This time Beverline answered. She informed me that Shirley was running the vacuum. "My, my, you certainly are keeping her busy these days," she remarked. "Let's hope she doesn't turn in her resignation."

I rolled my eyes. "I'm hardly working her to death, Mrs. Wilson. I believe *you're* the one who runs white gloves over the tables to make sure they've been dusted." As far as I was concerned, Beverline and I had agreed to loathe each other, and the gloves had come off. "I just need to speak with her about some arrangements for my luncheon. I'll try her again in an hour or so." The phone practically slipped out of my hand. As I rubbed my palm dry, I thought that all I'd need now was for Rosalind and Tanis to call and ask if they could bring their kids.

I quickly realized how unlikely that was. In the first place, Tanis had a pool at her home, plus she had a nanny who lived in. Rosalind had neither, but like Tanis, Rosalind knew it simply wasn't appropriate to ask to bring your children along to an adult luncheon. They also didn't have Marsha's predicament of being stuck in a ghetto. As for Valerie, she probably should have known better, but of course anyone who knew Valerie knew that she lived for her children. She was tickled pink to be a grandmother and to have a baby in the house once more.

Part of me wondered if I should tell Aaron about the extra guests. I ultimately decided against it. Aaron would be playing golf Saturday morning with John Hunter, Elias Ansara, and another friend. I knew he'd be surprised to see all those kids when he got home, but I would tell him it just came up at the last minute and I really had no choice, since all the preparations had already been made.

Still, the entire situation had me on edge.

On Saturday morning I made Aaron an omelet and had coffee with him while he ate. Right after breakfast he left for the links. I carried the dishes into the kitchen. Shirley was already at work, and the kitchen was filled with the scent of boiling shrimp. The shrimp were boiling in a clear Dutch oven, and I could see how large they were.

I was surprised to see bacon frying in a griddle that spanned two burners and Shirley mixing what appeared to be pancake batter. Why would she be making breakfast? She still had quite a bit to do before noon.

My confusion must have shown on my face. Shirley gave me a sheepish shrug and explained, "Mrs. Wilson buzzed me and asked me to make pancakes and bacon for her and the children, since I'm in this morning."

My jaw went taut. "Oh, did she?"

"I'm sorry, Emily. I couldn't really say no. But it won't take me long."

"You have nothing to be sorry for. It's not your fault." As much as I liked Shirley, I didn't feel it would be proper to complain to her about Beverline. Besides, it was pretty obvious that Shirley knew the deal. I suspected Beverline had no qualms about bad-mouthing *me*. "I'll help out to make sure we get everything done."

Just then the timer went off, and I reached for the pot holders Shirley had left on the countertop near the cooktop. "I'll take care of draining and rinsing the shrimp," I said. "You keep doing what you're doing."

Shirley let out a sigh. "Thanks, Emily."

"Good morning, Shirley," Beverline said as she burst into the kitchen. If she was surprised to see me calmly spreading fresh-made chicken salad on a large rectangular flatbread, she didn't comment. Instead she said, "How are the preparations for this afternoon going?"

"Just wonderful," I said in an equally bright tone. I put my knife down and picked up a sharper one and began to reduce a beefsteak tomato into thin slices. I felt Beverline's eyes on me as I arranged the tomato slices over the thin layer of chicken salad.

"What's that you're making, Emily?"

"Pinwheel sandwiches filled with chicken salad." I sprinkled lettuce that the efficient Shirley had already shredded on top of the tomatoes, then carefully rolled the bread up by the lengthwise side. I had to make a couple of efforts because the chicken chunks were so, well, chunky, but I refused to let Beverline see me get ruffled. I just kept trying. The rest of the sandwiches would be made with sliced London broil, which Shirley planned to make last so she could serve them hot.

"Everything's on the table for you, Mrs. Wilson," Shirley offered.

"The kids are eating already. I just came in to get my coffee. Uh, has Aaron left?"

I answered her. "Yes, about twenty minutes ago."

"Well, you're certainly up bright and early, Emily."

"Of course I am. It's nearly nine. My guests will be here at noon."

Beverline's eyes fell on the George Foreman grill Shirley had placed on the counter to cook the hot dogs in. "Oh, you're grilling, Shirley? I thought you were just making salad, sandwiches, and soup."

Shirley sent a pleading glance my way.

That was more than Beverline *should* have known about my menu, I thought with annoyance. She'd probably had Shirley up on the carpet and questioned her relentlessly. "Yes, we are," I answered, offering no further explanation. Then I pointedly added, "You know, Mrs. Wilson, if you hang around in here much longer your food will get cold."

"I suppose you're right," she said, getting the hint. But her sly manner told me she planned to find out exactly what would be prepared in that indoor grill.

# Chapter 28

"Oh, this is good," Marsha raved.

Rosalind and Valerie agreed, but Tanis merely nodded. "Where's Aaron today, Emily?" Tanis asked, just like I knew she would. I was sure she'd worn that pretty yellow and white halter sundress and yellow sandals for his benefit. Too bad she didn't know it wouldn't help, not even with the tops of her boobs peeking out from the top like giant stuffed pimentos.

"He's playing golf."

"John's with him," Rosalind added.

Valerie's gaze went to the pool. "Justin! Stop that splashing!" She turned and bounced her baby granddaughter on her knee. "Sometimes I wish they could stay this size."

Rosalind, Tanis, and I exchanged glances. Marsha spoke up. "You seem to be handling Melanie's having a baby pretty well, Valerie. I don't think I'd be as calm as you are if Cheyenne got pregnant at sixteen. Of course, she's only thirteen."

"I think a baby is the best thing that can happen to a woman," Valerie declared.

"Melanie's not really a woman yet, Valerie," Tanis pointed out. "Maybe physically, but not emotionally. Raising kids is hard."

"Is the baby's father involved?" Rosalind asked.

"He's fascinated and proud in a puff-your-chest-out kind of way, but he'll probably lose interest as she grows." Valerie shrugged. "Who needs him, anyway?"

"*She* does," Marsha said fervently as the rest of us exchanged quick glances.

"Excuse me," Tanis said. "I need to use your water closet."

She was in the house for about fifteen minutes. Either she could use a good laxative or she was chatting with Beverline. I suspected it was the latter.

Just a few minutes later Beverline came outside, wearing a sun visor, short-sleeved blouse, and Bermuda shorts. She walked over to the pool and said something to Kirsten, then went back inside with a quick, impersonal wave to my friends and me.

Beverline hadn't been outside since everyone had arrived, but I knew she'd been watching from the kitchen window and had seen all the kids. Everyone had been here for over an hour now. No way would she miss the opportunity to see firsthand who my guests were.

When I saw Kirsten, Arden, and Billy climb out of the pool and go inside, I wondered what Beverline was up to.

Aaron came home at one-thirty. I wasn't surprised to see John Hunter with him, but I didn't expect to see Elias.

I stood up to greet Aaron, whose eyes were focused on the pool and its occupants. "Emily, I thought you were just having your friends over. Where'd all these kids come from?"

"Both Marsha and Valerie asked if they could bring their kids."

"You could have said no."

I sighed. "Can we talk about this later?"

"That's probably best. I don't see my kids. Where are they?"

"Their grandmother came out. I think she asked them to get out of the water. They went inside right afterward. I haven't seen them since."

"I'm going to set the fellows up with drinks, and then I'll go in and find out what's going on." He gave my arm a little squeeze.

As the men walked over to the outdoor bar, Valerie turned around and with her free hand fanned the front of her blouse. "That Elias is one handsome dude, and he's not wearing a wedding ring. I'd like to talk to him a little more. Provided he's not a gynecologist, of course."

"No, he's a GI specialist." I said. None of us had to ask what was wrong with a gynecologist. Who wanted a man who had his hands in women's stuff all day?

Valerie giggled. "I went to the ER last year with what turned out to be a ruptured ovarian cyst, and the ER doctor was really fine. At first I was feeling too bad to look at his ring finger, and just before he discharged me I couldn't see it because he was holding my chart. Then, as he was discharging me, he wrote down a GYN I could follow up with. That's when I finally got to see the ring on his left hand. Then I saw the doc he recommended was a woman with the same last name as his."

"His wife," Rosalind guessed.

"You got it."

"It really wasn't your lucky day," Marsha remarked.

"No, it wasn't. I threw out his note and followed up with my own doctor."

We all laughed, and Rosalind got up to speak with John. When Aaron emerged from the house, I got up, eager to know what was going on.

He put an arm around me. "We'll talk later. Let's entertain our guests."

I shrugged. "All right. The guys are probably hungry."

I brought out the leftovers, glad I'd told Shirley to make more than what my friends could eat. No one had appeared to be in the house. Maybe they were all upstairs, or down in the basement bowling or something.

As I approached the patio with the tray, I noticed Elias

saying something to Valerie. Valerie looked especially attractive today, wearing oversize sunglasses and her hair pulled back, but wisps of it were blowing in the breeze, framing her face. Her grandson, who had been bouncing on her lap before she'd handed him over to a cooing Marsha, looked more like her son. Forty-four was a little old to have an infant, but Valerie could easily pass for being in her late thirties.

Elias held out his pinky for the baby to grab, then casually sat in a vacant chair next to Valerie. Could it be he was just as attracted to Valerie as she was to him? Her-ink black hair was about as far from blond as one could get, but it was obvious she had plenty of it; I'd seen Elias with only one girl with short hair. I had a hunch that his preference ran toward those whose skin was of a lighter hue. I didn't find this insulting. My own taste ran toward brown-skinned men like Aaron, or darker. That didn't mean I didn't think Kristoff St. John of *The Young and the Restless* wasn't handsome, because I did. He just wasn't for me. (I'm sure his wife would be glad to hear that.) Give me Idris Elba any day of the week.

Aaron, who'd been over by the pool talking to the kids, caught me on my way back inside. "They look good together, don't they?"

"I think so. Do you think he knows she's black?" Sometimes white people weren't too bright when it came to knowing who was black and who wasn't. Black people come with built-in antennae. We can look at someone like Mariah Carey and see black, whereas the average white person will see white.

"It doesn't matter, Emily. Elias has dated Latinas, Asians, Scandinavians, Africans, Australians, . . . you name it. The man just loves women. When I mentioned that you'd be entertaining your girlfriends for lunch Saturday he asked if Valerie was coming. Why do you think he drove all the way from Sands Point just to play golf?"

I beamed like searchlights. "I think that's great."

"Apparently, she made quite an impression on him New Year's Eve."

I hoped Elias was serious about getting to know Valerie. She was probably overdue for a real live man instead of a plastic stimulator. "Hmm. Not only is she older than the women I've seen him with, but she's got kids, even a grandchild. I wonder if he's really interested, or if he's just being flirtatious."

"He's the only one with the answer to that one. But I couldn't help noticing that none of Valerie's kids look alike, do they?"

"No," I admitted. "They all have different fathers."

People started leaving around four. Rosalind and John had promised their kids dinner out, "and I've got to take a nap first," John said, stretching his upper body in a yawn.

"I'm going to get going, too, Emily," Marsha said. "My mother doesn't really like me to be out with her car for too long." The sardonic way she spoke suggested that her late husband's money had paid for Mrs. Cox's Impala.

Tanis left shortly afterward. "Gee, what happened to your kids, Aaron?" she asked as she ran a comb through her curls, a little too innocently for my taste.

"Beverline took them on an errand."

"Well, I'm so sorry I didn't get a chance to say good-bye to them. I'm sure the other kids were sorry they had to leave. They seemed to be having so much fun together. Well, ta-ta for now."

We all said good-bye. Tanis set out, her effort to sashay her hips lost in her full skirt. She turned and said over her shoulder, "It was a lovely luncheon, Emily . . . if a little on the boisterous side."

I looked at Aaron. "She talks as if she knows something I don't."

"Oh, don't worry about her," Valerie said. She handed the baby over to Melanie, then began stuffing wet towels into a straw beach bag. "We're going to leave as well, Emily. I had a wonderful time, and so did all the kids. They're going to sleep really good tonight."

Aaron yawned. "I know what John meant about wanting to lie down. Between the sun, the eighteen holes, and the liquor, I'm dead on my feet."

Elias stood and offered his hand. "Don't stay up on our account, Aaron. I'm going to walk Valerie out and then be on my way."

"I'll see them out, Aaron," I added. I could tell he was tired. His eyes looked like they were barely open, but from fatigue, not from arousal.

"All right. Take care, Valerie," Aaron said.

"You, too, Aaron."

I waved as Valerie and Elias drove off in their respective vehicles, then stood where I was as Beverline's Buick approached. I recognized Kirsten sitting in the front seat. So she really had taken them out. That seemed . . . well, *unseemly*. I knew that Valerie's and Marsha's kids were technically my company and not Kirsten, Arden, and Billy's, but they all seemed to be getting along and having fun in the water. All of the kids except Valerie's youngest daughter knew how to swim. Marsha's son was about the same age as Billy, and Valerie's son just a few years older. Arden and Marsha's daughter were both thirteen, and Valerie's oldest daughter was just a little older than Kirsten.

"Hi, Emily!" Billy greeted with his usual gusto. "Grandma took us to the movies."

Kirsten and Arden said hello to me as well, although with more reserve. "Is everyone gone?" Arden asked.

"Yes. My friend Valerie just left a minute ago.

It took Beverline a little longer to get out of the car than her youthful grandchildren. "Go on inside, kids," she said. "Grandma needs to speak to Emily."

My eyebrows shot up. What did Beverline have to say to me?

She waited until the front door closed behind them. "I must say, Emily, I'm disappointed that you told Kirsten, Arden, and Billy that they couldn't use the pool for their friends and then opened it to your friends' children. Perhaps I need to remind you that my grandchildren *live* here."

"I'm well aware they do; you don't have to remind me of that," I said testily. "And that wasn't my intent. One of my friends asked if she could bring her children. I tried to convince her that wasn't such a good idea, but she was pretty insistent about it. There are special circumstances involved that I'd rather not go into, and I simply didn't have the heart to tell her she couldn't bring them. Then when my other friend found out that my first friend was bringing her kids, she asked if she could bring hers." I took a deep breath. My explanation was coming out like an Abbott and Costello routine. "It just kind of snowballed. I'm sorry if it caused any problems. But the pool was always open for the kids. *You* were the one who told them to come inside."

"Well, I had no choice once I got wind of whom you'd invited to our home."

I told myself to stay polite, at least until I found out what she meant, but already I didn't like the way it sounded. "Would you care to explain that, Mrs. Wilson?"

"Gladly," she said icily. "You invited the widow of a notorious drug kingpin here, plus her children. They live in the *projects* now that the Feds have seized all their ill-gotten assets. I guess those are the 'special circumstances' you spoke of?" She paused to let that sink in. "And if that's not bad enough, you also invited a woman who has had three children out of wedlock by three different men, plus *her* brats, who include, I might add, a girl barely older than Kirsten who just had a baby. I suppose your idea of the perfect playmates for my grandchildren are the son and daughter of a drug dealer and a bunch of bastard children. That might work in Euliss, but it won't work here."

I lowered my chin. How could Beverline possibly have known the backgrounds of Marsha and Valerie, whom she'd just met? "Have you hired someone to investigate me or something?" I wouldn't have put it past her. Anything to get rid of me.

"I have my ways of finding out things."

Suddenly I remembered how long Tanis had been gone when she went in to use the restroom. She'd probably been all too glad to answer Beverline's questions about my guests. "I think your way is named Tanis Montgomery."

"Tanis is a nice girl, and she understands my concerns."

She didn't deny it, I noticed. "She's from Euliss, just like the rest of my friends."

"She may be from Euliss, dear, but she's *not* like you and the rest of your friends. Those two women you run with, the drug dealer's wife and the one with all those baby daddies, simply aren't the type of people who belong here. At least your other friend didn't ask to drag her kids here as well. Of course, she's married to a white fellow and probably knows a thing or two about the right way to do things."

I couldn't believe she'd actually used the term "baby daddies." I'd had enough. "Mrs. Wilson, I explained what happened and apologized to you for it. I'll apologize to the kids as well. But I'm not going to stand here and listen to you put down my friends, *or* their children. Why don't you run and report what Tanis told you to Aaron? Tell him all about the horrible people I invited here." I knew Aaron would tell her to stop carrying on. "And while you're at it, you can try to convince him to dump me and take up with Tanis."

"Don't think I haven't tried." She turned to walk away, but not before checking out my reaction. She looked disappointed at my calm demeanor. She didn't know that Aaron had already told me he had no interest in Tanis.

Aaron knocked on the guesthouse door two hours later. No doubt Beverline had filled him in on our exchange the moment he'd woken up. I hadn't calmed down at all. How dare she criticize my friends!

"That'll be Aaron," Mom said in response to the knock.

She'd patiently listened to me ranting for nearly a half hour. "Now, calm down so you can talk this out with him reasonably." She disappeared into the bedroom.

I let Aaron in, and he took me in his arms. "Beverline told me what she said to you. I'm so sorry, Emily. She should have let me handle it."

"Aaron, I *told* her how it happened. It just kind of got away from me, got out of control. I felt so paralyzed . . . I didn't know what to do. I probably should have talked to you about it instead of trying to keep it hidden." Then something he said suddenly registered in my brain. "What do you mean, Beverline should have let you handle it? Handle what?"

He took my hand. "Emily, for once I have to tell you that I agree with Beverline, at least as far as the kids are concerned. Valerie and Marsha are fine with me, and they're welcome at any time, but I don't think it's such a hot idea for my kids to spend time with theirs. Kirsten, Arden, and Billy are as impressionable as any other kids, and who knows what ideas they might pick up. Kirsten was just telling me how cute Valerie's grandson is."

"So that means she's going to go get pregnant?" I said incredulously, shaking my head. "I can't believe I'm hearing this."

"You're not a parent, Emily."

"And you're not the man I thought you were."

He abruptly dropped my hand. "I think the best thing I can do right now is give you some time to cool off."

"Fine."

# Chapter 29

"**A**ren't you going out to Sag Harbor tomorrow with Aaron?" Mom asked me on a Friday night. I'd brought us a steak-and-cheese calzone for dinner.

"No. He's already out there. He left work early today and drove out this afternoon. I'll be here this weekend. Marsha and I are having dinner tomorrow night."

"You're engaged, but spending Saturday night with your girlfriend," she pointed out.

"She's treating."

"Don't make jokes, Emmie. I'm starting to get worried. Things haven't been right between you and Aaron for two weeks now. He hasn't been around on the weekends. Last week he went on that fishing trip with Rosalind's husband and their sons. Now he's going out to the island on Friday. I've never known him to do that. When is this going to end?"

I chewed my bite of calzone and swallowed it. "I don't know, Mom," I answered honestly.

"Mavis has asked me two or three times how you are. I know she's hinting for news about you and Aaron."

"Well, Tanis is the one who went in to blab to Beverline about Marsha and Valerie. I'm sure she wants to know what effect it had."

"Forget about her. If you're not careful, you're going to lose Aaron."

I spoke quietly. "And would that be such a terrible thing?"

"I want you to do whatever makes you happy," she said without hesitation. "But I do think you're overreacting, and maybe you don't fully understand Aaron's position."

"Why, because I didn't have kids?"

"That's right. I'm sorry, Emmie, but people are very sensitive when it comes to their children. It's much harder today to raise kids than it was when you all were small. Sex and drugs are everywhere. I wouldn't have wanted you socializing with a high school girl who'd had a baby or with the kids of the head of a huge drug empire when you were the ages of Aaron's kids, either."

"Mom, they're not going to be thrown together all the time. Marsha's and Valerie's kids were only here for a few hours. No one expects them to be best friends."

"That's all it takes sometimes to give kids ideas. Aaron's kids have lived pretty sheltered lives. Who knows what Marsha's kids have been exposed to, both when their father was alive and since they moved to Sherwood Forest. Valerie's kids are probably just rich kids who don't have a lot of supervision, but those are some of the worst ones."

I sighed. "Maybe it's best that I *didn't* have kids. Because I don't understand what all the fuss is about."

"Are you actually considering breaking up with Aaron over this?"

"He just doesn't seem as big a prize anymore."

Now it was Mom's turn to sigh. "Maybe it's a good thing Aaron isn't around again this weekend. I think the time apart will do you good."

"I suppose you're wondering what the occasion is, my treating you to dinner," Marsha said after we'd placed our order.

"Well . . . yes." I knew Marsha didn't have much extra money, even for eating at an informal place like the one she'd taken me to.

"I've made a decision, and I wanted to tell you about it. I'm leaving Euliss."

I drew in my breath. "You're *leaving?*"

"Yes. I hate it here, Emily. People are always pointing their fingers at me, usually kids who know who I was married to. The women stare daggers through my clothes, and the men look at me like they'd like to get me into bed. Those projects are just awful. Tiny bedrooms, no doors on the closets. Not that I have either or bedroom or a closet. The kids and I have been sleeping on air mattresses in the living room since we've been here. And both Cheyenne and Cameron are hanging out with bad kids."

I suddenly heard both Aaron and Mom telling me that parents had to be careful about whom their kids associated with, but that wasn't the subject at hand, so I pushed the thought away. "But, Marsha, where will you go?"

"James wants me to come down to South Carolina. The cost of living is lower there, and besides, that's where he is."

"Are you going to live with him?"

"In the beginning, yes. That's the only way I can afford to go. The kids are going to stay here with my mother while I go down and get a job." Marsha looked almost embarrassed. "I'll tell you the truth, Emily. James wants me to marry him, but I'm holding off. If we find that we can live together under the same roof, we'll probably get married. If not, I'll get an apartment for me and the kids, but by hook or by crook, I'm getting the hell out of Euliss."

"Wow. I'm flabbergasted, Marsha. I knew you and James talk a lot on the phone and stuff—"

"I've been down to see him a couple of times on the weekends. What can I say, Emily? It *feels* right. And the sex is great. Who knew he had all that talent?"

My heart wrenched, but at the same time I had to force myself not to make a face. James was buff, yes—there's no such thing as an out-of-shape Marine—but the thought of that ugly face with its big blubbery lips slobbering all over me was just plain revolting. Even Marsha had wrinkled her nose at him the night of the reunion. Now she'd done a hundred-and-eighty-degree turn. I didn't understand it, but *I* didn't have to sleep with him. I had Aaron . . . I thought.

*But do you really* want *him?*

The thought came hurling at me like an out-of-control baseball. Even if I got over his disapproval of my friends' children, was I kidding myself by thinking I could truly be happy with him when I wasn't getting all I needed? Half the time I didn't even climax anymore. And what about Marsha? Had she blinded herself to any shortcomings James might have just because he offered security for her and her children?

"All right; let me ask you this," I said, determined to get the truth out of her. "Do you love him, really? Or are you just telling yourself you do because the sex is so good?" *Just like* you're *trying to convince yourself that sex doesn't matter . . .*

The corners of Marsha's mouth turned upright in a dreamy smile. "I know it seems odd because of how we used to make fun of James when we were kids, but he's just wonderful, Emily. He's sweet and kind, generous. We get along great. He's good to my kids. And he wants to take care of me." She rolled her head back as if stretching her neck muscles. "I'll tell you something, Emily. If he'd joined our class before that day Tracy tore off my hairpiece, he would have kicked her ass on my behalf. Not because he liked me or anything, but because he's a gentleman. He just has strong feelings about people mistreating other people. How can I not love him, Emily?"

"I don't get it. If you love him so much, why not just marry him now?"

"Because I want to be sure, Emily. I have to be sure this is the right thing. Not just for me, but for the kids as well. I've got to get them out of Euliss, but I'd be stupid to think that

everything's just going to fall into place. I have to make sure
I can find a job. I'm willing to take this chance, but it has to
be done right," Marsha explained. "Marriage is a big step.
The foundation I build now will determine if it's going to be
for keeps." She paused. "And I *want* it to be for keeps."

I nodded. "I understand."

"You've been such a good friend to me. Valerie and Rosalind,
too, but especially you, since we were in grammar school. I
don't know what I would have done once I came back to
town if you hadn't been here. That's why I wanted to buy
you dinner, to say thanks for everything."

My eyes filled with tears. "I guess I can't believe it," I sput-
tered. "When are you leaving?"

"Next weekend. I gave my notice on Monday, and I already made my train reservation. Next week is going to be
real busy. I'll have to ship my clothes down there, plus I want
to spend as much time with Cameron and Cheyenne as I can.
I don't know how long it'll be until I see them again. I'm hoping I can bring them down and get them in school before it
starts, but I don't know." Marsha raised her shoulders for a
second, as if she'd had a sudden chill. "I'm very excited about
it, Emily. Following your heart always feels right."

"What about your mother?"

"She'll be sorry to see us go, but she agrees that the kids
should live somewhere nice. She even says that once I get settled she'll look into apartments down there, retire, and move
down there herself."

Mrs. Cox was in her early sixties, considerably younger than
my own mother. She'd gotten out of waitressing years ago and
now worked the reception desk at a social service agency.

"You know what they say," Marsha said brightly. "Mama
knows best."

"Not always," I said dryly, thinking of my own mother's
attempts to match me up with Aaron. "Sometimes they just
*hope* for the best."

\* \* \*

I kept thinking about our conversation as I drove home, and even after. Marsha was following her heart and was on the verge of a new life. She'd faced facts and made her move.

Maybe I needed to do the same.

When I woke up Monday morning I knew what I had to do.

I went in to work but told them I had an important legal matter to attend to and would have to leave at lunchtime. A little past one I got into the car and headed for Washington Heights. I could wait for Aaron to come home, but I thought it would be better if I talked to him in the impersonal setting of his office.

I arrived just before two. I hoped he'd be back from lunch by then. "I'm Emily Yancy," I told the receptionist. "I don't have an appointment, but if you can let Dr. Merritt know I'm here, I'm sure he'll see me." I'd never been to Aaron's office, and whenever I called him I dialed his cell number, so I doubted they had any idea I was his fiancée.

"Oh . . . um, yes."

The receptionist, who appeared to be in her midthirties, was acting flustered, like it was her first day on the job. She'd better get her act together if she expected to be a long-term employee.

"Just a moment, Ms. Yancy." She closed the frosted-glass slide, and I could see a blurred outline of her body as she got up and went into the rear.

I busied myself by looking at the waiting room, which looked like any other. Sturdy, nondescript pine tables and matching chairs covered with nubby fabric in basic beige. The coffee and end tables were covered with health-related magazines, plus those for fashion and sports.

I turned when the hallway door opened. One look at who walked in and my knees suddenly felt wobbly.

It was Aaron . . . and Shelly Muldoon.

The shock on their faces probably mirrored my own.

"Emily!" Aaron said after a few long seconds of silence. At that moment his cell phone began to ring. He ignored it. "I didn't . . . what're you doing here?"

"Hello, Emily," Shelly said uncertainly. She'd suddenly gone pale, and the expensive-looking beige knit dress and matching jacket—something that Jackie O. likely would have worn—made her look bland.

I simply stared at her. "Aaron, I need to talk to you about something important."

"Sure. We'll go into my office." He turned to Shelly. "Excuse us."

She nodded, worry in her eyes.

Aaron led me to his office under the watchful eyes of his staff, then closed the door behind us. "I'm sorry, Emily. I didn't know you were coming down . . . obviously."

"How long have you been seeing her?" I quietly asked.

"I haven't exactly been seeing her. Not in the way you're thinking. It's just that . . . things haven't been too good between us lately. Shelly called the week before last and invited me to lunch. I found that I enjoyed myself. You and I had just had our fight, and here was an hour when I could forget about all the turmoil in my life. We've been eating together pretty regularly since. That's all there is to it."

Eating together, he'd said—not lunch. So Aaron had been having dinner with her as well. And anyone could see Shelly wanted more than lunch from Aaron. "But there could be more," I prompted.

"Not while you and I are engaged. I'm not a cheater, Emily."

"I see," I said, realizing after the fact that I sounded just like Beverline. "Well, at least knowing you have a replacement lined up will make it easier." I slipped the engagement ring off my finger and put it in his palm. "I think both of us know that it's not going to work. Maybe Beverline was right. Maybe I'm not the right class." I thought of Shelly's expensive ensemble, the large but discreet gold square-linked chain around her neck, the beige and brown designer purse that dangled from her arm. *She* probably didn't run with, as Beverline put it, mothers of numerous out-of-wedlock children and widows of drug kingpins.

"I told you that class stuff is ridiculous, Emily. But you've closed yourself off to me. I don't know what to do, how to make things right."

"If you're finding solace in the company of another woman, there *is* no making it right, Aaron. I'm sure you already knew it was over between us and were just waiting for the official word to come down." I saw truth in his eyes. "Um . . . I'm going to talk to Mom and see what she wants to do. Under the circumstances, I don't think she should continue living on your property."

"There's no need—"

"No, it'll only remind you of me and will make you uncomfortable. The kids, too. I don't know the best way to handle that, but we'll figure that out." It made me physically ill to have entered their lives, especially Billy's, and then have to suddenly leave. I'd made Billy a promise to be his mother, and now I'd broken it. Worse, with him in Sag Harbor, I'd be gone when he returned, vanishing like the stains from wet paint once it dried. What if he had trust issues as an adult because of that?

"I'll take care of that. Emily, I don't know what to say."

"You can say that there aren't any hard feelings, and I'll be happy."

"No hard feelings," he said softly. "I'll never forget you, Emily. You taught me I can love again. I'll always be grateful to you for that."

"I won't forget you either, Aaron. And I'll be out just as soon as I can make arrangements."

"Will you go back to Indianapolis?"

"Yes." My next words brought a smile to my lips. "It's my home."

\*    \*    \*

Shelly was still in the waiting room when I reentered it, along with a few patients. She looked increasingly nervous as I approached her. "It's all right, Shelly. Aaron and I decided to break our engagement. You've got a clear path."

"Emily, I never planned—"

"There's nothing wrong with taking advantage of an opportunity," I said matter-of-factly. "By the way, do you like lobster?"

"I love it. Why?"

"Because you're going to be having a lot of it."

I smiled as I left the office. Shelly looked bewildered at my last statement, but she'd find out what I meant soon enough. She might have an easier time with Beverline than I did, but that didn't change the fact that she was in for a boring time behind the bedroom door.

Even lobster for dinner is going to get tasteless if you have it every night.

# Chapter 30

I set my plan in motion by first talking to Mom, who showed loving support. "As long as you're happy, and I must say, you're looking better now than you have in the past two weeks."

"I wasn't being honest with myself, Mom. I'll never do that again." From now on I was going to be satisfied, or else the man was gone. If he was sloppy, dishonest, a womanizer, or lousy in bed, I wasn't taking any less than what I deserved.

"Um, Mom, I don't think there's a rush, but you probably do need to think about moving out. I don't think it's healthy for the kids for you to keep living here. They'll probably have a hard time with the breakup. The saddest aspect of this whole thing, and the hardest part for me, is the effect it will have on Aaron's kids. Billy is bound to be disappointed, even heartbroken; and Kirsten and Arden, who'd just started to get used to the idea of me being their stepmother, might be embittered by the way it turned out."

"That won't be a problem, Emmie. I'm already on the waiting list for senior citizen housing."

"You are!"

Mom shrugged. "For months now. I didn't see how it would hurt. When we moved in here, no one knew whether it would work out or not, so one day I drove over there and signed up."

For a moment I was speechless. "Mom . . . you're a wise woman."

"It comes with living nearly eighty years. It shouldn't be too much longer for something to come available. It'll work out nicely, Emmie. A number of my friends from church live there, and Henry doesn't live far."

I nodded knowingly. "Ah, yes, Henry." I decided to put a voice to something I'd been worried about. "Mom, you wouldn't consider remarrying, would you?"

"Of course not. Maybe if I'd been widowed young, like Winnie." Valerie's mother, a little younger than Mom, had lost her husband about a dozen years earlier. "But it's too late for marriage. That would only create problems with our survivors after we die."

I called the people who managed rentals for my condo the next morning and told them I was coming back. The condo was vacant, and they assured me there would be no further rentals. I informed a disappointed Dr. Norman that I'd be leaving, and even though it was Tuesday he allowed me to make the following Friday my last day. All that awaited was for me to pack and ship my things . . . and tell my friends.

Before I could say anything, Valerie called and suggested we have a farewell dinner at her house for Marsha Friday night. I decided that would be an ideal opportunity to inform them about my broken engagement and impending departure. "And I'm not inviting Tanis," Valerie had said.

Perfect.

After Valerie, Rosalind, and I had toasted to Marsha's happiness and discussed her plans, I dropped my bomb. All three of them were shocked but respected my decision to keep the details to myself.

"I know you know what you're doing, Emily, but still, I'd hate to see Tanis move in on Aaron," Rosalind lamented.

"Me, too," Valerie added. "I think she's keeping that grip operator around just until she can land a big fish."

"Well, she'll be very disappointed to learn that Moby Dick is already taken."

Collective breaths were drawn in. "Is Aaron seeing someone *already?*"

"Yes, and before you get too excited, it didn't get started until we were on the rocks. Aaron insists it was just lunch—" I left out my suspicions about dinner—"and I happen to believe him. Everybody needs someone to talk to when they feel like their life is falling apart. But now they're free to take it to the next level."

"You're very understanding," Rosalind said, clearly baffled by my casual attitude.

"It doesn't matter. It's over with us, Rosalind. I'm just glad we realized it wouldn't work before we got married. The last thing I need is another divorce. But wait till I tell you who his new playmate is."

They all spoke at the same time. "Who?"

"Shelly Muldoon."

They howled so loud I was glad we were in a private home and not a restaurant, for if we'd been in the latter we surely would have been asked to keep it down.

I answered the rapid-fire questions that followed. Yes, Shelly first met Aaron at the reunion. She sold medical equipment, and he'd attended one of her seminars. I didn't know too much about what had happened after that, but she certainly seemed ready to take over once I was out of the picture.

"Well, who wouldn't?" Marsha asked. "Aaron is a real catch."

I smiled. Aaron would seem a lot less attractive to Shelly once she got to know him better—especially since she'd known Teddy.

After dinner, we all helped Valerie clear the table. Rosalind re-placed a vase of flowers in the center of the table. It had prevented us from seeing each other across the table, so we'd moved it. "What a lovely arrangement, Valerie."

"I can't believe how long it's lasted. Elias sent them last week."

Now it was her turn to be grilled as we pelted her with questions about Elias. None of us had even known they'd been seeing each other.

"Okay, stop!" she said, laughing. "We've just gone out twice. Stop trying to marry me off."

"Hey, twice is good for Elias," I managed to say between breathless laughter. "He usually loves 'em and leaves 'em."

"We're having fun. That's all," she said firmly.

"And are you going out again tomorrow?" Marsha hinted with a smile.

"As a matter of fact, yes." Valerie paused. "This time I'm getting my housekeeper to stay over."

We whooped again.

I went up to the dental offices to say good-bye to Teddy on my last day. He hadn't known about it and was understandably floored by my news.

"You're really going back to Indiana?"

I heard an old Jackson Five tune of that name playing in my head. "Yes. I'm shipping my things home Saturday, and my flight leaves Sunday."

"I can't believe it. I mean, I can't say I'm upset that you and Aaron broke up, but damn. Give a brother a chance, will you?"

"Teddy, it won't work. There're hundreds of available women out there. One is going to be perfect for you. You probably need to think about settling down."

"I'm sure one day I will."

"What, when you're fifty?"

"Sixty-five," he said with a grin. "Now stop worrying about me like you're my mama." He pulled me into an embrace. "I'll miss you, Emily."

*    *    *

How fitting it was that the last thing I saw on my mother's television before I left for the airport was a laxative commercial featuring Tanis, making a face and complaining about bloating discomfort before smiling and saying she was so much more comfortable now that she'd discovered No-Bloat.

I flicked the remote control. It was time to go.

I hadn't really felt bad about leaving until it came time to say good-bye to Mom. We'd grown a lot closer, she and I, in the past year, and this time our relationship had moved to a different level than the one from my youth. I had lived with her as an adult, and my father's absence had contributed as well. My parents had always been close, and I was happy to have been there for her, to have helped fill the huge void left in her life by his passing. I felt that our time together had given Mom a new respect for me as a woman, not just as her daughter, but as her equal. I was shocked when she pressed a check for twenty-five-hundred dollars into my palm. "Mom . . . you can't afford this."

"Sure I can. My rent is lower than it used to be, thanks to you. And it'll stay low even after I move. Your daddy took good care of me, Emmylou."

My eyes filled with tears at her using the name Pop used to call me.

"That's what I want for you, someone to take care of you" she said. Then she took my hands. "I'm proud of you, Emmie. It takes real courage to walk away from the type of life Aaron was offering because you weren't completely satisfied."

I bit my lip to keep from laughing. I knew her words were innocently chosen, but I couldn't help thinking . . . if only she knew how close she'd come to hitting on the truth.

"You've come a long way from the four-year-old who kept saying, 'Look, Mommy, she has blue hair!' when I ran into a friend from church on the street," she continued.

I remembered that day. My mother's gray-haired friend apparently used one of those old-style rinses that gave hair a bluish tint. Mom had tried her best to get me to shut up, but I insisted on being heard. That had been nearly forty years ago, and we still laughed about it.

"You take this check. It's my way of saying thank you for moving back and helping me out. I enjoyed having you here so much."

I sniffled.

"Now, don't you go getting emotional on me. You can use this money to support yourself until you start working. If you get a job right away, you can put it toward your new car." I'd decided against driving my Nissan back to Indy and sold it to one of my nephews. He was driving me to the airport. Mom had decided to stay behind.

Just thinking about her made my eyes puddle up. When I went to embrace her, I broke out into full-fledged sobs. I felt like a child being left at preschool for the first time. Mom cried, too.

"You have to fly out and visit me," I said. "Spend a week. Hell, spend a month. If you can bear to be away from Henry that long."

"It's not like that," Mom objected. "Henry and I are just friends. We cook together."

"I know, Mom. I'm just glad you're having fun."

It felt good to end on an upbeat note. I took one last look at The Big House, empty on this Sunday, the family all out in Sag Harbor.

I felt no regrets. I knew I'd done the right thing.

It looked like the flight wouldn't be full. At check-in I impulsively paid fifty dollars to upgrade to business class so I'd get a wider seat with more leg room. I accepted complimentary headphones and leaned back comfortably into the leather seat, listening to an old-school R&B station. I closed my eyes when Lionel Richie's soothing voice sang the lead on the Commodores's hit, *"Zoom."* I, too, felt convinced that happiness awaited me, and I sure hoped it was in Indy.

Movement nearby made me open my eyes. A dark-skinned man with a shaved head was settling into the seat next to me.

"Hello," I said.

"Hello. I hope I didn't wake you with my fidgeting."

"No, not at all." *He's rather nice looking,* I thought. *I wonder if he's married.*

"I promise you'll hardly know I'm here."

"It's not a problem." I went back to my music.

When we were airborne he pulled out a briefcase and began working, not with a laptop, but with a yellow lined legal pad. I couldn't help noticing his bold strokes in black ink, a letter and number combination that looked like some kind of physics. This man was becoming more interesting by the minute.

He put his head back, his chin raised and his eyes closed, deep in thought.

When I heard him sigh I glanced at him, only to find him smiling at me. I returned the smile.

"Are you going home or away from home?" he asked.

"Home." The simple one-syllable word gave me a wonderful feeling of contentment. I couldn't wait to see my friends. "You?"

"The same. My son was married in New York yesterday."

"How nice! Congratulations to you."

"Thanks."

I soon learned that his name was Michael Butler, that he was a chemical engineer, divorced with two grown sons. I decided he was probably a little older than I initially thought, maybe fifty or fifty-one. Here was a man who took care of himself.

The flight went by very quickly, and before I knew it the flight attendant was announcing our descent and imminent landing.

"It'll be good to get home, won't it?" Michael said after

the wheels of the landing gear touched the ground and we barreled down the runway.

My grin covered my entire face. "You have no idea."

"I've been meaning to tell you this, Emily. You have a lovely smile."

"Well, thank you."

"I was wondering . . . you did mention you sold your car before you left New York. May I offer you a lift home? We can stop along the way and have something to eat."

"That's sweet of you, Michael, but a friend is meeting me at the airport. But if you're willing to give me a rain check, I'd love to have a meal with you another time."

"That's a promise." He held my gaze. "Let's make it soon. I want to see that smile of yours light up the room."

"I'd like that, Michael." As I gathered my belongings, I thought how nice it was to have another shot at romance . . . with a man whose children were grown. Perhaps Aaron was just a pleasant interlude in my life that wasn't meant to be permanent.

Why shouldn't my spirits be high? I was back in Indy, where I belonged. Mom was fine. Sonny and my nephews would take care of getting her moved into her new apartment, and if she had any trouble with anything all she had to do was call her grandchildren, who'd hightail it to New Rochelle to come to her aid. She was happy and thriving in her new community, and with the help of family and friends, old and new, she'd continue to do so.

If Mom's happy, I'm happy, too. After all, that's how this whole thing started.

up on finding a husband way too soon in favor of deliberate single motherhood. What do *you* think?

8. Marsha did not learn her husband was not a legitimate businessman until well into their marriage. With no skills to fall back on, she chose to stay with him and risk the consequences, and she was left penniless after he was murdered. How do you think she *should* have handled the situation?

9. Teddy told Emily he believed they would make a good team. She was skeptical of this. Do you feel he was sincere or, just as Emily felt, looking for someone to help with his rent increase?

10 Are you, as a reader, content with the hopeful but undefined note upon which this story ended for the female characters? Would you like to know more about Teddy's and Wayne's relationships? (You'll actually have to e-mail me with the answer to this one. Go to my website at www.bettyegriffin.com.)

# DISCUSSION QUESTIONS

1. Emily's siblings felt she was the best candidate to return to Euliss because she was unmarried. Other families sometimes burden those judged to be the most successful with things like paying for family reunions and funerals. Do you feel this is fair? Why or why not?

2. Emily's middle name, Louise, came from her paternal grandmother. What are your feelings about giving a child an unfashionable name (Elmer, Sylvester, Gertrude, Mabel, etc.) in honor of a beloved relative?

3. Emily's disappointment in Aaron's performance in the bedroom led her into Teddy's arms. She felt reluctant to broach the subject with Aaron, worried that his limited sexual experience versus her more worldliness was too sensitive a topic. What would you have done in that situation?

4. Do you believe that Beverline would view any woman Aaron brought home as a potential replacement for her daughter and express dislike for her?

5. Did you empathize with Beverline's predicament at all?

6. Emily had been deeply hurt by her ex-husband's duplicity, and she divorced him because of it. Yet years later, she found herself doing the same thing to Aaron, even though she wasn't married to him. What are your feelings about her behavior and her efforts to justify it?

7. Both Emily and her mother felt that Valerie, who was twenty-seven when she had her first child, had given

# A NEW KIND OF BLISS

## BETTYE GRIFFIN

## ABOUT THIS GUIDE

The questions and discussion topics that follow
are intended to enhance your group's
reading of this book.